Great Dane
BRIDES

Heartlands
Library

A Bride's Portrait of Dodge City, Kansas © 2011 by Erica Vetsch
A Bride's Sweet Surprise in Sauers, Indiana © 2012 by Ramona K. Cecil

Print ISBN 978-1-62416-237-4

eBook Editions:
Adobe Digital Edition (.epub) 978-1-62416-413-2
Kindle and MobiPocket Edition (.prc) 978-1-62416-412-5

All scripture quotations are taken from the King James Version of the Bible.

This book is a work of fiction. Names, characters, places, and incidents are either products of the author's imagination or used fictitiously. Any similarity to actual people, organizations, and/or events is purely coincidental.

Cover image: © sima, Shutterstock

Published by Barbour Publishing, Inc., P.O. Box 719, Uhrichsville, Ohio 44683, www.barbourbooks.com

Our mission is to publish and distribute inspirational products offering exceptional value and biblical encouragement to the masses.

 Member of the
Evangelical Christian
Publishers Association

Printed in the United States of America.

Great Plains
BRIDES

TWO HISTORICAL ROMANCES

Ramona K. Cecil
Erica Vetsch

BARBOUR
PUBLISHING

A BRIDE'S PORTRAIT OF DODGE CITY, KANSAS

by Erica Vetsch

Dedication

To my husband, Peter,
a man of courage, character, and compassion

Author's Note

While most of the characters in this story are
fictitious, the characters of Charlie Basset, Luke Short,
and Bat Masterson are taken from the annals of Dodge
City history. I have tried to stay true to the historical record,
with one noted exception: Bat Masterson's proclivity
for keeping printed material stacked in his office is
fictional and entirely of my own creation.

Chapter 1

June 1, 1878

Uncle Carl had taught her that the customer should be accommodated no matter what, but surely there were limitations. Addie Reid pressed her fingertips against her temple. "You want to do what?"

"I want my picture made with my horse."

"Sir, this isn't a livery stable. I do serious portraiture."

The cowboy—so prototypical of the breed as to be comical with his wide hat, sunburned face, and bat-wing chaps—waved a scrap of newsprint in her face. "Read this here ad. It says 'Come to Reid's Photography to get your portrait taken with your trail pards and best friends.' This is your ad, ain't it? You are Reid's Photography?"

A small pang twisted Addie's heart. She was now. *What if I can't do this alone?*

"Well?"

"Yes, that's my advertisement, and this is Reid's Photography."

"Good. Then I want my picture made with my trail pard and best friend. I've got good cash money. Trail boss paid us off an hour ago. I got spiffed up down at the barbershop and headed right here."

"But sir, a horse? The advertisement is intended for humans."

"That horse"—he pointed through the open door to a dusty animal dozing in the sun on Front Street—"is the best friend and trail pard I've ever had. He's smart and gentle and has forgotten more about cow work than I'll ever know."

Which was either an accolade for the horse or an insult to the cowboy. She blew out a breath. "I can't haul the camera out into the street." Though she wouldn't risk moving the Chevalier for a simple portrait, perhaps she could use her smaller Scovill. Though the print would be smaller, too.

"I don't want no outside picture. I want it taken in the studio with one of those fancy backdrops. And I want the picture to be about this big"—he held up his hands about a foot apart—"so it will look good in a frame on the wall."

That ruled out the Scovill. A print that size would need the bigger camera. Her mind trotted back to what he'd said, and her jaw dropped. "You intend to bring a horse inside?" Jamming her hands on her hips, she shook her head. "No. Impossible. I'll take your picture, and it will be a good one, but the animal stays outside."

He tugged the corner of his enormous mustache. "I reckoned as much. No gumption. Should've known better than to come to a woman photographer. A man would understand. Guess I'll go over to Donaldson's. He offered to do it for me, but I wanted to give you a try at it first, since you're new in town and all. He said you'd be too timid."

Stung, Addie straightened. "Wait. Don't go." Donaldson's Photography three blocks down would be her biggest competitor, and Heber Donaldson had been the most vocal about the new photography shop on Front Street stealing his customers. "We can work something out." But it would have to be worth her while. She hesitated then quoted him a price.

The cowboy grinned. "That sounds fine to me. Donaldson was almost twice that. Don't you worry. My old Mudslinger's gentle as a spring breeze, and he'll stand quiet." He removed his hat and smoothed his hair. "You got a back door or something? I can lead him in that way."

"No, he can't come in through the back. That door's blocked off." She eyed the paisley-scattered rug in her reception room. "I suppose you'll have to lead him through here." This was ridiculous. Why was she even contemplating such a crazy idea?

Money. Pure and simple. She needed customers and couldn't afford to turn one away.

The cowpoke jammed his hat back on. "I'll fetch him in." He hustled outside as if afraid she might change her mind.

Which she should do. A horse in the studio?

Old Mudslinger's hooves clomped on the boardwalk and through the doorway, muffled on the carpet. She winced to think of horseshoe-shaped marks on the pretty red and blue rug but shrugged. *Worry about the bank manager. Worry about convincing him to let you assume the mortgage. And while you're at it, maybe you should worry about how you're going to get this beast to hold still long enough for the exposure.*

"This way." She hurried into the studio ahead of the horse and cowboy. The animal brought with him a whiff of sweaty hair and barnyard, hay and leather. Lovely. "Don't let him near the camera." In the center of the long room, her pride and joy, a glossy new Chevalier, stood on a tripod, the black drape hanging nearly to the floor. She crossed to a bench along one wall and pulled her order book toward her. Snagging a pencil from a jar, she held it poised above the page. "Can I have your name, please?"

"Call me Cracker. Everybody does."

"Very well, Mr. Cracker." She wrote the name and the date.

He guffawed. "Not mister. Just Cracker. It's a nickname I picked up because I love those little oyster crackers like they serve over at the Dakota House. Can't get enough of those tiny things. I been called Cracker for about as long as I can remember."

Cracker and Mudslinger. Fran was not going to believe this.

"Cracker, I've three backgrounds you can choose from, but I would suggest the landscape." She crossed the studio and tugged on the rope that raised the canvas curtain painted to look like a drawing room and lowered the heavy drape painted to look like rolling hills.

"Say, that's dandy." Cracker rested his arm across his saddle.

Mudslinger stood still, one hind leg tucked up a bit, his ears drooping. Perhaps getting him to stand still wouldn't be a problem. Might be more challenging to make him look alive.

Addie wrestled a plaster pedestal and a wicker chair out of the way and quickly folded a fringed piano scarf and tucked it away on a shelf. "Just what did you have in mind for a pose?"

Cracker rubbed his chin. "I want you to get all of us in

the picture. Head to tail and hat to hooves. And could you make sure you get my rifle in the picture, too?" He patted the gunstock sticking out of a scabbard on his saddle. "This picture's for my mama back in Uvalde."

Why a picture intended for his mother would need to be bristling with guns, Addie didn't know, but once again Uncle Carl's voice in her ear reminded that above all else, she must try to accommodate the customer.

"Lead him around here then, so the rifle is on the side facing the camera. Are you going to be astride?" She stepped back as Mudslinger's haunches came around. If the man wanted to be in the saddle, she'd have to move the camera back, which would reduce some of the detail. . . Her mind slipped into working mode, and she began to consider the lighting and the exposure time, the focal point, and how to achieve depth of field.

"Naw, I'll just stand beside him." Cracker looped the reins over the saddle horn and placed his hand on the pommel. He lifted his chin, shoved his hat back so it wouldn't shade his face, and stared off into the distance. "Like this. Like we're standing on a hill looking over a herd and dreaming of home."

Addie hid a smile. Cowboys might like to be thought of as firebrands and fearsome, but most were just boys with romantic notions and fierce pride. "That will be fine. You wait here while I prepare a plate. It won't take me a minute."

She ducked into the darkroom at the back of the building, struck a match to light the lantern, and lowered the red glass covering. Rosy light bathed the room, the workbench, the trays, and the rows of bottles and chemicals necessary to her job. She closed the door, shutting out all sunlight, and reached for a large glass slide to begin the process. Uncorking bottles and preparing the wet-plate washes, she shook her head again. A horse in her studio. If word got out, she might have a stampede of equine customers. Would that make the bank manager more amenable to her taking over the mortgage?

Just thinking of the meeting with the bank manager this afternoon made her hands shake. In her haste, she splashed a bit of silver nitrate on her cuff and wrist. *Grrr.* Grabbing the ammonia bottle and a rag, she dabbed at her skin. If she didn't get it off now, it would turn blackish blue and take ages to wear off. Twisting her lips, she scowled at the once-white cuff now blotched.

She took precious moments to roll up her sleeves like she should've done right away and donned her work apron to cover her straight blue skirt. She wouldn't have time to go back to her boardinghouse to change before meeting the bank manager, so now, in spite of the warm day, she'd have to don the matching jacket to cover the stain on her sleeve.

Finally, she had a prepared plate in the lightproof box. Entering the studio once more, she noted that neither cowboy nor horse had stirred. "I'll just get this into the camera. You'll both have to stand completely still until the plate has been exposed for the proper length of time. If you move even a little, the picture will come out blurred." She removed the lens cover and ducked under the drape to peer through the camera. She emerged, backed the camera up about a foot, and sighted again. Perfect. After replacing the lens cap, the black drape stifled all light. Operating by feel, she slipped the glass plate into the back of the camera and closed everything up.

When she emerged from beneath the cloth, she took a moment to tighten the combs keeping her upswept hair from teasing her face and studied Cracker. She approached him for some final adjustments. "Put one foot a bit in front of the other and let your left arm hang loose. You'll look more natural that way." She smoothed his collar and tilted his hat a bit more. The sunshine from the skylight overhead should provide enough illumination that she wouldn't need any flash powder. Just as well. The pop and glare of a flash might startle even the dozy Mudslinger into bolting.

"Make sure you get my pistol and knife in the shot." Cracker patted his gun belt.

"Of course." This was for his mother, after all. "Now relax, but hold completely still until I give you the word." She stepped back, surveyed the tableau, trying to see things through the camera lens in her mind, to see the finished product and predict if it would please the customer.

Gently, she unscrewed the lens cap. "Hold it." She counted off the seconds, added two more because the horse and saddle were so dark, then replaced the cap. "There. You're done."

Cracker relaxed a fraction then grinned. "Great. When will it be ready?"

"You can pick it up tomorrow, but you'll have to pay for it today." Uncle Carl always required payment from a cowboy before developing the picture, and she intended to follow his example. If she waited until Cracker came to pick up the photo tomorrow, chances were his money would've disappeared, siphoned off in one of the saloons or gambling halls. What took the average cowboy three months to earn on the trail up from Texas could be gone in a matter of hours in a cow town like Abilene or Dodge City, Kansas.

Cracker dug into his pocket and produced a wad of bills. He peeled off a couple, grinned at her, and added a third. "There you go, lady. A little something extra for you. And I'm going to tell everybody I know to come here to get their picture made."

He grabbed Mudslinger's reins and tugged. The animal roused, shuffled his feet, and ambled toward the door. When he came abreast of her camera, he paused.

Addie let out a shriek.

Cracker yanked on the reins, but it was too late. "Whoops. I sure am sorry about that. He ain't exactly housebroke, you know."

An hour later, Addie had scrubbed the studio floor and her hands several times. Praying none of the stable odor lingered on her clothes, she stepped into the Dodge City Bank. The sturdy, brick building faced Front Street, as her own shop did, the main artery into and out of town bisected by the Santa Fe Railroad tracks. North of the tracks only about half the businesses were saloons. South of the Santa Fe rails, saloons, gambling dens, dance halls, and houses of ill repute abounded.

The smells of ink and beeswax furniture polish drifted

over her. Everything in this bank bespoke prosperity, from the shiny woodwork to the burgundy velvet wallpaper to the gleaming brass hardware. A row of teller windows took up the left-hand wall. Patrons stood patiently in line waiting for their turns, and Addie took her place at the tail end.

Lord, please let the bank manager understand, let him give me a chance to prove I can do this. Because, truthfully, I have no idea what I'll do if he says no.

"Miss Reid?"

Someone touched her arm, and she realized she was standing in the middle of the bank with her eyes closed. Warmth spread across her cheeks, and she looked up into the bank manager's stern visage. "Mr. Poulter." She forced his name past her constricted throat.

"Please come this way. I'm glad to see you believe in being prompt. I despise being kept waiting." He sounded like he had a lemon rind stuck in his throat. Sour and raspy.

She followed, her pulse beating loudly in her ears. He led her to the half wall that separated the civilians from the cash and held open the gate. Not a squeak from the hinges. Darting a glance at his intense expression, she doubted the gate would have the nerve to sound off.

"Please be seated." He waved her to a straight-backed and uncompromising chair set square before his immense desk. Behind the nameplate and blotter, Mr. T. Archibald Poulter settled into leather luxury.

"I'm afraid I'm not sure why you wished to meet with me, Miss Reid. I am sorry for your loss, but I've looked over the agreement between this establishment and your deceased

15

uncle." He spoke slowly, as if she might have trouble keeping up with his words. "The terms are very clear. As I told you at the funeral, in the event of your uncle's death, the mortgage is due in full. If you cannot pay the loan, the collateral will be forfeit."

She hadn't forgotten how he had approached her as she walked away from her last relative's burial service and given her the news. He couldn't even wait until the next business day. Word had it that Archie Poulter had a heart of pyrite. Cold, yellow, and pretty much worthless.

Try nice first. The reminder, floating through her mind from a long-ago schoolteacher, surprised her. Trouble was, Miss Ambrose had never met this bank manager.

"I, too, have read the documents, Mr. Poulter." Though it irked her to be treated as if she had no more sense than a prairie chicken, she kept her voice reasonable and professional. "I understand the terms of that agreement. I am not here to dispute them. I'm here to negotiate a new agreement with myself as proprietor of the business. I wish to assume the loan at the current terms."

His thin brows shot down over his hawk-like nose. "Yourself as proprietor?" He shook his head. "I'm afraid that would be impossible. The bank has never loaned money to an unmarried woman to finance a business. Unless. . ." He leaned back in his chair and studied her. "Unless you have a male relative or business partner who would be a cosignatory on the loan?"

Addie moistened her lips and stifled the urge to roll her eyes. "No, there's no one else. But if you call in the mortgage now, all you'll get is photographic equipment and an empty building. The studio itself is collateral for the loan. Surely it would be in your best interest to let me continue running the business and paying on the mortgage."

He steepled his fingers under his chin. "Ordinarily, I would agree with you. It would be better to have another merchant assume the note. However, Heber Donaldson was in here just this morning, and he indicated he would be interested in purchasing the repossessed equipment from the bank. And a building on Front Street is never difficult to sell or rent. The bank wouldn't lose any money by calling in the loan."

Heber Donaldson. A thorn in their flesh from the moment she and Uncle Carl had stepped off the train three months ago. She throttled her handbag in her lap, clenching her fingers to stop them from shaking. "Mr. Poulter, please. The studio is my livelihood. It's all I know how to do. Without the studio, I have no way to support myself. I assure you, I'm a very good photographer. I know the business from the ground up. Photography, developing, bookkeeping. I've helped my uncle for years. If you won't give me a new loan, will you please give me time to pay off the debt? I'm only asking for six months." She'd have to live sparingly, and the summer season would have to be better than good, but she'd scrimp and save and scratch and claw to keep the studio. Six months would be pushing it, but she could do it if he'd only give her a chance.

"Six months?"

"Just until the end of this year. By January 1, I'd be

loan-free, and the bank would have the entire mortgage repaid with interest."

He squared up some papers on his immaculate desk and appeared to consider her request.

Hope sprang up when he didn't automatically shoot her down, but as the minutes crawled by, worry began to blot out that feeble hope.

Finally, he looked up. "I tell you what. I'm prepared to give you an additional three months to get your affairs in order. Ninety days. The mortgage will be due in full at that time, no excuses. The regular monthly payments will be due on the first of the month as usual, with a balloon payment on. . ." He opened a drawer and withdrew a small calendar. "August 29. That's ninety days from today, June 1."

"Ninety days?" She swallowed. "That's not fair. There's no way I can raise that kind of money in just three months."

"Miss Reid, it's more than generous when you consider it would be within the bank's legal rights to call in the loan today. When you view it in that light, I think ninety days is fair."

So, he was prepared to let her slave away all summer, making the monthly payments, then call in the loan and selling the studio to Donaldson. And she was helpless to stop it.

"I'd advise you, Miss Reid, to forget about trying to run a business and find yourself a husband. I realize you've barely had time to get settled in this town, and to be faced with bereavement so soon after arriving makes the situation more difficult." He toyed with the pin piercing his necktie just below his chin. "In fact. . ." He studied her face and let his eyes wander over what he could see of her from behind his desk.

She immediately wanted to scrub her skin with ammonia all over again.

"In fact, I wouldn't be averse to discussing an arrangement with you. You're a comely woman, and I have recently decided that it was past time I thought about getting married."

His audacity sucked her breath away. Threatening to yank her business, her livelihood, away from her one second and hinting at marriage the next? Addie rose and skewered him to his chair with her glare. "Mr. Poulter, I accept only the extension of the loan. In ninety days, I will pay the entire mortgage. Until then, I would prefer to keep our dealings entirely professional." She dug in her purse and produced a small roll of bills. "This is the payment that is due today. I will see you in one month with another installment."

Chapter 2

I had a hard time convincing him to lean against that pedestal, but I think it turned out perfectly, don't you?" Addie studied the photograph before slipping it into the cardboard frame. She ran her finger over the silver lettering in the corner of the frame and smiled.

Reid's Photography Studio, Dodge City, Kansas.

Fran Seaton looked over Addie's shoulder. "Bat Masterson has the most piercing eyes I've ever seen. They can turn my insides cold even on a day as hot as today."

Addie studied the portrait of the newly elected sheriff of Ford County. Though he wore a fine suit and natty bowler, and she'd posed him casually with his forearm resting on the plaster pillar, it was his eyes that drew attention. A hint of humor, a lot of grit, and absolutely no fear. Exactly what she'd been trying to capture with her lens. She doubted she'd even be able to tint a photograph to accurately capture the vivid blue of his eyes. Too bad there was no way to take color photographs. But it was one of the best portraits she'd ever done, color or not.

"Stop looking so smug." Fran poked her shoulder. "I know it's a good picture. I'm sure he will appreciate your skill. Let me see what else you've got." She scooped up a stack of newly developed portraits from the corner of the desk and plopped onto a red velvet settee Addie used for posing families. "Bat's handsome, but not what I'm looking for. Can you imagine looking across the breakfast table at those eyes every morning?" Fran shuddered. "I have a feeling any girl who tries to catch Bat Masterson will find herself trying to tame a tiger."

Addie put the sheriff's photograph into an envelope and fastened the clip. "Maybe you can go with me to deliver this after work. You might run into Jonas." A teasing smile tugged at her lips. It hadn't taken Addie long to find out Fran's views on nearly every male in town, especially Deputy Spooner.

"Ugh. No thank you. Bat might be a tiger, but Jonas is as scary as a bowl of oatmeal. Though you might be interested to know that Bat hired Miles Carr as a deputy. Jonas says he's getting his badge today."

"Is he? That's nice." Addie feigned nonchalance, but her ears pricked. The gunsmith had always been quietly polite when they'd passed on the street, but she'd never spoken to him.

"I think you two would make a lovely couple. He's so tall and—I don't know—watchful? I always get the impression he's kind of sweet on you."

"You're a romantic goose." Addie smiled fondly at Fran. "You see hearts and rainbows where none exist. Concentrate on your own affairs of the heart and leave me to my solitary existence. If you want to talk about how someone gets watched by someone else, let's talk about the way Jonas can never take his eyes off you."

Fran flipped through the photographs. "I've got my heart set on someone tall, dark, and handsome. Jonas is none of those things. Hey, this one has possibilities. What about him?"

Addie joined her on the settee and peered at the photo. "If you aren't careful, all your daydreaming about a romantic encounter is going to get you into trouble. Tall, dark, and handsome doesn't mean a man has a good character or is even nice. You can't judge a man by his portrait." And didn't she have reason to know the truth of that statement?

"I can tell plenty from the portraits you take. Look at Bat's. That picture tells you a lot about the man. You captured him perfectly."

Addie couldn't deny the pleasure Fran's compliment gave her, but she shook her head. "That's because we know Bat—at least a little. The papers are full of him, and we see him around town. You're reading into his photograph what you know of the man. These"—she tapped the stack in Fran's hand—"are total strangers. You should be careful. Not everything is as it seems in this life, and that goes double for men."

"Well"—Fran shrugged—"a girl has to start somewhere." She held up a photograph. "Tell me about him."

With a sigh, Addie took the picture. A young, sunburned, intense man looked back at her. "He's like half a dozen others in that stack. A Texan. Maybe twenty years old? Like all of them, he wanted to make sure I posed him so his gun and holster showed, and I couldn't talk him out of wearing those wooly chaps. They looked ridiculous and smelled worse."

She wrinkled her nose, remembering the pungent cow odor that had filled the portrait studio every time he moved. Cowboys made up the bulk of her business, and without exception, every man wanted his likeness struck in full regalia with his rifle or his handgun. Alone in the photograph or posing with his trail mates, every puncher wanted to look as fierce as possible. He wanted the world to know he was a cowboy and proud of it.

"What is this?" Fran held up another picture. "Are you serious?" She shoved a red-gold curl off her cheek and tucked it behind her ear, leaning over the picture. Her emerald eyes turned to Addie, wide and questioning.

"I knew you'd like that one." Addie laughed.

"A horse? You let someone bring a horse into the studio?"

Addie shrugged. "He said his horse was his best friend, and he fully intended to get his picture taken with his best friend. He even brought in the advertisement. Thank you for writing that up for me, by the way."

Fran held the picture up to the light streaming through the front windows. "Was he drunk?"

"Not at that time, though I have a feeling he hit the saloons pretty soon afterward. Most of them do." Addie shook her head. "I thought it might be a problem getting the horse to stand still for the length of time it would take to expose the slide, but he was so placid, I think he fell asleep. Though he did leave me something to remember him by." She pinched her nose and screwed up her eyelids.

"No!" Fran made a face. "He didn't!"

Addie sighed. "I do suffer for my art." She pantomimed agony, putting the back of her hand against her brow and fluttering her lashes until they both dissolved into giggles.

The photograph of the horse and cowboy had come out

even better than Addie had hoped. Almost as good as the one of Bat Masterson. She'd love to put the horse portrait in the window as an advertisement, but she was afraid it would give potential customers too many ideas. One horse in the studio was enough.

"With the way cowboys are pouring in here to get their portraits taken, you'll have everything paid for and enough money to last through the winter by the Fourth of July." Fran quickly made her way through the rest of the photographs. "What did Poulter over at the bank say yesterday? I meant to come by last night and get all the news, but I had to stay late at the store." She shrugged, shaking her head. "Will they let you assume the loan?"

Addie's middle clenched at the thought of Mr. Poulter and the loan. Eighty-nine days left. "Well, after I disabused his mind about marrying him—" She stopped to enjoy Fran's gaping and blinking. "He agreed to give me ninety days to pay off the loan."

"Wait, wait, wait. Marriage? Mr. Poulter asked you to marry him?" She grabbed Addie's arms and gave her a shake. "Tell me everything."

Addie laughed, though the bank manager's leering assessment still lingered in her memory, making her flesh crawl. "He didn't come right out and say it. Rather, he told me to give up ideas of running a business and find myself a husband. Then he said he'd given some thought to getting married, and I was, in his words, a 'comely woman.'"

Fran's eyebrows rose. "I hope you spit in his eye. Of all the nerve. He's old enough to be your father."

"I didn't spit in his eye, but I did agree to his terms on the loan. Somehow I've got to raise the money. I thought he might give me six months, and if I worked hard, I'd just about be able to do it, but he's already had an offer on the place. Heber Donaldson." Addie grimaced.

Fran sank onto the settee and let her head fall back to stare at the ceiling. She blew a puff of air that lifted her bangs. "What is this town coming to? Heber's been jealous of you since you arrived. He had most all the photography business sewed up before you came. A couple of photographers drifted into town last year, but he dropped his prices and they couldn't match him. But you've got him worried. And he and Poulter are friends." She shot Addie a concerned glance. "Be careful. There are politics and power and prideful men in this town, and they wouldn't hesitate to force you out if you had something they wanted."

Loneliness swept over Addie, a longing for Uncle Carl and for Abilene and the life she once knew. For the security of a home and someone to belong to, someone of her own to stand beside her to fight life's battles. Instead, she was alone.

Seeing Fran's troubled face, Addie put on a false bravado. "Don't you worry. I'm tough enough to take all comers. You wait. I'll find a way to pay that loan off, and Heber can go jump in the Arkansas River. He won't get his hands on this studio or the equipment."

"Then a lot is riding on you having a good season. I hope you can do it. I don't want you to have to close the shop. I've been waiting for two years to find a best friend in this town. I'm not giving you up." Fran shook her finger at Addie. "I wish I could help you, but we're just making ends meet at our place. The expansion of the feed business took all the money my brothers had saved up. Everything I make at the store goes to help pay the bills. Linc mentioned possibly looking for an investor or two to help out with the cash flow. Say. . ." She brightened. "Maybe that's what you need. An investor. If you had some backing, it would ease the burden. Maybe even pay off the loan entirely. Wouldn't that feel good, to go plunk the cash down right in front of that smug Mr. Poulter?"

Addie allowed herself a moment to imagine the satisfaction paying off the note early would have. But she shook her head. "I don't want an investor. I want to make it on my own. An investor would want to have a say in how I ran the business, and after the loan was paid off, I'd lose a percentage of the profits to a partner. If I'm going to be a success as a photographer, I have to do it myself."

The weight of the bank mortgage hung over her. All the equipment, most of the props, the backdrops, the glass slides, the development chemicals, even the frames and stationery, nearly everything had been purchased by Uncle Carl new when they came to Dodge City after losing his photography studio in Abilene. And then his heart had given out before they could open the shop.

Fran picked up the stack of portraits she'd tossed onto the settee and held them against her middle. "You want to be careful, Addie. Dodge City isn't exactly the best place for a woman on her own. I'm lucky my brothers let me out of their sight long enough to go to work, and they wouldn't if we didn't need the money. I wish you'd come live with me at our house. I'd feel better if you left the boardinghouse. My room isn't big, but it's got to be safer than Mrs. Blanchard's rooming house."

Addie shrugged. "My room is right next to Mrs. Blanchard's, and I haven't had any problems. Half the men who live at the boardinghouse are cattle buyers only here for the season, and they spend all their time downtown doing business. No one has given me any trouble."

"You haven't had much trouble because it's early yet. The trickle of cows and cowboys we've seen is nothing compared to the flood that's coming." Fran handed Addie the pictures and got to her feet. She smoothed her lace collar and straightened the pleats on her jade-colored dress. "When the herds start coming in every day, this town will bust wide open. That's why Bat's hiring new deputies, and I imagine the town marshal will as well."

"Then there's sure to be a deputy around when I need one. I'm not going to complain about the cowboys being in town. Nobody loves having his picture taken as much as a cowboy fresh off the trail. They're my bread and butter and some of the jam."

Addie stretched and brushed at her skirt. Uncle Carl hadn't approved of mourning clothes, said it flew in the face of everything the Bible said about eternal life for those who knew God. Consequently, Addie wore her customary plain ivory blouse and straight blue-gray skirt.

Though Fran fussed at her to wear more feminine gear and encouraged her often to come into the mercantile to see the latest inventory, Addie refused. Fran might be trying to catch a man, but Addie wasn't—not ever again. She was a businesswoman.

Besides, she didn't have the money for fancy clothes. Everything must go toward reducing the mortgage. If it wasn't for her, Uncle Carl wouldn't have lost the Abilene studio and had to start over. She owed it to him, and to herself, to make a success of this business.

Fran plucked a parasol from the prop box and opened it, twirling the lacy umbrella and tilting her head. "If you kept regular hours, one of my brothers could stop by to see you home safely when he came for me, but you're locked in your darkroom until all hours some nights."

Addie tapped the stack of photos into a neat pile and squared it up with the corner of her desk. She picked up a paper clip that had somehow found its way out of the box and returned it to the proper place so everything was neat and tidy. "Long hours are part of the job. When you're the only employee, you get to do everything. Photographs, developing, retouching, advertising, cleaning, bookkeeping, and sales."

"Speaking of sales, have you heard back about the Arden Palace?"

Grimacing, Addie propped her hip on the desk and began rolling down her sleeves. She frowned at the creases, but wrinkles were better than stains and acid pinholes. "Mr. LeBlanc said he'd let me know by tomorrow. I'm trying not to get my hopes up, but I can't help thinking what this would mean for the studio. The photos would appear on posters all over the state and maybe even in *Harper's* if you can believe what LeBlanc says. Heber put a bid in, and he let me know he expected to win the job."

"Wouldn't it be wonderful to see one of your photographs in *Harper's*?" Fran checked her reflection in the mirror, fussing with her hair and smoothing her eyebrows with her little finger, her heart-shaped face framed by the parasol. She wrinkled her nose. "You'd do a much better job than Heber Donaldson. He's too homely for words and an old crank besides." With an airy wave, she took in the studio. "You're so creative, and you've got that fabulous camera. Heber doesn't have anything that can touch it."

Addie smiled and walked over to trail her fingers down the heavy black drape hanging from the back of her Chevalier wet-plate monorail view camera. "I wanted Uncle Carl to start out a bit more cautious, but he was determined to make this studio as nice as the one he had in Abilene. He ran into some. . .difficulty in Abilene and lost his business. I think it was a matter of pride to him not to scale back when we got here." She sighed and caressed the gleaming wooden case. "It might be the best one in town, but it isn't paid for yet. With Poulter clamoring for the mortgage money, I really have to get the Arden commission."

The regulator clock on the wall chimed the hour. "Uh-oh." Fran snapped the parasol shut and tossed it in the prop box. "The mercantile calls. I'd better scoot." She headed for the door. Opening it, she turned back as the bell jangled. "Let me know how Bat likes his picture."

Addie's eyes returned to the portrait of the new sheriff. It was good work. Maybe if she showed it to Henri LeBlanc, it would provide the encouragement he needed to give her the commission to photograph the Arden Palace Theater.

Miles Carr lowered his right hand and shook Bat Masterson's. The weight of responsibility tugged at the brand-new badge pinned to his vest, even as a grin tugged at his lips. He glanced down at it and read: DEPUTY SHERIFF, FORD COUNTY, KANSAS.

Bat's eyes pierced him. "Deputy Carr."

"Congratulations." His friend Jonas stepped forward and shook Miles's hand, too. "I know you've wanted this for a while."

Jonas was right. Miles had wanted this for a long time. As long as he could remember. Now, to have the chance to serve alongside the likes of Bat Masterson, Charlie Bassett, Wyatt Earp, Bill Tilghman. . . His heart beat faster. Living legends all. Could he prove himself worthy to be counted among them? Could he live down his heritage and prove to himself and everyone else that he was good enough to be a lawman in Dodge City? The toughest, bravest young men in the West? Though at twenty-six Miles had a year on his new boss, Bat had such presence and reputation, he seemed much older.

Bat riffled through a set of keys and selected one. "I know you have your own sidearm, but a pistol and a rifle come with the badge. I find it handiest to keep the rifle here at the jail." He unlocked the gun cabinet behind his desk and withdrew a Colt and a holster so new the belt stood out stiffly and creaked as he folded it over before handing it to Miles. "You might prefer your own, but this gun has some stopping power. And it's intimidating to unruly cowboys." Bat slid the gun from the holster, cocked it, and sighted down the long barrel. Lowering the hammer, he flipped it in his hand and offered it, butt-first, to Miles.

Miles took the walnut-handled firearm, testing the weight. Guns were as familiar to him as a skillet to a bunkhouse cook. He'd been around them all his life, and until recently, he'd worked at the gunsmith's on Front Street. Whether shooting or repairing, there wasn't much about a gun he didn't know. "Can't go wrong with a Colt. You know the saying. 'God made men, and Colonel Colt made them all equal.'" He checked the cylinder, pointed the pistol at the far wall, and pulled the trigger. The click of the hammer coming down on an empty chamber snapped through the room. "The action is a little stiff. Do you mind if I file it?"

"It's your gun. If you want an easy pull, file away." Bat picked up his silver-topped cane. "You and Spooner will be working the same shifts, since you know each other well. The biggest chore is keeping the cowboys from ripping up the town every night." Light came into his pale eyes, and his mustache twitched. "They've been known to paint the town a very vivid shade of red. As county deputies, your jurisdiction is wider than the city police, but with the number of herds expected to come in, I've put you and Spooner at the disposal of the town marshal's office. Charlie Bassett will treat you right. County and city share the jail and the jailer responsibilities. I'll be around whenever I'm not out chasing horse thieves."

Bat handed him a box of cartridges, and Miles shoved bullets into the loops on the belt. Then he loaded five bullets into the gun, leaving the one under the hammer empty. Slinging the belt around his hips, he buckled it and holstered the gun.

"We give the cowboys quite a bit of leeway," Bat said. "That's the way the merchants and the mayor want it. Drovers roll into town, and the minute the herd is sold, they get paid off. Not long after, they're spending that money in the stores and saloons around town. We don't want to discourage this behavior." Bat tapped his cane on the floor. "Some of the townsfolk will bend your ear, telling you to come down harder on the cowboys, but don't let them sway you. Without those wild Texans and their cash, Dodge City would just be a former buffalo-hide camp."

Miles flicked a glance at Jonas. "So, go easy on the cowboys, but keep them from tearing up the town."

"It's a pretty tight line sometimes." Jonas shrugged. "For the most part, the men you'll go up against will be drunk, which works for you and against you. A drunk is usually easy to corral, but he's also unpredictable. You just have to use your judgment."

The door opened, and Addie Reid stepped inside. Miles drew a slow breath. Miss Reid had captured his attention the first time he'd passed her on the street, and he had found his mind straying to her more often than he wanted to admit. Foolish thoughts, since everything about her spoke of quality and class. If she knew who he really was, about his past, she'd run fast in the other direction. He couldn't seem to stop noticing the smallest details about her, though.

A few brown curls had escaped the coiled braid on the back of her head and brushed her cheeks. Gray-blue eyes widened, blinking to accustom themselves to the dark interior of the jail after the sunshine outside. A long strap slung crossways over one shoulder held a case at her hip.

"Excuse me, Sheriff. I was just on my way home and wanted to drop this by for you." She opened the case and withdrew an envelope. "I'm really pleased with how it turned out, and I hope you will be, too." She handed the sheriff the packet and turned to the deputies. Smiling first at Jonas, her eyes moved to Miles.

He had the odd sensation that she could see into his thoughts. He'd never been so scrutinized before, and he wanted to squirm.

Bat slid a silvery cardboard folder out of the envelope. "Miss Reid." He swept a glance at Miles and Jonas.

Miles realized his hands were fisted at his sides. He forced himself to relax.

"Have you met my deputies? Jonas Spooner"—he pointed with his cane—"and Miles Carr. I just swore Miles in a few minutes ago."

"Congratulations, Mr. Carr. I believe I've seen you in the gunsmith's shop next to my studio." Thick lashes fringed her eyes, and her lips were full and curved.

Before he could formulate an answer, Bat cut in. "An excellent likeness, don't you think?" He held the photograph up for them to see. "I had my doubts about the pose, but you've proven me wrong, Miss Reid."

"I'm glad you trusted me. It came out even better than I expected." She fastened the closure on her case.

Miles studied the tan leather box, an unwieldy accessory for a woman to carry, and realized it was a camera case. That made sense.

Jonas lifted a sheaf of papers from the corner of the desk. "I finished going through these Wanted posters and culled the ones we know are dead or in jail. Do you want me to burn them?"

"No, tear them in half. I'll use them as scratch paper." Bat continued to study his picture. "The city council was talking about having all the deputies' photographs taken soon. I'll recommend they consider giving the job to you, Miss Reid. If anyone can make silk purses out of a bunch of sows' ears, you can."

She didn't respond to his jest. Her cheeks paled, and her eyes bored into the paper Jonas held up. The Wanted poster of Cliff Walker. Train robber. Murderer.

Jonas caught her stare and flipped the paper over to study it. "Whew, he was a bad one, wasn't he?"

A cold finger of guilt stirred Miles's guts. He masked his features, turning to stare out the front window at the street. Of all the Wanted posters to turn up here on this day.

With a ripping sound, Jonas tore the paper across. "We don't have to worry about him anymore. Arrested, tried, found guilty, and hanged. One of that no-account nest of Walkers from up by Abilene. I sure would've liked to have been in on the posse that finally tracked him and his gang down."

Bat shoved at another stack of papers on his untidy desk.

"No, you wouldn't have, son. I was leading that posse, and it was the hardest ride and the closest shave I've ever had on a chase. Cliff Walker came within a gnat's eyebrow of shooting my head right off my shoulders before we cornered him, and he ran out of ammunition." He turned to Miss Reid. "One of the boys will see you to your boardinghouse, ma'am. Be a good idea if from now through the end of cattle season, you don't walk by yourself downtown."

"I'll see her home." Miles couldn't wait to get out of the sheriff's office. Bat and Jonas exchanged grins at his eagerness. Heat prickled across his chest. He didn't want Miss Reid to get the wrong idea, but she was a good excuse to leave. He didn't need any reminders about how lawless the Walker Gang had been. Not when he'd been considered one of them just a few short years ago.

Chapter 3

Fran chewed the end of her pencil and frowned at the ledger. Hap had been at it again, scrawling in her neat receipt book with his spidery, hurried penmanship. And it was up to her to make sense of the scribbles. Now, if it had been Wally, the numbers would be neat as a shiny new pin right out of the package.

Hap Greeley and Wally Price, cousins, business partners, and as different as chalk and cheese. And once more squabbling.

"Why did you order pickled beets?" Wally's fussy voice whined down the store. "You know we can get those locally."

"They were a bargain. Don't worry. We'll be able to sell them. I already got an order for a case from the Dodge House Hotel." Hap's voice, full of nonchalance and bonhomie, boomed. "You worry too much, Wally. We're primed to have the best season of our lives. The store's chock full of inventory, and cowboys are stampeding up the trail right to our doors."

Fran stood on tiptoe and leaned her elbows on the counter to see past the notions case to where her bosses stood by the cold stove.

Hap, big and loose limbed, with baggy gray trousers and a striped shirt, leaned against the counter. His sleeves were shoved up to reveal hairy, meaty forearms, and his boots had earflaps that slapped when he sauntered through the store. He took off his spectacles and rubbed them with his big red handkerchief. "It will be a good year."

Wally, immaculate in a starched white apron and black sleeve covers, held his clipboard against his snowy shirtfront. "If we don't have a good season, I'll know just where to lay the blame." Wally consulted the clipboard. His rosy face always looked freshly scrubbed, and Fran speculated that he used a ruler to part his greased hair. The white line bisecting his scalp was razor straight.

"Don't worry about it." Hap returned his glasses to his bulbous nose, dug his fist into one of the candy jars lining the counter, and popped a sourball into his mouth, rolling it until it made his cheek jut like a gopher's. "I told you, we're going to have a great season." He caught Fran leaning over the counter and winked at her. "With you and Frannie here seeing to things, there's not much chance of anything going wrong. Best thing we ever did, hiring Fran. The cowboys fall all over themselves to buy whatever she suggests to them."

Fran smiled. Hap had to be the most easygoing man in Dodge. He never scolded her if she was late for work, and when it was his turn to pay her, he usually managed to slip a couple of extra dollars into her pay envelope. The only person who ever got under his skin was Wally, and Wally had to work at it.

Wally squatted and began checking things off the list on his clipboard. "If you'd help out more around here, instead of hanging out over at Shanahan's or the Alhambra all the time, Miss Seaton and I wouldn't have to see to everything ourselves. You'd think, with a half interest in this mercantile, the store would garner more of your attention than a gambling hall."

Fran sighed and closed her ledger. Hap and Wally fought like an old married couple. And always about the same things. Hap's gambling and Wally's worrying. If they hadn't been left the store jointly by their grandfather, they never would've gone into business together, she was sure. But in the year since she started, Wally's harping rarely made a dent in Hap's good nature—or his gambling, and Hap's slipshod bookkeeping and fortune's favorite outlook hadn't rubbed off a bit on the straitlaced Wally.

"Miss Seaton, if you could clear some shelf space behind the flour bins, I'll put away some of these beets, though what we're going to do with more than two hundred cans of pickled beets, I'll never know." Wally's fussy, pencil-thin mustache twitched, and his nearly black eyes rolled.

"You'll think of something, Wally-me-lad." Hap smacked him on the shoulder, making Wally stagger and drop his pencil. "I believe I'll go out and drum us up some business. Fran, you hold the fort, right?"

The bell over the door jangled, and three cowboys strolled in. Wide-brimmed hats, easy rolling gait, tinkling spurs, and brash manners. Fran picked up her feather duster. Ignoring them, she went to the front windows and stretched to flick the duster along the top casing, being sure to raise her arms high enough to show just a hint of petticoat and ankle.

"Whooeee." One of the cowboys whistled low. "If I'd

have known there was a new clerk in this store this season, we'da made it our first stop."

Fran glanced over her shoulder and returned to her dusting. She stifled a sigh. Run-of-the-mill drovers. Again. When was someone exciting going to come through the door? Still, they looked ready to spend, so she should do her best by Wally and Hap and wait on them. She walked behind the counter and laid aside the duster. "What can I do for you boys?"

The tallest one grinned and leaned on the counter. "Well now, just a smile from your pretty lips would do for a start. We've been on the trail a powerful stretch of time. I haven't seen a pretty face in way too long." He jerked his thumb at his *compadres*. "Just these two ugly mugs and a dozen more just as homely, all the way from Uvalde."

One of his friends scowled and elbowed him over, jostling for room. "I ain't as ugly as you." He stuck out his hand, checked it, and then wiped it on his trousers before offering it to Fran again. "They call me Brazos Bill. And what would your name be, darlin'?"

She let him shake her hand and almost laughed when his pals demanded their own handshakes. Simple, uncomplicated cowboys. "You boys are just in off the trail? You must be in need of a lot of things then. New clothes? Candy? A gift to take back to your mothers or your sweethearts?" Fran always tried to steer the conversation toward mothers, wives, and sweethearts, just to keep the cowboys in line. Though they were high spirited and full of fun—as long as they hadn't been drinking—cowboys were fairly predictable.

She directed them toward the table in the center of the mercantile. Piles of shirts and pants in all sizes and colors lay in stacks on the long narrow top, and others hung from hooks and hangers on a rail overhead. "Everything you could want in the way of clothing, you'll find there. Boots and hats are on the wall here." Fran waved to the bank of shelves piled with boxes and the hat stand on the counter. She tilted her head and tapped her chin with her finger. "I think you'd look very handsome in brown. It would match your eyes." She held up a dark brown shirt with mother-of-pearl buttons.

As Hap had pointed out, cowboys had a tendency to buy most everything she suggested, and this group was no exception. She had to be careful not to abuse the power she wielded, though Hap encouraged her to use it. She didn't want to bilk the cowboys out of their hard-earned cash. It was a fine line, and she wasn't always sure she walked it correctly.

Wally beamed from behind the counter, totting up their purchases and taking their money. He wrapped the packages in brown paper and tied them with twine before disappearing into the back room.

When the Texans had their arms laden with purchases, two of them strolled out, but Brazos Bill stayed behind.

Fran returned to her dusting, but she was aware of Bill watching her every move.

"Say, when do you get off work here? I'd be pleased to buy you dinner at the hotel and maybe take in a show? I hear they put on a real good show over at the Comique." He pronounced it Com–ee–cue like most of the cowboys.

A tinge of excitement tugged at her, but at the same time disappointment encroached. She wasn't in the slightest bit interested in Brazos Bill or any of the Texas drovers. And while she'd love an opportunity to have dinner at the hotel and see a show at one of the theaters, she knew her brothers would never approve of her going out with a stranger. There was really only one man they would approve of her seeing. Her fingers curled around the handle of the feather duster.

The door chime rang out again. She glanced at the doorway and pressed her lips together. Speak of the devil.

She was at it again. Chatting with some cowboy.

Jonas used his heel to close the door and opened his coat so his badge and gun were on full display. "Afternoon, Fran." He nodded and sauntered up to stand beside the cowboy.

Fran shot him a "leave me alone" kind of glare and composed herself to looking all feminine and sweet again.

The cowboy straightened from lounging on the counter. "Fran, is it? Mighty pretty name for a mighty pretty girl." His grin had more than a whiff of wolf about it, and Jonas took a firm grip on himself so as not to shove the Texan's teeth down his throat. It wasn't this poor kid's fault he'd wandered into Fran's store and fallen for her looks. Fran was a mighty powerful draw.

Jonas tilted his head and raised his eyebrows at her. When she stared back at him with wide green eyes, he jerked his chin in the cowboy's direction, silently asking for an introduction.

She crossed her arms and huffed, blowing her red-gold bangs off her forehead. "Jonas, this is Brazos Bill. Bill, this is Deputy Jonas Spooner of the Ford County Sheriff's Office."

Bill nodded but didn't offer to shake hands, which was fine by Jonas.

"You just off the trail?" Jonas asked to be polite, though everything about the cowboy, from his work-stained clothes to his rank odor, shouted trail herd.

"That's right. Ramrod paid us off about an hour ago." Bill turned to face Jonas square, his muscles rigid. "I ain't doin' nothing wrong."

"I didn't say you were. Cowboys are welcome in Dodge City. We have a few rules, but most drovers don't find them too hard to live with."

"Rules? What rules? I don't remember too many rules last season." Bill scratched his hair over his right ear and squinted.

"Things change. The most important rule is: no firearms inside city limits. You can check your guns at the jail or one of the hotels." Jonas stared hard at the pistol tucked into the cowboy's belt. "Everything else is pretty much routine. Don't ride your horse into the saloons, don't cheat at cards, don't harass the womenfolk." Jonas tilted his head toward Fran, who gripped her feather duster as if she wished it was his neck.

"Since when is it harassing the womenfolk to talk to a store clerk?" Bill held his open hand out to Fran. "Have I said one harass-ful thing to you?"

"No, you've been most gallant. Deputy Spooner tends

to be overly cautious."

"Then you'll come out with me tonight?" The cowboy's face split in a wide grin once more.

Jonas pressed his lips together and folded his arms across his chest. "You talked to Linc this afternoon, Fran?"

Fran glared back for a moment and shook her head. "I'm afraid I won't be able to have dinner with you. My brothers expect me home right after work."

"Brothers? How many brothers?"

"Four," Jonas supplied. "They run the feed store over by the depot. You might've seen them. Seaton's Feed and Seed? Closest thing to grizzly bears we have around here, those Seaton boys."

Brazos Bill gulped.

Fran's brothers had as much of a name for themselves in Dodge City as Bat Masterson himself. Burly, surly, and without exception willing and able to take on a bull buffalo bare handed. They, more than any other, were the main reason why Fran hadn't gotten herself into more trouble with her flirting ways.

"The Seaton brothers." Bill rolled the idea around in his head for a minute. "You're their sister? Well, if they expect you home tonight, I'll just have to find other company, though it won't be as delightful as yours, I'm sure, Miss Seaton." He doffed his big hat. "You'll be certain to tell them I wasn't harassing you in any way, right? Good day." Snatching up his purchases, he all but bolted for the door.

Jonas laughed. "Works every time." He jerked when Fran whacked him with the duster. The cloud this produced made him sneeze. "What?"

"Why do you always have to ruin everything? You're worse than my brothers, even Stuart, and he's the worst of the lot." She plonked her elbows onto the counter and rested her chin in her hands. "It's not flirting to be nice to customers, and Wally and Hap won't appreciate you running off every man who comes in here and pays me some attention. You're not my keeper, you know."

"I do know." Jonas leaned down so his eyes were on the same level as hers. "Though I'd be happy to take on the role. Your brothers worry about some cowpoke getting the wrong idea. You're too pretty for your own good and their peace of mind."

She stuck her lower lip out. "They might as well be prison wardens, the way they order me around. And you are, too. Beats me why they don't mind you hanging around all the time."

"Your brothers and I have an understanding. I promised I'd look after you while you're in town, and that's what I'm going to do. You about ready to head home?"

Her mouth opened. "You have an understanding with my brothers? They've hired you to babysit me?" She sure looked cute when she was outraged, which was a good thing, since she seemed to be spitting mad more often than not when he was around.

"They aren't paying me to look out for you. It's part of my job as a deputy. I'd do it for anybody, so don't get all het up."

Wally Price came out of the back room. "This day has gotten away from me entirely. I didn't do half the things I wanted to. I suppose it's near to closing time. Miss Seaton, you did an excellent job with those cowboys. They bought far more than if I'd have been the one to wait on them." He seemed to notice Jonas for the first time. "Deputy Spooner."

"I've come to see Miss Seaton home. Her brothers just got a big delivery of feed at the store, and they asked me to come fetch her."

"Very good." The fussy little shopkeeper checked his clipboard then his watch. "You may go, Miss Seaton. I'll see you bright and early tomorrow morning, and we'll deal with these beets." His narrow mustache twitched like a rat's whiskers.

Fran grabbed her purse and hat from under the counter, stopping to check her reflection and pin the hat to her up-swept curls.

Jonas noticed the curve of her neck and the way a few wisps of hair played at her nape, and his heart bumped faster. Smothering his tender feelings for her, he took her elbow. "Quit primping. You look just fine. Every cowboy within eyesight of you will be gawking. You won't even have to flirt."

"You don't have to grab me up like a flapjack. I can take care of myself, you know."

He gentled his hold on her arm. "One of these days you're going to tangle with the wrong man and find yourself in a heap of danger."

"At least it would be an adventure. Better than the boring same-old, same-old I see every day."

Chapter 4

"The best thing about being a lawman is that no two days are ever the same." Bat leaned back in his chair and propped his feet up on the corner of his desk. His hat sat at a rakish angle, and he tapped the round, silver head of his cane in his palm. "There's always something popping up to keep things lively."

Miles dabbed his rag into the saddle soap and rubbed at the holster in his hands. "So, tell me more about what the merchants and saloon keepers have to say about enforcing the law on Front Street." He wanted to know exactly where he stood, so as not to run afoul of his new boss.

"There is a war going on in Dodge City. It's fought in the newspapers and at the polls. The mayor and myself and several others think we should—within reason—give the cowboys a free hand. Some of the local bigwigs want us to come down hard on the cowboys, keep them corralled, maybe even instill a curfew, if you can believe such a thing."

"A curfew, in Dodge? I don't know how you could enforce it without bloodshed." Miles held the leather belt up to the candlelight. Even this early in the season, hours after sundown, people still strolled the sidewalk outside, piano music rolled from the doorways of the saloons and theaters, and shouts and laughter ricocheted down the street. The theaters wouldn't close until about three in the morning, and the saloons wouldn't close at all.

"That's what I told him. The cowboys come to town expecting to let their hair down and play the curly wolf. They're looking to buck the tiger and get drunk and carouse with women of ill repute. All we ask is that they let us take their guns while they do it."

Miles's chest squeezed. Just because something was legal didn't make it right. The gambling, drinking, and immorality of Dodge City flew in the face of everything his newfound faith and God's Word told him. He didn't condone the behavior, but Bat was asking him to go light on the men who were doing the sinning. "What about the townsfolk? Don't they have a right to be safe?" He asked the question as innocently as possible. He didn't know his new boss well, and he didn't want to get him riled.

"Sure they do. But they live in Dodge City, the Queen of the Cattle Towns. If they want to be safe, they should go live in Topeka or somewhere. This is the West. The men work hard, and they play hard, too. Those same townsfolk like the money that rolls in every year, but they can't have it both ways. They have to take the cowboys as they are and the hijinks that go along with them. Dodge City is the last place in Kansas where Texans can bring their cattle. The legislature has pushed them out of Abilene, Ellsworth, Newton, and Wichita. They say it was the tick fever and the sodbusters who swayed them, but I have a feeling it was the preachers and the schoolmarms." Bat had warmed to his subject, and his eyes glowed.

"Most all the deputies and policemen in town side with the merchants and saloon keepers. In fact, most of the law enforcement in this county has investments in businesses on Front Street." Bat smoothed his mustache and ran his fingers down his lapel. "I've invested from time to time myself. I even owned a part of the Lone Star Dance Hall. You'd be wise to put your money into something like that. This town is a cornucopia of opportunity for a young fellow like you. Sink some money into one of the gambling houses or theaters and rake in the cash."

Miles bent to rub the leather harder, working the oil deep into the holster to make it supple and waterproof. "I'll have to have a look around." Investing wasn't a sin, though he'd steer clear of the saloons and brothels and such. Maybe the gunsmith's where he'd worked until recently. Or the saddle shop. Or even the livery. The buying and selling of horses was big business in Dodge City. A man could make a profit there. "Though I'll have to wait until I get paid." He grinned.

"Dodge City and Ford County pay their lawmen better than anywhere else in the West. You'll have a stake together in no time."

Jonas strolled in through the open doorway. He carried his rifle over his shoulder. "Things are livening up out there."

Bat swung his feet to the floor. "You can watch the jail, Spooner, though that won't be hard. Just the one prisoner, and he's asleep. Carr and I will take a stroll around, poke our heads in a few places, see what we turn up."

Miles's breath quickened, and his muscles tensed. His first patrol as a lawman. He made short work of slinging his gun belt on and holstering his weapon then checked that his badge was in plain sight. Forcing himself to relax, to steady his breathing, he took his hat from the rack by the door and settled it on his head.

The sheriff's boots rang on the boardwalk, and Miles matched his strides. Though Bat carried a cane, he showed no sign of a limp or any pain from the bullet he'd taken in the hip a couple of years ago. His eyes scanned the road and seemed to miss nothing.

Miles copied the action, sweeping the wide street and every window and doorway.

Cowboys clustered on the porch of the Long Branch Saloon. Rollicking piano music rolled through the open doors of the Saratoga, and down the street, the Alamo appeared to be doing a brisk business.

"There are more than a dozen saloons in town at the moment, and about twelve hundred residents. That number will more than double by midsummer. Both the residents and the saloons." Bat nodded to the cowboys as they passed through the crowd. "Evening, boys."

Miles searched every man with his eyes, looking for a weapon or signs of any mischief. Most of the young men had flushed cheeks and lurching movements, the beginnings of being knockdown drunk. They crowded into the saloon, laughing and jostling.

"They'll be sorry specimens by morning." Bat spoke mildly, as if he didn't care much one way or another.

"And broke, most likely. Nobody wins bucking the tiger except the dealer. I've never seen a faro game that wasn't crooked." Miles rested his hand on the butt of his pistol. "The saloons are fleecing the cowboys, and they're mostly too green and too drunk to know it."

"Gambling houses aren't running a charity. Nobody's making those boys go in there and gamble or drink. They could keep their money in their pockets and head home like good little lambs. All we're doing is providing a little entertainment. It's not like we're robbing them at gunpoint. They put up their money and take their chances." Bat frowned at him. "You sound more like a preacher than a deputy. You aren't against gambling and drinking, are you?" The smile that tugged at Bat's lips told Miles he thought the very idea a joke.

Miles's mouth went dry, and he scrambled for something to say that would be the truth and yet still keep Bat's respect. Nothing came to mind. "I think it's a shame that they risk their lives and break their backs getting longhorns up that trail, then, in the space of a couple of days or a week, everything they earned is gone."

His belly flipped. What a watered-down, tepid answer. *Where's your courage, Miles Carr?* But he had to keep his boss's respect, didn't he? How could they work together, count on each other in a pinch, if Bat thought he was some kind of weak-willed Bible pounder? Spouting off about how things were run in this town was his quickest ticket to losing his badge. He could do the job and keep his faith to himself.

"Might be a shame for them, but it's good for the merchants here." They passed the saddlery shop and paused before the windows of the photography studio. Though the blinds were drawn, slits of light appeared around the edges of the glass. Bat nodded toward the door. "She's working late again. I've warned her of the dangers of being downtown after dark, but she doesn't listen."

Addie Reid. Miles let a picture of her float through his mind. A pretty little thing and game, too. Trying to make a go of the photography studio in spite of her uncle's death. Though he admired her grit, he didn't see how a girl could run a successful business in this town. She didn't have anyone to protect her, and she seemed to have no fear letting cowboys traipse through the studio all day. Now that he was a deputy, he would make it a point to keep a closer eye on her place.

The gunsmith's shop next door was dark. Bat let the head of his cane trail along the siding until they got to the display window. "Shanky has some fine weapons. Does all the gunsmithing for the county. But you know that, I guess." Bat eyed a brace of derringers behind the glass. They lay in a velvet-lined box on a display shelf. Miles had worked on the pair himself just a few weeks ago.

They resumed their walk in the direction of the cattle yards. Far out on the prairie, the glow of sparks and steam announced the imminent arrival of the late-evening train. The long, mournful whistle rolled toward the town.

Miles touched the badge on his chest. A rush of pride washed over him, just as it had when he'd taken the oath and first pinned on the star. On the heels of that good feeling came a twinge of guilt. He had ducked voicing his views on the vice in this town. He should come clean. About that, and about his family connection to the Walker Gang. Then let Bat decide if he wanted to keep him on. He cleared his throat. "Bat."

The lawman stopped. He smoothed his mustache, his eyes piercing Miles.

At the last minute, Miles's courage failed him, as he envisioned Bat demanding the badge and gun back and, worse yet, hauling him to the jail and throwing him in a cell for being part of the Walker Gang. The law in Kansas had no love for the Walkers, and it wouldn't matter a plugged nickel that he hadn't done anything wrong. Being related to that nest of thieves would be enough to get his neck stretched in these parts.

Bat's eyebrows rose as he waited.

Miles voiced the first dumb thing that came into his head. "Anything else I should know about being a lawman in Dodge?"

The sheriff shrugged. "Mostly it's a case of being in the right place at the right time. Learn to smell trouble before it starts, and keep your gun handy."

Turning to retrace their steps, Miles's badge became even heavier. Being handy with a gun was second nature, and he'd long been able to smell trouble. But was he in the right place at the right time? He was new at this whole Christian thing. Could he be both a lawman and a believer? Would he have to give up one to be the other? If Bat ever found out who he was, being both wouldn't matter. He could find himself on the other side of a cell door faster than he could say, "Arkansas River."

Addie straightened and pressed her fists into the small of her back. She tended to lose all track of time when she was working, particularly when she was sequestered in the darkroom, but her rumbling stomach told her it must be past the supper hour.

Lifting the last print out of the warm acid fixing bath, she rinsed it and laid it on a sheet of glass. With her roller, she squeezed the excess water from the photograph and held it up to examine it in the rosy light of the red-glassed lantern on the wall.

Two more touch-up jobs awaited her attention, but that was fine, close work that needed a steady hand and sharp eyes. Better to leave it until tomorrow.

She lifted the red globe from the lantern, and golden, bright light filled the room. Clipping the last portrait onto the wire overhead to dry, she rolled her shoulders to ease the tension in her neck.

Working alone meant much longer hours than when she and Uncle Carl had split the developing duties. Tomorrow she would mount the dry photographs into cardboard frames for the customers to pick up. She inventoried the portraits she'd taken that day, judging the effects she'd tried to produce with each one.

By far, the best had been the Easton family. The butcher, his wife, and their three adorable sons. She'd posed them all together then persuaded Mr. Easton to allow her to photograph just the boys. At six, four, and two, they were stair steps in short pants. Golden halos of curls, rounded cheeks, sturdy legs, and engaging smiles. She'd set the middle boy on a brocade chair and placed the youngest beside him. The oldest boy she'd leaned against the plaster pedestal, much as she had Bat Masterson a few days ago. He'd been against the pose until she'd mentioned he'd look just like the sheriff. The picture had come out beautifully, and she had a feeling the Eastons would be very pleased. Maybe they'd even consent to letting her display a copy of the picture in the front window to entice other families to come in for a sitting.

Her final task was to store the chemicals and tidy everything up for the next day. This took her almost as much time as the developing, as some of the compounds used were volatile and, if treated casually, could injure or even kill. Uncle Carl's cautions and directions ran through her head as she closed up bottles of acid, lye powder, nitrates, and more.

Emerging from the dark room, she breathed deeply, trying to dispel the chemical smell from her nose. Working in such close quarters with so many strong emulsions and acids left her brain foggy. If only she could find a way to get clean air into the little room without letting in even the smallest bit of light.

Laughter and footfalls rang out from the boardwalk in front of the studio. A glance outside told her not only had she missed supper at the boardinghouse but darkness had fallen. She checked the clock. Eleven o'clock? She groaned and caught sight of her reflection in the mirror on the wall. "You've done it now, girl. Didn't Sheriff Masterson warn you about being downtown alone after dark?"

Four blocks to her boardinghouse. Between here and there, six saloons, two dance halls, the mercantile, and the jail.

And a gauntlet of cowboys.

They loitered on every porch, sauntered from saloon to saloon, and though most would treat a woman with deference, a few were truly dangerous—especially if they were under the influence of liquor. Life had taught Addie that coyotes often hid behind a mask of chivalry.

Still, she couldn't stay here all night. Taking one last look around the studio, Addie picked up her hat and bag and blew out the lantern. Things would only get worse if she waited. Last thing, she strapped on her camera bag. Though the Chevalier was her pride and joy, she would never leave her smaller Scovill behind. One never knew when a photographic opportunity might arise.

Locking the door behind her, she returned the key to her handbag and gripped the cloth sack close to her body. Petty thieves had been known to slice the cords of a lady's reticule to steal it off her wrist, and they weren't always careful with their knife. The camera case bumped familiarly against her hip. She wore the strap diagonally across her chest, which she knew wasn't ladylike, but carrying the camera that way ensured it wouldn't slip off her shoulder and also left her hands free.

Music rolled and light spilled from the windows and doorways of the saloons and dance halls. Her studio, tucked between a leather goods shop that boasted the "best fitting boots in the West" and a gun shop, was a good location for garnering foot traffic and drop-in business but not so good from a security standpoint. Still, it wasn't right next door to a saloon, which would've been much worse.

Squaring her shoulders, she stepped out of the recessed doorway and headed west. Clumps of men dotted the boardwalk between her and her destination. She took a deep breath, kept her chin up, and walked with purpose. If she acted scared, it marked her as easy prey.

When she reached the first group of cowboys, the odors of the stockyards, hard work, tobacco, and horses assailed her. They jostled, elbowed, and laughed. A match scratched off a boot sole, and one of them lit a huge cigar, puffing clouds of smoke into the night air.

Though they stood aside to let her pass, she could feel their eyes on her. Refusing to cower, she looked straight ahead, praying no one would stop her. She really needed an alarm clock in the darkroom. Something to help her remember the time and never get caught out like this again. Though once she'd started the developing process, she couldn't stop halfway through.

Her breath came a bit easier as she passed by the group. Perhaps she would make it just fine after all. Then she came abreast of the Long Branch.

A rowdy crew of firebrands lounged and joked on the porch. "Whooeee, lookit here." One cowboy elbowed his companion. "They sure do grow 'em pretty here." He stepped directly into her path, and she was forced to edge around him. "Hey there, little lady. Can I buy you a drink?" He had flushed cheeks and looked to be about eighteen. She kept walking, and he sidled along with her. His chaps flopped, and his spurs clanked with each stride.

"No, thank you."

He frowned and breathed beer fumes across her face. She kept walking, but he crab-stepped to get around in front of her. "There's no call to be uppity. Just one drink. No harm in that."

Addie started to inhale, but the alcohol on his breath hit like a blow. A cough exploded from her throat. She gasped. "Really, sir, I have to go. I don't want a drink. I just want to get home." Though she trembled, she tried to hide it. These men were like wolves. If she showed the least bit of fear or weakness, they would pounce on it. Her hands gripped the strap on her camera case.

"I'll go with you, then. Can't be too careful here in old Dodge." He shoved his hat back and tucked his thumbs into his belt. "My name's Brazos Bill. What's yours?"

His eyes were glazed, and his exaggerated gestures told her he was past halfway to drunk. Not only was he in no condition to protect her from anything, he might get the wrong idea the minute they were out of sight of the others.

"I'll be fine on my own, thank you. Why don't you go back to your friends?"

He scrubbed the side of his head and kicked his toe against the end of a bench under the window. "I think I'd rather make friends with you." His hand snaked out and grabbed her wrist. "I asked you polite to come in and have one little drink."

She tugged against his grip, but his fingers didn't budge. "Sir, please. You're hurting me." Her breath came fast, and her heart bumped. His friends had gone into the saloon. She didn't know whether to yell or not. Would screaming make him let go or would it bring more cowboys? Why hadn't she realized how late it was getting?

"You gonna have that drink with me?"

"Let her go." The icy command came from the darkness of the alley behind her.

She swiveled her head to look, but she couldn't see anything in the deep shadows.

Brazos Bill stiffened, and his grip tightened, making her fingers tingle. "This ain't none of your affair."

"I said, let her go."

Boots scuffed on the dirt, and she discerned a darker space in the blackness of the alley. Her throat tightened. Something sinister and powerful came from that shape.

"Mister"—Bill scowled—"I'm talking to the lady. You should move along and go find your own gal."

Addie wrenched her arm but couldn't break free. Her skin burned and the bones of her wrist ground together. She'd have bruises for sure.

The man in the shadows emerged. Light from a window gleamed off the star on his chest.

A breath whooshed out of her at the same time Brazos Bill sucked in air.

Miles Carr.

The cowboy's grip loosened a fraction, but he didn't let go. "What is it with you deputies? Can't a fellow talk to a girl in this town? First it was that clerk at Greeley's, batting her lashes and playing all flirty. Now it's this one"—he lifted her hand—"waltzing through town, offering herself as fair game, then crying when someone takes her up on it."

Addie gasped. "I did no such thing. I have a right to walk to my own home unmolested by drunken cowboys. Now unhand me, you. . .you Texan!"

Deputy Carr closed the distance between himself and the cowboy. "I've asked you twice to unhand the lady. If I have to ask again, I'll arrest you for assault."

Bill quivered.

The deputy stood his ground, and the look in his eyes chilled Addie and fired her blood at the same time. Gratitude, that was all it was. For his rescuing her. It had nothing to do with how handsome and courageous he was. Nothing at all.

Flinging her hand away, Bill backed up a step and raised his hands shoulder high. Disgust lined his suntanned face. "Fine. Take her. She ain't worth a night in a cell. This town sure has changed. Everywhere I look there's a deputy telling me what I can and can't do."

To Addie's amazement, Miles relaxed a fraction and slapped the cowboy on the shoulder. "I'm sure you'll find something else to do tonight."

Brazos Bill strode off toward the Long Branch, and Miles turned to her, a fierce expression in his eyes. "What do you think you're playing at, strolling through town after dark? You're lucky I came along."

She pressed her hand to her chest and gulped. "Thank you. I thought he was going to drag me right into that saloon."

The scowl painting the lawman's face eased. "C'mon. I'll see you home."

He took her elbow, and she could feel each of his fingers through her sleeve. She needed to remind herself of what had happened to her the last time a man made her heart flutter and her breath hitch. And she was of no mind to go down that road again.

Miles had wanted nothing more than to push his fist through that cowboy's face. The fire burning in his belly at the sight of Miss Reid trying to get out of that drover's grip didn't abate as they walked away from the scene. The only thing that had kept him from littering the street with the man's body had been Bat's caution to use a light touch where the cowboys were concerned. At least he hadn't had to draw his gun.

They walked in silence the remaining blocks to Mrs. Blanchard's Boardinghouse. Miss Reid didn't ask how he knew where she lived, and he didn't offer to enlighten her. The only rooming house on this end of town was Mrs. Blanchard's, and she was also the only landlord who had women residents—reputable women, anyway—so it didn't take much detective work to figure out.

They reached the porch of the boardinghouse, and Miss Reid turned on the step to face him. Their eyes were on the same level, and the starlight picked out the blue glint in hers. He backed up half a step.

She pressed her lips together, swallowed, and gave him a

polite smile. "Thank you for coming to my rescue. That man really frightened me."

"You had reason to be scared. You shouldn't be out this late without an escort." The gruffness in his voice surprised him, but it was better than the shouting he wanted to do. "Bat said he'd warned you about that."

She nodded, and he noticed the slight upturn to her nose. Some aroma clung to her clothes, like medicine or soap or something. Probably the stuff she used to make her pictures.

"I have orders to fill, and once I get into the darkroom, I tend to lose all track of time." She shrugged, spreading her hands like a little girl.

Her appeal made him even gruffer. "Next time you work late like this, raise the blinds in one of your front windows when you're ready to go home and me or one of the other deputies will walk you home. Good night, ma'am." He tipped his hat and strode away from her to resume his patrol, leaving her standing on the steps.

A block away, the lights and sounds of Front Street pulled him along, reminding him that he was a lawman and he couldn't afford any distractions, no matter how pretty they might be.

Chapter 5

"I have chosen you, *mademoiselle*, because I believe you have a gift." Henri LeBlanc waved his hands with all the fervor of his Gallic nature. "It is you who will capture the essence of my beloved theater, as you have captured my heart." He imprisoned Addie's hand, bent from the waist, and kissed the air just over the backs of her fingers. "The talent you displayed with your portrait of our esteemed sheriff convinced me you were the one I have been looking for."

They stood in the opulent foyer of the Arden Palace Theater, scheduled to open in just three more days. Addie withdrew her fingers and crossed her arms at her waist. "Mr. LeBlanc, what would your wife say?" She tilted her head and raised her eyebrows. Fran, standing just behind her, snickered. Knowing better than to take the Frenchman's words seriously, Addie waited for his response.

He laughed, flicked a handkerchief from his pocket, and dusted the gleaming handrail leading to the second floor. "You think she would lead me to the guillotine, no? Not my Gisette. She would agree with me, that you"—he nodded to Addie and included Fran in the gesture—"are like two beautiful roses. You complement my beautiful theater with your very presence."

Fran giggled again. Addie cast a glance over her shoulder

at her friend. Eyes wide, lips parted, Fran appeared to be trying to see everything at once. Not that Addie could blame her. Every surface in the Arden Palace shone with sparkling newness—plush carpeting, velvet drapes, textured wallpapers, gilt frames. The smell of new paint lingered.

The front door swung open, and Addie stifled a groan. Heber Donaldson, red faced and glaring, stomped in. "Le-Blanc, what is the meaning of this? You can't possibly choose *her* over me. I'm the most respected and experienced photographer in the county." He jabbed his finger toward Addie but didn't look at her. Instead, his eyes bored into the little Frenchman. "This is an outrage."

LeBlanc shrank back and patted his forehead with his handkerchief. He darted a look behind him to the safety of the office doorway and swallowed. "*Monsieur*—"

Donaldson ignored his protest, turning on Addie. "What did you do? Offer to take the photographs for free? That's the only way you could've undercut my bid. You're getting too big for yourself, girlie. Why don't you go back to the kitchen where you belong?"

"Monsieur, please, this is most inappropriate—" The proprietor tried to step in, but Donaldson rounded on him again.

"I'd like to know what you think you're playing at, Le-Blanc. I thought we had a deal." Donaldson shook his finger in LeBlanc's face. "You're supposed to give the job to me."

"No, no, nothing was certain." He raised his hands, his brow scrunching. "I discussed it with my wife, and she preferred the mademoiselle's portraiture."

"Ha! That explains it. Skirts usually stick together. I

might've known you'd be under your wife's thumb."

Addie shot a look at Fran, whose eyebrows rose and jaw dropped in a "do you believe this guy" expression.

The little Frenchman's dark eyes snapped fire. "That is enough, monsieur. You will not come to my establishment and insult me this way. Your bid was submitted and considered, but we have elected to give the job to someone else. I would prefer it if you would leave now. The mademoiselle has work to do." He pointed to the door, stuffing his handkerchief back into his pocket and smoothing his lapels.

Donaldson scowled, his face getting even redder. "You'll be sorry about this, girl. You'll be sorry you didn't quit and turn everything over to the bank. This job won't matter. You'll never make the payments, and by the end of the summer, you'll be washed up." He slammed the door hard enough on his way out to rattle the chandelier.

Addie took a shaky breath. "Where would you like us to start, and is there anything in particular you'd like photographed?" Her knees trembled, but she strove for a professional demeanor, as if getting bawled out by a competitor hadn't bothered her in the least.

She rested her hand on the cart she'd used to haul her equipment to the theater. A cart had been necessary, because for a job this big she'd packed up the Chevalier and brought it over from the studio. Anything less would be inadequate. This tableau called for a large print. But she had her smaller Scovill along as well. Best to be prepared.

LeBlanc's smile, though not as broad as before Donaldson's interruption, returned. "I should think you would know what is best. What I had envisioned, it is for the photograph to make the viewer want to see my beautiful Palace." Le-Blanc ran his hand down a lovely fluted column. "I should like to see some of the detail but also the grand openness of the theater. Yes?"

Addie nodded. "I would like to take a portrait of you as well. Perhaps here in the foyer, under one of the paintings? Or beside the ticket window. The scrollwork here would photograph beautifully."

"What about by these potted palms?" Fran touched the tip of one of the fanned-out leaves.

LeBlanc couldn't decide, posing himself in one place and then another before changing his mind altogether. "No, no, not a picture of me. It will be best to take only my beautiful Palace."

Addie, conscious of time ticking away, began lifting boxes of equipment. Fran followed suit. They entered the opulent auditorium and stood still for a moment. The grandness of the décor and the sheer size of the room sent a covey of quail darting around her insides. "Thanks for coming with me. With no natural light in the theater, I'm going to need someone to help me with the magnesium powder flash."

Addie unfolded the legs of her tripod in the center aisle. As she'd requested when LeBlanc had delivered the excellent news that he'd given her the commission, every chandelier had been lit and every wall sconce glowed brightly. Even the boxes on the second floor had lamplight streaming from them. "I'll take a few with the curtains drawn across the stage then a couple with them open."

"How many altogether?"

Addie grimaced. "I brought enough plates for twenty exposures. I know that's a lot, but I've never photographed something on this scale, so I want to try a lot of combinations. I wish Uncle Carl were here." Though she'd been confident enough when she put in her bid for the job, now that she was faced with it all her uncertainty and self-doubts came roaring back.

"I never thought Donaldson would show up here." Fran shook out the camera drape and handed it to Addie. "Bad enough that he stood in the middle of the mercantile yesterday and announced that LeBlanc was out of his mind to hire an amateur for such a job. He even hinted that you had used your 'feminine wiles' to get the bid. Though he did assure everyone that after you ruined the job, LeBlanc would be only too glad to come crawling to him, Heber Donaldson, a *real* photographer."

Addie grimaced and pressed her hand against her stomach. "I don't understand why he's so upset. There's plenty of work to go around."

"He's just jealous. Before you opened your studio, his was the only studio on Front Street, and he got most of the cowboy business. He knows he can't compete with you, not your photography and not with the cowboys. They would much rather have a pretty girl take their pictures."

"I just hope he's not right about this job being too much for me." She hated to admit the extent to which his tirade had rocked her.

"You can do this. And I'll stay, even if it takes all day."

Fran set the box with the wet-plate slides on one of the plush velvet chairs. She put her hands on her hips. "What should I do first?"

The preparations for the first picture took much longer than Addie had hoped, but thankfully, Mr. LeBlanc left them alone. She sighted through the camera and framed the shot to include the entire stage and the first two boxes on either side of the second floor. *Depth of field. Focus, exposure, angle, lighting.* Addie rehearsed everything her uncle Carl and her own practice had taught her and tried to forget how important this commission was. If she fell flat on her face, the bank would call in her loan, and her dreams and vision would disappear into the prairie air.

"Be careful with those two boxes. Keep them separated." She pointed to the two containers of flash powder ingredients. For safety's sake, she didn't carry them in the same box. Photographers had been known to burn down their own studios when flash powder ingredients got out of hand.

Fran helped where she could, and she put her own artistic talents to work straightening the folds of the stage curtains and even running upstairs to fuss with the drapes framing each private box. "What this place needs is some flowers." She leaned over one of the boxes. "Especially the foyer, but even in here. Imagine a couple of big vases of roses or carnations on either side of the stage. Wouldn't that look spectacular?"

"Where are we going to get those kinds of flowers in the middle of Kansas? How about a few Indian paintbrush stalks or sunflowers or yucca stems?" Addie set up her scales for measuring out the combustible elements she would need for the flash and paced off the distance between the camera lens and the curtain. She did a few quick calculations in her head.

"You're right." Fran's voice echoed in the vast room. "Too bad. They would look great." She disappeared from the box and soon emerged though a side door.

Addie finally had the magnesium powder and potassium chlorate measured out and in the holder. Her hands shook as she lit a long taper candle and handed it to Fran. "I'll be under the drape. When I point to you, touch the flame to the edge of the pan." She demonstrated with her finger. "Don't look at the pan when you do, or you'll be seeing black spots and stars. The flash powder will ignite and make a very bright light."

A tight band of tension wrapped itself around Addie's middle, and a sinking feeling of having bitten off more than she could chew started in her chest. With chilly fingers she loaded the first plate into the camera by feel, careful to keep it concealed from all light. She ducked under the drape, the familiar, closed-in, airless feeling of the heavy cloth isolating her from everything but the view through the lens. Allowing her eyes to accustom themselves to the darkness, she reached around to the front of the camera to remove the lens cover. She had to stretch, because she'd extended the accordion-pleated bellows on the Chevalier to full length, using every inch of the monorail mounting. With a dry mouth, she raised her right hand and pointed toward Fran, remembering to close her eyes.

Pop! Foof!

The familiar minor explosion of flash powder blasted the room with a light so bright she could see it even with closed eyelids. Her eyes popped open, and she reached around to cap the lens. When everything was dark and covered, she emerged from under the drape. Triumph trickled through her and loosened her stomach muscles.

"Wow!" Fran lowered her arm and peeked over her elbow. "Did it work?"

"I think so, but the proof will be in the developing." Addie tucked her thumbnail between her teeth and clamped down, surveying the room for an interesting angle. "I'm thinking we'll do another shot from here with a longer exposure and no flash powder. I'd like to capture the feel of an opening night with all the soft lights."

She set up and took picture after picture, from the balcony, from the foyer, from the stage looking outward to the seats and boxes. She even took one from well back in one of the boxes with only the stage in view, perfectly framed by the box curtains. Every photograph with the Chevalier took an age to set up as she had to prepare a new wet-plate and flash powder for each new location. As she held the watch in her palm timing the exposure, she knew in her heart the pictures would be good. She recapped the lens. Time for a little fun.

"Fran, go raise the curtain again and stand on stage. Pretend you're the actress you always wanted to be." Addie repacked all her equipment and lifted her Scovill. The dry-plate technique was so much quicker, though it didn't provide quite as sharp a detail nor could she print large photographs with it.

Fran grinned and vanished behind the drapes. A few thumps and bumps and the massive curtain parted to reveal a large stage. A painted landscape on canvas provided the backdrop. At least it wasn't advertisements as some theaters used. Fran struck a pose, lifting one hand, palm up as if beckoning to someone in the first box. She clutched the lace at her throat with the other hand and filled her expression with pleading.

"Hold that." Addie rested the Scovill on the back of one of the chairs and uncapped the lens. "Don't move or you'll just be a blur." She counted off the seconds in her head. "Okay, you can relax."

They took several more portraits, each one sillier than the last, before Addie announced she was out of plates. "That will have to be it. I think I used a whole month's allotment."

"Allotment?" Fran straightened from where she was almost hanging out of one of the balcony boxes and began braiding her hair. The Rapunzel pose Fran had suggested had sent them both into a fit of giggles that made taking the picture hard.

Addie removed the plate from the camera. "Yes. I'm on a strict budget, and photographs just for fun can be expensive. I've given myself an allotment of dry-plate money, and I think I've used it all up for this month." And she'd better cut that allotment back from now on if she was going to have any hope at all of paying off the mortgage. Only about ten weeks to go and she hadn't made much of a dent, though this commission would be a big step in the right direction.

Fran came down and sat on the edge of the stage between two footlights. She crossed her ankles and let her legs swing. "You haven't mentioned the little scrape you got into last week on the way home." Her green eyes held a slight accusation. "I've been waiting for you to tell me about it."

Addie repacked the Scovill, nestling it into the case and clipping it into place so it didn't slide around. The clips had been a good idea, even if the man who had thought them up and fashioned them for her hadn't been such a good idea for Addie.

"How did you hear about it?" She kept her voice neutral, though her heart did a little flip-flop. How many times since that night had her thoughts turned for no good reason to the newest deputy in Ford County?

"Jonas told me. I guess Miles must've told him." Fran hopped off the stage. "Did he really save you from a wild cowboy and walk you home in the moonlight?"

Addie turned away and wrinkled her nose at her friend's romantic notions. "It wasn't like that."

Fran hurried up the aisle until she stood in front of Addie. Placing her hands on Addie's shoulders, she gave her a little shake. "Then tell me how it was. Who was the cowboy?"

She shrugged off Fran's hands and sat in one of the plush seats. Fran plopped into the row behind her. Addie turned and stacked her hands on the back of the chair. She had been trying to forget about that night, and she'd been scrupulous about watching the time so as to be home before dark, but she could see Fran wasn't going to let her off without hearing the entire story. "He said his name was Brazos Bill, and he wanted me to go to the saloon with him for a drink."

"Brazos Bill?" Fran's voice shot high. "Are you joshing me? He came into the store and asked me out to dinner. I'd have gone, too, but Jonas shoved his big nose into my business and ran him off."

"You should be thankful. I wouldn't like to think about what might happen to a girl in the company of Brazos Bill when he's been drinking. Jonas did the right thing."

"Oh, pooh on Jonas Spooner. The man's worse than all my brothers combined. A mother hen has nothing on Jonas."

Addie shook her head and wondered what it would be like to have someone that protective of her. Though, come to think of it, Miles had done a very good job of protecting her that night. "When are you going to see that all Jonas's blustering is because he loves you?"

"But I don't want him to love me. I want him to leave me alone."

Addie looked up from stowing equipment. "Do you? Do you really?"

"Tell me what happened the other night." Fran evaded her question and got busy gathering things up.

"Brazos Bill grabbed hold of my arm and wouldn't let go. I thought he might drag me right into the saloon. But Miles happened on the scene and changed Bill's mind for him."

Fran sighed. "Romantic. And exciting. Like a knight rescuing a fair maiden. What did he say to you when he walked you home?"

"He told me I was foolish to be out alone after dark, and he was right."

"That's all? Surely he did something or said something that could be considered romantic."

He had arranged for her to signal one of the deputies if

she had to be in the shop late and needed an escort to the boardinghouse, but did that qualify as romantic? And if it did, was she willing to share that, even with Fran? "No, he just did his job, told me to be more careful in the future, and left me on the steps."

Fran frowned in disgust. "Men are so dense."

"You're dense if you don't get in on this." Deputy Ty Pearson counted a roll of bills.

Miles and Jonas stood on the front porch of the sheriff's office and watched the activity on the street. Ty had been going on for quite a while, and Miles was heartily sick of it. Jonas nudged him and jerked his chin. Miles followed his gaze and found Addie and Fran crossing Front Street, pulling a cart laden with boxes.

"Think we should go help them?" Miles whispered out of the side of his mouth.

Jonas shook his head. "I offered to help them when they headed out, but Fran set me back right quick. They were on their way to photograph that new theater of LeBlanc's."

At least Addie was doing business in the daylight when the streets were pretty safe. Miles didn't take his eyes off the pair until they disappeared into the photography studio.

"I'm telling you, it's the easiest money I ever made. You two won't ever get rich on a deputy's salary." Ty licked his finger and riffled through his cash once more. "Invest in one of the businesses. I started out south of the deadline because that's all I could afford, but now I've got enough to buy into one of the places on Front Street."

"There's nothing south of the deadline but brothels and booze joints."

Ty looked up, the gleam of greed in his eyes. "So? That's where most of the cowpokes spend their money. A little companionship and rotgut. No reason why I can't make a buck or two off it. They ain't hurting nobody."

Miles's gut clenched. "They're hurting each other. How many knife fights have we broken up down there? How many times does one of those girls get knocked around? I've only been a deputy for a couple of weeks, and I've already had to fetch the doctor for three of those girls."

Jonas nodded. "What they're doing is morally wrong and goes against everything God tells us is right in the Bible. It might not be against the laws of this county to visit the brothels or to get blind, stinkin' drunk, but it sure is contrary to the laws of God."

Miles wanted to squirm at the slack-jawed look Ty gave Jonas, and at the same time, he wanted to applaud Jonas's fearlessness in speaking up. Where Miles hid behind logic and reasoning as his motivation for standing against the avarice in Dodge City, Jonas came right out and said God didn't approve of the sinning. Though Miles was fairly new to his Christian faith, he wondered if he would ever be as bold as Jonas, as matter of fact and open. He hoped it would be a long time before he was asked point-blank to defend his faith.

Ty shoved his bankroll into his pocket and rested his

hands on his narrow hips. "I think you missed your calling, Spooner. You should've been a preacher. You should carry a Bible instead of a gun. Though I don't know as the Good Book would be much help down across the deadline when the bullets start flying." He threw back his head and laughed. "That the way you feel, too, Carr?"

Prickly sweat broke out on Miles's chest and his mouth went dry. He flashed a look at Jonas, but his friend's face was expressionless. He was saved from having to answer when Bat strolled out of the office and stretched. "Evening."

Ty wasn't ready to be done with the conversation. "Hey, Sheriff, I was just telling these boys they should get in on some of the action and buy into one of the businesses like you and me done. Tell 'em how dumb it would be to miss out on this opportunity."

Bat reached into his vest pocket and pulled out his watch. "I've mentioned it to both these gentlemen before. They're grown men. They can decide on their own."

"They're fools if they don't." Ty leaned against the hitching post, his expression clearly saying he already thought Jonas was a fool and that he wasn't so sure about Miles.

Bat snapped his watch shut. "I want you boys to stay close to Springer's place tonight. Dora Hand's performing down there, and it looks like it's going to be another packed house. Ty, I want you and Miles at the front door checking weapons, and Jonas, I want you in at the bar."

"Boss, why can't I be at the bar?" Ty took off his hat and ran his hand through his hair. "I'd sure like to see Dora perform. I hear she's good."

"She is very good. I want Jonas inside because I can trust him not to drink while he's in there." Bat bent his gaze on Ty, who squirmed.

Must be a story there. If Bat knew Miles well enough, he'd know Miles never touched the stuff either. But Bat *didn't* know Miles well enough, and Miles hadn't done or said anything to make Bat think he might be as devout as Jonas. Again he felt a thrust of guilt.

"As to the investing," Bat said, "I can understand Jonas's reluctance to buy into one of the more. . .salubrious endeavors here in town. Are you interested in something else? I've heard the livery is looking to expand, as well as the hotel."

Jonas shook his head. "No sir, I think I'll hang on to my money. I've got my eye on a little spread just south of here, and I've just about got enough money saved up to buy it. When I've got the money all put together, I'm planning on getting married and settling down to ranching." Jonas squared his shoulders as if he expected another ribbing from Ty.

Ty straightened and took a deep breath, but before he could say whatever he was bursting to say, Bat cut across the conversation. "I always admire a man who sets a goal and goes after it, regardless of what others might think." He clapped Jonas on the shoulder.

Miles knocked a dirt clod off the boardwalk with the toe of his boot. Not only had he missed a chance to stand up for his faith, but he'd also missed a chance to impress Bat. If he jumped in now, he'd just sound stupid. Why couldn't he be more like Jonas, who had no fear in just being himself?

But Miles didn't want to be himself. He wanted to be so much better than anything he'd been in the past.

Chapter 6

"What do you mean I can't go?" Fran set the coffeepot down on the stove hard enough to make the stove lids rattle.

Her eldest brother, Linc, tipped his chair back to lean against the wall and hooked his thumbs under his suspenders. "You can't go out at night by yourself, and none of us can take you. We've got to deliver four loads of feed to the fort, and we'll probably stay over."

"You could leave early. Nothing says you have to stay." She glared at each of her brothers. When Nathan grinned and ducked his head, she narrowed her eyes. "Just why are you staying over?"

Jack and Stuart, the twins, stood as one, mumbled their thanks for the meal, and scooted out the door like raccoons with their tails on fire. Nathan, pinned in the corner by Linc, looked like an animal in a trap. He studied his tin plate and dabbed his finger on a couple of corn bread crumbs.

Linc dug a toothpick from the pot in the center of the table and stuck it in the corner of his mouth. "We've been invited to a little shindig the quartermaster is giving."

Fran sucked in a breath. "A party at the fort?" She was immediately torn. A party at the fort with all those officers in uniform or tickets to opening night at the Arden, a gift from Mr. LeBlanc after they'd finished the photographs? "If you won't let me go to the Arden, then take me to the party."

Nathan snickered but subsided when Linc raised an eyebrow in his direction. Though Nathan was older than Fran by more than a year, sometimes he acted like a kid. Not so with Linc, who acted more like a father to them all than an older brother.

He turned his bland stare toward Fran. "You haven't been invited to the fort. It isn't that kind of party."

Frustration bloomed in her chest. "So I'm supposed to sit at home waiting for you while you get to go visit friends? I have an invitation." She dug the card from her pocket. "Mr. LeBlanc had them specially printed just for opening night. Addie's going. It's not like I would be alone."

"You might as well be. Two helpless lambs in a town full of wolves. You're not going out at night without a proper escort, and since we won't be here to do it, home you'll stay. If Addie goes, that's her business, though she should know better than to go alone."

"If you'd let me go with her, she wouldn't be alone."

"I've said all I'm going to say on this matter." Linc pushed his plate back and picked up his coffee cup to drain it.

Nathan shot Fran a sympathetic look, but he obviously wasn't so sympathetic he'd give up an overnight at the fort just to see her safely to and from the Arden.

She was going to have to do it. They left her no choice. And she'd have to hurry before Linc left for the day. Her lower lip trembled, and she turned her back to her brothers. After a second or two, she sniffed and let her shoulders shake just a bit. With little effort she squeezed two tears from her eyes and let them roll down her cheeks. She made a show of digging for a handkerchief. When she couldn't find one, she lifted the hem of her apron to dab at her eyes, though she was careful not to disturb the tear tracks. A sob escaped her throat. The more she thought about missing opening night, the easier the tears came.

She waited for it, almost smiling when Linc's chair scraped on the floor. "Now, Frannie, don't cry." His big hands engulfed her shoulders. "You know I don't like to see you cry."

She shrugged, but his hands didn't move. "I don't think it's so much to ask. After all I do around here. The cooking, cleaning, washing, not to mention working at the store." Though she kept the apron hem pressed to her lips, she made sure he could hear every anguish-infused word.

"You do work hard." Linc patted her shoulder with awkward tenderness, his voice so sad guilt poked her with pitchfork prongs.

"And I don't ask for much in return. One evening. I was looking forward to it so much. It isn't every day a girl gets an invitation to an opening night. Can't we reach some kind of compromise so I can go?" She lifted her face to him at the precise moment two more tears fell.

He all but crumpled.

At his pained expression, she did feel bad. But she was so close to getting what she wanted. . .

"We've already told the quartermaster when to expect us with the feed. I can't back out now." He looked tortured.

Her chin quivered, and she blinked her wet lashes.

"Please, Linc? For me?"

Nathan edged around the table. "Say, Linc, I have an idea. Why don't we get someone else to walk Fran to the theater? It doesn't have to be one of us."

Fran's tears stopped. The idea took hold in Linc's eyes, and the lines disappeared from his face. "That's a fine idea, Nate. We can ask Jonas to see her safely there and back."

Her jaw dropped. "Jonas?"

"Deputy Spooner would be just the man to ask." Linc folded his arms across his chest and looked down at her. "In fact, I wouldn't trust anyone else with the job."

Her mind scrambled to salvage the situation. "What about one of the other deputies? Jonas might be on duty or not available." She shot a glare at Nathan for coming up with the idea and putting it into Linc's head. The way Linc had grabbed onto it said not even a full-blown crying jag would dislodge it.

Nathan scratched the hair over his ear. "Jonas is free. I ran into him yesterday, and he said he was going to the opening night at the Arden anyway. He won't mind stopping by here to pick you up and bring you home." He grabbed his hat from the peg by the door. "We'd best scoot, Linc, if we're going to meet the train and unload that wheat."

"I don't want Jonas Spooner to accompany me." Fran jammed her hands onto her hips, all pretense gone.

Linc flipped his wide-brimmed hat onto his short red-gold hair. "You'll go with Jonas or you won't go at all." Nathan and Linc shared a conspiratorial look on the way out the door, and their laughter drifted through the open kitchen window.

Fran picked up a dishcloth and whipped it at the door. They'd planned this from the outset, and she'd fallen right into their trap.

Jonas Spooner. Fran sighed. It wasn't that she didn't like him, but he was so very. . .ordinary. She couldn't remember a time when she didn't know him. As kids growing up in Missouri, he'd always been around, frogging with her brothers or fishing or playing ball. And even then he'd carried her books and given her small gifts, never shy about showing his affection for her. When her brothers proposed moving west and opening a feed store and bringing Fran along to housekeep for them, it had seemed perfectly natural for Jonas to come along. That was the trouble. Jonas was more like a brother than a suitor. She just couldn't see him in those terms.

Aware of the clock ticking, she hustled through the kitchen chores. She had ten minutes before she needed to be at the mercantile, which was plenty of time. But only three days to decide what to wear to opening night, which wasn't much time at all.

Opening night. Anticipation feathered across Addie's skin as she checked her reflection in the mirror over the washstand. For such a special occasion, she'd piled her brown curls high, letting them fall in a cascade down her neck. A few tendrils lay on her cheeks—her much-too-pink cheeks.

"Stop it," she told her mirror-self. "You're merely following orders and using common sense. Miles Carr is only doing his duty as a peace officer."

Her mirror-self didn't appear to be listening, because her eyes glowed with anticipation and her mouth wouldn't quit smiling at the thought of seeing him again, and of having him see her dressed up for once.

Stepping back, she tried to get a full-length view of her gown, though the small mirror was a challenge. She smoothed her hand down the burgundy polonaise, her fingers bumping over the twenty cloth-covered buttons from her throat to her waist, feeling hollow and excited at the same time.

She'd bought this dress more than a year ago for the Cattlemen's Ball in Abilene, for *him*, for the night when she had been sure he would propose. A week before the ball, her world had fallen apart. And she'd never worn the beautiful dress, packing it away with her hopes and dreams and not taking it out of her trunk until today.

Determined to shake off the past and only look forward, she made sure the folds of her bustle and train lay just so and that the cuffs of the long, tight sleeves were straight. Fan, gloves, bag. Her Scovill lay on the end of the bed, snug in its case. Though she didn't feel wholly dressed without it, she knew she couldn't lug it with her tonight.

Picking up the invitation, she couldn't help the self-satisfied smile that tugged at her lips. Mr. LeBlanc had gone into raptures at the photographs she'd delivered to him. A fountain of French accolades poured from him, and he proudly presented her with the invitations to opening night.

Fran had been thrilled when Addie gave her one. Though she'd been less than thrilled yesterday afternoon when she'd announced that her brothers had maneuvered her into accepting Jonas's escort to and from the theater. Addie had almost gone to the sheriff's office to cancel her need for a deputy escort, figuring that Jonas could take her as well, but she'd decided against it. Jonas had her support in courting Fran, and she wouldn't do anything to derail his efforts.

The fact that Miles Carr would be seeing Addie to the theater had nothing to do with it.

Addie flicked the fan open and covered the lower half of her face, checking her reflection one last time. Too eager by far. She grimaced and headed downstairs.

Mrs. Blanchard sat in her rocking chair, her fingers flying, knitting needles clicking, creating yards and yards of lace. Addie had often speculated that if her landlady's knitting needles had been made of wood, she'd have long since started a fire. What she did with all that lace was a mystery. Nobody had that many petticoats.

Mrs. Blanchard looked over the top of her glasses and appraised Addie. "My, don't you look lovely, my dear."

"Thank you."

"Your gentleman is just coming up the walk." She craned her neck just slightly to peer out the window.

Addie flushed. "He's not my gentleman. I called in at the sheriff's office for a deputy to escort me to the theater, and Sheriff Masterson assigned Deputy Carr to the task." And that was all. Really.

Mrs. Blanchard's almost-nonexistent eyebrows rose, and her needles moved faster. The doorbell click-buzzed instead of ringing. "I should get that fixed someday."

Since she made this remark every time someone used the bell, Addie didn't put much stock in the comment. She gathered her skirts, told her heart to stop bumping so crazily, and opened the door.

Air crowded into her throat. From his brushed cowboy hat to the tips of his shiny boots, Miles Carr was immaculate. Even his badge gleamed. The only incongruous note to his attire was the gun belt slung low on his hips. "Evening, Miss Reid. You ready?" He offered his arm, a smile playing about his lips.

Though a warm evening breeze blew across her temples, her fingers tingled as if chilled. "Thank you for seeing me to the theater. I'm taking your warning not to walk through town alone to heart."

"I'm glad. You sure look pretty. Looking like that, I might have to draw my gun to fight off the cowboys tonight."

Pleasure shot through her. He thought she looked pretty. *Watch yourself, girl. You've had your head turned before. He doesn't mean anything by it, and you're not looking for a beau.*

She looped the handles of her fan and purse over her wrist and put her hand into the crook of his elbow. His formal dress set up a small panic in her chest. Did he think he was her date for the evening? She only had the one invitation, having given Fran the other. When she'd requested an escort to the theater, had someone misunderstood? But how did one ask without sounding ridiculous?

He matched his stride to hers, his eyes scanning the street ahead. Most of the windows along Front Street were lit, and cowboys strolled the boardwalks. The persistent lowing of cattle from the yards drifted on the breeze, as familiar to Addie by now as the all-night band music from the Long Branch.

She snuck glances up at Miles, hoping he wouldn't notice but unable to stop herself. Strength and integrity. Those words drifted through her mind, and she realized that had been her first impression of Miles, and that impression had strengthened each time she met him. But she didn't trust her own judgment. She'd been fooled before. Why didn't her heart seem to be listening to her head?

A steady stream of people headed toward the brightly lit Arden Palace, and Addie and Miles joined it. Women in fancy dress, men in suits, all with an expectant air. Cowboys wore their best clothes, some so new they still bore the creases from being folded in shirt boxes. The jingling of spurs mingled with the fluttering of fans.

LeBlanc had plastered the town with posters and flyers announcing opening night, each one bearing at least one of her photographs. The expense he'd gone to using such a new printing technique—he'd had to go all the way to Kansas City and back to find a printer with the necessary skills and equipment—must've been enormous, but it seemed to have paid dividends, judging by the size of the crowd.

"Looks to be a full house." Miles's eyes never stopped moving over the people on the porch. "Hope everyone behaves himself tonight."

The last person she wanted to see was Heber Donaldson, so of course they ran into him first. He glared, snorted down his long, hooked nose, and stomped away.

Mayor Kelley strode by, resplendent in evening dress, and Henri LeBlanc seemed to be everywhere in the crowd, greeting people, accepting congratulations, gesturing with large movements and a wide smile. "Ah, *cheri*, you came. I have reserved seats in a fine box for you. Number four." He took Addie's hands and kissed her cheeks. "It is going to be a wonderful night. Your photographs were *le magnifique*." He waved to a poster beside the front doors. Her name figured prominently, just as LeBlanc had promised it would.

Before she could thank him, someone clouted Miles on the shoulder. "You made it."

Jonas with Fran on his arm.

A pretty flush decorated Fran's cheeks, and she was exquisite in green, but she had a battle-glint in her eyes. "You've seen me to the theater, Jonas. I can take it from here." She tried to free her hand from his arm, but his shot up to cover hers.

"I wouldn't dream of leaving you here alone, Fran. I told your brothers I would see you to your seat." He smiled blandly, and Fran's protests bounced off him.

Addie darted a look at Miles. "Jonas can accompany me to my seat, too, if you'd prefer."

"It's no trouble." To her relief, he dug in his coat pocket and produced a ticket. "I had a hankering to see this particular play, and Bat expects us to make our presence known in the theater to keep the cowboys from breaking herd." He handed the ticket and her invitation to one of the deputies at the door. "Evening, Ty."

"Well, don't you look the curly wolf tonight?" The

deputy named Ty glanced at Miles's sidearm at the same time he tipped his hat to Addie. "Evening, miss." He jerked his thumb to the table beside him where three revolvers lay. "Already collected some firepower off some civilians."

Miles nodded and put his hand on the small of Addie's back to guide her to the stairway leading to the balcony boxes. She could feel each of his fingers as though he touched bare skin, and icy-hot chills raced along her arms and affected her breathing. The air grew close around her, and she flicked open her fan.

Fran and Jonas followed close. An attendant swept aside the heavy curtains to the box where Fran had pretended to be Rapunzel, and Addie almost giggled, not daring to look at Fran. Four chairs sat around a small table, and music from a string quartet drifted up from the orchestra pit in front of the stage.

Addie took the chair Miles held for her. Fran did the same, but with less grace for Jonas. The shorter deputy wore a dark suit that stretched across his broad shoulders, and everything about him exuded steadfastness and stability—the exact opposite of the ideal Fran dreamed about and often rhapsodized over. Addie shook her head, settled her belongings, and looked up to thank Miles for his consideration before he left to find his own seat. But instead of leaving, Miles and Jonas hung their hats on the rack in the corner of the box, and each took a chair at the table.

"What are you doing?" Fran's voice carried, and people from the lower level looked up at them. She flushed and glared at Jonas.

He scooted his chair just a bit closer to hers. "I'm going to watch a play. I bought a ticket." He waved the stub of pasteboard at her before tucking it into his vest pocket.

Addie turned to Miles. "You, too?"

He nodded. "LeBlanc said we could sit up here. I hope you don't mind."

She should, but she didn't in the least. Amazing how she'd gone from anxiety to relief to anticipation, all in a short amount of time. She hardly knew what to think or feel. All she knew was that she wasn't in the least disappointed that Miles was staying.

Scanning the crowd to give herself time to gather her thoughts, she took a few deep breaths. Her eyes lit on a face turned up and staring right at her. Her breathing stopped, and her heart started knocking against her ribs.

Vin Rutter's pale, almost colorless eyes bored into hers.

How had he found her?

Miles found himself staring at Addie. When she'd answered the door at the boardinghouse, it had been all he could do not to blink and stand there like a slack-jawed idiot. Whatever she'd done to her hair, it looked great. He wanted to bury his hands in those curls and let the silky strands twine around his fingers.

Rubbing his palms on his thighs, he turned his attention to the crowd below. Conversation hummed and people filed into the seats. Their box attendant appeared with a tray of fancy bits of food and offered them their choice of beverages.

Jonas ordered lemonade for everyone.

Fran looked like she wanted to wring Jonas's neck. She was sure pretty enough, but why Jonas continued to pursue her in the face of her obvious dislike of him was a mystery to Miles. Though when Jonas set his mind to something, he was awfully hard to deflect, and to hear him tell it, he'd had his mind and heart set on Fran for a long time.

He glanced at Addie again, taking in her profile. Her nose tilted up a little at the end, and her lips were parted. That dress she wore fired his blood. Not in the least revealing, it covered her from neck to toes and all the way to her wrists, but the cut of the reddish fabric showed off her womanly charms. She was the prettiest girl in the room, and she was with him. Sort of.

Something seemed different about her getup, though he couldn't pick it out right away. He almost snapped his fingers when he struck on what was missing. Her camera case. A laugh made it as far as his teeth before he choked it off. She went everywhere with that case, even to church.

A small commotion downstairs drew his attention. Two cowboys shoved at each other, but before Miles could even stand, LeBlanc was on the scene and the combatants sat down.

That's when he saw him.

Vin Rutter. He'd know those dead eyes anywhere.

Miles's mouth went dry.

Vin's eyes bored into his, and a smirk decorated his face. He sketched a wave and tilted his head in a mocking salute, and Miles's hands fisted on his thighs.

Addie sucked in a breath, and Miles broke eye contact with Vin. Her face had gone pale, and her hand pressed to her stomach. Her other hand gripped her folded fan until it shook. Was she unwell? He touched her shoulder, and she turned wide eyes to his face.

The houselights began to go out, and to his surprise, she scooted her chair closer to his. She beamed a smile his way brighter than the footlights, and his stomach muscles tightened. When she reached out and patted his hand where it rested on his leg, tingles shot up his arm, and he found himself clasping her fingers in his. They were chilly in spite of the warm room.

"I'm so glad you are here with me. It's going to be a wonderful night."

Fran's eyebrows rose from across the table. "Addie?"

Addie shrugged and kept her hand in Miles's. Jonas grinned.

Miles's mind reeled. Caught between apprehension at Vin's being in Dodge and the sensation of holding Addie's hand and sitting so near her, he couldn't think straight. He was grateful when the curtain went up and the performance began.

Addie clung to his hand through the entire first act and kept her attention on the stage. Miles couldn't have told anyone even the most rudimentary bits of the plot. His mind batted thoughts, tossing between Vin and Addie.

When intermission was announced, Fran bounced up without waiting for Jonas to pull out her chair. "I'm going to get some ice cream. Don't you want to come with me?" She sent a direct look at Addie, bombarding her with the message that she wanted Addie to come.

"No, thank you. I'd rather stay here." She turned to Miles. "You don't mind, do you?"

Far from minding, he had to quell his relief. The last thing he wanted was to run into Vin Rutter in a crowd. "We'll stay. You go on."

Fran and Jonas disappeared and returned in plenty of time for the second act. Fran's eyes shone, and it seemed she had forgotten her peeve at having to endure Jonas's company in favor of enjoying the evening. Addie remained quiet, only answering direct questions and those briefly. Fran finally gave up trying to draw her into the conversation and concentrated on her ice cream.

Miles watched the house seats below, keeping his eye on Vin. Rutter appeared to be alone, but in the crush, it was hard to tell. It was surely no coincidence that he'd landed in Dodge City, but what could he be after? Vin never acted without careful deliberation. It was the reason he was a free man at the moment and not languishing in Leavenworth. Wily and smooth, Vin Rutter knew how to wriggle out of trouble better than a greased snake.

By the time the play ended, Miles was a bundle of nerves. Addie had stayed so close to him he could smell her perfume—like flowers, though he couldn't have identified the particular bloom. Heady, and he would've loved to savor it if he wasn't so distracted.

When the last curtain call ended, the houselights came up again, and conversation replaced applause. The crowd stirred, gathering belongings, talking, and laughing, clearly in high spirits.

Fran sighed and sat back in her chair. "What a wonderful evening. Wouldn't it be something to have two buccaneers fighting over you like what happened in the play? How would you ever choose? Sebastian was so wickedly interesting and Barnabas was so brave and good." She sighed and fingered the string of beads at her neck. "Though I suppose Fiona made the right choice eventually. Oh, I never want this night to end."

Miles tried to gauge Addie's feelings. She'd been so quiet. Though this wasn't a by-the-book date with his asking her out and her accepting, he was still her partner for the evening, and he couldn't help but feel he'd somehow failed her, that she hadn't enjoyed herself. Yet, she'd held his hand for most of the play, staying with him in the box rather than escaping during intermissions, and still held his hand as if she never wanted to let go. That had to mean something, didn't it?

He gave up trying to navigate the maze of the female mind and stood. "I'm afraid we'll have to be leaving soon. I'm on patrol tonight." He pulled Addie's chair out as she rose.

Fran's face crumpled for a moment before brightening. She glanced down at their entwined hands and back at Addie's face.

Addie smiled, though her lips were tight. "See you, Fran."

Jonas and Fran left ahead of them, and Miles shepherded Addie toward the steps. She stopped at the head of the stairs and threaded her arm through his as if they'd been courting for months. His hand came up to cover hers in the crook of his elbow. He was at a loss to explain her behavior, but he was equally at a loss to stop himself from responding to it.

Threading their way through the thinning crowds, he led her through the lobby and out onto the porch. An evening breeze scudded up the street, whipping a bit of dust into the air and teasing the tendrils of hair on her cheeks.

Out of newly established habit, he scanned the area.

Vin stood across the street, his features clear in the light streaming from the Lady Gray Comique Theater. Miles gritted his teeth. When Vin stepped into the street and began sauntering his way, Miles, almost without meaning to, slid his coat aside to free his gun hand.

Then Addie laid her head against his shoulder, totally distracting him. "I'm tired. I think we should head to the boardinghouse, don't you?"

Her pale face so close to his threw all thoughts of Vin out of his head. He nodded and started up the street. For a whole block she kept her temple against his shoulder, and her closeness was all he could think about. When they turned the corner off Front Street, darkness surrounded them, and she straightened and took a deep breath. Her hand relaxed on his arm, and she gave him a trembling smile.

They stopped at the foot of the steps to Mrs. Blanchard's, and she turned her face upward. Moonlight bathed her features, making her eyes seem bigger and more lustrous than ever. "Thank you for seeing me safely home."

"You're welcome." His voice sounded gruff. Then, because he couldn't seem to stop himself, he did what he'd been wanting to do all evening—since he'd first laid eyes on her a few months ago, in fact. He slid his arms around her waist and drew her toward him. She fit perfectly into his embrace, and slowly, giving her time to run if she wanted to, he lowered his lips to hers.

Sweet. So sweet.

She sighed against his lips and returned the pressure, entwining her arms around his neck. He wondered if his head or his heart would explode first, and without breaking the kiss, his hands came up and buried themselves in her curls.

Soft.

His fingers tangled in the brown strands, and he cupped the back of her head, deepening the kiss. He never wanted it to end, and when he realized that, he knew he had to stop. He eased back and, before he could stop himself, snatched one more kiss from her pretty lips.

Her eyes fluttered open, dazed and dreamy. Manly pride that his kiss had so thrown her off balance made him grin. One of her hands lay against the flat of his chest, her fingers just covering the edge of his badge. Could she feel the thundering of his heart? They stood, locked together as if in a spell.

The curtains twitched, and the knob on the front door rattled.

Addie sprang back, and she touched her lips, her eyes still bemused and bewildered.

"Good night, Miles."

She disappeared up the stairs and into the house, leaving him standing in the moonlight, looking after her like a lovesick bull calf.

Chapter 7

Addie brushed past Mrs. Blanchard with her gaping face and blinking eyes and sought the refuge of her room. When she closed the door on the outside world, she leaned against it and pressed her hand against her chest to still the wild throbbing of her heart.

"Oh Addie girl, what have you done?" Fingers trembling, she struck a match and lit the lamp on her bureau. Immediately her reflection in the oval mirror caught her eye, and she gasped.

Her hair tumbled about her shoulders in wild disarray, and she remembered the feel of Miles's hands plundering her carefully arranged curls. Several hairpins dangled from the mass, and if she didn't miss her guess, she'd find more decorating the sidewalk. Her lips were pink and just a hint puffy, and she couldn't resist touching them again.

Closing her eyes, she was instantly back in his arms, his lips pressed to hers, the feel and smell and very essence of Miles Carr fusing to her. And she'd kissed him back with a passion that had both exhilarated and frightened her.

"Stop it!" Her eyes flew open, and she stared at her reflection. None of this was supposed to happen. She was playing with fire, and well she knew it. What had possessed her throwing herself at Miles that way?

The cause of her trouble seemed to superimpose his image over hers in the mirror. Vin Rutter, with his pale, dead eyes and narrow slash of a mouth. Here. In Dodge. Watching her. The minute she'd spotted him, cold, thorny terror had crawled up her windpipe and lodged in her throat.

Without really being conscious of it until now, she'd sought the protection Miles and his badge offered. Heat curled through her chest and flooded her cheeks when she thought of how she'd held his hand all through the play, trying to draw strength and courage from him, trying to tell herself that Vin and all he represented was in her imagination, or at the very least in her past and couldn't hurt her.

But that had been a fool's paradise.

Guilt followed hard. She'd shamelessly used Miles, leading him on, flirting outrageously—enough that even Fran had noticed and promised a reckoning in the morning. Addie swallowed. Vin had been waiting outside the theater. The terror had returned, and instead of telling Miles the truth, what had she done? Cuddled up to him and steered him away like some brazen hussy from one of the brothels south of the deadline.

Mortified, she clutched her hands at her waist and pressed her stomach to still the raging guilt. Shame licked at her skin, and she poured some water from the pitcher into the basin to bathe her hot face.

Dabbing at her damp cheeks with a linen towel, she went to stand by the open window, hoping the night breeze would blow some clarity into her head. Though her thoughts bounced around like tumbleweeds in a tornado, one remained paramount in her mind.

The kiss.

She couldn't get it out of her thoughts, but somehow she would have to. Somehow she would have to find a graceful way to retreat and pretend it never happened. It had been wrong to use Miles the way she had, and if Vin started any trouble, she might've just sucked Miles into it. "Addie," she groaned, "how could you be so stupid? You had no business getting involved with Miles."

Seeking to ground herself, to remember why she had to walk warily where all men were concerned, she reached for her Scovill case. The familiar scarred leather box brought her back to reality. Unbuckling the latch, she lifted the camera from its nest and set it on the coverlet. Though the room was dark and the interior of the camera case darker, she needed no light to find the small velvet tab along one side. She pinched the fabric and tugged, opening the false bottom of the case and tipping the fat, square photo album out into her hand.

She brought the lamp to the bedside table and turned up the wick. Her fingers traced the Moroccan leather cover and the gilt edges with their silver corner protectors. Sixteen photographs, her own work. Her first foray into portraiture. The first inkling that she might have a talent for capturing life through a lens.

The spine creaked as she opened the book. His face greeted her.

Cliff Walker. Not that she'd known it at the time.

No, when she'd taken this photo, he'd called himself

Clem Wilson. A traveling salesman for a sewing notions company.

Black hair, intelligent brown eyes, a smile that could turn a woman's insides to warm mush. And a tongue that ran with honeyed words to turn a girl's head.

She turned the page, and in spite of everything, a chuckle escaped her lips. Clem—*no, Cliff,* she reminded herself—leaned against the plaster pedestal he'd so proudly constructed for her. The same pillar she'd convinced Bat Masterson to rest his elbow on for his portrait. And what would Bat say if he knew the notorious Cliff Walker had posed in the same manner for her camera just over a year ago?

She studied the photograph again. His hat sat at a rakish angle, and his eyes burned with laughter—and what she'd mistakenly thought was love. All humor fled, and a lump clogged her throat. Flipping through the pages, she studied each well-known picture briefly before moving on. Rational thought began to trickle into her mind to replace the wild feelings Miles's kiss had engendered.

Cliff Walker, an accomplished liar, suckering her with his flattery, pretending interest in her work as a photographer, professing his love. And all the while, he'd been hiding his identity, hiding the fact that he was the leader of the bloodiest gang of thieves and killers Kansas had ever produced. He had courted her and promised her the moon, even while he and his gang robbed trains, plundered banks, and murdered innocents who got in their way.

She'd known nothing about his other life until the U.S. marshals arrived on her doorstep looking for him. Even now their disdainful looks and accusing comments made her squirm. They'd tried so hard to pull her into the investigation, sure she had known all along of his true identity, sure that she was an integral part of the gang. In the end, she'd been cleared, but it had been a harrowing time. The townsfolk in Abilene had withdrawn, those she thought were her friends separating themselves, leaving her alone to face the accusations with only Uncle Carl for support.

Addie pursed her lips and traced the edge of one of the pages. Cliff lounged under a tree beside a sluggish creek near Abilene, his long legs stretched out in the prairie grass and his hat tipped over his nose so that only the lower half of his face was visible. He hadn't even known she'd taken this picture until she showed him the developed print. A picnic blanket lay beside him. Such lighthearted fun, but under it all, a sinister secret that had ruined not just her life but Uncle Carl's as well.

How had she been so naive? She'd asked herself that question a thousand times. Cliff's arrest and trial had shocked her and killed any love she felt for him. Day after day she'd sat in that courtroom listening to the evidence and the testimonies of those Cliff had harmed. The prosecutor peeled away the layers of lies and deceit and revealed the killer behind the charming face. Justice had been swift, and Cliff had been hanged two days later.

Shattered, Addie had set about putting back together the broken pieces of her life. But healing wouldn't be possible in the hostile atmosphere of Abilene. Cliff had hurt too many people there for her ever to be free of the stain of her involvement with him. She couldn't even walk down the street without someone hurling harsh words or worse at her.

A week after the trial, someone threw a lit torch through the front window of the photography studio. The reception room and the workroom beyond had gone up in flames before the volunteer fire brigade got the blaze under control. The hostility toward the Reids had been so great, that if the neighboring buildings hadn't been in danger, Addie was sure they would've just let the studio burn. As it was, she and Uncle Carl only managed to salvage the props from the prop room and his boxes of glass slides. When the flames reached the darkroom, the developing chemicals ignited, destroying the rest of the building entirely.

The local police hadn't pursued the culprit too hard. Addie had the feeling they thought she and her uncle had only gotten what they'd deserved.

A black fist of remorse pressed under her rib cage. Everything destroyed, and the blame lay squarely with her. If she'd never taken up with Cliff, they'd still have the shop in Abilene, her uncle Carl might still be alive, and she wouldn't be so alone and scared.

And now Vin Rutter was here. She'd met him once when Cliff had brought him to town, though of course he'd introduced him as a business associate. She'd tried to like him for Cliff's sake, but his fishy eyes and lack of visible emotion had chilled her. If only Cliff had radiated that same dangerous essence, she'd never have fallen for his lies.

She had no illusions as to Vin's reasons for being in Dodge City. After Cliff's trial, at which he refused to name any of his accomplices, the gang had scattered, fleeing into Indian Territory rather than be caught in Kansas.

But Vin had returned, and only one thing would've brought him back.

Her. And what he thought she knew.

She was all he could think about.

Miles leaned against the clapboards of Greeley and Price Mercantile, careful to stay to the shadows of the alley while he watched the street. He'd shed his suit coat at the jail but still wore his best trousers and vest. The starch in his shirt chafed his skin, but the discomfort had been worth it. At least he hadn't looked out of place at the theater.

Horses galloped by, their riders anxious to get to the dance halls, saloons, and gambling dens before every last drop of revelry had been wrung out of the night. Music, laughter, shouts, voices. In the occasional lull, he could hear coyotes yapping out on the prairie, and the metallic clinks and pings as the steam engine sitting at the depot cooled.

He'd kissed her. And not just a brotherly peck either. He'd snatched her up like the last biscuit on the plate and crushed the breath right out of her. His blood raced at the memory, and he had to force himself to relax his tense muscles.

What had he been thinking?

He'd been thinking that he was with a beautiful woman who had intrigued him from the minute he first laid eyes on her. A woman who had changed from remote to receptive in the blink of an eye.

He frowned. The female of the species baffled him, but no more than he baffled himself. He had a list as long as his arm why he shouldn't get involved with a woman right now, and what had he done? Jumped in boots, badge, and all.

A door slammed across the street and footsteps rang out on the wooden outside staircase running up to the second story of the saloon. A woman entwined her bare arms around a cowboy's neck for a lingering good-bye in the moonlight, the tail end of a shameful transaction that had nothing to do with love. Disgust sloshed in his belly.

A snippet of scripture floated through his head. Something about the beam in his own eye.

Miles's face flushed, and he rubbed his palm against the back of his neck. An hour ago he'd stood not three blocks from this spot right here and kissed the daylights out of a woman he barely knew. A sigh forced its way past the guilty knot in his throat. He'd enjoyed every second of that kiss.

He wasn't good enough to court someone like Addie. With his more-than-checkered past, he'd only manage to drag her down if the truth ever came out. He needed to prove himself first, put some more distance on his unlovely youth, and ground himself as a lawman and a man of faith.

Though he'd done precious little on the faith front. He seemed to duck every chance he got to speak boldly about God and what God thought was right.

Lord, I'm asking for You to give me boldness to stand up for what's right, to speak up when the chance comes to identify myself with You. I've ducked it too much lately. I really want to be used by You, to be bold for my faith, but I need Your help. I need Your wisdom.

His plea for wisdom had his thoughts straying again to Addie. Surely there was some way to work this out, because he found himself wanting to court Addie, to make her his for always, thoughts that had never entered his head about a woman before. Maybe, after he'd shown her and the rest of the town that he was a man of good character—law abiding and upstanding—he could ask permission to call.

"You're looking good, Miles."

He whirled, his hand going for his gun, shocked that someone had snuck up on him so easily and even more shocked that it was the man he'd been on the lookout for.

Vin raised his hands. "Easy there, my dear boy. I'm not armed." The fake Southern accent Vin employed grated across Miles's skin. Though Vin found it useful for charming his way into and out of trouble, it made Miles's blood simmer.

Letting his gun drop back into his holster, Miles straightened. His unprofessional lack of attention galled him. Anyone could've walked up, stuck a knife between his ribs, and he wouldn't even have known. Of all the green, amateur, stupid mistakes.

"What do you want, Vin?"

Even in the dark of the alley, Vin's eyes glittered, reminding Miles of two pebbles surrounded by hoarfrost. "Is that any way to greet an old friend?"

"There's no friendship between us."

Vin's mirthless laugh pricked him. "And whose fault was that?" He stroked slender, pale fingers down one of his lapels. "You and your uppity mother, acting like you were too good for us. Old Man Walker said he'd never let either of you go, but I guess you both got out eventually. Such a tragedy, her taking that way out. How long's it been? Ten years?"

Miles shifted his weight, never taking his eyes off Vin's face. "He killed her. As surely as if he'd pulled the trigger himself. Poetic justice that he dropped dead a few days later. Doc said it was a heart seizure, but you'd have to have a heart first." Though he'd struggled to forgive his stepfather for the years of abuse and anger, he hadn't quite managed it . . .at least not for long. Forgiving the old man for driving his mother to take her own life—that was going to take a lot more prayer and effort.

"You disappeared before they threw the first shovelful of dirt into his face."

Miles shrugged. "Seemed the thing to do, with Cliff taking over for his father. Worst mistake my mother ever made, marrying into the Walkers. I'm glad I got out when I did, what with Cliff branching out into train robberies. Turned a bunch of mean dogs into a pack of killer wolves. He was vicious before I left, and he got worse after."

"Well, rest assured, the antipathy you had for your stepbrother was mutual. Cliff used to spit on the ground whenever your name came up."

Enough about the past. "What are you doing here, Vin? I thought you and the rest of the boys were hiding out in Indian Territory since the trial."

"I could ask you what you're doing here as well, though after tonight, I have a fair idea. You're such a dark horse, Miles. I never would've suspected it of you. All that talk about finding God and being forgiven." Vin sneered. "Clever of you to follow her here and insinuate yourself into her life. Tell me, does she know?"

He frowned. "Who are you talking about? Does who know what?"

"The delightful Miss Reid, of course. I saw you with her tonight, and very cozy you were, too. What did she say when she found out you were related to Cliff?"

Miles sucked in a breath. Vin knew Addie?

Vin feathered his fingers through his hair, his light movements reminding Miles of his dexterity, both with cards and with a gun. "Ah, I see from your expression that Miss Adeline Reid is once more clueless as to the true identity of her suitor." He tipped his head back and let out a derisive *ha*. "This is too rich. So smooth, too, coming from you. I always thought you were a tell-the-truth-and-shame-the-devil type, and here I find you insinuating yourself into Cliff's former paramour's life."

Miles's mind reeled. "What are you talking about?"

Vin's eyebrows climbed. "Stop playing games. I admit I'm chagrined that you should've arrived here first. I only learned of her whereabouts last week." He reached into his inner pocket.

Miles tensed, his gun filling his hand and training on Vin in a blur.

Vin stiffened and stilled. "My, my, you are a suspicious fellow these days. Allow me?" He inclined his head toward his hand still stuck in his jacket.

"Nice and slow."

A folded paper emerged. With excruciating patience, Vin opened the page and smoothed it out before turning it so Miles could see. A flyer for the Arden Palace. Miles had seen a hundred of them plastered about town. Vin pointed to the bottom right corner, and Miles didn't need to read it to know what it said. PICTURES BY ADELINE REID, REID'S PHOTOGRAPHY, DODGE CITY, KANSAS.

"What do you want with Addie?" He lowered his gun a fraction but kept it trained on Vin. Vin never wanted anything good for anyone but himself, and his interest in Addie made Miles's skin itch.

"If you must continue this charade, I'll play along." Folding the paper, Vin sighed. "Adeline Reid is the one-time fiancée of our dear, departed Cliff. The woman he claimed was his soul mate, the one person on earth who really understood him, who would make his life complete. Of course, their courtship met a rather abrupt end when the State of Kansas stretched your dear stepbrother's neck, but there it is."

Cold realization sluiced over Miles. "Addie?" Cliff's fiancée? His soul mate? Bile churned in Miles's stomach, burning hot.

Vin arched one eyebrow, a strangely black curve on his milky-white face given his pale hair. "Stop pretending you didn't know. Why else would you be here?"

"Addie and Cliff." Miles whispered the words, testing out the idea. It made him sick.

"That's right. The same little honey you were billing and cooing with tonight." Vin's narrow shoulders shook. Vin flicked the badge on Miles's chest, making him jerk back and raise the gun again. "I'd venture to say you didn't inform your boss either. I doubt the people of Dodge City would take too kindly to having a member of the Walker Gang—however much on the outskirts he might've been—on the county payroll."

Miles clenched his jaw, hating the knowing look coming from Vin's reptilian eyes. Vin thrived on wielding power over others. And everything he knew about Miles and about Addie gave him a great deal too much power.

Chapter 8

Fran tucked a stray curl up and clasped her hands against her chin, pressing her thumbnails against her front teeth, and feigned interest in the window display she'd been working on all morning, pretending she hadn't noticed the strikingly handsome man at the end of the counter who had been watching her since the moment he came in. She tilted the bonnet on the display stand to show the cluster of silk flowers better.

Curiosity wriggled up her spine. He perused the timepieces behind glass and moved on to the fobs, cuff links, and cigar cases before coming back to the pocket watches.

When he'd first entered, Wally had approached him with an offer of assistance, but the customer had declined. Lean and pale, he wandered the aisle and ran his hands over the merchandise. He dressed too fine for a cowboy but not flashy enough for a professional gambler. His skin was too pale for him to be a farmer or any kind of an outdoorsman, and yet he had an aura of capability to him that roused her curiosity. Indefinably not a drummer, a salesman, a banker, nor any of half a dozen other occupations that came to her mind.

Fran prided herself on being able to size up every customer—both their purchasing needs and their probable income—quickly, but this man had her baffled. Time to get some answers.

"Are you sure there's nothing I can help you with?" Fran approached him, fingering her lace collar and the two buttons she'd left open for coolness at her throat.

"I'm actually killing a little time before an appointment." His Southern accent flowed over her like melted butter. "Didn't I see you at the Arden Palace last night? In one of the private boxes?"

Pleasure feathered through her. "You might have." She studied his chiseled features up close, the straight nose, high forehead, intelligent eyes, finely cut lips. Handsome was hardly the word for it. His hair was as pale as the December moon, but his eyebrows were two dark slashes, and his eyelashes were equally dark, making his eyes seem even paler. Fascinated, she couldn't look away. "I attended opening night with friends."

"I knew it." He snapped his fingers. "One does not forget such a beautiful woman. A lady such as yourself, refined and genteel, stands out in one's memory." A slow smile stretched his thin lips. His eyes drew her, almost as intense as Bat Masterson's himself. "My name is Vincent Rutter. My friends call me Vin, and I do hope you will count yourself among that number. And you are?"

My, my, my. Very smooth, much more polished than a cowboy. "Fran Seaton, Vin." She caressed his name with just enough intimacy to draw another smile. A little thrill shot up her spine. Was this, at last, the mysterious stranger she'd dreamed about? The one who would sweep into town and carry her away for a life of romance and adventure? Though lately she'd become more and more aware that her adolescent fancies were silly, a part of her still longed for them to be true.

His eyes roamed over her face and form, and she swallowed. He had a knowing, practiced way about him, not awkward and overblown like most of the men who came into the store. This man was different, and that difference intrigued her like none had before.

"You've got a fine store here." He waved to the laden shelves and items hanging from rows of hooks overhead. "You must do a land-office business."

Fran picked up her feather duster. Dusting was a constant need in this windy, dirty town, but she also preferred to be doing something while she chatted up customers. "We do, though not usually until afternoon. The townsfolk drift through in the mornings, and the cowboys come in the afternoons, after they've slept off the night before." She tilted her chin and raised her eyebrows, inviting him to understand her meaning.

Though her brothers might try to hedge her around and keep her protected, she was no babe in the woods. No one could live in Dodge City for long without having at least an inkling of what went on. Some of her most frequent customers were the working girls from the saloons, dance halls, and "houses of negotiable affection" as she'd heard one of the girls put it. . .accompanied by a broad wink.

"A man could do quite well for himself in this town, I imagine. A businessman, that is."

She smiled and swiped the duster over a stack of Hap's

pickled beets on the counter. "That would depend on the business. Some do very well. Are you a businessman?"

His thin lips twitched. "You could say that. I'm in acquisitions, most recently with the railroad." Though he smiled, the humor didn't affect his eyes, which remained trained on her as if he had her in his crosshairs. Aha, why hadn't she considered he might work for the railroad? That explained his rather cosmopolitan air and the quality of his clothing.

Something thudded in the back of the store, and voices drifted toward them. "I'm telling you, Hap Greeley, if you don't stop, this partnership is through, cousins or not." Wally shouldered his way through the storeroom doorway, bent under the weight of the bag of flour on his shoulder. "I'm killing myself keeping this place open, keeping the shelves stocked, keeping up with the ordering. And what are you doing? You're sitting on your backside in some rat hole of a saloon playing poker. When was the last time you waited on a customer or checked a packing slip?" The bag of flour hit the floor with a powdery thump. Wally dusted his hands and wiped the perspiration from his forehead. "I'm working myself into an early grave to keep you in poker chips." He aimed his voice toward the storeroom doorway.

Hap, untidy and amiable as always, clomped out of the stockroom carrying an open can of peaches. He stuck his pocketknife into the can and fished out a slice of fruit. It plopped off the tip of the knife back into the syrup, and a glob of liquid splashed up on his glasses. "Confound it." He set the can and his knife on the counter, and out came the giant red handkerchief.

Fran made a mental note to wipe down the counter after they'd gone, since she was sure it now bore more than a trace of peach syrup.

"Wally, you worry too much. I told you I'd put the money back, and I did."

"But you didn't ask me before you took it. If you'd have lost that game last night, we'd be staring up from the bottom of a pretty dark hole."

"Well, I didn't lose. I'm on a hot streak right now, and I was lucky to get a seat at that table at all. It's a thousand-dollar buy-in, and you have to wait for a place to open. I'd still be there now if you hadn't come in screeching like a scalded cat. Made us look bad, Wally." He frowned and stabbed another peach. "Not exactly the best image to be leaving the businessmen of this town with, is it?"

Wally's face went from red to purple. He scanned the store, saw Fran with a customer, and grabbed Hap by the arm, dragging him to the storeroom and slamming the door behind them.

Fran sighed and set aside the duster in favor of opening her order book and ledger and making what she hoped were intelligent-looking marks in one of the columns.

Vin's dark eyebrows rose. "I take it those are the proprietors? You don't seem surprised by their bickering."

"Happens every day." His eyes had an almost reptilian quality that mesmerized her, especially this close. She tucked in her lower lip, and those eyes narrowed. "Nobody fights like family. They're cousins who inherited the store from their grandfather. Wally works, and Hap plays poker, and some-how they keep it all going, though Hap's getting worse. Last night, instead of depositing the day's receipts in the bank, he took them to a high-stakes poker game. Wally found out this morning and hit the roof."

"A thousand dollars to buy in for a poker game? This store must really be doing well." He rubbed his thumb across his fingertips, and for the first time, his eyes sparked to life. "I might have to see if I can get into that game."

She couldn't decide if she was disappointed or further intrigued. On the one hand, he had just admitted to being a gambler, but on the other, the thought of plunking down a cool thousand didn't seem to faze him. She came down on the side of intrigued. "The store does very well. Some days we take in so much money we need a deputy escort to take the cash to the bank in the evening."

He leaned in close, inviting her to do the same. With a slight huskiness to his voice, he whispered, "You know, it wasn't fair of you to go to that play last night."

"It wasn't?" She whispered, too, a delicious tremor playing across her skin.

"You completely distracted me from the actors on stage, and I imagine I wasn't the only one."

She fervently hoped the blush she could feel in her cheeks was the becoming kind and not the you've-been-out-too-long-in-the-sun kind. Though she scrambled for something coy and witty to say, she couldn't think of a thing.

"I noticed you had companions in your box with you. A couple and another young man? Perhaps the young man is your beau?"

"Oh no, Jonas is just a friend." She could've bitten her tongue off. Rushing to assure him she was unattached? Ugh.

"I see. Well, that relieves my mind. What about the others with you last night? Friends? They seemed most devoted to one another."

Fran frowned and toyed with her pencil. She hadn't had a chance yet to talk to Addie, but it was high on her to-do list. "Addie Reid and Miles Carr. Addie's my best friend."

"Oh? She seemed familiar to me. Is she new in town?"

"She's been here a few months. She and her uncle came here from Abilene, though her uncle passed away recently. She's running the photography studio up the street, Reid's Photography."

"She works alone?"

"She does, and I'm so proud of her. If it had been me, with that whopping big mortgage and all alone, I think I would've just folded up and died. But she's making a go of things. And she'll get that note paid off before it's due. She told me she would, and I believe her. Come the end of August, she'll own her business free and clear."

He leaned his elbows on the counter. "I think you're made of sterner stuff. I imagine you would've come up with a plan to survive." Again his slash of a mouth lifted at the corners. "Perhaps your friend has a nest egg put away or she knows she's going to come into money soon, and that's why she's so certain she can repay the loan."

It wasn't quite a question, and Fran shrugged. "Addie doesn't have any extra money that I know of, but we're coming into the busiest part of the season. She's got lots of customers every day, and she's getting some attention because she took some fabulous photos of the new theater. That was her work on the posters. Did you see it?"

Wally emerged from the back room, his face still dusky red, and opened the flour sack to empty it into a bin. Hap shuffled out, looking sheepish, his hands in his pockets and his glasses sliding down his nose. He hitched them up and sidled out of the store, keeping his head down as he passed Wally and giving Fran a quick wink before stepping out into the sunshine. Wally watched him go and folded the flour sack into precise squares. He frowned in Fran's direction.

She grimaced and closed the ledger. Though her bosses wanted her to chat up the customers, particularly the male customers, dawdling with someone who didn't look like he was going to make a purchase at all was another matter. "Vin, as much as I am enjoying talking to you, I do have to get some work done. This window display is driving me crazy. Something's not right about it, but I do have to get it finished before the afternoon rush."

Footsteps sounded on the boardwalk out front, and Jonas walked through the doorway. Though with the light behind him she couldn't see his face, she knew his silhouette as well as she knew her own name. Her lips pressed together. Couldn't she go a day without his coming in to check on her? Bad enough that she'd been finagled into letting him escort her to the theater last night.

Several of the ladies who had come in this morning had asked if she and Jonas were now keeping company. As if she would! And now Vin might think she wasn't telling the truth about Jonas not being her beau.

Jonas put on his most pleasant expression, hoping for once Fran wouldn't bite his head off. They'd parted amiably enough last night to give him a glimmer of hope that she was coming around to her old self, the girl he'd fallen in love with. When his eyes lit on her chatting with yet another strange man, his resolve to be pleasant slipped a notch.

"Morning, Fran." Jonas sauntered toward her, smitten as always with her fresh, golden beauty. Would it ever pall on him? Would he ever get used to it? Would she ever outgrow her flirtatious ways and see that they were perfect for each other?

He eased back his jacket lapel and hooked his thumb in his vest pocket. "Howdy." He nodded to the stranger. "Don't believe I've had the pleasure." This man definitely wasn't a cowboy, but what he was remained to be seen.

Fran braced her palms on the counter and leaned forward. "Jonas, this is Mr. Vin Rutter. He works for the railroad."

Jonas sized him up. Lean, well dressed, pale as a catfish belly, and with a pair of eyes that reminded him of ice-cold nickels. Rutter. He'd heard or read that name before, but where? It teased his gray matter, but he couldn't quite lay hold of the thought he sought for. Jonas filed it away to think about later. A railroad man. Hmm.

"Vin, this is Deputy Jonas Spooner." She said his name with just a hint of exasperation. "Was there something you wanted, Jonas?"

Rutter stepped back from the counter. "Miss Seaton, it's been a pleasure. I hope you're able to solve the dilemma of the front window display, and I look forward to seeing you again. . . ." He paused, and his eyes roved over everything he could see of her behind the counter. "Soon."

Jonas fisted his hands and straightened. Jealousy writhed in his gut, and he had a fierce desire to send a right hook through Vin Rutter's leer. Warning bells went off in Jonas's head, an instinctive reaction that this man could be danger-ous. Where had he heard that name? He kept his eyes on the man all the way out the store before he turned to Fran. "You're playing with fire. Again."

Her wide green eyes got wider. "I have no idea what you mean." Her heels tapped on the floor as she headed toward the front of the store.

He strode after her. Catching her elbow, he stopped her and spun her around. "That wasn't some cowboy you were flirting with. When are you going to realize you can't play with a wolf and expect it not to bite you?"

"Vin's no wolf." She shrugged off his grip. "He's a per-fectly nice gentleman who works for the railroad. And I wasn't flirting." Her conscience twinged. "And even if I was, there's no law against being nice to customers. You coming in here to harass me is getting to be a tired old habit. I can take care of myself, regardless of what you or my brothers think."

"That's just it, Fran. You can't. You're too beautiful for your own good. The cowboys are bad enough, but you can't play your little games with a man like Vin Rutter. There's something about him that gives me the creeps."

"Do you know something specific that makes you say that, or is it just your jealousy?" Her pointed chin went up as it so often did around him lately.

He sighed and lifted his hat to thrust his fingers through his short hair. "I don't know anything specific, no, but I plan to find out everything I can about him. Until I do, you stay away from that man."

She gasped and turned her back on him, shoving things around in the front window, toppling bonnets off hat stands, and knocking a beaded purse to the floor. Her shoulders quivered, and her back was so straight he thought it might snap. "Jonas Spooner..." His name came out sharp as a sewing needle. She turned, and if glares could start a fire, his face would be smoldering right now. "You have no right to say who I will and will not see. You don't know anything about Vin, and yet you're willing to malign his character. You're jealous, and that's that." She pointed to the door. "Get out of here. I don't want to see you right now."

He backed off, shaking his head. He'd come in determined to be pleasant, and now she was chasing him out like a stray mongrel. Shoving his hands into his pockets, he nodded. "I'll go, but mind what I said. You try to pet a wolf, and he'll bite you."

When he walked out into the sunshine and past the window, something inside the store smacked into the glass at his eye level. Little spitfire. Prickly as a box of straight pins. If he ever did manage to win her heart, he had a feeling he'd never be bored again.

Chapter 9

Miles wiped his palms on his trousers and gripped the door handle. For days, he'd rehearsed what he would say to Addie when he saw her, but everything he came up with made him sound like a donkey.

He'd meant to see her sooner—the day after their kiss, in fact—but Bat had rousted him before dawn to ride with a posse chasing a pair of horse thieves. Riding for hours in the blazing early summer heat had given him plenty of time to think and prepare what he would say, but he wound up chasing his thoughts and running in mental circles. The memory of their kiss would distract him, followed hard by the knowledge that she had been Cliff's girl. . .and round and round he went.

Twisting the handle, he let himself into the studio. Armchairs flanked the door, with some potted ferns and small tables. Photographs hung on every wall of the front room, mostly portraits but a few landscapes and buildings and such. Centered on the right-hand wall, a large picture of the interior of the Arden Palace held pride of place.

But it was the portraits that drew his eyes. Dozens of cowboys, singly and in groups. Lots of hats and chaps and spurs and guns. There were some businessmen—he recognized a couple of local lawyers, one of the town's doctors, and the preacher at the Methodist church. Children stared solemnly back at him, in their best clothes. Then he turned to study the pictures on the left-hand wall.

Miles sucked in a breath. These were completely different. Like moments caught in time. A cowboy down near the stockyard stroking his horse's mane, his eyes keen on the horizon. A black woman bent over a washboard with a hundred lines and wrinkles bearing testimony to the long journey her life had been. Deeply seated in her dark eyes, he saw wisdom and long-suffering.

Another picture made him smile. A baby sat in a washtub in someone's yard. Sunlight gleamed off the halo of blond curls, and a perfect little hand, like a star-shaped rowel, reached for a sunflower bobbing near the tub. Soap bubbles surrounded the tot, and he could just make out the edge of a calico apron fluttering on a clothesline. The picture was so natural, and the baby looked so real and happy, Miles thought if he touched it he could almost feel the soft skin and the slick of bubbles.

A dozen other photographs hung on the wall, each one a sliver of life caught unaware. Unlike most photographs where the subject faced the camera in awkward stiffness, Addie seemed to capture her customers in a relaxed moment, as if they had no notion a camera was pointed their way at all. Her skill impressed him.

"Miles?"

His chest squeezed. Turning, he tried for nonchalance. "Afternoon."

She stood, framed by the doorway that led to the back

of the studio. One graceful hand held the doorjamb, and the other propped a heavy book against her waist. Those blue-gray eyes made his stomach do flip-flops. "Good afternoon."

He rubbed his hands on his trousers again. "I'm sorry I didn't come to see you before now."

"Jonas told me you were out of town." She looked him in the eye, and the only indication that she might be thinking of their last meeting was a bit of color in her cheeks. Of course, that might be caused by the warm day, too.

"Horse thieves." Why did his tongue feel like a wooden shovel?

"I understand you apprehended the offenders?" She shifted the book on her hip, and he read the words FAMILY ALBUM on the velvet cover.

"They're in the jail, or the 'Hotel de Spooner' as Bat's calling it." Jonas was currently splitting jailer duties with one of the town policemen while several of the county deputies followed up on leads. The horse-thieving ring was proving bigger and broader than they had imagined.

Miles remembered with a jolt why he was standing in her parlor and dug in his pocket. "This here's my chit for getting my portrait taken. From the sheriff's office." He swallowed against his tight shirt collar. "Bat thinks it's asking for trouble posting the names and pictures of all the peace officers, but he's been outvoted by the county board."

She looked up from scanning the paper he'd given her. "Why is that asking for trouble?"

He shrugged. "Why give out the names and faces of the lawmen to a bunch of cowboys full to the skin with ruckus juice? They might look at it more as a shopping list of who to shoot than any deterrent to crime." Miles realized he still had his hat on and snatched it off. *The manners of a prairie dog.* He smoothed his hair, conscious that in his haste he'd dragged it all askew. "So, can you take my picture now, or should I come back later?"

Neither one of them mentioned the big bull buffalo in the room—the kiss. And crowding to the front of his mind was everything Vin had told him about her. Her innocent air might be a hoax. Was the fact that she hadn't mentioned the kiss they had shared a sign that she was a cool customer when it came to men? How could he find out without revealing his own connection to Cliff?

Had she loved his stepbrother?

He shoved that thought away as unworthy. It didn't matter in any case. Everything Vin had told him meant she could never be his.

She folded the paper and tucked it into her skirt pocket. "Now is a good time. I don't have another appointment until after three."

Miles followed her into the back room, his innards warring over what he wanted to believe and what might actually be the truth. He stepped through the doorway into her studio, and his eyebrows rose.

A large room with a skylight surprised him with its open, airy feeling. Various pieces of furniture sat around the perimeter—a settee, several chairs, and an assortment of stools like the ones the piano players used in the saloons with seats that screwed up and down. Blankets, tapestries, and drapes hung from a row of hooks along one wall, and at the rear of the studio, several canvases hung from the ceiling, ready to be pulled down or rolled up for backdrops. A huge, boxy camera on a tripod dominated the center of the room with a black cloth hanging from the back almost to the floor.

He breathed in the smell of fresh pine and paint mingled with a faint chemical odor.

"This is quite a place." He rotated his hat brim in his hands. "Really nice."

"You sound surprised. What did you expect?"

"I don't know. I heard you had a mortgage you were try-ing to pay off. I figured"—he raised one shoulder—"you'd be scraping by without so much equipment or something. . . ." His voice trailed off, because he hadn't really given it much thought, just assumed from the bits and pieces he'd heard from Fran and Jonas that money was tight for her. And here was all this stuff, everything shiny new and fully stocked.

"You can't sell anything out of an empty cupboard." She dragged a stool to the area before the camera. "Without the proper equipment, a photographer can't take the kinds of pictures that will please the customers and have them com-ing back for more. I also cater to a wide clientele. I have to have the right props and furnishings to suit everyone from cowboys to city commissioners and everyone in between."

He sat where she indicated, still holding his hat. "Do you take a lot of pictures of commissioners?"

"I take photographs of whoever wants one. Family por-traits, cowhands who want to commemorate their trip up the trail. This morning, I took pictures for the girls from the

Lone Star Dance Hall." She lifted the drape on the back of the camera and flipped it to the side.

"The Lone Star?" His voice shot up. "What kind of pictures would those girls be wanting?" Surely she hadn't taken any of those risqué ones some of the women in that part of town liked to pass out as advertising. His face got hot at the thought.

Her eyes appeared over the back of the camera. "They were perfectly respectable photographs. Did you know that several of those ladies have families back east? Families who have no idea what those girls do for a living? Every single one who came in here today was dressed like she was ready to go to a church supper and she stayed that way." Addie stepped around the legs of the tripod, her hands resting on her hips. "I do good work in this studio, respectable work. They wanted pictures of themselves to send home. To let their families know that they were all right. I don't condone lying, and I have no control over what those girls tell their families, but those were good, decent pictures I took."

Miles held his hands up, palms facing her. "All right." He wanted to laugh at her spitfire answer, but the fighting light in her eyes told him he'd be safer not to. "I understand. I didn't mean anything by the question." Her vehemence both reassured him and discomfited him. She didn't condone lying. Was it lying not to tell someone something? Not to mention that he knew her former fiancé? More than knew him, in fact?

She relaxed and let her hands drop. "I'm sorry. It's just that every photographer is approached at one time or another about taking pictures that should never be made. I don't hold with provocative poses or pictures taken to advertise what they're selling, and I don't want my name associated with such a sordid practice as taking pictures intended to lure and inflame. It makes me a little. . .defensive."

He could understand that. Just like he didn't want his name associated with the doings of the Walker Gang. Just thinking of what Addie might say if the truth came out made his guts squirm.

"If you'll wait here, I'll get a plate started in the darkroom." She whisked away, disappearing behind a door to his left.

He studied the capped camera lens, like some great, black, lidless eye, and let his gaze wander the room again. So much new equipment. Had Addie been in collusion with Cliff and his nefarious activities? Or was she an innocent casualty in the war the Walker Gang had waged on decent people for the past few years?

She reemerged, wiping her hands on a cloth and checking a clock on the wall beside the darkroom door. "That will hold for a few minutes while we get everything situated out here."

"How'd you get involved with photography?"

"My uncle Carl was a photographer. He worked for Matthew Brady as a photographer during the war and struck out on his own afterward. My father was a Union soldier. He died at Chickamauga, and my mother died not long after the war ended. Uncle Carl came for the funeral, and afterward, he packed up my valise and took me with him in his caravan wagon. We lived out of that wagon—a converted ambulance from the war—for a couple of years, traveling from town to town where he'd take portraits and I'd help him develop them. We finally settled in Abilene when the first herds came up the trail. He opened a studio, and we lived there until recently." She fussed with something on the back of the camera, not looking at him. "Then we moved to Dodge City. Uncle Carl thought the prospects would be good here."

They'd left Abilene not long after Cliff's trial and execution. Did that mean Cliff had meant so much to her she couldn't stay in the town where he'd died? Or had the citizens of Abilene made it too difficult for her to stay? His thoughts milled like a herd bedding down for the night.

She stepped close and took his hat from him. "We don't want this in the picture." Tilting her head, she studied his face until he grew uncomfortable.

"Do I have dirt on my face?"

"No." She smiled, but it seemed detached. "I'm framing the portrait in my mind to get just the right angles and lighting."

"Are all those pictures in the front room yours?" He tried to ignore the warm feeling of her fingers as she placed them under his chin to raise it just a fraction and turned his head to the right.

"Yes." Addie stepped back then approached again to push his shoulders down a hair. "I'm thinking a three-quarters shot."

"How do you make them look so..." He sought the word. "Relaxed?" That wasn't quite it, but he couldn't think of how to put it.

"The trick is in not telling the subject to relax." A real

smile teased her lips this time, and something warm sprang into his chest. "Portraits aren't about how the person looks in real life. A good portrait shows the subject as they think they look or even more as they wish they looked. A skilled photographer uses every weapon in her arsenal to produce a portrait that diminishes a customer's faults and showcases their strengths."

"Weapons? Like what?" Did she think he had a lot of faults that needed diminishing?

She rummaged in a box on a table and pulled out a square of cardboard with an oval cut into it. "Like this. I put this over the lens to diffuse the edges and give me an oval exposure. A photographer uses light, angle, exposure, props, filters, diffusers, and especially her knowledge of the subject to take a portrait. It also helps greatly to know what the portrait is to be used for. Commercial photography like the Arden Palace shots or the posters of Dodge City lawmen won't be staged the same way a portrait of a deceased baby or a woman who wants a picture to send to her sweetheart." She ducked behind the camera and peered through the lens. "A portrait can hide or reveal, and both can be a result of a photographer's skill."

What did she see when she looked through her camera at him? And what did she know about him that would be revealed by her obvious skill? He shifted and grimaced, then tried to get back to the way she'd positioned him.

"You can move for now, but once I get you into your final pose, you'll have to be still for the exposure or you'll come out all blurry." She emerged from the drape, smoothing her hair into the twist on the back of her head.

"You take pictures of dead babies?"

She sighed, crossed her forearms on top of the camera, and rested her chin there. "I do. It may seem gruesome, but for the families who commission the picture, it's often the only reminder they have of a loved child who passes away. I often prefer, if possible, to take a picture of the mother holding the child, so she will always have that link to her baby. I can't imagine the pain of losing a child, and if I can mitigate it in any way, then I try." She went back to work adjusting, focusing, posing his shoulders again, and tilting his chin. A few cranks pulled a shade partway across the skylight to shield him from some of the glare.

There was a lot more to photography than he'd ever imagined. And a lot more to Addie Reid than he'd imagined, too.

Addie looked through her lens at Deputy Miles Carr and tried to maintain her professional air. It was the only way she could think of to get through this first awkward meeting since the night he'd walked her home from the Arden. The night when she'd practically thrown herself at him out of fear of Vin Rutter. The night Miles had kissed her senseless.

She needed to stop babbling about photography and think, or his portrait would come out all wrong and everything she'd said about being a skilled photographer would blow up in her face. If he sensed her unease, he would tense up. Instead of talking about herself, she should talk about him. "How are you adjusting to being a deputy sheriff? Do you like the work?"

For the first time, his eyes lost their wary look and took on a shine. "It's the best job I've ever had. I can't believe I get to work with men like Bat and Jonas. Most everyone likes them, and those that don't at least respect them."

Ah, her first inkling of what he would want in a portrait. "I read the article in the paper about the posse and capturing those horse thieves. It sounds like you acquitted yourself well."

He shrugged. "We worked as a team. Bat knows his onions. Though they had a head start, he had a feeling they were headed to Trinidad, since one of them had family there. We went across country and got around ahead of them near the state line. Then it was just a matter of waiting until they showed up."

"You make it sound so simple."

"I'm learning that being a lawman can be simple if you do it right and everything falls the way you hope it does. I read once where someone said that chance favored the prepared mind. That's a big part of being a lawman in Ford County. Being prepared for just about anything. It isn't enough to have a reputation. You have to be able to back it up with a quick hand, a steady nerve, and determination to succeed." Passion for his job glowed in his expression. His hand fisted on his leg, and he leaned toward her a bit.

This was just what she wanted to capture. "Wait right here while I get a plate." She hurried to the darkroom, closing the door behind her before parting the heavy woolen curtains. By feel, she reached the pan holding the plate she had just washed with collodion. Lifting it dripping from the solution, she slid it into the box that would protect it from light until she could get it into the camera.

Slipping from the darkroom, she hurried to the Chevalier and ducked under the smothering drape. With instinct born of much practice, she inserted the plate into the back of the camera. Silver nitrate dripped from her fingers, and she wiped them on the edge of the drape.

"All right. We're ready." She approached Miles once more and readjusted his pose. "Tuck your thumb just under your jacket at the waist to hold it back, because I want your badge to show up well in the picture."

The gleam of pride leapt into his eye once more, and his jaw lifted just a hitch. Exactly as she wanted. Stepping back, she removed the lens cap, counted to five, and replaced it. "Perfect."

He smiled at her, the same smile he'd given her the night of the play, and her heart bumped harder. "Thank you. I've never had my picture taken before, but you've made the whole process a pleasure."

"You've never had a portrait taken?" She blinked. "Not ever?"

Miles retrieved his hat from the chair where she'd placed it earlier and held it before him. "There wasn't much money for that kind of thing when I was a youngster, and what with one thing and another, I guess I never got around to having one taken since I left home. Nobody to send it to anyway." He shrugged. "When will the picture be ready?"

"I promised the county board I'd have them done by this weekend if they could get all the officers to come in. You're the last one, actually."

"Do you think I could get a copy of my picture? I'd pay you for it of course."

"Sure. You can drop by for it on Monday, or I can bring it by the jail."

"I'll stop in for it."

She tried not to let herself feel glad that he'd be coming by again. Neither of them had mentioned the kiss or that night at all. And what did that mean?

Miles stared at his likeness. It was him, and it wasn't.

When he'd stopped by for it on Monday morning, unable to hide his eagerness, Addie had been setting up for a family portrait and couldn't spend time with him. He'd handed her his coins and taken the little cardboard folder, tipping his hat and escaping the rowdy kids and harried parents. How she would ever corral them into sitting still for a picture was a mystery, but he didn't doubt she could do it.

He traced the silvery scrolling letters on the bottom of the frame while staring at the photograph. Addie's skill made him take a deep breath and shake his head. Everything she'd said about capturing people the way they wanted to be, how they wanted to see themselves, was present in this picture. For the first time in his life he saw more than a dirt-poor kid with no prospects or a weedy offshoot of a larcenous family tree. Looking back at him was a lawman. Someone who stood for something good and decent. Someone who could command respect. Someone with a future.

For the first time he really believed he could overcome his past and be the man he wanted to be.

Chapter 10

Firecrackers went off in the street for the hundredth time that day. July Fourth, cowboy-style.

Fran held the lengths of dress goods high to allow her passage through the throng in the mercantile and stepped into the comparative calm behind the counter. She ripped a length of brown paper from the roll and reached above her head for the string holder. It hung just out of her reach down the track, and Fran grabbed the metal cage and dragged it toward her before snipping off a length of twine. The paper crackled as she wrapped the fabric into a neat bundle and tied it up. "Here you go, Mrs. Blanchard. Three lengths of calico and one of the bombazine." She set the bundle next to the thread and yarns Mrs. Blanchard had already selected. Why had the woman chosen today of all days to brave the store? "Is there anything else I can do for you?"

"Thank you, dear." Mrs. Blanchard dug in her purse. Someone jostled her elbow and coins plopped onto the counter.

Fran slapped them to keep them from rolling off onto the floor. They'd never find them in this crush if they escaped.

"Such a lot of people in here."

"It is the Fourth, Mrs. Blanchard. Every cowboy and rancher and farmer and businessman in Ford County is here to celebrate."

She saw the elderly lady to the front door and hurried on to the next customer. They stood three and four deep all along the counters, laughing, joking, and for the most part under control. Spurs jangled and wide-brimmed hats blocked her view of the back of the store where she'd last seen Wally.

Divide and conquer was the order of the day. Fran manned the counter with the patent medicines, housewares, cloth, and sewing notions, while keeping an eye on the center table of ready-made clothing. Wally took care of the other long counter with the tobacco, foodstuffs, and candy. The demand for new clothes kept Fran hopping, and Wally made several trips to the storeroom to replenish the stacks.

"Hello, darlin'." A sunburned cowboy leaned on the counter. "You sure are a sight for these trail-weary eyes."

Since he was at least the tenth drover in the last hour to pay her a compliment and she was already tired to death, she had to force herself to smile at him. "What can I get you?"

"How about a dance tonight? You will be at the dance, won't you?" He put an extra-thick drawl into his words. "A lady as pretty as you can't be sitting home on the Fourth."

A flutter jumped to life in her middle, not because of this ordinary cowboy but because Vin Rutter had been in first thing to see her and asked her to save him a dance. "I'll be there. If you're lucky, you might get a dance, but you're not the first cowboy to ask."

"Lady, if you're going to be there, there's probably going to be a fight." He winked at her. "There might even be bloodshed, as pretty as you are."

And so it went until she finally closed the front door on

the last customer. As the bell overhead jangled, she turned and leaned against the door. Wally dropped into a chair near the cold potbellied stove and stretched his feet out.

Fran walked slowly toward him. The store was a mess. What had started out as neat stacks of clothing and precise pyramids of canned goods, now looked as if a tornado had blown through. The shelves were nearly bare behind the counters. As unladylike as it was, she was too tired to care, and bracing her hands on the counter near where Wally lounged, she hopped up to sit. "A cloud of locusts couldn't have made a neater job of it." She tucked a strand of hair up into a hairpin.

"I do believe we must've set some kind of record." Though he drooped with tiredness, Wally's eyes gleamed. "We even got rid of almost all those ridiculous pickled beets, though what cowboys would want with them I can't imagine."

"It's like they had buying fever. I sold the most bizarre things today. Patent medicine and scarves and gloves and every last pair of suspenders." Fran laughed, trying to ignore her aching feet. How was she going to get through an entire evening of dancing? "I don't know when I've been this tired."

Wally smoothed his oiled hair, the part still razor straight even after the day they'd put in. "You've done a marvelous job today, Miss Seaton. I'm sorry Hap wasn't here to be more helpful. Why he had to choose today of all days to go over to Fort Dodge is beyond me. Though, after the row we had last night, I told him he could stay over there for all I cared. Things are going to change around here. I need a partner I can count on, not one who bleeds us dry and sponges off my labor."

Fran hadn't actually been sorry Hap wasn't with them today, though she liked him well enough. Hap Greeley wasn't on speaking terms with hard work, and if he'd have been here underfoot, he and Wally would've been scrapping instead of waiting on customers. For the first time that day the chimes of the wall clock could be heard. Four o'clock. Only an hour to go before the town supper and dance.

"Do you want me to help you count the tills?" Though she longed to head home and soak her feet, she wouldn't miss the dinner and dance for anything. The sooner she got out of here, the sooner she might see Vin.

As she'd hoped, Wally waved her away. "No, you head home and get ready for tonight's festivities. I'll count the receipts. Bat promised me a deputy to see me safely to the bank, and Banker Poulter is holding the vault open for me. I think we must've cleared more than two thousand dollars. Be sure to lock the front door on your way out."

Fran hopped off the counter, her sore feet yelping as they impacted the board floor. "Do you want me to be here first thing in the morning to help clean everything up?"

He put his hands on his knees and forced himself to his feet with a slight groan. "No, I think we'll open at noon tomorrow. You don't need to come in until about ten, I should think. Hap might be back by then, and he can help us. I'm tired of slaving while he loafs around. He can bend his back for once."

She left him counting stacks of bills next to the register, making careful notes in his receipt book. If Wally got Hap to work tomorrow it would be the first time since she'd known either of them.

Rushed for time, she didn't wait for one of her brothers to show up. She wove through the throngs on Front Street and hurried to her house. Nobody was home. She quickly heated water for a sketchy bath then brushed and restyled her hair.

Vin had been a frequent customer at the store the past week, and she couldn't quell the thrill she got each time he stepped into the mercantile. Though he hadn't asked formal permission to call on her, she knew he would soon. And she had a feeling he wouldn't be intimidated by her brothers.

Donning her best dress, sewn by her and Addie—with Mrs. Blanchard's help—just for tonight, she knew she looked her best. The pale green fabric scattered with tiny white flowers exactly matched her eyes and highlighted her red-gold hair. She didn't need to touch her lips and cheeks with any color—though her brothers would be scandalized to know she even possessed makeup. Bad enough the fit they'd thrown when she'd pierced her ears. She swung her head a little, feeling the tug of the silver and peridot dangling from her lobes.

A knock sounded on the door.

She inserted the last hairpin and went to answer.

Jonas Spooner stood on the doorstep, hat in hand. "Evening, Fran. You sure look nice. I came to take you over to the dinner. I was going to walk you home from the mercantile, but you left before I got there."

She held on to the door. "Did one of my brothers send you?"

He shook his head. "Nope, thought it up all on my own.

You don't have someone else calling for you, do you?"

Irritation scratched at her. "No. But I've arranged to meet someone there."

"A man?" His brows narrowed together, and his lips flattened.

"A gentleman, yes." Fran reached for her fan and bag.

"Do your brothers know?" Jonas stepped back as she closed the door behind her then offered his elbow.

She took it with bad grace, and not for the first time noticed the muscles under his shirtsleeve. Where Vin was lean, Jonas was sturdy. And where Vin had all the excitement of the unknown, Jonas was as familiar to her as her brothers. . .and as annoying. "I don't have to get their approval for everything I do."

His shoulders relaxed, and he blew out a long breath. "Fran, I'm tired of arguing with you. Let's bury the hatchet, call a truce. We used to be such good friends."

He was right. They had been good friends, until he messed everything up by declaring his love for her. To tell the truth, she was weary of fighting with him, too. A truce sounded nice. He tilted his head and gave her a smile, making something spark in her heart. He could be endearing, charming even, when he tried. Why couldn't he accept that friends was all they would ever be?

"I'd like that. To be friends again."

"I was hoping you'd say that. Let's have a good time tonight." He tucked her hand more securely into his elbow and gave it a pat. "I'm hungry. Are you?"

The dinner held little appeal for her. It was the dance

that occupied her thoughts. When would Vin get there? How many dances could she have with him before people started talking? What would her brothers say?

They strolled up the street, following the crowd toward the church where the supper would be held. They ran into her brother Stuart, and he seemed glad enough to relinquish any responsibility for her to Jonas. Fran searched the dinner crowd for Vin's pale face, but he didn't appear to be among the diners.

As soon as a seat opened up at one of the long benches, someone filled it. Women carried laden dishes to the tables and empty plates back to the kitchen.

"I'm glad I didn't volunteer to serve. This is worse than the crowds we had at the store today."

Jonas found them two seats near the door, and throughout the dinner he saw to her every need and chatted easily with her and those around them. She couldn't help but notice how several of the single ladies serving the dinner stopped to say hello to him and ask if he would be at the dance later. By the time the fourth young lady had stopped to inquire, Fran found herself becoming irritated. Couldn't they see he was escorting her? Brazen, that was what it was.

The minute Jonas finished his slice of apple pie, she took his arm. "Let's go. I don't want to be late for the dance."

Jonas smiled and led her outside and down the way toward the Arden Palace where the dance was being held.

Once inside the building, she scanned the packed seating areas and the dance floor. The orchestra, borrowed from the Long Branch Saloon for the night, sawed away at a reel.

Women pivoted and swung, their dresses like bright flowers in a sea of big hats and bandanas. Fran tapped her foot along with the music as she searched for Vin.

Jonas surveyed the crowd. "I better get in before you get mobbed. Dance?"

She nodded, still searching for Vin, until Jonas fitted his arm around her waist and drew her toward him. Her eyes widened. Had she ever danced with Jonas before? She couldn't remember.

Her glance bounced off his, and her breath hitched. Under her fingers, the muscles of his shoulder felt as solid as a draft horse, but his steps were light and fluid leading her in the waltz. Though he maintained several inches of space between them, the iron band of his arm made her feel as if he held her against him. Heat flared in her middle, and uneasy, unfamiliar feelings began sloshing, as if her heart were a bottle of sarsaparilla being shaken.

She tried to concentrate on the steps and rationalize her inner turmoil. When she closed her eyes, she could feel his hand on her back, warm and strong. Her eyelids bounced up. He swung her in a perfect pivot, leading with confidence, as if they were floating.

"You look surprised." He grinned. "Didn't think a country boy like me could dance, did you?"

She shook her head and gave herself over to the enjoyment of dancing with Jonas. The man had hidden depths. Not that she was interested, she reminded herself, but at least he wasn't murdering her feet like a lot of the cowboys. Passing a group of ladies on the fringes, Fran wasn't unaware of their envious looks.

The music swirled to an end, and Jonas's arms dropped from around her. Why this action should give her such a feeling of loss baffled her, and she squelched it by clapping a smile on her face and following him off the floor. She was a muddleheaded fool, that was what.

They reached the seating area, and her heart gave a jolt. Vin stood there, tall and slim, his pale hair brushed smooth and his clothing immaculate. Though several ladies encircled him, he looked over their heads and locked eyes with her.

Her heart thundered and her mouth went dry.

He threaded through the women and smiled down at her. "Ah Fran, you look delightful."

Jonas's jaw tightened. "Evening, Rutter."

"Thank you for occupying my girl until I could get here, Spooner." He lifted Fran's hand and kissed the air over her knuckles. "There goes the music, my dear. Shall we dance?" He didn't wait for her consent, swinging her into his arms and joining the throng on the dance floor.

She caught sight of Jonas watching her for a moment before being surrounded by females. A strange emptiness grew in the pit of her stomach.

"Am I such a poor dance partner that you should look so sad?" Vin bent and whispered against her temple. His warm breath stirred the fine wisps along her hairline and dragged her mind away from Jonas.

"No, of course not." He was an accomplished dancer, though not in Jonas's class. She gave him her brightest smile. "I've looked forward to being with you all day."

He held her a bit closer. "You stand out like a flower in a cornfield. Have you ever thought of leaving Dodge City? Your face and form"—his voice dipped—"are more suited to society balls in Kansas City or St. Louis, or even New York, rather than this little prairie stomp." His lips drew into a sneer as he took in the cowboys and calico.

Stung that he should think so poorly of the biggest event she'd ever been invited to, she bit her lower lip and tried to see it through his eyes. If he'd been to those cities, she could understand perhaps why he didn't think so much of a cow town celebration.

"Do you think so? Dodge is the biggest city I've lived in. I grew up on a farm near Springfield, Missouri, and came here with my brothers two years ago when herds first started trailing into Dodge."

"I assure you, my dear"—again his breath tickled her temple—"you would make a sensation in a big city. Have you ever thought of traveling?"

Had she ever? Only every night before she drifted off to sleep. "I suppose with your job you travel a lot." She couldn't keep the wistfulness out of her voice. What would it be like to swing aboard the AT&SF and let those clacking wheels take her to all the places she dreamed of seeing?

"You could say I move around a lot."

"It sounds lonely, always moving like that."

He shrugged, and his eyes bored into hers. "Maybe I didn't know I was lonely until recently."

Her breath hitched. "When will you move on, and will you be back through here often?"

"I'm not sure how long I'll stay. I'm expecting to come into a great deal of money in the near future, and I plan to use some of it to travel." A smile tugged his lips. "Maybe when I do pull out of here, I won't be going alone. You dance beautifully." He turned his head just enough that his lips brushed her forehead, leaving her skin tingling.

Vin Rutter was a man who could give her all the things she dreamed of—adventure, travel, excitement. She gave herself over to enjoying the evening.

Vin kept her to himself and refused to allow anyone to cut in, but in the middle of their third dance, a grubby boy snaked toward them through the crowd and tapped Vin on the arm.

"It's time."

Vin's arms dropped away, and he lifted her hand, squeezing her fingers. "I do apologize, but I have an appointment I can't possibly break. I shall turn you over to the tender mercies of these gentlemen." He waved to the men standing on the sidelines waiting for partners. "But I shall expect your heart to remain true to me." He followed the young messenger toward the doors.

After his departure, the spark went out of the evening. Though she laughed and flirted with her partners, nothing seemed as fun. It didn't help at all that Jonas swung past again and again, each time with a different girl in his arms.

Addie slipped another wet-plate into the Chevalier and removed the lens cover to capture the man staring so intently at the camera. She counted off the seconds. The knot between her shoulder blades reminded her that she'd been preparing plates and posing subjects for almost ten straight hours. Every drover in town seemed to have stomped through her studio to commemorate the holiday with a portrait.

The cowboy paid her and sauntered out, and with thankfulness, she flipped the sign in the front door to CLOSED and snicked the lock. Though weary, a thrill ran through her at how her coffers had swollen today. This thrill was quickly followed by a twinge of apprehension. Even with such a boost to her cash flow, the final mortgage payment loomed like a tyrant.

Another tyrant stalked her as well, contributing to her weariness. Ever since spying Vin Rutter at the Arden ten days ago, her nerves had been on edge. Sleep eluded her, and food tasted like sawdust, though she hadn't seen him since that night. Maybe his coming to Dodge was a coincidence. Maybe he was just passing through. Maybe she was worried for nothing.

And maybe he was just biding his time until he confronted her.

If only she could confide in someone. Fran would be her natural choice, but telling Fran meant revealing how gullible she'd been to fall for the likes of Cliff. The pain was too raw. Besides, Fran had been too consumed with a new beau—a mystery man that had her all aflutter—to pay much attention to Addie. According to Fran, the man was more exciting than an Italian count, better looking than Bat Masterson, and more fascinating than a magician. Addie shook her head.

Nothing with Fran was ever simple, especially when it came to men.

She supposed she shouldn't throw any stones. Every time she thought of Miles Carr—and she seemed to think about him way too much—her heart did strange things and her mind ran in a dozen different directions. She had no idea what he might feel for her.

When he'd come to her studio for his portrait, he'd been composed and businesslike. He hadn't mentioned their kiss, and she would've rather died than bring it up first. She blushed, remembering the bliss of being held in his strong arms, the way his presence had calmed her fears and made her feel safe. Had it meant nothing to him? Had she let it mean too much to her?

The portrait she'd taken of him was good—better than good—if she did say so herself. Would he mind that she'd printed a copy of the photograph for herself?

Stop these foolish thoughts. You seem to be forgetting that he'd drop you like a hot rock if he knew about your past. You have other things to worry about. Though this was far from the first time she'd given herself a stern talking-to regarding Miles, her heart didn't seem to want to listen any better now than before.

She gathered her things and prepared to leave. If she hurried, she might make it to the church in time to get some of the community dinner, though by now most of the tables were bound to be cleared as the town dance had been under way for more than an hour.

Her hand brushed the camera case at her side. The

contents of the hidden compartment reminded her yet again that she needed to avoid getting involved with a man. With the mortgage payment hanging over her head like a sword, she couldn't let her attention be diverted from her work, even by someone as handsome and kind as Miles Carr. She'd been fooled once before, and she wasn't minded to play the fool again. If the bank knew of her past, the manager would call in the loan and put her out of business quicker than igniting flash powder. And there was the complication of Vin Rutter to contend with.

She stepped out onto the boardwalk and locked the door. Dust and noise filled the air as riders, wagons, and pedestrians clogged the street. Everyone was dressed in their best, and red, white, and blue bunting hung from every porch and balcony.

In spite of the high spirits and joviality all around her, a feeling like cold fingers brushed across the back of her neck, and she turned around. The crowd parted for a moment. Her breath snagged in her throat. Vin Rutter leaned against a hitching post, staring at her. His thin lips twitched, and he bowed slightly before the crowd obscured him again.

Shaking, she gripped her camera case. Anger burned bright, incinerating her fear. How dare he come here and by his very presence threaten to disrupt her life all over again? She wasn't minded to play the victim again. Marching toward him, she vowed to get to the bottom of his reason for being in Dodge City and make sure he knew she wanted nothing to do with him or the tangled past.

When she finally made it through the crowd, he had vanished.

Miles strode down the street, alert to trouble but feeling pretty good about how things had gone today. Though Dodge City teemed with people, so far the skirmishes had been few. But like a pot of water on a stove, the air held a sense of impending action, as if something might boil over at any time. The quickly approaching nightfall might bring with it everything the lawmen of Dodge could handle.

As he passed the bank, he stuck his head in. "Everything set here? I'm just headed to the mercantile now."

Ty Pearson lounged against one of the teller windows, cradling a shotgun in his arms. The bank manager, Archie Poulter, jingled some keys or coins in his pocket, his heavy eyebrows overhanging his eyes. "Hurry him up if you can. I can't wait here all evening."

"I'll do my best to chivvy him along." He nodded to the banker and to Ty and headed up the street. His antipathy toward Archie Poulter had been an irrational thing until he learned from Jonas via Fran that the pompous old man had made an offer of marriage to Addie. Then his antipathy had solidified into active dislike.

Miles rapped on the mercantile door and shaded his eyes to peer through the glass. Wally sat at the counter surrounded by stacks of coins and bills. He looked up, frowned, and nodded. Miles turned his back to the door and watched the street as he waited for Wally to round the counter and come let him in.

"Come in, come in. Sorry, I didn't recognize you at first."

The little shopkeeper stepped aside to let Miles enter.

Miles scanned the shelves and tables. "Looks like a stampede went through here."

Wally scuffed his way back to his stool behind the counter and tapped some bills into a neater pile. "It feels like it ran right over me, though I shouldn't complain. This is the single best day we've ever had. Nearly twenty-three hundred dollars in sales. I'm about cleaned out for inventory."

"I checked on the way over, and they're waiting for you down at the bank." Miles hooked his thumbs into his belt.

Wally mopped his forehead with a wrinkled handkerchief and made a couple more notes in his ledger. "I'm sorry to keep everyone waiting. It's taken me longer to count the receipts than I thought." He reached for a canvas bag and began lifting stacks of bills into it.

A faint popping sound caught Miles's attention. He strode to the door to see several men running down Front Street. More popping. He wrenched the door open, and the sound got louder. Gunfire? Bat and two of the town policemen charged past.

Shouts echoed. Should he go help, or should he stay with Wally? His job was here, but what if Bat needed help? More gunshots. So many it sounded as if an army advanced on the west end of town.

"Wally, lock this door behind me and wait here until I get back." Miles drew his gun, checked his load, and hurried after his boss.

Crowds jostled past Miles and headed east, and he fought against them to get through. When he finally found himself on open ground, he realized the ruckus was coming from the livery stable on the far end of Front Street. Bat and two deputies had their guns drawn, watching the scene from cover.

Miles cut across the street to join them, diving behind the edge of the building they crouched beside. "Who's in there, and who are they shooting at?"

The door to the livery rattled. Bat shook his head. "Maybe someone in there shooting off a shotgun?"

The firing stopped. The smell of gunpowder hung in the air, and slowly they emerged from cover. Silence.

"Do you think he shot himself?" one of the policemen asked.

"Or he's out of ammunition." Bat motioned for Miles to follow him. Before they were halfway across the street, smoke began leaking under and around the livery door.

"Fire! Fire!" the two city policemen yelled and ran for the water barrels nearby.

Miles followed Bat. Wrenching the doors open, Miles covered the lower half of his face with his arm. A wall of smoke billowed out into the street, and an orange glow made shadows dance on the wall. Horses neighed and stamped.

"You take the right!" Bat ducked into the first stall on the left.

Miles dodged the hooves of a draft horse and yanked at the halter rope. Removing his hat, he swatted at the face of the animal, backing him out of the stall and shooing him out of the livery.

His eyes streamed water and stung, and his throat rasped on the heavy smoke. Six more horses on his side of the immense barn. Men rushed past him with buckets of water, shouting and splashing, kicking at the straw and soaking the walls.

In the last stall, so near the flames, the horse bucked and plunged, terror stricken. Miles darted in and got shoved back. He tried to gauge his leap this time and managed to get halfway into the stall before the horse jerked and side-stepped again. The animal pinned him against the side of the stall, grinding Miles's ribs and shoving the breath out of his chest. Already short of breath because of the smoke, Miles saw stars and blackness crowded the edge of his vision.

Of all the stupid ways for a lawman to die.

Addie's sweet face swam in his vision, peeping at him from over the top of her camera, and his vision darkened further, until he could see nothing but swirling smoke and blackness.

Mercifully, the horse yanked back once more on the halter rope and managed to break free. Miles sank against the stall divider, cradling his ribs and gulping in thick, smoky air that made him cough painfully, unable to stand, unable to even crawl to safety away from the thrashing hooves. He felt himself sliding toward the straw, felt the heat of the flames encroaching, but in his dazed state, he couldn't move.

The air this close to the ground was better, and mercifully, someone managed to get the horse out of the stall. The sound of flames engulfing the barn and showers of sparks illuminating the scarves and blankets of smoke overhead prodded him to do something about getting out. Miles rolled onto all fours and got to his knees.

Hands reached out of the smoke and grabbed his lapels, dragging him up and toward the door. Wobbling, clutching at the stall dividers for support, they made toward the lighter square of smoke that must show where the doorway was. He and his rescuer stumbled into the street where other hands hauled them out of the way of the fire brigade.

Miles's knees gave out, and he found himself sitting on the ground, his head hanging, gulping great lungfuls of fresh air. The frenetic activity around him slowed, and the shouting and tumult died.

Bat leaned against the building next to Miles, his hands braced on his knees and his face streaked with soot. Red spidery veins surrounded his piercing eyes, and smoke-induced tears made tracks on his cheeks. "Thought we lost you there," he said through coughs.

Miles rubbed his squashed ribs and groaned. "I thought you did, too." His head swam, and he had a hard time focusing through the tears pouring from his eyes.

Someone squatted before him, holding his shoulders. "Are you hurt?"

Addie.

He coughed, trying to answer her, but finally had to settle for shaking his head.

She disappeared for a moment then returned, holding a dipper and splashing water onto his pant leg in her haste. "Here, drink this." She cupped the dipper around his hands, holding them steady while he tipped it up to take a long, smoke-clearing draft.

Coolness slid down his irritated throat and improved

things considerably. He stopped with half the water still left and offered it to Bat, who took it, spitting and coughing before downing the rest of the contents. "What happened?" Miles rubbed his hands down his face.

One of the city policemen flopped down between him and Bat. He held a bucket, but this one would never carry water again. Jagged holes of ripped metal jutted out on all sides. "A prank."

"A prank?"

"Looks like someone threw a handful of bullets and shotgun shells into this bucket then built a fire on top. Left it to burn and ran away. When the fire got hot enough, the bullets started exploding. Ripped through the bucket, the door, and injured a couple of the horses."

Addie gripped Miles's upraised knee. "You mean to tell me these men risked their lives, *nearly died*, because of someone's stupid prank?"

Gratified at her indignation, Miles covered her hand with his and squeezed. Now that he could breathe again, the dizziness abated, and his eyes quit leaking. With a swipe, he ran his sleeve over his cheeks and chuckled. "You once told me, Bat, that this job was never boring."

"Speaking of jobs, did you get Wally to the bank before this little shivaree?" Bat straightened his coat and accepted his hat from a bystander, brushing the crown with his sleeve before setting it on his head.

"No." Miles pushed himself upright, trying to ignore the squashed-bug feeling in his chest. That horse had really worked over his ribs. "I'd best get up there and see to it. Wally and Mr. Poulter are probably champing at the bit." He adjusted his gun belt and jacket and headed up the street with Addie at his elbow.

Dozens of people stood observing and talking. The firemen and volunteers had managed to douse the flames before too much damage had been done, and now they raked piles of charred straw out into the street where others wet it down further.

Addie tucked a strand of hair up behind her ear. "I was headed to my studio when I heard the gunfire. Then someone yelled that the livery was on fire. I got there just in time to see you and Bat disappear into the smoke." She took a deep breath. "I thought you'd never come out of there."

Miles rubbed his ribs. "For a while there, I thought I might not either." Smoke-smell clung to his clothes and hair.

The block where the mercantile sat was nearly deserted. Everyone was either still at the dance or milling around the livery, it seemed.

He checked his watch. Less than half an hour since he'd run out of the store. He glanced at the sun, nearly to the horizon, and swallowed against the rasp in his throat. The sun could've easily set on his life back there in that barn. Seeing Addie's face in his mind's eye when he thought he was dying made him realize how much she had come to mean to him. Perhaps he should say something to her. He stopped walking. "Addie, I. . ." What about Vin and Addie's history with his stepbrother, Cliff?

"Yes?" A breeze stirred her hair, and the sunset gilded

the brown strands. She reached out and picked some straw from his shoulder. He stood still, and she brushed her fingers down his cheek, leaving a trail of sensation where she touched him. "Yes, Miles?"

Until he knew for sure, he'd be a fool to commit to anything. And there was always the chance that she'd lump him in with Cliff if she ever found out they were related. Better to keep things impersonal.

"Nothing." He stepped up on the boardwalk to bang on the mercantile door. "Wally? Open up. It's Deputy Carr."

No answer. Perhaps he was in the storeroom. Or maybe he'd gone on to the bank without an escort.

Addie fiddled with her camera case. "I think I'll head to my studio. I have some pictures to develop. Will you be at the fireworks later?" He didn't miss the uncertainty in her voice or the question in her eyes, asking him to explain his odd behavior.

"I'll be around." Her eyes widened at his abrupt answer, and he tried to soften it. "I'm on patrol tonight."

She stepped away. "Maybe I'll see you there."

He nodded and banged on the door again, rattling the glass panes. "Wally!" Cupping his hands, he peered into the store. He rattled the knob, and it gave in his hand. His gut clenched.

"Addie."

She stopped a few yards away. "Yes?"

"Wait here for a moment, will you?" He entered the store, looked around, squatted for a moment, and went back to the door. "Go get Bat. And be quiet about it."

"Is something wrong?"

"Wally's been killed, and the store's been robbed."

Chapter 11

Addie's camera case bounced against her hip, and she grabbed it up, holding it pressed to her middle as she ran up the street. Plenty of people still milled around the smoldering livery, and at first, she couldn't find Bat in the gathering dusk.

Finally, after she'd about given up hope and decided to head for the jail, she spotted his bowler. He stood talking with Mayor Kelley and the editor of the *Globe*. Mindful of Miles's warning to be discreet, she moved around behind the mayor, caught Bat's eye, and jerked her head away from the group before strolling to an open space in the crowd.

Thankfully, he excused himself after a couple of agonizingly long minutes. "What can I do for you, Miss Reid?"

She swallowed. "Deputy Carr needs you at the mercantile." She kept her voice so low he had to bend close.

"What happened?"

"Mr. Price has been killed, and the store's been robbed."

Bat took a deep breath through his nose, his lips pressed together. Cinders had charred holes in his fine suit, and the odors of smoke and burned straw clung to him, as they had to Miles. He scanned the crowd. "I'll head right there. Go tap Deputy Spooner on the shoulder and ask him to follow me."

Addie sidled up to Jonas and whispered her news in his

ear, and together they sauntered up the street as if they'd both lost interest in the fire. They weren't alone, as others, now that the excitement had abated, headed back toward the town dance.

Addie and Jonas found Bat and Miles squatting beside the body. Though Addie had known Wally must be dead, nothing prepared her for the shock of seeing him that way.

Bat braced his hands on his thighs and rose.

Miles handed him a dented can.

"Not much of a murder weapon." Bat set it on the counter.

A dark red stain marred the label, but not so much that Addie couldn't make out the picture and words. Pickled beets.

"A crime of opportunity?" Miles studied the shelves and counters. "It looks like whoever did this picked up whatever was handy and bashed him in the head. The place is such a wreck, it's hard to say if Wally put up any kind of a fight. I was in here just before the fire, and it looked pretty much like this. I guess they had a banner day with customers."

Bat set the can on the counter and snapped his fingers to Jonas. "You'd better find the town marshal. This is his jurisdiction, but do your best to keep it quiet. The last thing we need is a bunch of gawkers." He turned to Miles, who stood and dusted off his hands. "Get a pencil and paper and start writing things down. When we catch the killer, we'll need to keep the evidence straight for the courts."

Addie frowned, and an idea blossomed in her head. She relaxed her hold on her camera bag, letting it rest against her hip. "Sheriff?"

"Miss Reid? I forgot you were there. This is no sight for a lady. I trust you won't broadcast this until we've finished here?"

"Sheriff, I have my camera. Would it be helpful to have a picture of the. . ." She waved her hand over Wally's body, sickened but willing to be of aid if she could. "It might help later when the case goes to trial."

Bat smoothed his mustache, his keen eyes studying her. "An excellent idea. You have the equipment you need?"

She patted her case. "Everything's here. I just need some light."

Miles stood on a chair to light the overhead kerosene lamps, as well as the ones behind the counter. Their reflectors magnified the illumination until it was bright enough for her to get a good picture.

With a lump in her throat for Wally, and for Fran, too, when she heard the news, Addie readied the Scovill. Her hands shook, and she had to steady the camera on the edge of a flour barrel, sighting through her loop to frame as much of the store as she could while still capturing the details.

She didn't have to tell poor Wally to hold still for the exposure.

The instant she replaced the lens cover, the door burst open, and Mr. Poulter strode in with Deputy Pearson on his heels. "Really, Price, I've waited as long as I can. You're more than two hours overdue—" He halted, his mouth falling open and his hands reaching out to clutch something solid to steady himself. "Dear me, what happened?"

"Mr. Poulter, you need to leave."

Pearson took one look at the body, ducked out the door, and before anyone could stop him, he yelled into the early evening air, "The storekeeper's been murdered! Wally Price is dead!"

"That fool!" Bat charged through the doorway, but the damage had been done.

The dozens of people passing the store on their way back to the dance stopped, and as one, they tried to crowd into the store for a look at the gruesome crime scene. Women shrieked, men shoved and shouted, pushing Bat back into the store.

Addie found herself nearly carried toward the back of the mercantile on a wave of curious onlookers. Someone grabbed her arm, and she tried to wrench free, until she realized it was Miles.

"Go out the back way and get to your studio. Develop that picture and bring it to the jail. Hurry."

Glass broke, and cans toppled as more people wedged into the store.

Addie slipped out past the storeroom and into the alley, panting and shaking. She'd never seen anything like it. First the murder, and now a stampede. Bile rose in her throat at the callous disregard of Wally's life, the cheap thrill the townspeople sought at his expense. Tears burned her eyes, and she clutched her camera. At least she had something she could do to help Bat and Miles track down Wally's killer.

Bodies pressed in through the doorway, men shouted, women screamed, and Miles battled to keep his feet. His ribs ached, and his head pounded. The curious onlookers gawked and jostled their way inside, flooding the store and trampling the crime scene. At least he'd gotten Addie out safely.

Through the throng, Bat's voice reached him, trying to reason with the crowd, but Miles couldn't tell that it made any difference. Two dozen, three dozen? He grabbed a man and shoved him toward the back door. "Get out of here. There's nothing for you to see here."

The man fought back, taking a swing at Miles. They scuffled, knocking against a cabinet. Glass broke, and Miles heaved the man away from him.

A gun blast went off, and everyone stilled. The crowd parted until Bat stood alone over the body, his pistol in his hand emitting a thin stream of blue smoke. A fresh bullet hole decorated the pressed-tin ceiling. "Now that's enough. I want every last one of you to get out of here right now before I lay this barrel upside a few noggins." His eyes seemed to cut through the onlookers. He nodded to Miles, who drew his gun as well. "You folks back there, head out that door and don't come past the body." He barely turned, keeping his gun pointed slightly up but ready to jerk it down if need be. His body quivered, like a panther ready to pounce. "You up here by this door, get out onto the street." He started shoving people out the door with his gun, and they went, like chastised sheep, until only Miles and Bat remained.

"What happened?"

Bat holstered his gun, his face a mask of disgust. "Mob behavior." He wiped his hand across his cheeks, smearing the soot there. "With the whole town keyed up for the celebration, then the fire, I knew if word of this killing got out tonight, the lid would blow off. People do strange things when they're in a group. Panic's going to spread fast, and I wouldn't be surprised if rabble-rousers didn't make the most of it. Remind me to have a word or two with Pearson. Of all the stupid things to do, running into the street and crowing like a rooster."

The city marshal, Charlie Bassett, shouldered through the door. "What's going on?"

Bat pointed. "It's Wally. Got himself robbed and killed."

Charlie scowled. "I thought one of your deputies was looking after him."

The guilt that had peppered Miles the moment he saw Wally sprawled on the floor stung like buckshot. "I was supposed to walk him to the bank." He waited, his hands fisted, for them to say all the things he'd been thinking himself.

What kind of lawman are you?

Your negligence cost Wally his life.

You're a sorry excuse for a man, trash. You'll never be anything but a waste.

"I just heard about the fire." Charlie squatted beside the body. "I was down at the Alhambra breaking up a fistfight. The only casualty down there was the mirror behind the bar."

The mob had knocked Wally even more askew than he'd been, and merchandise littered the floor. The marshal, a good friend of Bat's, shook his head. "If I hadn't had my hands full in the saloon, I'd have helped you out down at the livery."

"There's going to be plenty of accusations and blame-shifting over this." Bat blew out a long breath. "We're going to take a beating in the papers."

Miles grimaced. If he would've stayed at his post, Wally would be alive. Should he turn his badge in first, or should he let Bat have the satisfaction of firing him? He stared at the floor. Every hateful accusation his stepfather had ever hurled at him sat like a fistful of rusty nails in his gut. Worthless, useless, no-account. What had ever made him think he could be a lawman?

Bat checked his watch, holding it to the light of one of the lamps. "By now the whole town knows about this. Any evidence here has been ruined. No mystery how Wally died. He's got a dent in the back of his head." Bat searched around him. "Where'd that can go?" He found it behind the counter and showed the bloody label to the marshal. He took it and set it on the floor beside the body. "We'd best go get the undertaker. This is terrible timing. You and I are supposed to leave on the night train, Charlie. We have to transport those horse thieves over to Wichita and testify at the hearing."

"This can't afford to wait. Store got robbed, too?"

Miles spoke up. "Wally said it was more than two grand. I was in here just before the fire at the livery. He was counting the money. I told him to lock the door behind me, but he must not've. It wasn't locked when I got back here, and you can see it hasn't been forced." He pointed to the latch, as normal as a nickel. "I don't know how long I was away. Half an hour maybe?"

Jonas appeared in the doorway, and Bat beckoned him in. "Spooner."

"The undertaker's waiting outside, and the city police are standing guard on the porch. Most of the crowd has taken off toward where they'll be setting off the fireworks."

Charlie tilted his head and appraised Miles. "So you were the last one to see Wally Price alive?"

Miles stilled. "Except for the killer." Was Charlie Bassett accusing him?

The marshal's eyebrows rose.

Bat rolled his eyes. "Easy there, both of you. Miles didn't kill Wally. He was down at the livery helping me."

Jonas stepped farther into the store. "Miles wasn't the last to see Wally alive. I was on the front porch of the Arden when I heard the ruckus at the livery. I headed down Front Street, and when I passed here, Wally was standing in the doorway looking up the street. That had to be after Miles raced out. I didn't pay too much attention at the time, but I did see Wally, and he was very much alive."

Relief coursed through Miles. At least he wasn't going to have to stand trial for murder.

Charlie shrugged. "All right, that clears Miles." He jerked his chin. "Sorry about that, but we have to consider everything."

Miles nodded, his jaw tight. "The door wasn't locked when I got here, so either Wally forgot or the killer got in before Wally relocked it."

"If I was the killer, I'd have come in the back door." Bat pointed his walking stick to the back of the store. "Carr, you and Spooner go check it out. We'll get the undertaker in here."

Miles and Jonas filed into the narrow hallway that led to

the back door. When they were out of earshot of Bat and the marshal, Miles whispered, "Thanks for backing me up."

Jonas nodded. "Good thing I saw him at the door as I ran by or you might be in a real fix." He opened the back door and studied the lock. "No sign of trouble here, but we don't know for sure if it was locked at the time of the killing."

"And I sent Addie through here when the crowd came boiling in the front. She took a photograph of Wally for us, and she's gone to develop it. We should ask her if the door was locked when she tried to get out."

They returned to the store in time to see Wally being covered with a sheet. The undertaker, a rosy-cheeked man who looked more like a fairy-tale gnome than a mortician, lifted the head and shoulders, while another man lifted the legs.

Bat checked his watch again. "Charlie and I have talked it over." He smoothed his mustache with his thumb and forefinger. "Since you are technically being seconded to the city marshal's office for the cattle season, we don't see any reason why you, Miles, shouldn't be in charge of the investigation. We'll be hauling those prisoners over to Wichita and waiting to testify. No telling how long that will take. That leaves you to find Wally's killer."

Miles blinked. "Me?"

The serious light in Bat's eyes compelled Miles, and he couldn't look away. "Tomorrow morning, the papers will be full of how we failed to protect Wally Price. It will be all over town that you were the deputy tasked with seeing him safely to the bank. I think you should be the man to bring the killer in. Take Spooner with you. Until this man is caught, you have no other duties, the pair of you. Use whatever means necessary within the law, and don't be afraid to interpret the law pretty broadly if need be. If you don't bring in the killer yourself, Miles, you'll never have the respect of this town or the cowboys who ride in here. You might as well hang up your badge and get out of Dodge."

Miles swallowed, the weight of responsibility, the weight of his whole future as a lawman now resting on tracking down a killer and bringing him to justice. The rightness of Bat's words rang true. If he couldn't do this, if he couldn't find the murderer, he'd never be able to walk down Front Street with his head up again.

Chapter 12

"Any idea where we should start?" Jonas spoke above the rattle of wagons and music and laughter as he and Miles stepped out of the store. He took a deep breath, trying to ease the tension in his shoulders. How was he going to tell Fran about Wally? She'd be crushed.

"Undertaker's first, I suppose. Then ask around if anyone saw anything."

"The town's chock full of strangers, even more than usual, what with it being the Fourth and all."

Miles dragged his hand down his face, leaving streaks in the soot. His clothes smelled of smoke and horses, and red rimmed his eyes.

"I think we should take a good hard look at Vin Rutter." Jonas spat the name. Seeing Rutter fawning over Fran and her lapping it up made Jonas's stomach roil.

"Vin Rutter?" Miles stopped, and Jonas collided with him.

Revelers flowed around them, all heading in the opposite direction, toward the prairie on the west side of town where the fireworks display was set to begin around ten o'clock. Riders on horseback and wagons and buggies clogged the street. Nightfall had brought about a whole new wave of celebrants, and things were livening up.

Jonas nodded. "He's a fellow who hit town a couple of

weeks ago. Been hanging around the mercantile, bothering Fran some." Though Jonas tried to quash his jealousy, it still writhed like a ball of rattlesnakes in his chest. "She let it slip once that he had asked how much money the place made. He's been in that store half a dozen times or more, but he never buys anything. He was at the dance for a while, but he left before I did."

Miles braced his hands on a hitching rail. The light from the Alamo Saloon fell across his face. Lines creased his forehead, and the tightness around his eyes spoke of the stress he was under. A muscle worked in his jaw. His chest swelled as he took a deep breath. "It's as good a place to start as any. We'll see if we can track him down after we talk to the undertaker."

Mr. Givens met them on the front porch of his mortuary establishment, wiping his hands on a towel. His eyes shone bright as new pennies behind his round glasses, and his cheeks were rosier than ever. "Come in, come in."

Jonas let Miles take the lead, and they threaded their way through a front room full of coffins. A spidery-legged chill ran across Jonas's chest. He'd never been too comfortable with the trappings of death, and standing in a room full of caskets did nothing to put him at ease.

"I've just started the laying-out process, deputies. Doc Meyer is with him now." Givens entered a back room, and they followed into the brightly lit space. On a table in the center, Wally Price lay, half-covered by a sheet.

Miles leaned against a counter and crossed his arms. "Anything you can tell us, Doc?"

Jonas dug in his pocket for his pencil and notebook, licked the lead point, and prepared to jot down relevant details.

Dr. Meyer bent over the body. "Probably nothing you don't already know. He died as a result of a blow to the head. I don't see any signs that he put up a fight. No bruises or split knuckles. At a guess, I'd say his attacker surprised him." He pulled out a pipe and tamped it full of tobacco.

Jonas blinked at the clouds of smoke soon wreathing Doc's head. "Ambush?"

"Possibly. Either that or he knew his attacker and had no fear of turning his back." Doc shrugged and tossed a spent match onto a tray. "But that isn't saying much, since Wally knew pretty much everyone in town, and he was a trusting soul. The most I can say is that his attacker was tall. At least taller than Wally, and he's right-handed."

Jonas wrote down the doctor's words. "How can you tell?"

Using the stem of his pipe, he pointed to the wound. "The fracture is above the curve of the back of the skull and it's on the right side of the head." He turned the undertaker around. "If this is Wally, and I'm the killer. . ." He lifted his right hand and made a chopping motion from above.

Miles nodded. "Thanks, Doc. If you find anything else, let us know."

They stepped out onto the street together. Jonas tucked his notebook away, grateful to be out of there. His mind returned to the subject that had occupied him for the past couple of weeks. "Rutter's tall, and I bet he's right-handed."

A cowboy galloped past whooping, scattering people before disappearing up the street. Music spilled out of the saloons and dance halls, and pedestrians clustered on the sidewalks.

Miles rested his hand on his gun and surveyed the street. "So are more than half the men in this town. And you're making an assumption. The killer doesn't have to be a man. It could've just as easily been a woman. Wally wasn't very tall, and he wouldn't have feared turning his back on a woman."

Jonas stepped close to allow a couple to pass by on the boardwalk. "Call it a gut feeling. There's something not right about Rutter. He's too smooth." He scowled. "Fran said he was in acquisitions for the railroad, whatever that means, but I've never seen him at the depot or in the railroad office upstairs at the bank."

Miles turned troubled eyes his way. "Are you sure this isn't just jealousy because Fran seems to prefer someone else? It's a far cry from poaching a fellow's girl—even lying to a girl about your job in order to impress her—to robbing a store and killing a shopkeeper."

Though Jonas knew Miles spoke the truth, he stubbornly clung to his belief. "There's something there that I don't trust, and it has nothing to do with Fran. That man is up to something shady, and I aim to find out what it is. He's been nosing around the store, and Fran might've been the excuse he needed to scout the place before robbing it."

"Okay. It won't hurt to track him down, I guess."

Familiarity with Vin's proclivities led Miles to begin the search south of the deadline in the red-light district. A couple of discreet inquiries and a few dollars to a working girl, and he had the information he needed. Fortunately, people tended to remember Vin with his pale eyes and fancy clothes.

Miles's skin itched. He hadn't told Jonas that he knew Rutter, that Jonas's instincts were telling him the truth that Vin was hatching some sort of plan that boded ill. And the longer Miles withheld that information from his friend, the more he encroached on having to tell an outright lie.

And Jonas's motives bothered him. Pursuing a suspect he had a personal grudge against blurred his objectivity. . . though Miles was in no position to judge. He didn't want Vin convicted of murder if he was innocent, but he wouldn't mind finding a legitimate reason to throw Vin behind bars or run him out of town and away from both Addie and Fran. With Vin gone, maybe he could squash the guilt gnawing at him for hiding the truth.

Miles and Jonas entered a narrow, dark, smoke-filled saloon. No piano music, singers, or performers of any kind. This establishment was for serious drinking and gambling. Two steps into the place and Miles longed for fresh air. Stale beer and cigar fumes assaulted him.

A doxy sidled up to him with pouty lips, and her cheap toilet water added to the miasma. "Buy me a drink, cowboy?" Her husky voice slurred, and she put her hand on his arm.

Miles motioned for Jonas to stay by the door and keep watch. "I think you've had enough."

"If I'm still standing, honey, I ain't had enough." She gave his forearm a squeeze, leaned in, and whispered a coarse suggestion.

"Not interested, ma'am." Grimacing, he removed her hand from his arm and walked to the bar.

A cadaverously thin man wiped glasses with a dirty towel. "What'll it be?" He didn't bother looking at Miles.

"Information."

The man's head swiveled, and his focus glanced off Miles before returning to the glass in his hand. "We don't deal in that here. Beer and whiskey we got. Information you'll have to find elsewhere."

"I'm just looking for a fellow. Goes by the name of Vin Rutter. Tall, pale, talks with a Southern accent."

"Askin' after a man in these parts of town ain't exactly healthy. Almost as unhealthy as answering those kinds of questions."

Miles eased back his lapel so the edge of his badge showed. He studied the bartender. "When was the last time you had your liquor license reviewed by the city council? I hear the city's coffers are getting kinda bare. Might be time for some more raids so they can gather in some fines to pay for running the town."

The towel and glass slowly descended to the stained and gouged bar top. "There ain't no call to play rough."

"Then talk straight. Have you seen him?" Miles inclined his head to where Jonas stood by the door with his hand on his six-gun. "My friend's getting tired of waiting."

The bartender leaned close, and for the first time in the dim lighting, Miles got a look at his eyes. One brown and one green. Disconcerting. "He's in the back room playing poker." The bartender jerked his thumb, and the woman who had approached Miles when he came in sidled over. He tried to ignore her bare arms and low-cut dress.

"Rosabelle, take this gentleman to the back room."

Her eyebrows lifted. "He don't look like no high roller to me."

"Do as I say, woman," the bartender growled, and Rosabelle scowled right back, but she did as she was told, leading Miles past several closed doors to a cramped room near the back.

Miles glanced back down the hall at Jonas and jerked his head. Jonas disappeared out the front door. He'd cover the back to make sure Vin didn't bolt out that way.

Rosabelle didn't bother to knock, just shoved the door open and stepped aside to let him enter.

Six men sat around a green felt table, cards, cash, and chips covering the surface. On a low settee in the corner, a woman sprawled, snoring softly.

Vin sat on the far side of the table, eyes gleaming over his cards. He lifted his glass and tossed back the contents, then froze, sighting Miles.

Heads turned. Miles recognized some of the other gamblers. "Evening, gentlemen."

"This is a private room." A burly teamster lifted his chin, jutting his wild beard over his cards.

"Sorry to interrupt. Just need a word with one of your opponents." Miles stared at Vin, whose mouth had thinned to the point his lips disappeared.

"I've waited too long for a chair to open up at this game. I have no intention of leaving it, especially not when I'm on such a hot streak." Vin fanned his cards then picked up some chips. "I call."

The bearded man scowled, stared at his cards, and threw them facedown on the felt. "Take it."

Vin's long, pale fingers raked in the pile of bills and coins and separated them with lightning-quick dexterity.

"Deal him out." Miles glared at the dealer, a bare-armed girl with sallow skin and stringy hair. She regarded him soberly and skipped Vin as she tossed out the pasteboards.

Vin's jaw tightened, and he blinked slowly.

Miles stood his ground. "Up to you, Rutter. Either you come with me, or I have to shut the whole game down and run you all down to the jail."

"Here, what for?" The teamster bristled.

"I'll think of something."

The gamblers all scowled at Vin. Tension mounted until all at once Vin relaxed.

"Thank you, gentlemen, for a most profitable evening." He shoved his chips toward the dealer who counted them up and exchanged them for cash. Carefully folding the money, Vin inserted it into a gold clip and pushed the bundle deep into his trouser pocket. "Let's take our discussion outside, shall we?"

Miles stepped aside to allow Vin to precede him and accidently kicked the leg of the woman on the settee. An apology flew to his lips, but the woman didn't even stir. Though she snored, dead to the world, her eyes were partially open, rolled back a bit in her head. Disgust and pity tangled in his belly. Drugs or drink or both.

Vin led him out the back door and stopped when he spotted Jonas waiting in the alley. "A pincer movement." He leaned against the wall, cool and bored. "To what do I owe the pleasure, gentlemen?" He glanced at Jonas. "Surely this isn't about Fran?"

Was his cool exterior a front to hide the fact that he'd bashed Wally Price over the head and robbed him, or was he nonchalant because he had nothing to fear from answering their questions? Miles couldn't tell.

"It's nothing to do with Fran, but it is to do with you hanging around the store asking questions." Jonas stepped closer.

The alley was dark, and Miles glanced up and down the narrow passageway. "Why don't we continue this conversation up at the jail?"

"The jail?" Vin straightened. "What is this about?" His drawl diminished.

Jonas shoved Vin toward the front of the building. "At least let's get out of the dark here so I can see your face. Get moving."

Light from the saloon's front window bathed the porch, and Miles positioned Vin so he could see his face. Vin's fishy, pale eyes locked onto Miles. "What is this about?" he asked again.

"Where were you tonight between six and seven?"

"Why?"

"Just tell me."

"Am I under arrest?"

"Not yet." Miles examined Vin's clothes as best he could

for any telltale evidence that he'd killed Wally. "A shopkeeper got murdered tonight. Mr. Price from the mercantile. You've been seen hanging around there, and tonight I find you in a high-stakes poker game. It's well known around town that particular game has a steep buy-in. Where'd the money come from, and where were you at six tonight?"

"Well, I can assure you I wasn't murdering Price or anyone else. There are more ways of acquiring stake money than robbing someone."

Though, in Miles's experience, it was a favorite method of members of the Walker Gang. He set his jaw. "If you don't have an alibi, I'm going to have to run you in. You were seen leaving the town dance not long before the murder, so where did you go?"

Vin studied his fingernails, completely relaxed. A knowing smile dragged at his lips, and his eyelids lowered to half-mast. "I came straight here. At six o'clock, I was sitting down to the first hand of the night." He indicated the saloon. "I had to wait two weeks for a chair to open up in that game." He smirked at Jonas. "The opportunity came at a most delicate moment. I do hope Fran wasn't too upset when I left her."

"Anyone else see you here?" Jonas never took his eyes off Vin. He had a stillness about him that some might be foolish enough to interpret as indifference, but Miles recognized it as steel-strong control, keeping a tight lid on his temper.

"Everyone at the poker game, I expect."

Miles wanted to bash the smug look off Rutter's face. "You haven't explained how you came by the money to get into the game."

A gleam shot into Vin's eyes. "As I told you, there are plenty of ways to get cash in this town. It's all in knowing where to look."

Dread slithered through Miles. The knowing gleam in Rutter's eyes set up a gnawing worry. "We're going to have to verify your alibi."

Vin shrugged. "Go ahead. Everyone in there will vouch for me. As for the money, I parlayed a small stake into a big one playing poker at the Alhambra today. You can check with the bartender there. I bought a round of drinks for the house when I cashed out for the day."

Miles glanced at Jonas. Vin's alibi for the time of the murder was solid.

"If that's all, gentlemen, I believe I'll be going. I have a few things yet to accomplish tonight."

Jonas's hands fisted until Miles thought he might hear the knuckles crack. "Rutter, we're going to track your every move. And I'm warning you, stay away from Fran Seaton."

Stepping just in front of Jonas, Miles rested his hand on his gun. "You're free to go for now. Don't make any plans to leave town just yet."

"No worries there, my dear Miles. I haven't finished what I came to do." He sketched a wave and sauntered away toward Front Street.

Jonas stared after him. "You two sound as if you know each other."

Miles's chest tightened. "We've crossed trails before." He tried to refocus the attention on the investigation. "Let's head back into the saloon and check his alibi. After that, you can go meet Addie and walk her over to the jail. I'll meet you there after I check on Vin's story about hitting it lucky at the Alhambra this afternoon."

Addie wiped her hands on her apron and studied the still wet print in the light of the red lantern. Even with rosy illumination and the unfortunate subject matter, she knew the picture was flawless. Every board in the floor, every wrinkle in the clothes, every letter on the canned good labels stood out in sharp detail.

Careful not to bang into anything in the crowded space, she rolled her head and shook her arms, forcing herself to relax. Developing photographs was a precise and tedious business, as the knot between her shoulder blades and the band of tension around her forehead testified. Though she wanted to snatch the picture off the drying line and race with it to the sheriff's office, she had to wait until it was dry enough to move without damaging it.

She checked her timepiece, holding it up to the glow of the lantern. Nearly ten. She grimaced. Darkroom work always took longer than she wanted.

Arranging jars and draining solutions through filters and funnels, she tidied her workspace. Chemicals were unforgiving and demanded to be cared for correctly, something that Addie had no trouble with, being neat by nature. Touching her finger to the edge of the print, she judged it not quite ready.

With a sigh, she swept aside the heavy curtain and

opened the door to the studio. The light from the studio lamps dazzled her for a moment after the low, red light of the darkroom. She blinked, feeling like a burrowing owl.

"I thought you were never going to come out of there."

She jerked.

Vin Rutter stepped from the front room into the studio.

Her heart lodged in her throat then dropped to stampede around her chest. "What do you want?"

He produced a wicked little cheroot and a match. With a *scritch*, he struck the match against his boot sole. It flared to life, and he lifted it to the cigar, puffing and filling the air with acrid smoke. "That's hardly a gracious greeting."

Her mouth went dry as flash powder. "How did you get in here?" She was sure she had locked the front door.

He patted his pocket. "Oh I have plenty of talents. A simple lock like that didn't deter me for long." He came closer, crowding her between a plaster pedestal and the darkroom door. "It's good to see you again, Addie. You're as lovely as ever." His cold, pale eyes raked over her face and form. "I've been asking around town about you."

"I can't imagine why. And put that cigar out. It's a hazard in here, and it smells terrible."

He stared at the glowing end of the cheroot. "I can remember a time when you didn't complain about the smell of a good cigar. Someone we both knew and loved had a fondness for them."

"I don't wish to discuss anything from that time in my life. Anyway, that cheroot isn't even remotely a good cigar." She wrinkled her nose and waved her hand in front of her face.

"Ah, I see you've gained some spirit since last we met. I always thought there was more lurking behind those guileless eyes than you let on."

"Mr. Rutter, if that is your real name, I want you to leave. I can't imagine why you sought me out, but we have nothing to discuss." She lifted her chin, praying he would go. If anyone saw them together, it could open the door to a lot of awkward questions that would eventually reveal all her secrets. Then she'd be forced out of town again, and she couldn't face that.

He held up his hands, palms outward, and spoke around the cigar clamped in the corner of his mouth. "Addie, is that any way to treat Cliff's best friend?"

"Don't talk about him." A bitter shudder rippled through her, and she gripped the edge of the pedestal.

"Is he still so dear to you that you can't bear the sound of his name?" A chilled laugh came from his thin lips. "Or is it another reason that makes his memory painful? You've certainly kept your past association with him a secret here in Dodge. I haven't heard so much as a whisper, not even from that chatty friend of yours at the mercantile. Is your reticence caused by shame, or are you truly mourning the loss of your lover?"

"We were never lovers." The idea made her skin crawl. "If he indicated otherwise, you can add it to his long list of lies."

Vin rose from the settee and circled the studio, touching drapes and running his hand over the back of a wicker chair. "You've done quite well for yourself here. No one would suspect you were practically run out of Abilene without a penny to your name. I really am impressed. It must've taken quite a lot of money to get started again. And without the help of your uncle now, too. You must be lonely." He tilted his head and smiled, trying to coax a response from her.

The calculating look in his lizard eyes put her nerves on alert. "Vin, I have no desire to relive any of that, especially not with you. Cliff Walker robbed me of everything. I lost my home, my business, and my only family member. I've rebuilt here, and I want my new life to be free of reminders of the past. That includes you. I don't know why you came to Dodge, and I don't know why you're still hanging around, but hear me clear. I want nothing to do with you or anyone else even remotely related to Cliff. Leave me alone." She moved toward the front room.

He followed her to the reception area and leaned against the doorjamb. Crossing his arms, he raised his hand to adjust the cigar and blew a cloud of foul smoke toward the ceiling. "He really did love you, you know, whatever his other faults."

"I asked you to put that nasty thing out." She jerked up the heavy canvas window shade.

"You were all he talked about when we were on the road."

"When you were out robbing banks and trains and stagecoaches, you mean." Addie peered out the window. The street had cleared considerably while she'd been in the darkroom. The fireworks were scheduled to begin soon, and it seemed most folks were already assembled at that end of town.

"Addie."

He spoke from so close behind her, she jumped. An army of ants ran through her veins. She moved to the other window and snapped the shade up to allow lamplight to spill into the street. "Vin, leave me alone. You and your ilk have done enough harm to me and mine."

"Perhaps I'd like to make amends. Smoke the peace pipe, as it were."

She whirled and shoved him backward. "I don't smoke."

He grabbed her wrists and hauled her close, breathing cigar fumes across her skin. His eyes bored into hers, and his grip stung. "Enough. I'm tired of sparring with you. I had intended to go slowly, tread softly, but something happened tonight to let me know I might need to cut my time here in Dodge City short. So the kid gloves come off. I want to know where it is."

"I don't know what you're talking about." *Though she knew very well. It was the only reason he'd be sniffing around.*

"Don't play games with me. I want that money."

"I don't have it." She gritted her teeth and strained away from him. He smelled of smoke and liquor and cheap perfume.

"Then where is it?" The words hissed from his slash of a mouth like steam.

"I never had it. I don't know where it is, and even if I did, you would be the last person I'd tell." She tried to wrench her arms from his cold, hard grasp, but his strength made a mockery of her attempts.

"You must have it. I've searched everywhere else, all our hideouts, all the places we stayed after the last robbery. He was devoted to you. You played a pretty part at the trial, pretending to know nothing of his real identity, all dewy eyed, protesting your innocence. It was a beautiful performance.

But you can't fool me. I know you have that cash, and I'm not leaving Dodge until I get it." He loomed over her.

Since the trial and Cliff's execution, she'd had nightmares about someone coming after her, seeking the treasure she didn't have. "Vin, I don't know where it is." The quiver in her voice gouged her soul. Hadn't she vowed never again to be the victim of a low-minded man, and here she was, cowering? She straightened her spine and swallowed. He might be stronger of body, but she would be stronger in mind and spirit. She would not beg.

The glass in the door rattled, and the knob twisted. Vin's hands dropped away, and he stepped back as the door swung open.

Addie had never been so glad to see anyone in her life. It was all she could do not to launch herself into the arms of Jonas Spooner.

"Any trouble here?" His sandy eyebrows lowered, and his eyes went stony. "Addie, are you all right? I saw the shades were up and figured you were waiting for someone to walk you out."

"Thank you, Jonas. I'm just about ready to go." She rubbed her stinging wrists. "Mr. Rutter was just leaving."

The deputy stepped farther into the room, leaving space for Vin to get by. The two men eyed one another until Vin shrugged, readjusted his cheroot, and headed for the door.

As he passed Addie, he whispered, "I'll be back."

Chapter 13

Addie sagged into an armchair in her waiting room, swallowing hard and trying to calm her racing heart.

Jonas closed the door, twisted the lock, and came to squat beside her. "What's going on, Addie? Was he causing you trouble?"

The urge to spill the entire story pressed against her throat, but the price tag of unburdening was too high. If Jonas knew, he would despise her, and it would only be a matter of time until he told Fran. . .and Miles. Her mind quailed at the thought. "No, no trouble."

His eyes flicked to her reddened arms. "Addie, you can trust me, you know."

She stood and untied her apron. "I know, Jonas. You're a good friend. If I ever have a problem you can help me with, I'll come running. I promise. Can you walk me down to the jail? The photograph I took should be dry now."

Jonas stood, opened his mouth to say something, but thankfully closed it, not pressing the issue.

She hurried to the darkroom, tucked the photograph into her camera case, and blew out the lamps. Jonas waited while she lowered the window blinds.

"You should lock that door while you're in there working alone at night." Jonas tested the knob.

She slipped the key into her pocket and frowned. The lock had proven no obstacle to Vin. She would need to see about bolstering her defenses with a sturdier model, though she couldn't really spare the money.

"The picture turned out all right?" Jonas steered her down one set of steps, across a side street, and up onto the next stretch of boardwalk.

"Yes. Poor Wally." She kept her hand on her camera case. "I can't imagine anyone killing him. He was such a nice man."

"Money's a powerful motivator. The store did a great business earlier today. There are more than a few men in town who would kill for that kind of money, and they wouldn't care if Wally was a nice man or not."

They approached the end of the block, the same end where Price and Greeley's Mercantile sat. Lamplight shone through the windows. "The marshal posted a couple of deputies. With Wally dead and Hap out of town, the place is defenseless. Looters would ransack the place like buzzards on a carcass."

As they drew abreast of the opening, Hap Greeley himself stumbled out, colliding with Addie and nearly knocking her off her feet.

She yelped and grappled with her camera case, clinging to Jonas's arm to regain her balance. "Mr. Greeley."

He raised trembling hands to his face, shoving his glasses up and wiping his eyes. His shoulders shook, and he gulped. Blinking, he seemed to notice them for the first time.

"It's terrible. Poor Wally." Hap dragged out his red handkerchief and rubbed his bulbous nose.

Addie put her hand on his arm. "I'm so sorry."

Hap nodded and shoved his glasses up to swipe his eyes. "I just got back into town and heard the news. Couldn't imagine why the store was lit up at this hour." He jerked his thumb toward the doorway where two city policemen stood. "I just can't believe it. It's like a bad dream. The store is such a mess."

"Sorry about the ruckus in there. Folks sort of stampeded through the place when they heard about the killing. We got them out as soon as we could, but not before they trampled stuff pretty good." Jonas shook his head. "Did you see anything in there that would tell us who did this?"

Quivering, his eyes still moist, Hap dropped onto the bench beneath the window. He cradled his head in his hands. "Poor, poor Wally."

Addie looked at Jonas, who seemed at a loss how to deal with the devastated man. She blew out a breath and joined Hap on the bench. "Hap, we're going to find out who did this. In fact, Jonas and I were just on our way to the jail to take some evidence in."

Hap straightened, his eyes locking onto hers. "Evidence?"

She smiled encouragingly and patted her camera case. "Yes. I don't know if it will make any difference, but I did photograph the crime scene. I just developed the picture, and we're taking it to the sheriff. I hope it helps find who did this to Mr. Price."

The mention of his former partner's name sent him into another bout of the shakes. "Even if you do find the killer, it won't bring Wally back. He wasn't just my cousin. He was my best friend."

Jonas shifted his weight. "Hap, I know this is a hard time for you, but you have to pull yourself together. Come down to the jail with us. I know Miles and Bat will want to ask you some questions."

"Questions?" He scrubbed his nose with the hankie again. "But I wasn't even in town today. I don't know who did this. If I did, I'd shoot him myself." His big hands fisted around the red cloth, and his ashen cheeks bloomed with righteous color.

Jonas took his elbow and got him to his feet. "You never know. Anything you can tell us might be helpful, and it's better than sitting here wallowing."

Hap rolled these words around for a minute. "You're right. If I can do anything to help, I will." He rumbled along behind them toward the jail, sniffling and occasionally muttering, "Poor, poor Wally."

Addie realized her sleeves were still rolled up and unrolled them, buttoning the long cuffs to hide the marks where Vin had squeezed her wrists. Though she had been waiting for him to make his move, she hadn't expected him to accost her so forcefully. Cliff had never laid a hand on her, never given her any indication of his violent side. But Vin Rutter was apparently a cat of a different color. Though he wore the trappings of civilization with his nice suit and cultured voice, pure meanness lurked close to the surface.

What would it take to convince him she didn't have the stolen money? Railroad detectives had searched her home in Abilene and gone over every inch of the studio looking for the cash, more than thirty thousand dollars in bills and gold coins. Though she and Uncle Carl had protested, they were helpless to stop the search. By the time the jury reached a verdict, their future in Abilene was over.

Addie shook her head. That wouldn't happen here. She couldn't let it. Though Dodge was a wide open, volatile town, she loved it and wanted to stay. She'd made a dear friend in Fran, and she was succeeding at her business, fulfilling her dream of being a good photographer. And there was Miles to consider. Her feelings for him had grown in spite of her efforts to quell them, to be reasonable. She wanted her life and future to be in Dodge City. Vin had no part in that, and she refused to let him destroy her dreams. Somehow, she would convince him she didn't have the money, and he would leave town.

They approached the jail shared by the city and county law officers. The upstairs of the two-story building was dark, but the door stood open on the first floor. Behind them, the first boom and explosion of light from the fireworks blazed across the sky.

At the first explosion of fireworks, Miles looked up from his notes. "Finally getting started. I have a feeling nobody in town is going to get much sleep tonight." A faint glow flickered across the window as the firework faded. Another blast soon followed. "I heard they had enough rockets to last for more than an hour."

Letting his feet slide off the corner of the desk, Bat

straightened in his chair and yawned. "That's just the ones the volunteer fire department is lighting. There will be plenty of others throughout the night. How long did Miss Reid think she would be?"

Miles shrugged, feigning nonchalance, though his mind had returned to her again and again while he worked on writing down everything he could think of regarding the investigation so far. "She said she would hurry."

"A fine woman, Addie Reid. A man could go farther and fare worse." Bat tugged the corner of his mustache. "Yes sir, a smart man wouldn't let much grass grow under his feet where Addie was concerned. Some young jackanapes might ride up the trail and throw his loop at her."

Prickly warmth hitched its way over Miles's chest. "You thinking of courting Addie?" He wouldn't stand a chance against someone as handsome and fascinating as Bat Masterson. *Whoa there, pard, where did that come from?*

"Me?" Bat's eyes twinkled. "I was just making a general observation, not a declaration of intent." A smile twitched his mustache, and Miles winced, realizing he'd risen to the bait. "I was just thinking what a nice couple you two would make."

Miles's muscles relaxed by increments—muscles he didn't know he'd tensed. Shaking his head, he returned to his notes. He was going to have to confront his feelings about Addie sooner or later, but for now, he needed to focus on finding Wally's killer. After that he'd deal with Vin and telling Addie about his relationship with Cliff. If, after all that, she still wanted to be with him—and he hardly dared hope she would—then he'd—

The door opened, dragging him from his thoughts, and Addie entered the jail followed by Jonas and Hap Greeley. Miles shot to his feet a fraction before Bat. He reached up to loosen his tight collar only to find the top buttons weren't even closed.

She lifted the camera case strap over her head and shoulder, freeing a few wisps of hair from the knot at her neck. They drifted down and teased her cheeks, and he had to check himself to keep from reaching out to tuck a strand or two behind her ear.

Her slate eyes locked with his, and his tongue quit working. All he could think about was how beautiful she was to him, how courageous and talented, and how much he wanted to protect her from Vin. How much he wanted her to be innocent in all of this.

Jonas cleared his throat, and the sound broke the spell and allowed Miles to look away. His friend dragged a chair from beside the door. "Here you go, Addie. Do you want some coffee?"

"No, thank you."

Why hadn't he thought of that? While Jonas took care of her, Miles stood there like some plaster pillar. He shoved aside a stack of papers and perched on the corner of the desk as she unbuckled the case.

"I've got the picture in here." She lifted a four-by-six-inch print from a compartment at the bottom of the box. Must be where she kept the extra plates for the camera.

He took the photograph from her and passed it first to

Bat, though he itched to snatch it back and study it for clues. "Thank you. I'm sorry you had to see such a terrible thing."

"I only hope it helps catch the killer."

Hap took a staggering breath. "Poor Wally."

Jonas stepped close to Miles. "He's pretty worked up. Guess I might be, too, coming home to news like this. I don't know how much help he'll be, rattled as he is."

Miles nodded. Known for his excess of emotion, Hap wouldn't be any different in grieving his cousin. "Take notes for me, will you?"

Jonas nodded and dug in the desk drawer. He came up with several sheets of torn paper, remnants of the Wanted posters. Miles's palms grew damp. *Please, God, don't let him use one with Cliff's name or face on it.*

Bat looked up from the photograph. "This is excellent, Miss Reid. Of course, knowing your work as I do, I expected nothing less." He smiled at her, and Miles quelled a thrust of jealousy. According to the ladies about town, Bat was considered quite handsome and a prime catch. He glanced at Addie to see what effect the sheriff's blue eyes and charming manner might be having.

Addie merely nodded. "I got it here as quickly as I could."

"A shame we weren't able to keep people out of the store until we had time to look things over more thoroughly." He smoothed his mustache. "Pearson's ears are probably still burning from the dressing-down I gave him." He handed the picture to Miles. "I'd best head toward the fireworks. I promised the mayor I'd stay handy in case there was trouble down there."

"Don't you want to stay and question Hap?"

Bat shook his head. "I believe in hiring capable men. You're in charge of the investigation." He tipped his hat to Addie. "Miss Reid, it's been a pleasure."

Miles blinked at this vote of confidence and stared after Bat's back as he stepped out of the jail. The responsibility pressed against his chest, but a thrust of pride battled for space there, too. "Addie, I'm sorry to bore you with all this, but I can't spare anyone to see you home just yet. If you can wait until I'm done here with Hap, I'll see you safely to your boardinghouse."

She nodded. "I'd like to stay, especially if you have any other questions about the photograph."

Jonas handed her the sheets of paper and the pencil. "How 'bout you take notes for me then. Miles always makes me write everything down, but my penmanship isn't much better than his."

Addie took the implements, cleared a space on the desk by setting a stack of papers on the floor, and poised the pencil over the sheet of paper.

Shifting his attention, Miles tried to clear his mind of everything except asking the right questions. "Hap, you feel up to answering a few things?"

The storekeeper nodded. "I'll do whatever I can, but like I told Deputy Spooner, I was out of town since yesterday, so I don't know how much help I'll be."

"I understand. Have you noticed anyone hanging around the store? Anyone you didn't know?"

Hap pinched the bridge of his nose. "I'm in and out of

there all day. Lots of folks come through the store, some are buyers and some are lookers." He glanced at Jonas and shrugged. "A lot of them come in to see Fran. Our business has really grown since we hired her."

Jonas nodded, grimacing.

"Do you recognize the name Vin Rutter?"

Addie jerked, her hand coming up to cover her lips. It stood to reason, with her history with Cliff, she might know Vin's name and might even have met him. Maybe having her here wasn't such a good idea. Though what harm could she do to Miles's investigation? Vin already knew Miles suspected him in the crime.

Hap's chair creaked as he shifted his weight. "I don't know that name. Who is he?"

"Tall, lean fellow with really pale eyes. He's been hanging around the store asking questions. Jonas here overheard him asking Fran about how much money the store made." Low thuds came from outside, the fireworks show punctuating the discussion.

Hap's watery eyes shone. "He must be the man then, the one who done in Wally." He surged to his feet. "You'll arrest him, right? Is he still in town? Why aren't you chasing him? Is there a posse forming? I want to ride with them."

"Easy, Hap. We're looking into it. He's been questioned, and he has an alibi for the time of the murder." The poker players had corroborated Vin's claim that at the time of the murder Vin was flashing a roll of cash that would choke a cow.

Jonas tapped Miles's shoulder. "What'd they say down at the Alhambra?"

Rubbing the edge of his fist against his thigh, Miles rolled his eyes. "Just what Vin told us. He hit a hot streak at poker and raked in a bundle. Stood a round of drinks for the whole place and left. That was about three o'clock."

"And we already know he was at the town dance for a while." Disgust laced Jonas's words. He slammed his fist into his hand. "I wish it had been him."

"We can't arrest him just because we don't like him. His alibi is solid."

Hap stood and paced the small space between the desk and the door. His movements were jerky and sharp, so unlike his usual genial self, and with each ricochet from the fireworks, he flinched. "We were best friends, me and Wally. Lifelong friends. And where was I when he needed me most? Over at the fort chewing the fat with the quartermaster." He wrung his hands. "If I was any kind of a partner, I would've stayed to help out on our busiest day."

"Why didn't you?" Jonas voiced the question Miles had been going to ask.

A sheepish frown tugged down Hap's face. "I was peeved. Wally and I had a fight." He shrugged and shuffled again between the door and the desk. "I know, that's nothing new. We've always fought, from the time we was kids. I was sore at him for something. I can't even remember what now." He stopped and blinked hard. "I'll never forgive myself. My best friend gets murdered, and my last words to him were said in anger."

A huge sigh lifted his chest, and he fought for composure, his cheeks and throat quivering. When he mastered himself, he continued. "I figured I'd punish Wally for the fight by leaving him high and dry on the Fourth. I knew the place would be swamped with customers, and I guess I thought he might be more appreciative of the work I do around there if he got a chance to miss me when things were busy."

Miles glanced at the picture beside him on the desk. Hap was so worked up at the thought of Wally dead, he wondered if it was wise to show the poor man the photograph. "Sit down, Hap." Miles stalled for time by going to the water bucket. He brought a dripping ladleful.

Hap sank onto the chair, grabbed the dipper, and slurped, spilling water down his shirtfront and swiping at his lips with the back of his sleeve. "Thanks."

"I have something I want you to look at. You need to tell me if you see anything that might be out of place, anything that might help us identify who did this to Wally." Miles picked up the photograph, glanced at it, and handed it to Hap.

He sucked in a huge breath. His jaw dropped open, and his Adam's apple bobbed. "Who would do such a thing?" he whispered. His hands shook so hard, Miles thought he might drop the photograph.

"Take your time. Look it over carefully."

"He's seen the store," Jonas said. "That's where he was when Addie and I came by on our way here. There are still two city policemen down there to stop any looters or busybodies."

"Everything is such a mess. This never should've happened." The big man's shoulders shook, and he lurched out of his chair again, as if his body couldn't sit still with all the sorrow pushing at him.

Guilt that he hadn't been there to protect Wally rose up as far as Miles's neck, and he swallowed it down. Bat had told him not to blame himself, but it was proving harder than he thought.

"I think that's enough." Addie rose and rounded the corner of the desk, brushing past Miles. She reached for the photograph. He gripped it, and she tugged again until, reluctantly, he let go. She passed it to Miles, and her look accused him for distressing Hap so much. "I'm so sorry, Hap." She patted his arm.

At her touch, he seemed to pull himself together. "I need to go. I need some fresh air."

Miles nodded. He couldn't think of anything else relevant to ask, and Hap was in no condition to think rationally anyway.

At the door, Hap turned around, a frown creasing his forehead. "I still don't understand how this happened. Wally had made arrangements for a deputy to walk him to the bank. How was it no peace officer showed up to look out for him? He was killed just after closing time, wasn't he?"

Miles gritted his teeth and forced himself to tell the truth. "Hap, I was the one supposed to get Wally to the bank safely, but there was a fire down at the livery. I told Wally to lock the door and wait for me to get back, but by the time we had the fire out and I made it back to the store, Wally was dead."

Hap's chest rose and fell, and his ham-sized hands drew

into fists. "You? You let Wally get killed?" His eyes spread wide, and with a quickness belied by his bulk, he lunged.

Miles jerked his head backward, narrowly escaping a haymaker to the jaw. He scrambled off the corner of the desk, toppling stacks of paper and leaping away from the onrushing shopkeeper. "Hap, stop!"

Addie skittered out of the way, taking another sheaf of pages with her.

Jonas leapt around and encircled Hap with his arms. "Enough! Hap, calm down."

With Jonas's weight on his back and his arms squeezing so hard they shook, the bull rush slowed. Not until Hap's shoulders relaxed did Jonas loosen his grip.

Hap sank to his knees. He braced himself on his palms, gasping for air, great, choking sobs wrestling their way out of his throat. The Wanted posters, letters, and paperwork strewn across the floor crunched and rustled under his weight.

Miles's own chest rose and fell faster than he would like to admit. The speed behind the attack still had him rattled.

When Hap had control of himself once more, he pulled himself upright, digging for his handkerchief. "I'm sorry. I'm so sorry. I don't know what came over me." He struggled to his feet. "It's just so terrible. I—" Hap dove through the open doorway into the night.

Jonas tugged his jacket sleeves down, and Miles rubbed his palm across the back of his neck. "That is one rattled man."

Addie spread her hands. "Look at this place." Papers

littered the floor, Hap's chair was overturned, and an inkwell had given up the fight all over the desktop.

"Great." Miles jammed his fingers through his hair. "I have to clean up this mess before Bat gets back. If he sees this, Pearson won't be the only deputy in his doghouse. It might not look too great, but it looks better stacked up than spilled all over the floor."

"I'll help." Addie set her camera case on a chair and bent to a stack of papers that had fanned all the way underneath the desk. "Where does all this stuff come from?"

Miles scooped up a handful of scrap paper and tossed it onto the ink puddle. He couldn't deny a thrust of satisfaction when India ink obscured half of Cliff Walker's picture on one of the scraps. Lifting the waste bucket, he crumpled a paper up to protect his fingers and swiped the drippy mess into the metal container. "This blotter will never be the same."

Jonas snorted. "Good thing it was there at all or you might find yourself sanding and refinishing the desktop." He edged past Addie, his arms full. "Bat never throws anything away. Newspapers, flyers, Wanted posters, circulars, advertisements. And he jots notes all the time. I told him he had a future as a writer if he ever gave up lawing."

They tidied the worst of it, but it couldn't really be called clean. Miles shoveled another sheaf of papers onto the corner of the desk. "What this place needs is a good fire."

Two city policemen came into the office for the night shift, freeing Miles and Jonas.

Jonas lifted Addie's camera case. "I think we've done

enough. We can still take in the last of the fireworks if we hurry."

Miles gladly turned his back on the jail and followed Addie and Jonas onto the porch. "I wonder where Hap got to. I've never seen a man cry like that. Men don't do that where I'm from. A man caught crying. . ." He shrugged. "He'd never live it down. He'd lose all respect."

A firework burst on the night sky, red and blue stars of color. They watched it together until it faded away. Miles offered Addie his arm.

Jonas fell into step on her other side. "Hap's an emotional man. I guess that's why he and Wally always fought so much. Hap is as likely to cry or yell as laugh. He wears his emotions where everyone can see them."

Addie settled her camera case on her hip and threaded her hand through Miles's arm. He tried to ignore the thrill her touch gave him. It might be foolish, but he clung to her innocence, needing it to be true as much as he wanted it to be true. "I suppose. Everybody's different, but all that emotion makes me uncomfortable."

Chapter 14

The smart thing would've been to ask to be taken home, but Addie was loath to miss a chance to be with Miles for a while longer.

Refusing to examine her reasoning, she strolled between the two deputies, eager to embrace at least a little of the holiday festivities that she'd missed by working all day. But by the time they reached the edge of town, the last firework had been lit and the crowds were dispersing. Scores of people came toward them, some to their homes and more toward the establishments waiting to help them celebrate further.

"Sorry, Addie, looks like we missed it." Miles guided her to the side of the road and out of the traffic.

"That's all right. It's been a very long day." She stifled a yawn.

Miles and Jonas watched the passersby, alert to trouble, lawmen even when they were supposed to be off duty.

Warmth spread through her, and a bit of pride, too. Miles was a good man, honorable and true. Perhaps, if she told him about her past, he would understand. It was only a matter of time before someone connected her with the trial of Cliff Walker. Coming clean first would be better than being found out. And somewhere in town Vin Rutter lurked like a mountain lion, ready to pounce.

When the majority of the revelers had dispersed, they followed, walking up Front Street toward her studio and her boardinghouse beyond. They passed a saloon and the brightly lit Arden Palace, and as they walked in front of the drugstore, someone shouted.

"Addie!" She barely had time to brace herself before Fran launched herself into Addie's arms. "Isn't it terrible? Wally's been killed!"

Addie hugged Fran and patted her shoulder. "I know. I'm so sorry."

Fran's brothers stepped off the Arden porch, casting uneasy looks at one another. "Evening, Jonas, Miles." Linc Seaton shrugged and jerked his head toward Fran. "She's been crying pretty much since she got the news. We were just flipping a coin to see who got to take her home."

Fran snorted and dabbed her eyes. "Who *had* to take me home, you mean."

The brothers shared a guilty look. One of the twins slapped Jonas on the shoulder. "Now that you're here, you wouldn't mind walking her back to our place, would you?" A grin split his face.

Jonas nodded. "Be glad to."

The Seaton brothers scattered like quail.

Fran stared after them, her cheeks wet. "Like schoolboys let out early for summer vacation. Only too glad to be rid of me."

Jonas took her hand. "That's all right. I never mind seeing you home. You know that. Though I'm surprised. I thought you might be with someone else. Men were lining up to dance with you the last time I saw you."

Fran lowered her chin and studied her crumpled handkerchief.

Addie glanced from her to Jonas. Something had shifted there. Fran usually bristled like a hairbrush when Jonas was around, but tonight, she seemed shy and uncertain. Was she softening toward Jonas at last?

"My escort had to leave. Then I got the news about Wally, and I haven't been able to think of anything else." Fran dabbed her eyes again.

Jonas caught Addie staring at their linked fingers and shrugged. "We've declared a truce. We're friends, just like we used to be."

Miles's eyebrows rose. He appeared about to say something but must've thought better of it and closed his mouth.

Addie, too, chose to say nothing, but her thoughts swirled skeptically. Could two people be friends when one was so obviously in love with the other? Her heart went out to Jonas, and for a moment, she wanted to shake Fran. Everything a woman could want in a man was right in front of her, and she couldn't see it. Jonas's heart was hers for the taking, but she spurned it, hankering after a girlish, gossamer fantasy. Imagine settling for something as tepid as friendship when love—true, honest, glorious love—was within her grasp.

Two riders galloped up the street, scattering pedestrians and whooping into the night air.

Miles took Addie's elbow. "Let's get moving. Things are getting rowdy."

They walked a block in silence. She couldn't blame Miles for being preoccupied, here at the outset of a murder investigation. At least she'd been able to do something to help him, taking that photograph. They'd have a record preserved for when he found the murderer and the case went to trial.

Thoughts of Wally brought Hap to mind. His and Wally's fights had been common knowledge around town, but Addie had been surprised to realize how close they were. Hap's emotions had been so raw her heart had gone out to him.

She remembered the bewilderment and shock when Uncle Carl died. The fear of facing life without him, of having to run a business all alone.

To hear Fran tell it, Hap didn't do a lot around the store, relying on Wally to take care of the details. Hap had been more interested in shooting the breeze, swapping stories and tall tales, making the customers feel welcome enough to come back over and over.

Miles guided her up the steps onto the boardwalk in front of the gunsmith's, and out of habit, Addie's eyes strayed to her own studio's front windows. The shades were drawn just as she had left them. Thankfully, her signal earlier that evening had worked. She didn't know how she would've gotten rid of Vin if Jonas hadn't come by. She would have to have a new lock installed tomorrow, or she wouldn't feel safe in her own place of business.

A patter of unease scampered across her skin. Something wasn't right. She blinked. A dark outline showed around the edge of the door.

"What is it?" Miles looked down at his arm where her grip had tightened.

"The studio. I think the door is open. I know I locked it when I left."

Miles stopped, guided her into the recessed doorway of the gunsmith's, and pushed Fran in after her. "You girls wait here, and if you hear any gunfire, keep your heads down." He motioned for Jonas to catch up and drew his pistol. Moonlight raced along the barrel, and his face hardened. He was so intent and alert, he seemed a stranger, and Addie caught a fresh glimpse of the lawman steel she'd captured in his portrait.

Jonas drew his own weapon. "Is there a back way out of the building?"

Addie shook her head. "No, I nailed the back door shut because it is in the darkroom. I didn't want someone opening it at the wrong moment and ruining developing pictures."

Fran clutched Jonas's arm. "You'll be careful?"

His eyebrows rose, and his eyes gleamed. "I will." He pushed her farther into the doorway. "You wait for us to come and get you, you hear? Don't follow us, even if you think it's safe."

He and Miles disappeared into the studio before Addie could warn Miles to be careful. Her hands found Fran's, icy cold, and her heart thundered. "I *know* I locked the door." A sick, breathless, swoopy feeling settled into her stomach. *Please, God, protect Miles and Jonas.*

Time stretched out, though only a few moments had passed since they had entered the studio. Though many businesses along Front Street were doing a lively business, spilling noise and light onto the boardwalks, the silence from the studio deafened her. Visions of Miles and Vin coming face-to-face in the dark made her insides quiver.

"I hate it that we can't see what's going on." Sheltered in the doorway of the gunsmith's, the front door of her place was out of their sight. There had been no light around the window shades. Did that mean whoever had been in there was now gone? The unsteady feeling increased, and she closed her eyes, reminding herself to take deep breaths. Fran's hands stayed clutched in hers as they waited what seemed a long time, though Addie had no way of measuring other than her racing heartbeats.

Where were they? Had the intruder somehow overpowered both deputies? Were they hurt or hostage? Her imagination grabbed the reins and took off at a gallop. Maybe it wasn't Vin. Perhaps Wally's killer was hiding out in her studio, and somehow he'd done to Miles and Jonas what he'd done to the shopkeeper.

Addie nearly went right up in the air when someone touched her arm. Quelling a scream, her eyes popped open, and her knees buckled.

"It's all clear." Miles holstered his gun. "But you'd better come inside."

Fran stepped out of the doorway first. "Is Jonas all right?"

"Yes. He's still in there looking around."

Addie found her voice. "What happened? Did you find someone in there?"

"No, whoever it was cleared out." The gravity in his

expression sent her heart plummeting.

Fran headed toward the faint light spilling out of the now wide open studio door, and Addie followed, her footsteps ringing on the boardwalk, but her mind not registering the impacts.

Miles stopped her at the threshold by putting his hand on her arm. "Addie, I'm really sorry."

She pushed past him, needing to see what had happened. The worst case would be if someone had stolen the Chevalier. She nearly collided with Fran, who stood in the center of the front room with her fingers over her lips. Jonas, in the doorway to the studio, held a lantern high. Addie recognized it from the darkroom, though he'd removed the red glass shade so yellow light spilled over everything.

Her reception room was in a shambles. Stuffing protruded from long slashes in the upholstered chairs, and not a single picture remained on the walls. Broken glass crunched under her feet, grinding into the rug. Her two Boston ferns had been uprooted and lay in bedraggled heaps of dirt and fronds, stomped to death beside their smashed planters.

"Oh no," Fran breathed. "Your beautiful portraits."

Mangled frames wrenched from the walls lay in discarded heaps, glass shattered and photographs ripped into random fragments. Miles took Addie's hand, but she could hardly feel his touch. Her breathing sounded harsh in her ears, but she couldn't seem to get enough air.

Jonas moved the lantern to reveal more damage. "It's worse in here." He backed up a few steps into the studio proper. "I'd light more lamps, but I couldn't find any others that hadn't been broken." The smell of kerosene drifted from the studio, mixed with the tang of developing chemicals so familiar to Addie.

With dread, she allowed Miles to lead her. The weak light from the lantern and the skylight revealed devastation reminiscent of a tornado. Her eyes went first to the center of the room. The beautiful glossy Chevalier lay in a heap of splintered wood and ripped leather. The lens lay faceup, a sunburst of cracks spidering across it. The legs of the tripod had been snapped like kindling. Bits of glass winked back from the floor, all around what was left of her portrait camera.

Slowly, Jonas toured the room. The painted canvas backdrops had been gouged with a knife, leaving long ribbons of fabric hanging. Shards of mirror decorated the settee, and the prop box would never hold another prop again. A puddle seeped through the open doorway to the darkroom.

"The darkroom?" Her question rasped out of her dry throat. The chemicals, the glass slides, the pans and equipment...

"There, too." Miles's hand tightened on hers, and she realized he still held it.

Fran picked up the parasol, her favorite accessory, and fingered the bent and broken ribs. "Who would do this? Was it drunks out of control?"

Miles shook his head. "Whoever did this was fast and thorough. I don't think anything escaped destruction. This doesn't feel like random vandalism. This feels personal."

Jonas stepped closer, throwing the perimeter of the room

into shadow, blanking out at least some of the horror. He nodded his agreement with Miles. "It's so methodical. Almost as if the person was looking for something, and when they couldn't find it, they went into a rage and busted the place up."

Vin.

The realization echoed through her head. He hadn't believed her about not having the gold, and the minute she left the studio undefended, he'd snuck back in to search for it. When he didn't find it, he decided to pay her out for denying him.

"Any idea what someone might be looking for?" Miles bent an intent gaze on her. "Did you keep anything of value here? Can you tell if anything's been stolen?"

Jonas used his toe to nudge the pile of kindling that had once been a fabulous camera. "There's such a mess in here, maybe the vandalism is to keep us from noticing whatever was stolen. Can you tell if anything is missing? Where do you keep your money?"

She shuddered and clasped the camera case at her waist. "I put the day's receipts in here to take to the bank tomorrow. The Chevalier"—she pointed—"was the most expensive thing I had here." At least she had the money she'd made today, but how far would that take her? The bank manager would be furious when he saw the damage. Her collateral had disappeared.

Though she tried, she couldn't focus on anything but the gaping loss. How was she going to make the mortgage payment? How was she going to take portraits when her camera was ruined? How could she explain Vin, Cliff Walker, the money he'd stolen and hidden somewhere, and everything else to Miles?

Fran put her arm around Addie's shoulders. "It's too late and too dark to sift through everything tonight to see what might've been stolen. Tomorrow will be soon enough."

"Fran's right." Jonas nodded. "We should get you girls home."

They crunched their way through the broken glass toward the front door. Miles motioned for Jonas to bring the lamp closer. "Look at that." He pointed to the latch. "It wasn't forced. Either someone had a key, or someone picked the lock."

"Just like the mercantile. That door wasn't broken or kicked in either."

"You think the two are related?" They put their heads together.

"I don't know, but it's awfully strange that they both happened today." Jonas scanned the street. "I don't have any reason to link the two except that neither place had a damaged lock. It's possible Wally let whoever killed him into the store. This. . ." He gestured to the doorknob. "Who knows?"

Chills formed in Addie's middle and radiated outward until she trembled. The sense of violation, of trespassing on not only her property but on her peace of mind, overwhelmed her.

How could he do this to me? What have I ever done to him? And why was I naive enough to hope that he would take me at my word? He wouldn't find the cash, because I don't have it. I've never had it. I wish I'd never even heard of it.

Addie let Fran guide her into the house, grateful she'd allowed herself to be talked into spending the night. The last place she wanted to be was her boardinghouse, alone with her thoughts.

Fran lit a lamp beside the door and pushed Addie into a rocking chair. "You poor thing. Your teeth are chattering."

Stove lids rattled, a match scraped, and the pump handle squeaked as Fran filled up the kettle. She disappeared into her bedroom and emerged with a shawl, which she draped around Addie's shoulders. "I know it's a warm night, but you're shivering. You just sit quiet. Tea will be ready in a jiffy." She yanked open a drawer, rattling the cutlery, and with quick movements, she sliced some bread. "I'll be right back." Hoisting the trapdoor to the cellar, she disappeared, reemerging with a plate of butter.

Addie clutched the soft woolen shawl around her shoulders and tangled her fingers in the fringe, though she knew it wouldn't bring any warmth. The cold she felt was so deep inside, it would take something hotter than a blacksmith's forge to melt it.

You have to tell him. You have to tell Miles about Vin.

The teakettle whistled, and Fran dragged it off the stove. "Here," she said as she held out a mug of fragrant tea, "drink this."

"Thanks." Addie whispered the word and cleared her throat. "Thank you."

"What a rotten thing to have happen. I'm so sorry, Addie. It's just been a miserable day all around." Fran blew across the top of her own cup. "I can't decide what to dwell on first. If I think too long about Wally, I'll just break right down and cry. Then there's your beautiful studio, all smashed up. Who would do such a terrible thing? Not to mention Jonas. I will never understand that man."

Sipping the hot tea, Addie strove to sound normal. She grasped onto something to divert her mind from the depredations inflicted on her poor studio. "What happened with Jonas?"

"He asked me if we couldn't be friends. Like we used to be." Fran toyed with a sugar spoon. "And I said I'd like that. I am tired of fighting with him. We used to be so close, until he changed."

Addie knew she shouldn't meddle, that they should be left to sort it out themselves, but perhaps because her own life was in such a mess, she felt the need to do what she could to straighten out Fran's. "You better be sure of your feelings, that there's no hope that you could ever return Jonas's love. Otherwise, once you get those foolish notions about romance out of your head and face reality, you might find you've lost the most precious thing you've ever had."

Fran gave her a not-you-too look. "I *am* facing reality. I know what I want, and it isn't Jonas. Can you imagine me and Jonas together?"

"Yes. Everyone seems to see it except you. You two are perfect for each other."

"You can't be serious. Jonas is so. . .so. . ." She stopped, frowned, and finished, "He's too good to be interesting."

"I take it the mystery man you've been going on about for the last week or so isn't a good man?"

"I didn't say that." A wistful look came into her eyes. "He's not bad, just. . .mysterious. It's exciting." She picked up her tea and challenged Addie. "Is it wrong to want a little adventure? To want something other than to be a housewife, producing a new baby every year or two, a slave in my own house? I want to travel, to see the world and do something exciting. I think Vin could do that for me."

Addie's teeth rattled on the rim of her teacup. "Vin? Did you say Vin?" *Please, God, don't let it be him.*

Fran chewed her bottom lip and nodded. "His name is Vin Rutter, and he's the most interesting man I've ever met. I don't know what it is about him, but he's got this. . .I don't know, presence? And he's so charming."

Her heart sank. That rat. That utter and absolute rat.

Fran, now that she'd divulged his identity, burst open like a sack of beans. "He's tall and slim, and he's got this sort of swagger to him." Her expression softened, and her voice got dreamy. "And his eyes are so pale. The first time I saw them, I thought of icicles, but now that I know him better, I don't think of them as cold. He comes into the store every day, just to see me."

"Fran, I don't—"

"Jonas told me to stay away from Vin, but he's just jealous." Fran hugged herself. "I get all churned up whenever I see Vin, and my heart does cartwheels. That's how love is supposed to feel, all giddy, like you're flying. I don't feel that when I'm with Jonas. I just feel. . .ordinary."

Addie remembered that swooping feeling, like her heart had grown wings. The moment she first saw Cliff Walker, she knew her life would never be the same. And here was Fran, about to make the same dreadful mistake.

"Is that love? Is that enough to carry you through a lifetime? I have a feeling that real love burns like a candle with a steady flame. What you're describing is more like a firework, bright lights and sound that burst across the sky but fade away to a few floating cinders before you can blink. Real love is lasting. It will stand the test of time. I think real love is recognizing in someone else everything you need to be complete."

Even as she said the words, Addie knew she'd found that in Miles. The spark had been there from the moment they first met, and in every encounter since then, the realization had grown. He was everything she wanted and needed, and her feelings for him burned steady, like a candle, obliterating anything she might've felt for Cliff.

"You make it sound so boring." Fran refilled her cup. "Do you think Hap will sell out now? He's going to be devastated when he gets back from the fort. I wonder if anyone has ridden over to tell him. Surely someone did."

Typical of Fran to change the subject if things weren't going the way she wanted. Addie sighed and let her get away with it for the moment.

"Hap already knows." His collapse on the jail floor pressed on her heart. "Devastated just about sums it up. He was in a bad way when I saw him. Crying. . .sobbing, actually.

I had no idea it would hit him that hard."

Fran's eyes filled up and glistened. "Oh, I knew this would happen if I thought about Wally at all. Poor Hap. They scrapped all the time, but they really were best friends." Groping for her handkerchief, she sniffed. "He'll want some help with the funeral arrangements."

Addie set her cup aside. "Fran, we should talk about Vin."

"No, we shouldn't. At least not tonight. I know you were hoping I'd choose Jonas, but that's not going to happen. Vin is completely different from Jonas, and he's so charming. You'll understand when you meet him."

She understood right now, but how much could she tell Fran without jeopardizing their friendship? Would Fran turn on her—like her friends in Abilene had—when she found out about Cliff and the trial and the stolen money? Or would it merely fuel Fran's thirst for adventure, pushing her into Vin's arms? And how soon after she told Fran would the entire town know? The bank would undoubtedly call in the loan right away, not that she had any way of paying the note back now that the studio was in ruins.

Her mind scampered from one fruitless thought to another, while weariness poured over her. Listening to Fran rhapsodize about Vin made her stomach lurch. Had she sounded the same way about Cliff once upon a time? Regardless of what it might cost her, she had to save Fran from making the same mistake.

"Fran, about Vin—"

"No, we're not going to talk about him any more tonight. I'm being selfish. You've been through a terrible time this evening, and I'm prattling on. You're going to go straight to bed. Don't worry if you hear something in the night. It will be the boys coming home late." She pushed herself up from the table. "You can borrow one of my nightgowns."

Before Addie quite knew where she was, Fran had her tucked into bed. A wave of sleepiness engulfed her, but she shoved it away to make a promise to herself.

First thing in the morning, I'm going to sit Fran down for a long talk.

Miles let Jonas precede him into the room Miles rented at the Western Hotel. He followed and dropped down onto his bed and flopped backward across the quilt. The room wasn't anything to brag about, but it was cheap.

Jonas scrubbed his palm across his short hair. "I'm tired, but my mind is too full to sleep just yet. I figured we could talk about the case or something."

"Seems like it's one thing after another." Miles pressed the heels of his hands against his forehead. "And I'm no nearer finding Wally's killer than I was when I first knelt over the body, and now there's this new thing at Addie's. With Bat and Charlie out of town and half the county deputies sorting out that horse thief situation. . ."

Jonas didn't reply. Turning up the lamp, he reached for Miles's Bible lying on the dresser, but instead of opening it, he laid it back down and walked over to the window to stare through the opening in the drapes. The tension around his eyes told Miles he had plenty on his mind, too, and it might not be related to their jobs.

Miles frowned. He didn't want to pry, but if Jonas wanted to unload, he was willing to listen. "Anything you want to talk about? Fran maybe? You two sure were quiet tonight."

Jonas didn't turn away from the window, and he didn't answer for such a long time Miles thought he might be mad. Finally, Jonas sighed. "I've loved Fran for about as long as I can remember. Since we were kids. I always thought she'd be mine, you know? I never figured it any other way." He shrugged and shook his head. "Last night, I couldn't sleep, thinking about her. I wrestled with God, asking Him why He didn't change Fran's heart when I knew I'd be a good husband to her."

Pushing himself upright, Miles rested his forearms on his thighs and waited. Jonas was always so open about his relationship with God, something Miles admired.

"God made me realize that if I truly loved Fran, then I had to want what was best for her, what would make her happy." He pivoted and sat on the sill of the open window. "I don't know if you've noticed, but Fran has been anything but happy when I'm around lately." He grimaced. "I wanted her to be something she obviously can't be. And I needed to realize that I can't force her to love me. If friendship is all she can give me, then I need to be happy with that."

"How's that working for you?"

Jonas grunted and gave a wry grin. "It hurts worse than getting gored by a longhorn. But I'll survive."

Laughter drifted up through the open window, harmonizing with piano music from the saloons and the occasional lowing of cattle in the pens near the depot. Nighttime in Dodge City.

Miles shrugged out of his vest and gun belt. "I admire you, Jonas." He spoke softly, not used to voicing feelings. "I wish I had your courage."

"What are you talking about? You're one of the bravest men I know. Bat thinks so, too. He told me when he was thinking about hiring you that he thought you had a lot of sand."

Miles tucked that compliment away to savor it later. "There's brave and there's brave. I don't seem to have any trouble facing down rowdy drunks or chasing horse thieves, but there are some things that scare me rigid."

"Such as?"

The need to tell someone, to share his burden with someone who would understand, surged through Miles. "There are things I should've told you, that I should've told Bat, before he hired me. If he knew the truth about me, he would send me packing."

It was Jonas's turn to wait while Miles marshaled his thoughts. Now that he'd begun, though he was tempted to retreat, he forced himself to get it out, to be as courageous as people thought he was—as he wanted to be.

"I spent my growing up years with the Walker Gang. Cliff Walker was my stepbrother. My mother married his father when I was about five." He sat up straight and looked Jonas in the eye, not flinching from whatever judgment he might see there. "I got out when I was sixteen, almost ten years ago, after my mother died and before Cliff took over and started robbing trains. I turned my life over to God, and I've tried to put all that behind me, but it keeps following me."

Jonas pursed his lips in a silent whistle and raised his eyebrows. Crossing his arms, he studied Miles until he wanted to squirm. "Is that all?"

"All? Isn't that enough?"

Miles couldn't have been more surprised when Jonas chuckled. "I thought you were going to tell me something really bad. Sounds like you were a kid stuck in a bad situation, and you escaped as soon as you could. You should tell Bat about it, though he won't care. Bat hasn't exactly been a choirboy, you know."

"There's a little more." Actually, a lot, and he needed to get it out tonight.

"Go ahead, but I don't think it can be as bad as you think it is."

"It's about Addie."

"If you're coming to me for advice on women, you might as well know I'm not exactly a font of knowledge, but you're welcome to get it off your chest."

"Before she moved here, Addie was Cliff Walker's girl."

"What?" Jonas shot upright off the windowsill.

Miles put up his hands, motioning Jonas to sit down again. "And I haven't told her that I knew him—that he was my stepbrother."

"How is it that you know this? Did Addie tell you?"

"No, it was Vin Rutter. Rutter was Cliff's best friend and a member of the gang. He was arrested at the same time as Cliff, but he got off because someone messed up on the warrant. For some reason, he followed Addie here to Dodge, but I don't know why. Vin never does anything that doesn't benefit himself somehow, so whatever his reason for hanging around, it can't be good. I haven't seen him in ten years, but he hasn't changed."

This time, his revelation made Jonas rub his hands down his cheeks and stare at the ceiling, blowing out a long breath. "That explains why it seemed you two knew each other when we questioned Vin and why you haven't gone ahead and pursued Addie, though it's plain that you're in love with her."

Miles jerked, but before he could protest, Jonas rolled his eyes. "Don't try to deny it. I've been there. I *am* there. From one hopeless case to another, trust me, you're in love."

In love. "I don't have time to be in love. I have to solve Wally's murder."

Pacing the area between the window and the door, Jonas clasped his hands behind his back. "Vin's been hanging around Fran a lot. She's fascinated with him. But she wouldn't take a twenty-four-carat suggestion from me right now, so I can't warn her off. It would be like throwing kerosene on a fire."

"I'd much rather find a way of dealing with Vin that kept the girls out of it. I'd hate for it to get around town that Addie had been tied up with Cliff. And please don't talk to Fran about this until I can sort things out with Addie. Her past is her secret, just as my past is mine, and she should be allowed to choose who she talks to about it."

Jonas stopped pacing. "You've been carrying around a lot

of burdens. I stand by my earlier assessment. You're one of the bravest men I know."

"I sure don't feel like it. Have you ever tried not to be something you've been your whole life?"

"Every day."

That answer, when Miles expected a denial, made him blink.

"Every day I have to let God be in charge and change me. It's when I try to do the changing, or when I get bucky and refuse to change, that things get fouled up." He clapped Miles on the shoulder. "Get some sleep. You're going to need it. We've got quite a few mysteries to solve."

Miles closed the door after his friend. When he put his head on the pillow, he thought he'd have trouble getting to sleep, he had so much to think about and work through, but as his eyelids grew heavy, he realized that in sharing his troubles with Jonas, he'd lightened his burden.

Would he experience the same easing of his troubles when he confessed everything to Addie?

Chapter 15

Fran eased out of bed at sunup, careful not to disturb Addie. Indignation at the destruction caused in Addie's studio burned through her. As if Addie didn't have enough troubles. Whoever did it should be horsewhipped.

She took pains with her hair and dress, anticipating seeing Vin sometime during the day. A line formed between her brows as she studied her reflection. Jonas disapproved of Vin, and his motive was plain, but from what Addie said, she disapproved of him as well. The way Addie had spoken of love being a steady flame, a recognition of something in the other person that she needed to complete her...

Fran sighed and smoothed her eyebrows. Every time she ran those words through her head, though she wanted to see Vin's face in her mind, it was Jonas's features she saw.

A cold biscuit sufficed for breakfast. Anything more would necessitate building a fire and making enough noise to rouse the house. She slipped outside, breathing in the cool morning air that already held a harbinger of the heat of the day still to come. Odd on a Friday morning not to see more bustle and signs of life, but Dodge City drooped, victim of the celebrations of the previous day.

She used her key to let herself into the store, swallowing hard and bolstering her courage. "Just get in, get the book, and get out."

The store looked like cattle had stampeded through. Goods lay strewn and toppled on the floor and across the tables and counters. What on earth had happened in here?

Though she didn't mean to look, her eyes went to the floor in front of the cash register. She yanked her gaze away from the place where Wally had breathed his last and scuttled behind the counter. Though she didn't have a lamp and the early morning sunlight barely penetrated the front windows, she knew exactly what she was looking for. But as she groped on the shelf below the register, her hands found only bare wood.

Stooping, she reached well back under the counter and was rewarded with only dust on her fingertips. She stood and put her hands on her hips, searching the disheveled area, but didn't find what she sought.

With a shrug, she skirted the center of the room and let herself out, careful to lock the door behind her. It was in there somewhere, but she didn't have time for a thorough search. Time to go face Jonas at the jail.

"Morning, Miss Fran." Ty Pearson tipped his hat and leaned on his broom on the front porch of the jail.

"Good morning." She tilted her head. "Bat's got you sweeping today?"

A dusky red tinted his neck. "Yep, I'm on jail duty. Somebody's got to do it." He shrugged and jabbed at the porch with his broom.

She'd heard from Jonas in the past that sweeping out the jail was reserved either for a prisoner or someone Bat was peeved at and wondered what Ty had done to earn Bat's disapproval. "Is Deputy Spooner in yet?"

"He's in there."

Jonas met her at the door. He wore a guarded expression, and tiredness lurked around his eyes.

A twinge of guilt pricked her. He was handsome, in a steady, solid sort of way. She tried to imagine her life without him and drew a blank. He was always there, like the sun coming up in the morning, like the breeze that blew across the prairie. Though she wasn't in love with him, she didn't want him to go out of her life. She wanted the friendship he'd offered yesterday, and yet, that, too, left her strangely dissatisfied.

"I didn't expect you so early." He brushed his hand down his vest front.

"Do you want me to come back later?"

"No, don't go." He swept some papers off a chair and turned it so the back rested against the front edge of the desk. "Miles isn't here, but I can take you through some questions. If he thinks of anything else, we can find you again. How is Addie this morning? I realize now we left you off at your door kind of abruptly last night."

"She was still sleeping when I left, and don't worry about last night. You had plenty on your plate, and we went right to bed after we had a cup of tea." *And quite a talk about you.*

"Let's get started then." He dug in his pocket and withdrew a small notebook. "I wrote down some questions for you last night."

"Did you sleep at all?" The words popped out before she could stop them.

He shrugged. "A few hours." Pages rustled as he thumbed through the little booklet until he found the page he wanted. "Now, I want to walk you through yesterday at the store, who came in, what they bought, who was hanging around."

She settled herself in the chair and crossed her ankles, resting her hands in her lap. "I thought you'd want to know that, and I stopped by the store this morning to get the receipt book, but I couldn't find it. The store is a mess."

He nodded. "A bunch of folks forced their way into the store to get a gander at what had happened. They ended up shoving each other, and some goods got damaged. You couldn't find the receipt book?"

"It wasn't under the counter. That's where Wally would've put it when he finished counting the money."

"Probably got stolen along with the cash. Whoever did it probably scooped everything off the counter into a bag or a sack." He licked his pencil and held it over his notebook. "Try to remember who was in the store. If you don't know the name, a description will do. Pay particular attention to anyone who might've had an altercation with Wally."

She chuckled. "The one most likely to have an altercation with Wally was out of town. Hap was over at the fort, and we were rushed off our feet serving customers. There wasn't time for disagreements. We were practically shoving packages at people to get to the next customer in line."

Starting with opening the store in the morning, she went through the day, describing regulars, cowboys, ranchers in town for the Fourth. "I know I'm missing a lot of people, folks Wally waited on while I was busy, and I didn't know everyone, not even half."

"It's all right. This just gives us a place to start."

"Do you really think the killer was in the store yesterday, that he was one of the customers?"

"It's possible. That's why it's important that you try to remember as much as you can."

She taxed her memory. "There were so many people. I can't possibly remember them all. That's why I wanted the receipt book."

"Was anybody upset?"

"No more than usual, I guess. You always get a few difficult customers. A couple of cowboys got a little rowdy. You know how they do. But Wally smoothed things over, convinced them to take it outside. It was all very good natured."

Jonas consulted his notebook. "What about Vin Rutter?"

She stiffened. "What about him?"

He wiped his hand down his face. "I meant, was Vin in the store yesterday? In the morning maybe? I know where he was in the afternoon."

"You don't think Vin had anything to do with this?"

"We've checked his alibi for the time of the murder. If he's involved, it isn't directly." His tone left no doubt that he thought it possible if not probable that Vin was somehow tied to Wally's death.

"You questioned him?" She knotted her fingers, striving to hold on to her temper. "You had no call to do that, Jonas. I thought you were my friend. Vin didn't kill Wally, and I won't let you accuse him." Defiance bloomed in her chest. If everyone wasn't careful, they'd drive her to do something drastic where Vin was concerned, like elope or something.

The color drained from Jonas's face as his expression tightened. "I'm beginning to think you don't know me at all. Especially if you think I would frame a man for murder out of jealousy. I asked you a straightforward question. Was Vin in the store yesterday morning?"

She nodded. If he thought she was going to help him implicate an innocent man, he had another think coming.

"Did he buy anything?"

She shook her head.

"Nothing?" His jaw tightened and his eyes narrowed.

"Not from me."

"What did he want, then?" The patient tone in his voice, as if she were a badly behaved toddler, grated.

"He just wanted to talk."

"About what?"

"It's not relevant to your investigation."

"I'll be the judge of that." He leapt up and pinned her by putting his hands on the edge of the desk on either side of her and leaning close. "When are you going to get it through that beautiful head that I'm trying to protect you? Stop being so stubborn, or I'll have to throw you in a cell for obstructing an investigation." His eyes gleamed like ice chips, and his lips were only inches from hers. With a growl, he pushed himself away, and her breath started again.

She swallowed. "He asked me to save him a dance. I told him I would." Shrugging, she twisted the drawstring on her handbag. "And he asked if business was as good as we expected, since it seemed there were a lot of people in the store. I didn't have much time to talk to him, and I think he realized that, because he said he'd see me later at the dance and left."

"Did he say anything else to you? Did he talk to Wally at all?"

"I don't think so."

"It's important, Fran. I wouldn't ask if I didn't have to. It isn't as if I *like* hearing about you and another man. I'm doing the best I can here." The bleakness that entered his eyes and voice rubbed a fresh, raw place on her heart.

Her shoulders sagged. "There was one other thing. He asked about Addie."

"Addie?" Jonas's eyebrows rose.

"Yes. He said he was thinking of getting his portrait taken and was Addie as good as he'd heard. I told him she was the best in town, but not to take my word for it. I told him to stop by there and see for himself. She had lots of her work hanging up in her front room." Remembering the devastation from the night before, she bit her lip. "Though all that's ruined now."

Jonas snapped the notebook shut and shoved it in his pocket.

"Whatever you're thinking, it's wrong, Jonas."

"You couldn't possibly know what I'm thinking right now."

"Then why don't you tell me?" It disturbed her to know he was right. For much of her life she'd known exactly what he was thinking, but now, she hadn't the faintest idea. The niggling suspicion that Addie might've been right—that Fran had lost something precious forever—irked her.

"All right." Jonas hauled her to her feet, his hands hard

on her arms, his eyes demanding that she look at him. "I'll tell you, though you won't like it. I think you've let your romantic notions color your good sense. A stranger starts hanging around asking questions about the kind of money the store is taking in, and the next thing you know, your boss is murdered and the place is robbed. Now you tell me this same man was asking questions about Addie, and lo and behold, her place is ransacked that same day. Even a simpleton could see the connection."

Tears smarted her eyes. When she struggled, he let her go, hanging his head and turning his back on her. She wanted to reach out to him, to return somehow to the familiar relationship she'd found so irritating only days ago, but when she touched him, he moved away.

She left the jail trying to convince herself that she'd made the right choice. Vin was her ticket out of there, her ticket to a life of adventure. If Jonas couldn't understand that, then there was no friendship between them anymore.

Chapter 16

Miles shouldered the shovel and broom he'd borrowed from the hotel and headed to the photography studio. The morning sunshine almost hurt his eyes. There were probably a lot of revelers who wouldn't welcome the daylight, but he needed it. Everything always looked worse at night. In the daylight, despair dissipated, or at least diminished to a manageable level.

Lord, help me to help Addie. Help me find out who did this to her. Help me find who killed Wally, and whether the two are related. And above all, help me to be the man You want me to be, to act with honor and not let fear keep me from doing the right thing.

With a brisk knock on the photography studio door, he let himself into the reception room. Though daylight had improved his outlook, it shone cruelly on the havoc wreaked here. Nothing had survived the devastation except the window and door glass. He frowned. All that plate glass would be hard for a vandal to resist. Why hadn't it been smashed, too?

A scrape and thump from the other room drew his attention. "Addie?" He headed that direction.

Sunlight streamed through the skylight, illuminating dust motes in the air and cascading over Addie. Though she'd put her hair up, strands were already finding their way out of the pins and framing her face. She straightened from bending over the pile of debris in the center of the room that had been the big camera. "Miles." Telltale tear tracks left damp streaks on her cheeks. She swiped at them and wiped her hands on her skirt. "What are you doing here?"

Lowering the shovel and broom, he surveyed the room. "I came to help." He indicated the tools. "Where would you like me to start?"

She took another swipe at her cheeks. "You don't have to do that. You're too busy."

"I'm here, and I'm not too busy. Jonas is questioning some of the people who were in the store yesterday. If we can discover if anything was stolen here, it might give us a lead into who did this. Now, what do you want me to do first?"

Her bewilderment at the chaos surrounding her made him want to hug her and assure her everything would be all right. But how could he make such a promise? Perhaps a little physical labor would help him marshal his thoughts.

He couldn't shake the feeling that the mercantile and the photography studio were somehow linked, but how? And what role did Vin play? He had a solid alibi for the time of the murder, and so far this morning, Miles hadn't been able to run him to earth. All he knew was that Vin was still in town. His horse was at the livery, and Miles had checked at the depot. Vin hadn't boarded the night train.

She looked around the room. "I guess it would be best to see what can be salvaged."

"Leave the heavy stuff for me, and don't throw anything

out. If we sort as we clean, maybe you'll be able to discover if anything is missing." His boots crunched on broken glass, bits of plaster, and wood with every step. He put his hands on his waist and considered the shattered furniture, mirror shards, and the camera carcass. "Wait here. I'll be right back."

He ducked outside and around the back of the building to the rear door of the Alhambra Saloon.

One of the bartenders opened the door to his knock.

"Hey, Jethro, I need some crates. Do you mind if I take some of these?" He pointed to the pyramid of beer crates stacked in the alley. About twice a week a wagon went through and picked them up to be put on the train and sent back to the distilleries for reuse.

"Take some. Boss won't care."

Miles grabbed three and returned to the studio. "We can use these to sort stuff."

"Thank you." Addie took one of the boxes and began placing shards of looking glass in the bottom. The sadness in her eyes tore at him, as did the droop to her shoulders.

"Be careful. You could get a nasty cut." He took another box and stacked the camera into it. A shame. Such a nice piece of equipment, and she was so gifted with it. Miles used the side of his boot to scrape together a pile of broken glass.

She scanned the room, brushing her hands against her skirt. Finally, she shrugged. "I don't think anything is missing, just destroyed. All the props are here and the equipment." Returning her attention to the settee, she lifted another jagged piece of mirror and dropped it in the box. It shattered, and she gave a suspicious sniff.

Seeking to distract her from tears if he could, he said the first thing that came into his mind. "If this is some random vandal and not a targeted attack, why not bust out the front windows?"

She stopped and turned, her eyebrows bunching. "I've no idea. Maybe he ran out of time? Maybe he didn't want anyone to suspect anything too soon? I wouldn't have known until this morning that anything had happened if I hadn't seen the door open last night. But you can bet that someone would've seen or heard something, and certainly someone would've noticed if the front windows shattered."

The precariously growing stack of broken furniture shifted and crashed to the floor, startling both of them.

She squeezed her eyes shut and pinched the bridge of her nose.

"You said he."

"What?" She tucked a strand of hair behind her ear.

"You said he, not they. You think this was the work of one man?"

She shrugged and poked at the bits that used to be a stool, possibly the one she'd had him sit on for his portrait. "He, they, does it matter? The studio is destroyed." Emotion thickened her voice, but she blinked a few times, marched to the darkroom door, and wrenched it wide. A cry escaped her throat, and she turned away.

Miles crossed the room, his hand going to his sidearm. Shoving her aside, he peered inside, ready to confront anyone who might be hiding there. His mind boggled. Even in the reduced light, the destruction awed him. Glass lay in glittering snowdrifts amid globs of sodden paper and dented metal trays. A cabinet had been overturned, and photographs and papers soaked up whatever had been in the bottles that lay broken everywhere. Over all, a pungent chemical smell bathed the air. He relaxed and let his hand drop away from his gun.

Sobs reached his ears. Addie stood a few feet away, her head bowed, arms limp at her sides. Her shoulders shook, and a tear fell from her cheek to the wood floor and splattered.

Instinctively, he gathered her into his arms and pressed her head into his shoulder. "Shhh, Addie. I'm so sorry." If the fury of the destruction bludgeoned his senses, what must it be doing to her?

"He didn't leave me anything at all." The words, muffled against his shirtfront, tore his heart. "All my uncle Carl's work was in there. All his slides. Everything he managed to save from the Abilene studio."

That explained all the glass. He rubbed his chin on the top of her head, holding her close, trying to take some of her sorrow. Her light scent drifted to him, reminding him of the last time he'd held her, and he felt a heel even thinking about kissing her when she was in such distress.

Rubbing small circles on her shoulder, he let her cry. Anger burned hot in his belly. He would find out who did this, and he would pay.

Addie soaked in the comfort of Miles's embrace even as she soaked his shirtfront with her tears. Though mortified at breaking down so thoroughly in front of him, she couldn't seem to help it.

The loss of Uncle Carl's work was like losing him all over again. He'd spent the better part of twenty years accumulating a body of work—portraits, still-life photographs, experiments with development techniques and exposures, and hardest to bear, all his war photographs—and now everything lay in splinters. All because of her.

She didn't doubt for a minute Vin Rutter was responsible for the vandalism. But if she hadn't fallen for Cliff Walker, none of this would've happened. She and Uncle Carl wouldn't have had to move away from Abilene, Uncle Carl wouldn't have been put under such strain with a heavy mortgage and the shame of all but being run out of town, and Vin Rutter would never have shown up again to harass her.

A victim again, at the hands of one of the Walker Gang.

The realization dried up her tears. The sobs slowed to a few hiccups and sniffles.

Miles pressed his handkerchief into her hands, and she dabbed and swiped. He kept his arms around her and his chin against her temple, and she savored the contact. When she had herself well under control, she tried to step out of his embrace, but he held on.

With one hand he tipped her chin up, and she looked deep into his brown eyes. Questions lurked there, ones she hoped he never asked. Something else tinged his expression, something that reached out to a vulnerable place in her heart and stirred it to life. Heat curled through her.

Run away, Addie. You can't love him. Your life is too broken.

But as his lips lowered to hers and her eyes fluttered closed, she realized that being with Miles was beginning to mend the broken places in her heart. The comfort of his arms around her and the warmth of his kiss wrapped her in a feeling of peace and safety that she'd never felt with any man before.

He ended the kiss long after he should have and long before she wanted him to. Her skin tingled when he brushed his fingertips against her temple, trailed them down her cheek, and rested them at her throat. "Addie, I'm sorry this happened to you, and I'm going to do everything I can to find out who did this. Is there anything you can tell me to help narrow the search?"

It was on the tip of her tongue to blurt out that she knew who had done it and why, but her fingers tightened, and she realized she had placed her hand over his badge. Deputy Marshal, Ford County. Miles Carr stood for everything Cliff Walker had despised. Would he think her a fool to have fallen for Cliff's charms? Would he, as his fellow peace officers had up in Dickenson County, assume she had been in on Cliff's crimes? Pointing the finger at Vin meant opening all those old wounds. She swallowed her confessions. "No, there's nothing I can tell you."

He eased her out of his arms and stepped back, leaving her feeling more alone than ever. "I guess I'd better be on my way then. I'm supposed to meet Jonas down at the jail and see what he found out about business in the mercantile yesterday. I'll check back in with you later."

"If I'm not here, I'll be at Fran's. I promised I'd stay with her at least one more night. She's coming to help with the cleanup."

"That's good. I was going to suggest it myself, that you might be better off with her for the next little while. Don't try to move the heaviest stuff. Jonas and I will help you carry that out later." He tipped his hat and left.

Rubbing her upper arms, she tried to talk sense into herself. *What you need is to take another look at those photographs of Cliff and get your head on straight about Miles.*

Even as she thought it, her heart decried the comparison. Miles was nothing like Cliff. Miles hadn't misled her, deceived her, or used her. He'd been honest from the first. She could trust him.

Then why didn't you? You had the perfect opportunity to tell him the truth about Vin and Cliff and why the studio got ransacked, but you held back. Ashamed to be truthful with him about your past, afraid he would reject you.

"Oh hush up," she whispered. "Get to work. You've got more than enough to think about without swooning over Miles or wrestling with the mess Cliff made of your life a year ago." The mess Vin had made was more than enough to be going on with.

Though she repeated this dictate to herself several times over the next few hours, she couldn't get Miles out of her mind. . .or her heart.

Miles spent the rest of the day questioning people who had visited the mercantile on the Fourth. Just finding some of them was proving difficult, since some folks had come to town only for the day and returned to outlying ranches and farms, and others were sleeping off the effects of the previous night. Still, tracking down the customers gave him a good excuse to continue his search for Vin, though that, too, proved fruitless.

Not a single person he questioned raised any warning flags or produced any solid leads. Housewives, ranchers, cowboys, ordinary citizens who had seen nothing out of the ordinary. By evening, Miles had nothing to show for his questions but a headache and a nagging sense of futility.

"The more I look at it, the more it looks like a crime of opportunity." He tossed his pencil down onto the paper-strewn desk and rubbed his temples.

"What about the door? It wasn't locked." Jonas tipped his chair back to lean against the wall and propped his boots up on the corner of the desk.

"Wally probably forgot to lock it behind me when I ran up the street. He was concentrating hard on the cash and ledger book. Or maybe a last-minute customer came in to get something, and he opened the door for them, forgetting to lock it when they left and allowing the robber inside."

"Without that receipt book, we can't know if he had a late customer."

"And we wouldn't know anyway unless this customer had a charge account. According to Fran, if you pay cash, Wally doesn't write down your name."

"Do you think the killer might've been a charge account customer, and that's why he took the receipt book?"

Miles planted his elbow on the desk and his chin on his

fist. "I don't know. It was right there with all the money. If the killer swept the money into a sack or a bag or something, stands to reason the book would go, too."

"And we're no closer to finding the killer."

"I'm not licked yet. There's one other trail we can follow."

"What?" Jonas sat up and dropped his feet to the floor.

"The money. Somebody's flush right now when they were spare yesterday morning." Miles stood, stretched, and reached for his hat.

"Money isn't easy to track in this town. Too much gambling." Jonas rose and checked his gun.

"Every place that has gambling has a gambling boss. We'll ask them which way the money's flowing. I figure we should start with Luke Short over at the Long Branch."

They found Luke sitting in the lookout chair at the Long Branch. To those who didn't know him, his slight frame and quiet manner seemed to put him in the no-account column. Miles knew better. Luke Short was one of the toughest, sharpest-eyed, intelligent men Miles had ever come across. Which made him perfect as a gambling boss for the busiest saloon in Dodge.

"Hard to say." Luke never took his eyes off the faro table. "Lotsa cash floating around this week especially. Four herds hit town the day before yesterday, and most of the cowhands are still here. Money is changing hands faster than fleas swap dogs."

"What about cowhands that have more money than you'd figure they would, even just getting paid off?" Miles pitched his voice low to get under the music and chatter.

"Nobody's come in with more money than I'd expect them to have. Several riders have lost their whole pay and gotten a little unruly about it, but nothing I couldn't handle." He patted his sidearm.

"Any big winners?"

"Just that fellow we talked about before, Vin Rutter. He hit a hot streak in a poker game and fleeced a few swellheads. Walked out with a pocketful of money. Too bad he didn't switch to faro. I could've gotten some of it back." Though he didn't smile, a half-humorous, half-predatory gleam lit his eyes. "I was dealing while he was in here, but he wasn't of a mind to buck the tiger."

Miles flicked a glance at the oil painting of a tiger that graced the wall over the faro table—an advertisement to all that the saloon offered faro, the same way the longhorns mounted over the bar indicated a patron could get a full meal in that establishment if desired. Several cowboys crowded around one of the faro tables, even this early in the afternoon. He shook his head. If faro was played fair and square, the odds were even between the house and the gambler. Which didn't suit the house at all. Consequently, there wasn't a faro game west of the Mississippi that wasn't rigged, crooked, or otherwise tilted in the favor of the gambling establishment. "If you hear anything you think might be helpful, let us know."

"I will. It's a bad business, what happened to Wally. I'll keep my ear to the ground."

Miles stepped out into the evening air, and Jonas joined him. Whenever they went into one of the saloons, they always split up. No sense bunching targets if things were going to get unruly.

"Where to next?"

"Might as well keep working in a straight line. The Saratoga and the Alhambra."

Checking in with the bartenders and gambling bosses netted them no new information.

As they crossed Front Street toward the river, a gaudily dressed young woman hurried toward them. She might've been pretty if not for heavy makeup and a world weariness in her eyes that made her look old before her time. "Scottie sent me to get you. That fellow you're looking for is down at the Lone Star. Weird-looking man. Pale eyes, like a fish." One of the straps holding up her dress slipped, baring her shoulder, and she yanked it up. "Scottie said for you to hotfoot it down there, because this fellow was drinking pretty fast, and he was packing a gun."

Miles locked eyes with Jonas. Bat was zealous about enforcing the law of no guns inside city limits, and rightly so, considering his brother had been gunned down disarming a drunk. What was Vin thinking?

Jonas nodded. "Thanks, ma'am. We'll head right down there."

The girl led the way but stopped on the porch of the Lone Star Dance Hall, so named to appeal to the hundreds of Texans who came through each season. From the looks of things, they were doing a roaring business for so early in the day. They entered the barnlike structure, and the girl blended into the crush.

"Mighty crowded." Jonas sidestepped a bowlegged cowboy and a giggling woman who looked to be staggering more than two-stepping. A haze hung in the air from cigar and cigarette smoke, and men stood three deep at the rail waiting for a dance. "You see him?"

"Nope." Miles grabbed an empty chair along the wall and stood upon it to survey the crowd. Wide-brimmed hats, fancy dresses that didn't cover enough of the dancing girls, in a couple of cases a pair of enormous, wooly chaps. Music, the stomping of boots, laughter, and clapping. Then he spied a familiar figure over by the bar.

Miles hopped down and nudged Jonas. "Swing around thataway, and I'll come at him this way." He waited until Jonas had time to thread his way through the crowd to come up on Vin's left.

"Gimme another."

Coins clinked onto the bar, and Scottie, the bartender, slopped whiskey into a glass. Miles noted the bulge under Vin's jacket. The girl had been right. Drunk and carrying a gun.

Vin tossed back the drink and smacked the bar. "Another."

Miles put his hand on Vin's forearm and pressed it into the bar. "I think you've had enough." He jerked his head at Scottie before slipping his hand into Vin's coat and relieving him of a pistol.

" 'Bout time you got here." Scottie grabbed the bottle and headed toward the other end of the bar to serve waiting customers.

Vin's thin nostrils flared. He wheeled around, blinking.

"Deputy." He lurched slightly, corrected, and leaned against the bar.

"Vin, I think you'd better come along with me."

His eyes narrowed. "Where?"

"Down to the jail. You're under arrest for carrying a gun inside city limits." Miles latched on to Vin's elbow. "Let's go."

"Jail? I don't think so."

"I do think so."

Vin leaned close and hissed into Miles's face, "I'm not leaving until I get drunk as a skunk. I'm in mourning." His whiskey-soaked breath wafted around Miles.

"Mourning? For what?"

"I'm mourning the demise of my brilliant plan. I arrived too late. The cupboard is bare." He waved his arms in an exaggerated swoop, and the force of the motion carried him staggering sideways.

Miles grabbed his arm.

The patrons of the dance hall seemed to realize that an arrest was in progress, and they formed an interested ring.

"We'll talk about it at the jail. C'mon."

"I'm not going anywhere with you." Vin's hand jerked into his jacket, where he groped under his arm. Blinking, he lifted aside his coat to look at his shirt.

"Looking for this?" Miles patted the pistol he'd taken off Vin, now safely tucked into his waistband.

Jonas handcuffed the prisoner, and between the two of them, they got him to the jail. He collapsed on the bunk in the first cell and began snoring.

Miles tossed the key into the top drawer of the desk. "I don't know what else Vin might have been planning, but he did accomplish one thing."

"What?" Jonas scowled through the bars at the prisoner.

"He got drunk as a skunk."

Mr. Poulter lifted a shred of canvas that had once been part of a lovely backdrop and let it fall from his fingers. "Why didn't you come to me first thing this morning? I had to hear about this from Heber Donaldson."

Heber stood in the doorway, a supercilious smirk on his face.

Addie took a deep breath and counted to ten so she wouldn't fly right over there and smack it off. He couldn't wait to spread the news of her misfortune, she bet.

At least most of the damage had been cleared away, though the empty place where the Chevalier had stood mocked her as much as Heber's smirk. Her muscles ached from the hours of cleaning, and she knew she was too tired to be rational about business matters.

She had been locking up before heading to Fran's house when the banker had arrived with Donaldson on his heels. It was hard not to imagine buzzards circling over a dying animal.

"I'm afraid the bank will have to call in the loan." Poulter dusted his hands. "Without equipment, you have no way of paying off the loan and the bank has no collateral. You will have to close immediately and surrender whatever can be salvaged to satisfy the note."

His eyes drifted to her waist, and her hands instinctively covered the Scovill's case, as if to shield it from his mercenary eyes. Though his words were no more than she'd expected, hearing them was like a hammer blow.

"We had an agreement, Mr. Poulter, that I expect you to honor. I have until the end of August to pay the balance on the loan, provided I continue to meet the mortgage payments on time between now and then." She'd fought this battle in her head all afternoon, and she was more than prepared. "Unless or until I miss a payment, you cannot call in the loan."

"But, my dear"—his patronizing tone smeared over her, making her want to shudder—"you have nothing with which to earn the money. I knew I never should've extended the loan to a woman. They just don't understand business."

Donaldson snickered. "She'll understand soon enough." He sneered. "You thought you'd bested me when you stole that Arden commission, but who's laughing now?"

Addie stood her ground, determined not to cry or show any weakness. "This building is mine for the time being, and I want you both to leave. If you don't, I'll have you arrested for trespassing."

Poulter snapped to attention, indignation contorting his features and blood suffusing his cheeks. "How dare you! Nobody talks to me that way, young lady."

"Don't they? Well, it's high time, don't you think? Now get out. We have nothing more to discuss until the end of next month." She held on to her bravado, even as she smelled the smoke of her bridges burning.

Chapter 17

Addie looped her camera case over her head and adjusted the strap across her chest. "Thank you for letting me stay over again last night." She'd been so bludgeoned by her encounter with Poulter and Donaldson, she'd practically stumbled to Fran's place and collapsed into bed. She hadn't even heard Fran come in.

Fran pinned her hat on her upswept hair and checked her reflection one last time. "You know it's no trouble. Are you headed right back to the studio this morning?"

"No, I have to go to my boardinghouse. I need a change of clothes."

"I am sorry I wasn't able to help you clean up yesterday. Hap corralled me as soon as I was finished at the jailhouse and demanded an inventory of the store so we can determine just how much money was stolen. It took much longer than I thought it would, mostly because Hap doesn't have a clue how to run the store. He'll probably need me there for most of the day today, too. He's so distracted, and he keeps breaking into tears."

"Don't worry about that. You have an obligation to Hap to get the store open as soon as possible. I won't be at the studio much today in any case, at least not until I've talked to a few people. I have to raise some money and fast. I'm only sorry we don't have time for a talk, because, Fran, we need to discuss Vin. There are some things you don't know about him. Some things that you won't like hearing."

Fran's jaw set, and a steely look invaded her green eyes. "How are you planning to raise money to restore the studio?"

Addie sighed. "Fine, but we're going to talk about Vin sooner or later. As for the money, I guess I'm going to have to look for an investor or two. I need to get back into business fast, or I'll lose too many customers to even think of meeting the mortgage payment."

"Where are you going to look for investors? You know if I had the money I'd give it to you." Fran threaded her hand through the strings on her bag. "And my brothers, too. Maybe you could ask Linc, though I don't know as he has any cash to spare." In a flash Fran went from angry and stubborn to generous and caring.

"Don't worry, and don't ask your brothers." Addie linked her arm with Fran's and gave it a squeeze. "I'll find someone." She spoke with more confidence than she felt. So many of the men in this town who had money chose to invest in businesses of a tawdry nature. She didn't want to link her studio to any of that, which cut down on her options considerably.

"How was Hap when you left him last night?" Addie shielded her eyes as they stepped outside. She needed to remember to get a hat from her room.

Fran shook her head. "He's in a terrible state. I never realized what an anchor Wally was for poor Hap. And the funeral is the day after tomorrow. If it wasn't for the church ladies, I don't know where we'd be. They've handled all the arrangements. Hap just wanders around picking things up and setting them down. He won't even come to the front of the store where it happened. Said he can't bear to walk over the place where Wally died. The longer he stayed in the store, the more upset he got. Truthfully, I was glad he finally left me to it. It's looking more and more like he won't be able to keep the place going alone. I imagine he'll either sell up, or like you, he'll be looking for a new partner."

"Poor man. And he's all alone. If he was married, things might be easier for him. He would have someone to take care of him and help him through his grief."

"Up to now I was always glad neither of them was married. No bossy wife coming into the store to tell me how to do my job, but now, I think you're right. I wish Hap had someone. Right now he looks like a calf that got separated from the herd and can't find its way home."

Addie parted ways with Fran at the mercantile and walked the remaining blocks to the boardinghouse, her mind spinning with her to-do list. She mounted the stairs and opened the front door. "It's just me, Mrs. Blanchard."

Her landlady, usually knitting away in her rocker at this time of the morning, wasn't in the parlor. Shrugging, Addie lifted her hem and trotted up the stairs, relieved not to be dragged into a long chat session with Mrs. Blanchard, who would insist on knowing every last detail of the break-in at the studio. Word had spread yesterday, and people had knocked on the studio door and rattled the knob, trying to get a look inside.

She turned to head along the hallway to her room at the

end and nearly collided with her landlady.

Mrs. Blanchard grabbed her by the arms, her breath coming in gasps. "Miss Reid, oh thank the Lord you're all right! I was on my way right this minute to the marshal's office." White ringed her eyes, and her hands made quick, jerky movements like a scared bird.

"What's happened?"

"Your room. Oh my stars and garters, your room. It must've happened last night when I went over to my sister Gertrude's house. The only one here was Marley Jacobs, and he was so drunk he couldn't have hit the ground with a hat. He never heard anything at all."

Addie's throat closed up, and she plucked Mrs. Blanchard's bony fingers off her arm. Fearing what she would find, she forced herself to open the door to her room.

Chaos.

She stood, frozen, in the doorway.

Mrs. Blanchard nudged her aside to look as well. "I was just coming in to change the towels, and I found all this."

Every drawer hung open, every cupboard door gaped wide. The bedclothes were strewn on the floor, and the mattress had been dragged off the frame. Long slashes eviscerated the pillows, and goose down dusted every surface. The mirror from the washstand lay in shards on the rug, joined by pieces of pitcher and bowl.

Mrs. Blanchard wrung her hands. "Everything's ruined. Look at my drapes." The dusty-rose velvet hung in ribbons, all the silvery fringe ripped away and long rents sliced into the panels. "I'm so glad you weren't home when this happened, but who's going to pay for this? The bedding, the china, even the wallpaper." She waved to the wall beside the door.

Addie stepped farther into the room and turned to view the damage.

Where Is It?

The letters, nearly a foot high, had been carved into the wall, marring the muted cabbage rose and ribbon pattern. Addie's hand went to her mouth, and tears stung her eyes. The violence in those slashes, the vindictiveness and malice, made her insides quake.

"Addie dear, who would do such a thing? And what were they looking for? What is 'it'?"

It was something she didn't have. *It* was something she didn't know how to get. And *it* was something she wasn't willing to die for. Up until now, even with the vandalism of the studio, she'd not really feared for her safety. But this, the invasion of her room, the destruction of her personal items, and especially that message hacked into the wall. . . She swallowed. This felt like more than anger. It bespoke an unbalanced mind. Had he been drunk? If she had been here when Vin ransacked this room, she had no doubt but that he would've killed her.

"You know, don't you? You know what he was looking for. I can tell by your expression that you do." Mrs. Blanchard grabbed Addie's arm.

Her hands shook, and she took short, jagged breaths. "Mrs. Blanchard, please don't let anyone else into this room until I get back. I'll go report the break-in at the jail." Once more she peeled the woman's fingers off her arm.

Her landlady returned to wringing her hands at her waist, balling them in her apron. "Addie, I don't like to do this, but you can't stay here anymore. For the first time in my life, I don't feel safe in my own home. First your studio, now your room? I have an obligation to my other boarders, too. It's obvious that whoever did this didn't find whatever he was looking for. That means he'll keep looking." She blinked, her lips quivering, but her head high. "I don't want him looking for it here ever again, whatever it is."

Addie's throat tightened, and her heart dropped down to her stomach. How many more shocks could she take before she lost her mind? A glance told her the few dollars she'd stashed under her mattress had disappeared. Penniless, homeless, and thanks to Vin, the only possessions she owned that hadn't been destroyed were on her back.

"Addie? You understand why I can't have you here?"

"I understand." And she did. She understood that she would never be free of her past until she brought it into the present. Vin couldn't be allowed to terrorize people this way, no matter what it cost her to admit to being Cliff Walker's girl. She would put an end to this today.

"I probably shouldn't have hit him." Jonas flexed his fingers. "I just couldn't take it anymore."

Miles stared down at the unconscious form now sprawled across the bunk in the first cell. "I'm surprised you stood it for as long as you did. He had no call to say those things about

Fran. He's a sloppy drunk, and he's mean afterward." And more slippery than a pickled onion. Vin's alibi for the time the studio was ransacked was as unassailable as for the time of the murder. Luke Short had verified that Vin had been in the Long Branch from ten o'clock on the night of the Fourth until dawn. Which left Miles exactly nowhere as far as solving the crime.

Cowboys on a tear didn't make sense, because they would've broken the front windows. Robbery wasn't the motive like at the mercantile, because nothing had been stolen, only destroyed. He jangled the cell keys, spinning them on the ring while his thoughts spiraled.

Jonas gripped the bars and rested his forehead on his hands. "What's Fran thinking of, hankering after someone like this? Can't she see he's no good?"

"I doubt Vin Rutter has shown this side of himself to her. You've seen him around town. He acts cultured and smooth. Whatever fascination Fran has with him will wear off soon. She's like a rabbit, mesmerized by a rattlesnake."

"But will she realize the danger before the snake strikes? I've tried to warn her, but she won't listen to me. I didn't break your confidence or Addie's, but unless one of you tells Fran about who Vin really is, I'm afraid for her." Jonas straightened and let his hands fall away from the cell door. "I've already lost all chance of winning her love. Now I just want to keep her safe."

Miles shoved his hands into his pockets and stared at the floor. If he hadn't been such a coward about trying to hide his past, maybe he could've saved people he cared about a lot of heartache. But no more. "Keeping Fran safe is more important than trying not to hurt her feelings. I'll talk to her. At least while Vin's in jail he can't be causing anyone any harm."

His mind blanked at what Addie would say when she found out. But keeping her safe from Vin was more important than her feelings. . .or his. He'd have to tell her the truth.

He nearly dropped the keys when the door opened and Addie slipped into the jail. She stopped just inside the doorway, clutching the strap of her camera case. Her eyes glistened, and she blinked, sending a couple of tears tracking down her cheeks.

In two strides he was before her. He grabbed her by the shoulders, checking for an injury. "Are you hurt? What's wrong?"

She shook her head, gulped, and swiped at the tears in an angry, little-girl gesture. "I wasn't going to cry." Which seemed a silly thing to say, since she clearly was crying.

"What happened? Are you still upset about the studio?" That was understandable.

"No. I mean, yes, of course I am. But that's not all. I need to report another break-in. And. . ." She gulped another big breath of air. "I know who did it."

His eyebrows rose? "Another break-in? At the studio?"

"No, not at the studio. At my boardinghouse."

Jonas swept a pile of papers up into his arm and offered her a chair. "Here, Addie. You look about all in. Sit down and tell us what happened."

Miles let his hands drop away, and she sank onto the chair. Her camera case knocked against the desk, and absently, she tugged it around to let it sit in her lap. "I spent last night with Fran at her place, and this morning when I went to my room at Mrs. Blanchard's to get something, I found that someone had broken in." She clutched the camera case, her knuckles going white. "Sometime after seven last night, someone got into my room and tore it apart. All my things are ruined, the furniture is broken, the drapes and bedding destroyed."

Jonas perched on the edge of the desk and touched her shoulder. "And you know who did it?"

She nodded and moistened her lips. "The same man who broke up my studio."

A low moan came from the cells, and Vin sat up, rubbing his jaw and scowling.

Addie's eyes widened and her jaw fell open. "You've arrested Vin? But—" She stopped. "How did you know?"

Miles's thoughts spun. "Slow down and tell me what happened and what Vin has to do with it."

"Mrs. Blanchard says sometime after seven last night someone broke into my room. If anything, it looks worse than the studio." She shuddered and renewed her grip on the camera case. "So much hate." Her blue-gray eyes trained on the prisoner. "How could you? What did I ever do to you?"

"Me?" Vin grimaced and touched his swollen left eye. "I've never been to your boardinghouse, and I certainly wasn't there last night."

Addie shot out of her chair. "Don't try to deny it. I got your message. Why won't you believe me when I tell you I don't have what you're looking for?"

"Message? What message?"

"Don't play ignorant with me. The message you carved into the wall of my room. 'Where is it?' Not exactly subtle. I knew it was you the minute I saw it."

He scowled, wincing. "You've got a problem."

"I'll say I do. I'm being preyed upon by a malicious, yellow thief."

"Maybe, but it isn't me."

"Addie." Miles put his hand on her arm.

She shrugged it off. "I don't know how you figured it out so quickly, but thank you for arresting Vin. I want to file charges."

"Addie, we arrested him early last night."

"Did someone already report the break-in?" She tore her eyes away from her tormenter and looked up at Miles. "Is there a witness? Mrs. Blanchard said the place was empty except for Marley Jacobs, and he was sleeping off a drinking binge. Did someone see Vin leaving?"

"No, what I'm trying to tell you is we arrested Vin last night at about six. He was carrying a firearm inside city limits. If your break-in didn't happen until sometime after seven, it couldn't have been Vin who did it."

Vin put his head back and laughed, making Addie want to reach through the bars and slap his face. "Hoo hoo!" He wiped his eyes and dragged himself off the floor to sit on the bunk. "This is great. All of you trying so hard to pin something on me, and every time I've got an alibi. I never thought I'd say this, but"—he waved at Jonas—"thank you for arresting me last night." He tipped his head back and laughed again.

"Shut up, or I'll black your other eye." Jonas stepped forward, his hands fisted and a dull red flush climbing his cheeks.

Miles jammed his fingers through his hair. How had things unraveled so quickly?

Chapter 18

Addie groped for the chair and sank into it. If what Miles said was true, then Vin couldn't have been the one to break into her room. But if it wasn't Vin, then who? One of Cliff's other gang members? A chill shot through her. Vin was right. She did have a problem.

The door crashed open, and Addie jumped. Fran marched into the jailhouse. "Jonas Spooner, you rat, what's the idea of locking Vin up? Have you lost your mind?"

Addie pressed her fingertips to her temples. She loved Fran dearly, but now was not the time for histrionics. "Fran, please."

Fran didn't stop until she stood toe to toe with Jonas in front of the bars. "This is outrageous. Did you think I wouldn't hear about this?" Jamming her hands on her hips, she looked into the cell. "Oh Vin! What have they done to you?" Her jaw dropped. "Jonas? You hit him? How could you?" She rounded on the deputy.

Miles inserted his arm between Fran and the bars. "You need to step back."

"No, not until you tell me what happened here. I want this man released. He hasn't done anything wrong, other than make Jonas jealous." Hectic color decorated her cheeks, and her eyes snapped fire.

Jonas said nothing, but neither did he move to open the cell door.

"Fran"—Addie rose—"it isn't what you think."

"It's exactly what I think. It's shameful of Jonas to abuse his office this way. I never would've suspected it of you. It's so unlike you to use violence."

Addie tried to catch Miles's glance. Everything was coming apart at the seams, and Fran's dramatic protests weren't helping.

Vin grinned through the bars. "Fran, my sweet, how lovely of you to be concerned. I shall come and find you the minute I get out of this. . .establishment. Then we can be together."

Jonas started forward. "Now see here, Rutter. If you come anywhere near—"

Fran slapped his hand off her arm. "I can take care of myself, Jonas Spooner, and don't you—"

Miles tried to speak over the argument. "Let's all calm down and talk this over—"

"Hush up!" The words barreled out of Addie's mouth and everyone froze. Before they could gather themselves, she continued. "Fran, sit down." Pointing to the chair she'd just left, she marched to the cells and grabbed her friend's wrist. "You're going to sit still and listen to a few home truths about Vin Rutter. Then you're going to apologize to Jonas and go home."

Fran gasped, but Addie was mad clean through and tired to the point of recklessness. She dragged Fran to the chair and pushed her into it. "Now, listen to me, all of you.

Fran Seaton, you're treating a decent man shamefully. Jonas has never had anything but your best interests at heart. The reason Vin Rutter is in jail has nothing to do with you. He's in jail because he broke the law." She poked Fran in the shoulder. "I have news for you, the entire world doesn't spin around you. It's time you dropped these girlish fantasies about a white knight riding in to rescue you from your life and realized the best man for the job is standing right here."

"Um, Addie. . ." Jonas shuffled his feet, his face going even redder.

"Don't. You've been too patient with her. It's time she got a dose of reality before she does herself some real harm."

"I don't have to sit here and take this." Fran gathered herself, but Addie pushed her back down.

"Yes you do. I've been too patient with you, too. I've let you weave dreams about a man I know is bad, and all because I was afraid to tell the truth. Afraid you'd think less of me. I've let you change the subject and skirt the topic every time I bring it up, but no more. I can't stand by any longer. Your precious Vin Rutter is a former member of the Walker Gang, a liar, and a criminal." She took a deep breath and forged on. The time for hiding had ended. She didn't dare look at Miles, afraid of the disgust she would see there. "I was once romantically involved with Vin's saddle pard and boss, Cliff Walker, the leader of the gang."

Fran's eyes widened, and Jonas stepped forward.

Addie held up her hand. "I didn't know about the gang or the killing or stealing. Cliff kept me completely in the dark, using a fake name and telling lies on top of lies. He was handsome, smooth, fascinating—all the words you've used to describe Vin. I let my head be turned. When the U.S. marshals showed up at my door, I was stunned, and I didn't want to believe them." She swallowed, remembering. "They were convinced I was an accomplice. The marshals badgered me for hours, trying to get me to admit to being part of the gang. They were trying to find the money Cliff and his gang stole during their last train robbery."

Her knees wobbled, all the humiliation, the exhaustion, the confusion, and the hurt piling back. "They questioned me and Uncle Carl extensively, and in the end, they had to let us go. But not before all of Abilene knew and became convinced of our guilt. Our photography studio was burned, people called me names, and eventually, they ran us out of town. It ruined my uncle's health, and my reputation."

She walked to the cell and glared in at Vin. "And Vin was one of the gang members. He was arrested with Cliff, but the sheriff released him. Cliff was tried and executed for robbery and murder. I thought I was done with all of that, that I could put it all behind me and start a new life here, but a few weeks ago, Vin showed up looking for the stolen money. The cash has never turned up, and Vin is convinced I have it or I know where it is." She gripped the bars until her hands shook. "I'm telling you all now, I don't have it, I don't know where it is, and I wish I'd never heard of Cliff Walker or any of his gang."

She let her hands fall away and turned on her heel to approach Fran once more. "I should've told you before, when you first mentioned Vin, but I was afraid. I was afraid I would lose your friendship if you knew I'd been the girlfriend of a killer. I'm sorry I didn't tell you, but I'm telling you now. Vin Rutter is rotten clear through. He's a liar, a thief, and probably a killer himself."

She swayed. "When my studio was ransacked, I thought it was Vin. He came to my studio after the gold once before." She glanced at Jonas, whose face looked carved from stone. "The night of Wally's murder, when you came in and Vin left. He'd been pestering me to tell him where the money was. And this morning when I saw the destruction in my room, I thought it must be Vin still searching. But if he was in a cell here last night, he couldn't have broken into the boardinghouse." She swallowed. "But if he isn't the culprit, then there is someone else out there looking for the money. One of Cliff's gang members or someone who has heard about the trial."

"Addie." Miles put his hand on her arm, but she eased away, still unable to look at him, afraid to see the disgust in his eyes.

"No, Miles." Her breath hitched in her tight throat as she fought for control. "You deserve to know the truth. Here I am accusing Fran of mistreating Jonas, but I'm to blame as well. The night the Arden Palace opened, I took advantage of your chivalry. I spied Vin in the crowd, and I was afraid of him. I used you as a shield, hoping he would leave me alone if he saw me with another man—and a deputy at that. And I haven't been truthful with you about my past. At first, I thought it wouldn't matter. I was trying to get a fresh start here in Dodge City and forget about Cliff and everything he'd done to my life. I thought if I ignored it, it would go away." A bitter laugh surprised her. "Then, when I realized I was. . .becoming fond of you. . .I didn't want you to know about Cliff because I was afraid you'd despise me."

"Addie, I wouldn't—"

She straightened her spine, the strength of resolve coursing through her, giving her courage. "I'm not going to be Cliff's victim anymore. He's had far too long a reach—all the way from the grave—holding on to my life. Well, no more." She squared her shoulders. "Fran, I'm sorry I had to speak so harshly to you, and I'm sorry I didn't tell you the truth about Vin sooner. Jonas loves you, and I know you love him, if you'll just grow up enough to realize it. He's worth a hundred Vin Rutters."

Fran stared hard at her, her face pale and her hands knotted in her lap. Her chin was tilted at a dangerous angle, and she looked from one face to another.

Addie's shoulders slumped. Telling the truth had cost her Fran's friendship, just as she had feared. Her only consolation lay in the fact that at least Fran knew about Vin now. Any choice she made wouldn't be made out of ignorance. She wouldn't fall into the same trap Cliff had laid for Addie.

She risked a look at Miles, who stood with his hands jammed in his back pockets, staring at the floor. Though she had never admitted to herself how much she hoped he wouldn't care about her past, that he would somehow say it didn't matter to him, that he loved her anyway, his posture and his refusal to look at her made her face reality. She had been foolish to hope. When he did look at her, his eyes were so tortured, she couldn't bear it.

Jonas shifted his weight. "Fran, how's about I walk you home? I think Miles and Addie might have some things to talk over."

Fran rose, cold and fiery all at once. "Leave me alone. I can find my own way home." She skirted Addie without a glance and stalked to the cell bars. Her glare could've started the corn-husk mattress on fire. "Vin Rutter, you're pathetic. I don't want to see you again. Whenever you get out of here, I'd advise you to keep on riding." She marched to the door but paused to deliver one parting shot. "I don't want to see *any* of you again."

Miles winced when Fran slammed the door on the way out.

Jonas closed his eyes for a moment and tilted his head back, and Addie sank onto the chair Fran had vacated and put her face in her hands.

"What a little spitfire." Vin eased back onto his bunk. "I love the women in this town."

Anger flared through Miles. "Be quiet. You've done enough harm here."

Jonas's fisted hands shook. His throat worked against his collar, and his jaw muscles bulged. "I believe I'll go get some air." He met Bat at the door coming in.

"Boys, what progress have you made on finding Wally's killer?" He slung his bag under his desk and leaned his cane against his hip to remove his leather gloves. "Hap's on his way over to look at the picture again. Maybe something will jar loose. Hello, Miss Reid." His piercing eyes bored into Miles.

Great. The boss was back early. Miles could hardly catch his breath from one crisis to the next. What he wanted to do was sweep Addie out of here and find someplace quiet where they could talk. Where he could tell her how much he loved her, how he admired her bravery in telling Fran the truth, and where he could confess to his own relationship with Cliff Walker. Then he wanted to come back to the jail and haul Vin outside and run him out of town. After that, he'd come back and admit to Bat that he had made no headway on the case, that he was related to Cliff, and that he would turn in his badge if Bat wanted him to.

Oh, that was a great plan. Turn his back on everything he'd ever dreamed of being and doing and hope Addie would overlook the fact that he was a coward, a liar, and jobless.

Jonas hovered near the door, but he stepped aside when Hap Greeley entered.

"Sheriff, I'm willing to look again at the picture, but I don't know what I can tell you." The big shopkeeper removed his glasses and rubbed them with his red handkerchief. He looked terrible, as if he hadn't slept or bathed in days. His clothes bagged, and his thinning hair ran amok. Bloodshot eyes held a world of inner turmoil. "I can't stay long though. I have to take care of some of the details for the funeral tomorrow."

Bat snapped his fingers. "Where's the picture, Miles?"

Miles frowned and looked at heaps of papers covering every flat surface. He sorted back to the last time he had seen it. "It was on your desk."

"I don't want to know where it was. I want to know where it is." The sheriff lifted a sheaf of pages and ruffled them. "Did you start a file? Why are all these reports and fliers mixed up?"

Jonas shrugged. "There was a little accident with one of the piles. They fell onto the floor. I scooped them up the best I could."

Bat's mustache twitched, and his eyebrows came down. "Well, both of you, get your hands in here and sort through this mess. I want that picture. Hap, you have a seat. I'm sure it's around here somewhere."

Addie rose, and Miles thought she might make her escape, but instead, she took a pile of papers and leafed through them. "When was the last time you had it?"

Miles considered. "I guess the last time I saw it for sure was the night you brought it over here. That's when Hap—when the papers fell off the desk. Since Hap didn't see anything in the picture that would tell us who killed Wally, I didn't give it another thought." Wanted posters, newspapers, arrest reports, telegrams, receipts, train schedules, his fingers flew through the papers. He could feel Bat's eyes on him, judging, assessing. The cane started tapping, and a trickle of sweat beaded at Miles's temple and ran down his cheek.

Hap throttled his handkerchief and mopped his red face. "I hope you find out who did the killing. Poor Wally must be avenged."

"Jonas, did you show the photograph to Fran when you questioned her?" Miles scrabbled to catch a cascade of newspapers determined to slide onto the floor.

"No, I didn't get a chance. She kinda left abruptly."

The longer they looked, the more desperate Miles became. Losing the photograph was just another black mark against him. What had ever made him think he could be a lawman? He couldn't even run an investigation without losing evidence.

Addie set aside another bundle of pages. "Sheriff, you really need to invest in another filing cabinet. Your papers and the city marshal's are all mixed up, and there're enough old newspapers here to fill a wagon."

Bat grimaced and spread his hands. "I know it. I'm terrible about such things. Never seem to get around to throwing out the old stuff."

Jonas kicked an empty ammunition box over beside the desk. "Maybe we can throw out some things now and whittle this down. I imagine the photograph is on the bottom of one of these stacks."

After half an hour of sorting while listening to Hap moaning, Miles was ready to put a match to the entire works. Vin remained mercifully quiet, no doubt not wanting to be noticed by Bat. Eventually, the scarred and battered desktop emerged. Miles's shoulders sagged.

No picture.

"Why are you pawing through papers when you should be out finding Wally's killer?" Hap rose, his sweaty, balding head almost brushing the ceiling. "I didn't see anything helpful in that photograph, and you're wasting time."

Miles gritted his teeth.

"Now Hap, don't worry." Bat took a cigar from his vest

pocket and clamped it between his teeth. "I'm sure the boys are doing all they can to find Wally's killer."

"But what about opening the store again? With a killer on the loose, I won't feel safe. What if he comes back? You don't have any leads." He swiped at his pate with the handkerchief, his face quivering. "You can't even hold on to a single piece of evidence."

"Hap, take it easy. I'm sure we'll find it. And if we don't, we'll have Miss Reid make us another copy." Bat kept calm, no doubt trying to stem the emotional river flowing from Hap before it burst its banks. The man had a crazed edge to his voice, so near the breaking point he shook.

Miles cleared his throat. "As to that, I don't think she can. The photography studio was ransacked, and all the plates and equipment destroyed."

Bat's eyebrows rose. "When did this happen?" He directed the question to Addie.

"Late on the Fourth. Sometime after the murder but before the end of the fireworks show. But—"

"Why didn't you report this to me?" Bat's eyes pinned Miles. He dug a match from his pocket and lit it, holding it to the end of his cigar and creating clouds of blue smoke.

"I would've reported it, but you'd already left on the night train by the time the vandalism was discovered."

A sinking feeling, like bogging in quicksand, floundered in Miles's chest. The harder he struggled to do things right, the more of a hash he made of it all. Exactly as Jonas had described when he tried to change without God's help. *God, I could use some of that help right now.*

"Then tell the truth and don't hold anything back. The only way to be free of a lie is to tell the truth." "What have you done about finding Wally's killer?" Bat stroked his mustache.

"We questioned folks who were in the store the day of the murder, but nobody seems to have seen anything. We've also been putting out feelers looking for the money. Luke Short is keeping an eye out, as are several of the other gambling bosses. So far, nothing's turned up."

Bat nodded. "That's what I'd have done, too. What about the break-in at Miss Reid's? Any leads there?"

Miles fisted his hands. "It's not just her studio. Last night someone ransacked her room at Mrs. Blanchard's place. Addie came in to report the crime, and I haven't had a chance to go over there and take a look yet."

Vin rose off the bunk and came to the bars. The swelling around his eye had darkened. "How much longer will you detain me?"

"What's he in for?" Bat frowned. "Anything related to the case?"

Hap jerked and his watery stare bored into Vin. "Did you kill Wally?"

"I didn't kill anyone. I've been harassed by the deputies, questioned, followed, and suspected of everything from murder to spitting on the sidewalk, but I'm innocent, and it's killing them." Vin smirked at Miles.

"We arrested him for carrying a firearm inside city limits. He's been here since last night." Miles swallowed. "He's a former member of the Walker Gang who's been hanging around for a few weeks, and he's made himself a bit of a nuisance with Miss Seaton and Addie here. Addie thought it might've been Vin who tore up her place, since he's been so troublesome, but he was locked up when the second break-in occurred."

Bat motioned to Jonas. "Turn him out." He leveled a stare at Vin. "You strike me as a man who enjoys making trouble for others and not paying for it. I'd recommend you make yourself scarce in Dodge City. We don't hold with your kind around here. If you venture into this county again, I'll make a punchboard out of your hide."

Miles shook his head at the quick summing-up. Bat was astute, no mistake. He'd described Vin perfectly and on short acquaintance.

Jonas rattled the keys as he opened the cell door. Vin gathered his hat and coat and marched out with his chin high.

When he'd departed, Bat jerked his head toward the door. "Spooner, I suggest you follow our friend there and make sure he gets on the train or forks his horse."

With a nod and a slight smile, Jonas left.

Addie had her arms crossed at her waist, tapping her toe. "Sheriff, about the picture. . ."

"That's a grievous loss. I'm vexed that we can't find it." Bat removed his hat and smoothed his hair. "And now we can't even get a duplicate made." He turned to Hap. "I apologize. It's sheer negligence, and I share a part in it for keeping such a derelict office. We'll keep looking. Perhaps it will turn up."

Hap nodded, hanging his head. "It's all so terrible. I'm

absolutely lost without Wally to take care of all the details. I imagine I'll have to sell up. I don't know that I could go on trading there anyway, not where Wally was killed. I don't think the horror will ever fade. If only I'd been in town, maybe I could've stopped it. It's too bad about the picture."

Addie blew out an exasperated sigh. "That's what I've been trying to tell you. I've got the glass plate here." She patted her camera case. "If I can get some chemicals and get into my darkroom, I'll make another print."

"What?" Hap's eyebrows rose nearly as high as his voice. "You mean—"

"Don't lose hope, Mr. Greeley. Miles and Jonas and Sheriff Masterson are doing their best. I'm sure they'll find out who killed Wally." She removed the camera and flipped open a little compartment in the bottom of the case. "See, the slide's intact. It won't take me long once I get set up, and we'll have another picture for you to examine. Maybe this time something will stand out."

Her face glowed with such conviction, Miles wanted to hug her. She'd suffered so many blows, and yet, here she was, still standing.

Bat nodded. "Carr, go with Miss Reid and see what you can do to help her. I'm going to go talk to Luke. He might've come across something. You were smart to enlist his help. I don't put much importance on the picture, but I don't like loose ends. If the case comes to trial, we'd best be able to lay our hands on the photograph or the defense might argue that we've handled the evidence poorly. Don't want the killer to get off because a jury thinks we can't do our jobs."

A lot of white showed around Hap's eyes behind his glasses, and he twisted the handkerchief until Miles thought the fabric would rip. He caught Miles looking at him and took a deep breath, as if trying to calm himself. "I hope you can find something, anything. This not knowing is driving me to distraction." He checked his watch and wiped his head once more. "I need to be getting along. There are some things to see to for Wally's service and all."

Miles plucked his hat off the peg by the door. "Addie, where can we get the chemicals and such that you need? The pharmacy?"

She glanced up from repacking the case. "The quickest way will be to go to another photography studio, though I don't know that any of my competitors will be interested in loaning me the chemicals." She looked down at her hands. "With all that's happened at the studio and at my boarding-house, I can't afford to pay for new supplies just yet."

"What about a place to do the work?"

"I could develop the print in someone else's darkroom, but I prefer my own. I was able to salvage most of the pans and trays I'll need."

"Let's go then."

"Wait." Bat grabbed a piece of paper and a pencil. "I'll write you a requisition for what you need, just in case anyone gives you any trouble over getting the supplies." He scribbled a few lines and signed his name. "There, that should smooth the way."

Addie glanced at the paper and tucked it into a pocket. "We'll be back as soon as we can."

Miles stopped at the door. "Bat, there are a few things we need to talk about later. And I apologize for misplacing that photograph. I don't seem to have made any headway with this case."

Bat settled his hat and picked up his cane. "I think you're doing a fine job on the investigation. It was a rotten set of circumstances to begin with. Too many strangers in town and too few clues to go on. It's lucky Miss Reid can give us another copy of that picture, but I wouldn't put too much stock in it changing things. Unless we come up with a witness, or some of the cash shows up, it's likely the killer is already out of town."

Miles nodded, discouraged by the lack of progress but encouraged by the vote of confidence from his boss. He'd been half-afraid that Bat would fire him on the spot for not having made an arrest already.

Addie was half a block up the street before he caught up with her. "Where're we headed?"

"Donaldson's. He's the closest, though he won't be glad to see me."

They entered the shop, and Miles couldn't help but compare the place to Addie's before the break-in. No welcoming reception area, just a bare counter in front of a dividing curtain. No bell rang out over the door, and no one appeared from the back of the studio.

Miles rapped on the counter. "Donaldson? You in?"

Heber Donaldson emerged from behind the limp drape. "What can I do for you?" he began with a hopeful smile. His expression darkened when he saw Addie. "Miss Reid, what do you want?"

Putting himself slightly in front of Addie, Miles addressed the pompous photographer. "We're here to get some chemicals for developing a picture. As you might've heard, Miss Reid's studio was vandalized. She's in need of some supplies, and while you're at it, a little courtesy would be appreciated."

Addie's hand pressed against his back. "It's all right, Miles. I didn't expect a warm welcome." She offered the note from Bat. "Heber, the sheriff wrote this requisition. You'll be reimbursed for everything."

He took the note, running his hand down his beard and scowling. "What is it you need?"

"Chemicals for developing a dry-plate, and a few pieces of equipment."

He nodded. "Those supplies ain't cheap. I'll be making careful notes of everything you take."

Miles held on to his temper. "Just get the stuff. We're in a hurry."

Twenty minutes later, Donaldson all but shoved them out the door with his bad grace. Miles carried a crate of clinking bottles, and they made short work of getting to Addie's building.

"I'm afraid things are still a mess. I don't know if I'll ever get all the glass swept up." Addie produced the key and let them inside.

Miles surveyed the room. The plants had been swept up and the photographs in their frames all stacked against the right-hand wall. The rug at the front door had disappeared, and the drapery in the doorway had been removed.

"This is as far as I got. The front room and the darkroom. Fran was coming to help later today." She bit her lip. "I suppose I've lost that friendship forever. I spoke too harshly to her." Blinking quickly, she lifted her chin. "I just couldn't have her thinking Vin was her hero when I know what a skunk he really is."

"I didn't even know she was in love with him until recently."

Addie led him into the studio. "I don't know that she was really in love with him. More like she was in love with the idea of him. In love with love. I feel badly for Jonas, so patiently waiting for her to grow up."

"Where do you want me to put these?" He indicated the bottles and jars in his arms.

"This way. Put them on the bench in the darkroom. Be careful though. Some of those are quite dangerous, especially if you don't know what you're doing." She set down the jug of water she carried—special filtered water from Donaldson's for mixing chemicals.

He skirted the stacks and boxes of debris in the studio and entered the little room. The narrow workspace looked better than the last time he'd seen it, but even his untrained eye picked out the barren places on the bench and shelves. He put the crate on the work surface, carefully set out the containers in a row beside some dented trays, and returned to the studio.

"I lined up the supplies. Anything else I can do?" He tucked his fingers into his back pockets.

Addie unbuttoned one of her cuffs and began rolling it up in precise folds. Her slender wrists and delicate hands drew his attention, and he forced his gaze away. "It's really a one-person job." She started in on the other cuff. "The room's so small I'd be tripping over you in there. But"—her lashes flipped up, and he caught a glimpse of worried blue-gray eyes—"I'd really appreciate it if you stayed in the studio. With all that's happened, and Vin not responsible for the vandalism here. . ." She spread her hands and shrugged.

"I don't blame you. I won't leave." He reached for a broom. "I can work on some of the cleanup."

"Thank you." She hoisted the gallon jug again. "Please don't come into the darkroom once I've started or the print will be ruined. I'll do my best to hurry, but it takes a while." She flashed him a smile that sent his pulse galloping and disappeared into the darkroom.

He grabbed a broom. *Don't be a fool. Once she learns you're related to Cliff, any hope you have of winning her is gone. Keep your mind on business. Protect her as you would any other citizen and forget about anything else.*

Talking to himself didn't change his feelings one bit. He still hoped and prayed she would forgive him, that somehow she could see past the man he had been to the man he wanted to be, the man he felt he could be with God's help and her by his side.

Jabbing with the bristles at a stubborn line of broken glass along the base of a plaster pedestal, he scowled. She was right. She might never get to the end of all the broken glass scattered through this place.

He leaned the broom against the wall and took hold of the pedestal. Something stung his hand, and he yanked it back. Examining his palm, he noted a bright red dot at the base of his thumb. One of the corners of the pillar had broken off, and a jagged piece of wire protruded from the crumbled edge. Frowning, he horsed the pillar out of the way, careful not to grab the wire again. Maybe he could patch it for her somehow.

The pile of junk in the center of the room grew as he added broken furniture and props. Maybe he and Jonas could get a wagon from the livery and help her clear out the room so she could start fresh.

Chapter 19

Fran scowled and leapt back as the box of coat buttons slipped from her fingers and crashed to the floor. Shiny black wooden circles skidded and rolled across the floor, racing toward the most inaccessible crevices and hiding places. Tears burned her eyes, and she smacked the counter. Why was she even bothering to continue the inventory? Her life was in ruins and here she was chasing buttons and counting hay rakes. She pressed the heels of her hands to her eyes and calculated the revelations that had brought her to this place.

Addie hadn't trusted her enough to tell her about Cliff Walker and had shamed her in front of everyone at the jail.

Vin Rutter had used her and manipulated her, and she'd fallen for his lies like a naive schoolgirl.

Her boss had been murdered, and her job was in jeopardy if Hap didn't keep the store open.

Jonas despised her for a fool.

Her throat tightened, and fresh tears pricked her eyes. Though each part hurt, the last one ached most. Addie had been right in that, at least. Fran had let herself get carried away with girlish fantasies and driven away the most precious thing she'd ever had. The look in Jonas's eyes when she'd stormed out of the jail—disgust, resignation, repulsion—made her feel as small and foolish as she had been acting.

The front door rattled. Ignoring it, she swiped at her cheeks. Whoever it was would have to go to the store up the street. Hap hadn't given her leave to open for customers, and she wasn't in the mood to fill orders anyway.

The knob jiggled, and the person knocked. Couldn't they see the sign in the window? Fran headed for the storeroom, but before she got halfway down the aisle, the front door opened.

"I thought I might find you here."

Her stomach flared like a blacksmith's forge, heating her blood. "Did you just pick that lock?"

"It's one of my many talents."

"That figures. A criminal like you. What are you doing out of jail?"

Vin closed the door behind himself and leaned against it, snicking the lock. "I was released, though I've been commanded by our illustrious sheriff to vacate the county." He'd dropped the smooth Southern accent. Now he sounded like the common outlaw he was.

"If Bat ordered you to go, why are you still here?" She crossed her arms at her waist.

"I came to see you." He straightened and started toward her, his stride as smooth as a panther's.

"I can't imagine why. We have nothing to discuss." Skirting the end of the counter, she stepped behind the solid, wooden barrier, wanting to keep something between her and this. . .rat. . .skunk. . .coyote. . . No word seemed bad enough.

"I have something to do before I leave this town." He followed her progress along the counter, staying opposite her.

"I wanted to give you something to remember me by."

"You cannot be serious. You have nothing I want or need, nor do I want to remember you." The man not only had no scruples, his arrogance took her breath away.

"What you want isn't relevant. It never has been. That was always your mistake, thinking any of this was about you. You were so easy to manipulate. A very pretty pawn, but a pawn nonetheless. And you're still a pawn in my game. Miles and Spooner have blocked me at every turn, but I'm not finished yet. I have one more hand to play before I depart."

His words hit like darts. "You're out of your mind. Now get out. I wouldn't want to be you if Bat finds you still in town."

"Not to worry, what I have in mind won't take long." His face hardened. How had she ever thought him handsome? His lizard eyes glittered, making her flesh crawl. "I have no intention of leaving empty handed." His bold leer raked her face and form, and he laughed.

For the first time she knew real fear. Malice flowed off him in waves. "There's no money here. We were robbed, remember?"

He placed his palms on the counter and leaned toward her. "It's not money I'm after. It's something better."

She pressed her shoulders and hips into the shelves behind her and shot a glance at the door. The smirk dragging his lips sideways left her in no doubt of his intent. Her heart thundered in her ears, and her mouth went dry. She judged the distance to the door and knew she wouldn't make it. He would be on her before she went two steps.

"Ah, I see you understand at last. That's one of the most appealing things about you, Fran, your delightful innocence. Though I shall rectify that condition soon enough. Now, don't be tedious enough to try to run. It's undignified."

She groped behind her for a weapon. Fear and anger warred in her, surging and making her mind blank. "If you touch me, I'll scream." Her hands closed on glass, and her fingers gripped the neck of the bottle, the ridges and size telling her it was Dr. Pettigrew's Cure-All Tonic.

"Who will hear you, my love, after I gag you?"

"You don't love me. Why are you doing this?" She edged toward the door, keeping the bottle behind her back.

He kept pace, cutting off her escape route. "Of course I don't love you. This isn't about love. It's about revenge. Revenge on Spooner for punching me. Revenge on Miles for blocking my attempts to get near Addie. Revenge on Addie for keeping the money from me." With each statement his voice rose and his eyes got wilder. "Killing Spooner wasn't enough. I want what he treasured most."

"What?" Her heart stopped. "Killing Spooner?" The words came out a strangled whisper.

"That's right." He sneered and advanced around the counter, grabbing her arm and hauling her up against him. "The sheriff set Spooner on my trail—I suspect to make sure I left town quickly—and he followed me to my lodgings. I had to get rid of him. I'm only sorry he won't be around to learn about what I did to you."

His breath scraped her cheek, but she barely felt it. Jonas was dead? "You lie." He couldn't be dead. Not Jonas. "You're a liar."

He laughed again, a slimy, sickening laugh—the snake. "I am an accomplished liar, that's true, but in this instance, I assure you, I'm telling the truth. It gave me great pleasure to kill him."

"Let me go." She paused between each word, forcing the syllables through her clenched teeth. His grip on her arm stung, but she knew it was only a precursor to what he intended.

"Soon." He dragged her a couple of steps. "I think the storeroom."

She went limp, hoping to catch him off guard. Tears she didn't have to fake flowed down her cheeks. "My brothers will avenge my honor. Bat and Miles will hunt you down and shoot you like the rabid dog you are."

"Stop sniveling. You might even enjoy it."

She wanted to throw up.

He dragged her down the center aisle, bouncing her hip off the corner of the clothing table and yanking her after him in spite of her yelp of pain.

It's now or never, Fran. If he gets you into the storeroom, you're a goner.

She braced her feet and swung her arm up. The bottle of patent medicine connected with his temple and burst in a cascade of glass and pungent fumes. Vin dropped like a stunned ox, sprawling on the floor and knocking over the bean barrel. Thousands of rock-hard navy beans shot across the floor.

Had she killed him?

She shook with violent tremors, turning from him and pressing the back of her hand to her mouth to stifle the sobs crowding her throat. She didn't care if she had killed him. Part of her hoped he was dead for killing Jonas. Good riddance.

Weariness weighted her limbs, and she realized she still gripped the neck of the broken bottle. She needed to get outside, to call for help, but her legs refused to move.

Jonas was dead?

A hand grabbed her ankle, and she screamed. Vin struggled to sit upright, glass shards raining off his shoulders. Though she tried to kick away from him, he hung on. In a blink, he lunged up toward her. "You're going to pay for that!" He reached into his coat and withdrew a pistol, ratcheting back the hammer and aiming it at her face.

The door crashed open, and Vin spun his gun toward the sound, dropping his grip on her ankle.

Fran froze. "Jonas!"

Two guns crashed simultaneously, drowning out her scream. Splinters flew from the door frame. Vin rocked backward and collapsed, a bright red blossom spreading on his snowy shirtfront.

A haze of blue smoke drifted toward the pressed-tin ceiling, and Fran blinked.

Jonas. Blood flowed from a cut over his eyebrow, but there he stood, living and breathing.

The bottle neck slipped from her fingers and shattered at her feet. She raised her hands to cover her face, giving in to sobs.

"Fran?"

She found herself cradled in his arms. He pulled her hands away from her eyes and peppered her face with kisses.

She clung to him, and when his lips found hers, her response rocked her to her core. The kiss bore no resemblance to the platonic pecks he'd placed on her cheek from time to time. Instead, it was a giving, a receiving, promises, and apologies. It took her breath away.

Breaking the kiss, he crushed her to himself and whispered against her hair, "He didn't hurt you, did he? I was so afraid I'd be too late."

She leaned back in his arms. Though his face was as familiar to her as her own, she couldn't stop herself from touching his features, drinking in the sight of him. She brushed her fingers near the cut on his brow. "What happened?"

He winced, though her touch was light. "He ambushed me in an alley. I wasn't paying enough attention. He must've thought he knocked me clean out. I was dazed, but I could hear him. He told me what he wanted to do to you." His voice thickened, and he held her tighter. "He didn't hurt you?"

She wrapped her arms around his neck and buried her face. "No, no, I'm fine." And she was, better than fine. "I'm so sorry, Jonas. I'm sorry for everything."

"Shhh, we'll talk about all that later. For now, just let me hold you." He stroked her back and rocked gently.

Fran absorbed his comfort, his presence, and his love, and in that moment, the last remnants of her childish fantasies slipped away. Here was everything she wanted and needed to be complete.

Miles dumped another dustpan full of broken glass into a crate and straightened. Sliding his timepiece out of his pocket, he checked it. Again. The darkroom doorknob rattled. At last.

Addie poked her head out of the doorway. "I'm almost done. You can come in now if you want."

He shrugged through the curtain, getting hung up on the shredded fabric for a moment.

"Sorry about that. I put the drape up over the door just in case someone accidentally opened it at the wrong time. It blocks out the light, but it's a nuisance, too, especially now that it's all ripped up." Addie raised the red shade on the lantern and blew out the flame. "You can leave the door open. The light from the studio skylight will be enough."

Two clear prints hung clipped to a line over the workbench. Strong chemical smells pricked his nose, and he resisted the urge to sneeze. "Everything went all right?"

"Yes. I made an extra, just in case." She poured liquid from a tray back into a bottle. Her slender hands moved with such grace, his heart pounded. A hank of hair slipped onto her cheek, and she used her wrist to push it back, but with little success.

He reached out and tucked the silky strands behind her ear. At his touch, she stilled. "Addie, we need to talk."

She nodded. "I'm sorry I didn't tell you before. About Cliff, about Vin." Her throat lurched, and she looked down. "I'll understand if you don't want to have anything to do with me now."

Wanting nothing more than to take her into his arms and tell her he wanted everything to do with her for the rest of her life, he forced himself to grip the edge of the counter.

"Addie, you don't owe me any explanations, but I sure owe you one. Vin Rutter told me a few weeks ago about you being Cliff's girl. He thought I already knew. You see, I've known Vin and Cliff for a long time."

Blinking, she shook her head, frowning.

"It's true. I'm sorry I never told you. I was. . .ashamed." He touched her arm.

She stiffened. "How is it that you knew Vin and Cliff?"

"My mother married Cliff's father when I was a kid. Cliff was my stepbrother." There, it was out. And despite all it would cost him, he was glad. Though painful, telling the truth did set him free of the weight of guilt and shame he'd carried for so long. "Addie?"

She was silent for what seemed a long time, a myriad of thoughts and emotions playing across her face. Finally, her shoulders sagged. "Was it the money?"

He frowned. "What?"

"Was it the stolen money you were after? Is that why you paid attention to me, pretended to care about me?" Her hands shook. "Is that why you kissed me?"

"No." He grabbed her upper arms and forced her to look at him. "I didn't know about the money until you told me about it at the jail this morning. That's the truth."

"The truth?" She reeled back. "How can I believe that? You're part of the Walker Gang. You, Vin, Cliff, you've done nothing but lie to me. I can't trust anyone, least of all you."

Though it was no more than he'd expected, her declaration was a dagger to his heart and hopes. "Addie, I can't tell you how sorry I am."

"Go away."

"Can't we talk about this?"

She sniffed, and he felt more of a heel than ever. "There's nothing to talk about. Just tell me this one thing."

"Anything."

"Are there any more of you?"

"Any more of who?"

"Walkers. Can I expect a visit from anyone else in the Walker clan intent on ruining my life?"

He knew she was lashing out because she'd been hurt, because she'd been buffeted beyond bearing, but her words hit like body blows. "For the record, I'm not a Walker. I'm a Carr. My father was an honorable man. My mother was tricked into marrying Cliff's father. She regretted it from the first, and finally took her own life to escape his cruelty. I left soon after she died, and I never went back. You aren't the only one to have your life blighted by the Walkers. I know you won't believe this, but I love you, Addie Reid, and it has nothing to do with Cliff, Vin, or any stolen money."

He knew he should stop, but the words poured out anyway. "Before you start hurling accusations and holding grudges, perhaps you should remember that you weren't exactly forthcoming about your relationship with Cliff either. A lot of trouble could've been averted if I'd known what Vin was after when he hit town."

Unable to stand the hurt in her eyes—knowing he'd caused it—he ducked through the curtain.

The brightness of the sun streaming through the skylight dazzled him, and he only had an impression of a large shadow in the doorway to the front room before a gun blast slammed into him and knocked him back into the darkroom.

Addie could hardly see for the tears pouring from her eyes. Miles's words had opened all the old wounds, tearing away half-healed scabs and making her heart bleed anew. Cliff once more reached from beyond the grave and stirred up a tornado of devastation in her life.

She jerked at the boom of a gunshot and knocked the bottle of carbonate of soda over onto the counter. A poof of white powder shot up. Before she could right it or comprehend where the shot had come from, Miles careened backward through the doorway, scrabbling at the curtain for a handhold, but falling heavily to the floor, a shred of fabric ripping away in his hand.

"What happened? What is it?" She knelt beside him, touching his shoulder, and her hand came away wet.

"Stay down." The words came out clipped as he rolled to his side and drew his gun.

"Is it Vin?"

"Shh."

"Carr? That you? The girl in there with you?"

She recognized the voice, but why he would be shooting a gun in her studio baffled her.

Miles struggled to his knees, checked his gun, and gently pushed her behind him. "Get under the workbench."

"You're bleeding."

Another shot ripped through the curtain and shattered

the lantern. Ruby glass rained down.

Miles shrugged off her hand and shoved her under the bench. He used the barrel of his pistol to edge the curtain aside, and the instant the cloth moved, a bullet ripped through it.

Addie screamed and ducked back, hitting her head on the underside of the workbench.

"What does he want? Why is he shooting at us?" Addie's skin rippled as if someone had trailed an icicle down her back.

"Hap Greeley! What are you doing?" Miles edged around until he was beside the door. His left arm hung limp, and blood soaked his sleeve, dripping down his fingers and splashing to the floor.

"I want that picture and the plate." The voice was Hap's, and yet it wasn't. He sounded...crazed, out of control. "Throw out your gun and come out of there."

Miles shook his head as if to clear it and blinked. "That's not going to happen."

"You will! You have to!" A shot whipped through the curtain and thudded into the back door—the back door she'd nailed shut and blocked with a filing cabinet.

Addie's fingernails bit into her palms. "Why does he want the picture? Is he crazed?"

Peeking out again, Miles returned fire for the first time. The acrid smell of burnt gunpowder filled the room. "He's tucked in behind that pillar. I can't get a good shot. I should've thrown that thing in the alley when I had the chance." Sweat beaded on his forehead, and his skin had a pallor that appalled her.

"Hap." He raised his voice, but his chest rose and fell sharply with the effort. "Is there something in that photograph that proves you killed Wally?" He swayed and pinched his eyelids shut.

Hap's answer was another bullet.

Addie inched toward Miles. "You have to let me stop that bleeding."

"Stay back. Someone will have heard the shooting. Help's coming if we can hold him off." He sent another barrage into the studio, the bullets thudding dully. "Need to reloa—" His gun slipped to the floor, and he sagged after it into a heap.

Addie grappled with his broad shoulders, trying to drag him out from in front of the door and under the workbench. She could barely budge him. The slickness of the blood pouring from his shoulder didn't help. She had to get him out of here, or he would bleed to death. "Hap."

"That you, girl?"

"Miles is shot. He needs a doctor." She tore at her sleeve, ripping it away from her shoulder. As quickly as she could, she folded it into a pad and pressed it against the wound. Red soaked it immediately.

"Throw out that plate and whatever pictures you made. No tricks, or you both die."

Her mind whirled, stalling, trying to find a way out of this, anything to hold on until help came. "Were you the one who broke up my studio? And my room at Mrs. Blanchard's?"

"You gave me no choice. I had to have that plate. Now throw it out here along with that gun."

Anger flared through her. How many times in her life

would she be a victim? Well, not this time. She pressed her knee against Miles's wound, knowing she must be hurting him but needing both hands to rip a strip off her petticoat. She wrapped his upper arm as best she could, praying it would be enough to stop the blood.

Her mind raced. "Hap, can't we talk about this?" She placed her hand on Miles's chest, reassured by the heartbeat throbbing there. If they got out of this alive, she was going to throw herself into his arms and beg him to forgive her. *Please, God, give me the chance.*

His gun lay on the floor near the curtain. She'd never shot a pistol in her life and wasn't certain she even knew how to load one properly. Miles had been reaching for more bullets on his belt when he keeled over. How many times had Cliff offered to teach her to shoot, and she'd laughed it off as unnecessary?

Well, if she couldn't use a gun, what could she use? She inched out from under the workbench and knelt, coming eye-to-eye with the bottles and pans of developing chemicals. Quietly, she lifted a glass tray off the workbench, careful not to slosh its contents over the side.

"No tricks now, girlie. Throw out the gun and come out of there."

She put as much fear into her voice as she could, allowing a sob that wasn't all pretense to escape from her throat. "Hap, I'm too scared. You hit Miles, and he passed out. He landed on his gun. It's underneath him somewhere, and I can't find it. Please. I can't get it for you."

He growled and snapped another shot through the

doorway. The bullet narrowly missed her, and she screamed, almost dropping the glass basin. Wood chips flew as the filing cabinet took another direct hit. "All right, I'm coming out. I have the plate with me."

She stepped over Miles's legs. *Please, God, don't let him die. Please help me. I need to tell him how sorry I am. I need to tell him I love him.*

Edging the curtain aside, she tried to still the tremors in her hands. The liquid sloshed and rippled.

Hap rose, pushing over the pillar. It crashed to the hardwood, and bits and chunks of plaster flew off and skittered across the floor. "Where is it?" White ringed his eyes behind his spectacles, and his hands jerked as if he was a puppet with no control over his movements.

"It's here. In the tray." Addie raised the shallow container.

"Bring it here." He motioned with his gun for her to come to him.

She sobbed, hoping she looked at least as frightened as she felt. "I can't. I'm scared. Come take it." She held the tray flat on her hands, keeping her fingers away from the edges.

Through the doorway into the reception room, she glimpsed a crouched figure at the front door. Another dark shadow passed behind the glass in the door.

Hap growled and started toward her. When he was only a step away, she flipped the tray, sending the contents cascading over him. He screamed and grabbed his red, sweaty face. Scrabbling at his eyes, he dropped the pistol, howling in pain and rage.

Addie leapt away from his staggering form, and the front

door crashed open. Bat and Deputy Pearson tackled Hap and wrestled him to the floor, and Addie's knees gave out. Jonas caught her before she hit the floor.

Chapter 20

Miles stirred, wishing whoever was pushing a red-hot poker through his arm would lay off.

"Easy, Miles. I'm almost finished."

Gentle hands restrained him when he tried to rub at the pain. He cracked one eyelid, which seemed to weigh a ton. "Doc?" A blurry face slowly came into focus. "Where am I?"

"You're at the jail." The sawbones knotted a bandage on Miles's left arm. "The bullet went clean through. You lost a lot of blood, but you'll be fine."

A gasp caught Miles's attention, but he couldn't see who was there. He made out the bars of one of the cells. He was on a cot inside. Someone in the next cell moaned.

"I'd better see to my other patient. You rest quiet, you hear?" The doctor rose, and Addie came into view.

She had tears on her cheeks. Had she been crying for him? She knelt beside the cot and took his hand. It felt pretty good. She brushed the hair back from his forehead, and that felt even better. Her eyes were so sad, he wanted to hug her, to kiss away the hurt, but he couldn't muster the energy.

Something clanked in the next cell. "Now Hap, stop that. I have to bathe your burns."

Miles jerked his thoughts away from Addie, and the events of the day came rushing back—getting shot, being pinned down in the darkroom, fighting to stay conscious. "Addie?" His dry throat rasped.

"Shhh. Rest now. We'll talk later." She lifted his head and held a glass to his lips. "Doc said you'd be thirsty and tired, and that you're not to worry about anything."

Cool water. The best he'd ever tasted. His head touched the pillow again. There was so much he needed to say to her. So much he needed to know. But darkness crowded around the edges of his vision, and he knew he was going to succumb again.

"Stay. Stay with me, Addie." He gripped her hand like a little child.

She leaned close and brushed a kiss on his forehead. "Forever, Miles, if you'll let me."

When next Miles woke, it was nighttime. His shoulder felt like a mountain lion had been chewing on it, and something tugged against his hand when he tried to move. He opened his eyes and looked down.

Addie sat on the floor beside his cot, asleep with her head resting on their clasped hands. Contentment like he'd never known filled him, and he knew he must be grinning like a simpleton. She had stayed, and if he hadn't been dreaming a while ago, she had promised forever. With his right hand he reached across and touched her glossy brown hair.

She stirred, raising her head and locking clouded blue eyes with his. Her cheeks were flushed, and her hair had come out of its braid to lie in ripples on her shoulders. The sight of her all sleep tousled made his heart race.

She seemed to become aware in an instant, blinking, and scrambling to her knees. "You're awake."

Since he was looking right at her, he didn't see the need to confirm her statement. Though moving awoke new pain under the bandages, he lifted their locked fingers.

Her sleep-flush deepened to a rosy glow. "Miles—" She broke off, confusion flashing in her eyes.

"Later, Addie. We'll sort all of that out later. Tell me what happened after I passed out."

The cell door clanged. "I'll tell you what happened." Deputy Pearson edged inside. "Your ladylove here pitched a pan full of lye water into Hap Greeley's face." Pearson carried a cloth-covered tray. "Doc said for you to wake up and eat something. Said you needed to get your strength back." He used his boot to drag a chair close. "Addie, how's about you sit there and spoon some of this stuff into him."

A moan ripped through the air, and Miles turned his head. Cuffed to the bars in the adjacent cell, a man he assumed must be Hap Greeley lay on a cot, his face swathed in wet bandages.

Jonas sat beside him. He soaked another cloth and placed it over Hap's eyes.

"Here, let me help you sit up." Addie leaned over him. He inhaled her perfume as he struggled upright—difficult considering Doc had used enough bandages on his upper arm for a hospital.

"How does that feel? Doc said if you got dizzy to stay lying down."

The room did wobble for a minute, and his arm throbbed, but he refused to give in to it. "I feel like a rag doll with half the stuffing drained out, but I'll be fine. I have a powerful thirst though."

Addie helped him drink and insisted on feeding him, though he felt like a fool. Addie wouldn't quite meet his eyes and kept herself busy with trays and napkins.

He wanted to grab the spoon and hurl it away so he could kiss her senseless and somehow convince her they were meant to be together, that their pasts didn't matter, only their future. He wanted her promise that she'd meant forever.

Miles forced himself to be patient. By the time he'd finished the soup, strength began to return to his limbs, and the grogginess in his head lifted.

Bat came into the jail and entered Hap's cell. "Greeley, it's time to answer some questions."

Miles started to swing his legs to the floor, but Addie stopped him by putting her hands on his chest and pressing him into the pillows. "You're supposed to rest."

He captured her fingers with his right hand. "I feel fine." It wasn't strictly true, but he wasn't going to let a little pain stop him. "I won't go far. I need to hear what Hap has to say."

Miles edged down the cot until only the bars separated him from Hap. Bat took Jonas's place near Hap's head, and Jonas leaned against the wall in Hap's cell and opened up his notebook.

"What happened to your head?" Miles noticed the swollen and bruised cut on Jonas's forehead for the first time.

"Had a little run-in with Vin Rutter." Jonas shrugged.

"Don't worry. He won't be bothering anyone ever again. I'll tell you about it later."

Addie scooted her chair closer to Miles, and he reached over to hold her hand.

Bat leaned over the prisoner. "Hap, Doc says you can talk just fine, so go ahead. What happened?" He unlocked the cuff from Hap's wrist, freeing him from the bars.

A moan filled the air, and Hap dragged the wet bandages off his face. Red welts and blisters covered his skin.

Addie's breath hitched in her throat, and Miles squeezed her fingers.

"I killed him. I killed Wally." Hap's red, weeping eyes blinked, but his voice was strong and controlled, not like the demanding, demented voice from the studio. "He was going to dissolve the partnership."

"Why?"

"My gambling. He said he couldn't trust me anymore, not after I took some money out of the till to gamble."

"Take us through everything that happened on the Fourth."

With a sigh, Hap began. "I was over at the fort for a party at the quartermaster's. Gambling, drinking. There was a lawyer there, too. He said Wally had come to see him the day before about breaking up the business. I was so mad I hopped right on my horse and headed back to town to confront Wally and talk him out of it." He shuddered, and Bat handed him another wet cloth, which he pressed to his cheek. "When I hit town, there was some kind of ruckus going on at the livery, so I went around back of the store and tied my horse up. I let myself in, and Wally was there, counting money, just like I figured he would be."

Jonas's pencil scratched as he recorded every word. Miles pictured Wally alive as he'd last seen him, counting out stacks of bills. Then his mind drifted to those smoke-filled moments in the livery when he nearly got himself trampled to death.

Hap's voice brought him back. "We argued—I know we fought all the time, but this time was different. Wally wouldn't budge. Said he'd had enough of working like a dog to keep me in gambling chips, and that the next day, he was going to file the papers. I was so upset I hardly knew what I was doing. I don't know exactly what happened, but all of a sudden, I was standing over Wally with a can in my hand, and he was on the floor dead. I panicked. I never meant to kill him." He moaned again, pressing the cloth into his face. "It was an accident. I just wanted to make him listen to me."

Bat's eyes glittered in the lantern light. "Then what did you do?"

Hap sucked in a big breath. "I tried to make it look like a robbery. I unlocked the front door, and I took the money off the counter. Wally had most of it bagged up to take to the bank. I ducked out the back and hid just outside of town until it got dark. I figured I'd stroll into town and pretend to be shocked when I heard the news."

"Which you did."

"That's right. I went to the store, and there were deputies there, and it wasn't hard to act like I was upset. I *was* upset. Like I said, I didn't mean to kill him. Just being in the store made me want to throw up." Tears tracked down his ravaged face. Though he was upset, he seemed to be in his right mind. Did madness come and go? Miles tucked that question away to ask the doctor sometime.

"What about the picture? Why attack Miss Reid and Deputy Carr?"

"I thought I'd gotten away with it until I saw that picture she took. I knew I had to destroy the photograph and the plate, or eventually, someone might put me there at the time of the murder. I pretended to get upset when Carr showed me the picture, and I tipped a bunch of papers off the desk. In the mess, I shoved the picture into my pocket."

Miles grimaced. So that's where the first photograph had gone.

"I figured Miss Reid would have the plate at her studio."

Addie's hand tightened on Miles's shoulder. "How did you get inside? The lock wasn't broken."

He shrugged. "Skeleton key. Wally changed locks on me once, trying to keep me out of the store when he wasn't there, so I ordered a skeleton key a few months ago. I used it to get into your place."

"And you ransacked my studio."

"I couldn't find the right plate. There were hundreds of glass slides and photographs."

Addie's hand shook. "So you ruined everything you could find?"

Hap's shoulders hunched. "I was mad. And scared. It was like I couldn't stop myself once I started breaking things."

"What about my room at the boardinghouse?"

He scowled and winced. "I was afraid that I'd missed the plate somehow at your place. What if you kept it in your room? When the old woman left, I went in and searched, but I couldn't find it. And the anger took over. I don't remember what all I did to your room. It was like I was out of my head."

Out of his head was right.

The door opened and Fran slipped inside the jail. Miles's jaw dropped when she made a beeline for Jonas in the cell doorway. Jonas grinned at Miles and put his arm around Fran, who didn't seem to mind in the least. Something drastic had happened there, and Jonas jerked his chin, a promise to divulge all later.

Fran tugged something from her pocket. "Here they are. I found them hanging in the darkroom and brought them both." She turned the papers to reveal two copies of the photograph of Wally sprawled on the mercantile floor. "And I noticed right away why Hap would want the picture destroyed. I wish you'd shown me the photograph sooner. It would've saved us a lot of trouble."

Hap groaned and sank back onto the bunk.

"What is it?" Bat reached for one of the pictures.

"Look beside the register, just at the edge of the photograph." Fran ducked out of Jonas's arm and pointed over Bat's shoulder. "Right there."

"A pair of glasses?"

She nodded. "Hap's glasses. He never went anywhere without them, but he was always taking them off and rubbing them or shoving them up on his forehead. He often took them off when he fought with Wally. Like a habit, you know?"

Bat tugged at his mustache, studying the picture.

"Was that it, Hap? The glasses?"

"Yes."

Jonas shook his head. "But when Addie and I met you at the mercantile, you were wearing your glasses. I remember because you kept taking them off to wipe your eyes."

Miles nodded. "That's right. You had them when you came to the jail."

"The minute I got out of town to hide, I realized I'd left the glasses behind. I knew I'd have to get them back or someone would be bound to notice. When I snuck back into town, I went right to the mercantile. There were two deputies in there, so I had to act shocked. The place was a mess, and someone had knocked the glasses onto the floor behind the counter. The deputies didn't even notice when I picked them up and pretended to take them out of my pocket before I put them on. I was caterwauling and carrying on, and they were only too glad when I left."

Bat scowled. Miles wouldn't want to be either of those two deputies when the boss caught up with them.

Fran shook her head and returned to Jonas's side.

"I thought everything was fine," Hap continued. "When no new picture showed up, I figured I must've destroyed the right plate after all when I hit the studio. Then *she*"— he pointed at Addie—"chimes in about how she had the plate with her the whole time."

Addie shuddered and stood up, as if she couldn't bear to be near him anymore. Miles levered himself up and put his good arm around her waist.

Bat shook his head. "So you went to the studio to kill them and get the plate once and for all?"

Hap nodded.

"How were you going to cover up killing them?"

"I don't know!" His hands fisted on his thighs. "I wasn't thinking. I just had to get that plate!"

Bat stood. "That's enough for now. Hap, you're under arrest for the murder of Wally Price, the attempted murders of Miles Carr and Addie Reid, the destruction of property, and about half a dozen other things."

Miles guided Addie out of the cell toward Bat's desk, and Jonas and Fran followed. He leaned against the desk, careful to keep hold of Addie's hand and not to tip over any stacks of paper still cluttering Bat's workspace.

Jonas ripped out the notebook pages and placed them into a labeled file folder, along with the two copies of the photograph. "Not going to lose anything related to this case." He tucked the folder into a cabinet and took Fran's hand.

"You two look like you have a lot to tell us." Miles raised an eyebrow in Jonas's direction.

Jonas grinned, and Fran blushed. "Let's just say things worked out all right in the end." He raised Fran's hand and brushed a kiss across her knuckles. "We're going to be getting married in a couple of weeks and moving out to my new ranch." Without another word, they walked outside together.

Addie sighed. "It sure took them long enough."

Bat locked the cell door and tossed the keys onto his desk. "Carr, why don't you get some air? Take Addie home. With Hap in jail, no reason why she won't be safe over at

Mrs. Blanchard's place. At least for the time being until you two sort some other arrangement out." His eyes twinkled as he took in their clasped hands.

Glad for the excuse to get her alone, Miles didn't hesitate.

Addie breathed in the cool night air, still unable to fathom all that had happened. It would take a long time to sort through all Hap had said and put all the pieces together. Some things they might never know. "Jonas killed Vin. Did you know that?"

Miles stilled. "Did he?"

"Jonas followed Vin to his hotel, and Vin bashed Jonas on the head and left him for dead. Then Vin tried to attack Fran. Jonas got there in time, but he had to shoot Vin. Over at the mercantile."

"I always figured he'd wind up getting killed by some lawman somewhere."

"I guess coming that close to losing Jonas for good made Fran see things clearer." Standing on the jail porch, she soaked in the touch of Miles's hand in hers. "Are you sure you shouldn't be resting? You lost a lot of blood. Does your arm hurt?"

He led her down the steps and up the street. "I'm fine. Not up to running any races, but I can see my girl home."

Addie stopped.

His girl.

They walked in silence the two blocks to her boarding-house, and Miles drew her into the deeper shadows of the cottonwood tree beside the house.

"Miles, about what I said to you in the studio. . ."

He turned to her and put his fingers to her lips. "Shh. I don't want to hear an apology. We both said things we shouldn't have because we were hurt and scared and churned up."

She blinked, caught sideways by the warmth and forgiveness in his voice. His hand dropped away, and she felt the loss of his touch on her lips. "Everything happened so fast, I was angry and confused. I thought you were only after the stolen money, that everything between us had been a lie. I'd already been told so many lies. And then you were shot, and I thought you might die. I was afraid I'd never get the chance to tell you how sorry I was."

He shook his head. "No, I told you, no apologies. This is one time when I think we should just let the past go. Both of us have let things in the past determine who we are and what we do. We can't change the past, but there's no sense in chaining ourselves to it and letting it drag us around." His arm slipped around her waist, and he pulled her close. "I love you, Addie Reid, and I've been waiting a long time for you to say you love me, too."

Careful of his wound, she eased her arms around his neck. Happiness sang in her veins, and she tunneled her fingers into his hair, drawing him close. In a whisper, just loud enough to be heard over the tinkling sigh of the night breeze in the leaves overhead, she gave him the words he needed to say. "I love you, too, Miles. Forever."

Chapter 21

"How do you like living on a ranch?" Addie dug through excelsior to find another bottle. She lifted the jar, studied it in the sunshine, and placed it on the darkroom shelf.

Fran, her hair tied back with a kerchief, put her hands on her hips. "It's wonderful. But you know what? I'd live in a rabbit hole as long as Jonas was there."

"You talking about me?" Jonas stuck his head into the darkroom. "Wife, what are you doing standing around while we labor away moving all these boxes?"

"Standing around? I'll have you know. . ." Fran started after her husband of two weeks, swatting him with the cloth in her hand, sending clouds of dust into the air.

Jonas beat a hasty, laughing retreat.

Addie shook her head and went back to arranging supplies. She smiled when Miles came into the darkroom and slipped his arms around her waist. She leaned back, reveling in his strength. "Did you get everything from the depot?"

He nuzzled her neck. "Mmmhmm."

"Are those two still squabbling out there?"

"Nope."

"What are they doing?"

He pressed a kiss under her earlobe. "Pretty much the same thing we're doing."

Addie laughed. "Deputy Carr, don't you have work to do? We have to get everything unloaded and set up before the grand opening tomorrow. I've got customers lined up."

His arms dropped away. "You're a tough taskmistress, Mrs. Carr. I thought new brides were supposed to like billing and cooing with their husbands." He tilted his head, giving her a reproachful, forlorn look. "Married for a week, and she's already tired of me."

She grinned, leaned into him for a quick, dusty kiss, and gave him a playful push. "Someone around here has to keep us on task. I can't count on those two." She waved to the studio where Fran's laugh reached them. "And you're just as bad, trying to distract me when I have so much work to do."

Taking her hand, he tugged her out of the room. "Come see what all we brought."

A half hour later, a shining new Chevalier stood on glossy tripod legs in the center of the studio. Miles and Jonas dragged packing material and crating out to the alley, and Fran pirouetted with a new parasol from the replenished prop box.

Tears pricked Addie's eyes. God had been so good to her. To all of them, but especially to her. The court had ordered Hap to make restitution for all the damages, as well as compensating Addie for her distress and all the business she had lost as a result of his actions. She'd immediately paid off the mortgage—much to Archie Poulter's and Heber Donaldson's chagrin—and set about ordering new equipment with the money.

Fran studied her reflection, dragged the kerchief off her

hair, and shrugged at her disheveled appearance. "You never told me what Poulter said when you went in to pay off the mortgage."

Addie grinned. "He looked like he'd swallowed a hedgehog and it got stuck halfway down." The satisfaction of counting the bills and coins out on his desk down to the last copper penny had stayed with her for days.

"You know," Fran said, "my first thought when I saw the studio that night was that Donaldson must've done it. He was so mad at you for getting the Arden contract, and then everyone on opening night was buzzing about your fabulous photographs." Fran snapped the parasol shut. "I thought he destroyed this place out of revenge."

"I thought about him, too, but it didn't make sense. Why destroy the equipment you had already put a bid in to buy? He was sure I wouldn't get the note paid off, and when I didn't, he would get everything for a fraction of the cost. He and Poulter had it all worked out. He wouldn't have gained anything by smashing up the studio."

"I suppose. He won't be any happier now that you're going to be up and running again. Still, there isn't much he can do about it, not with all the publicity you've had over Hap's agreeing to plead guilty to avoid a hanging. You've got them lining up in the street to get their pictures taken here now."

Addie went to the desk and patted her appointment ledger. She had so many sittings scheduled she would be hard pressed to keep up with everything.

Miles came back with Jonas. "That's the last of it. Except for this stupid thing." Miles planted his hands on his hips and nudged the broken plaster pillar with his boot. "Since Jonas is here, he can help me haul it outside. It's awkward to carry very far by yourself."

"You don't have to tell me." Addie nudged the pillar with her toe. "I just scoot it around when I need it."

Miles and Jonas each got on an end and hoisted it horizontally between them. A chunk of plaster broke off and crashed to the floor, followed by a metallic *clink*. The men stopped. A bright gold coin rolled across the floor, traveled in a lazy circle, and wobbled to a stop.

Addie blinked.

"Is that—?"

"Did you drop—?"

"Addie?"

Miles motioned for Jonas to put his end down. When the pillar stood upright again, he poked his finger into one of the bullet holes he'd made when shooting it out with Hap. Fran bent to pick up the coin, and Jonas took it from her, studying it in the bright August sunshine pouring through the skylight.

"Gimme a hammer." Miles held out his hand, trying to peer into the hole. Addie handed him the hammer they'd used to open crates and gasped when he smashed it into the plaster. Wrenching it out, he hit the column again. Dust exploded and bits of wire and plaster shot across the floor. With one more blow, he caved in the whole side.

A fistful of gold coins trickled out. When the flow stopped, Miles reached into the hole and withdrew a paperbound bundle of banknotes, then another, and another.

He grinned. "I'd say that was about thirty thousand dollars' worth, wouldn't you?"

Addie gaped. "Vin was right. I did have the money." A cloud of fear encroached on her happiness. "I didn't know it was there, I swear."

Miles kicked coins in all directions getting to her. He grabbed her by the arms and shook her. "Adeline Reid Carr, don't think for a minute anyone here suspects you. This is Cliff's doing, not yours."

She searched his face, seeing only trust and assurance there. . .and love. Lots of love. Nodding, she moistened her lips. "The pillar. Of course. Cliff made it for me. I should've known." She shook her head at her blindness. "Where is my camera case? The Scovill?"

Fran found it hanging by its strap in the darkroom. "Here it is."

Addie unlatched the compartment in the bottom and withdrew the photo album. Swallowing hard, she gripped the book. "I meant to throw this away, but with the trial and the wedding and everything, I forgot. I want you to know, this means nothing to me, and I am going to destroy it. I kept it for a reason, but that reason no longer exists."

Miles took the book, scowling when he saw the first portrait. He flipped through the pages. "These are all of Cliff."

"I kept them to remind me how foolish I had been. But I don't need them anymore. Everything Cliff was means nothing to me now because when true love comes, lies fall away." She held Miles's gaze.

He nodded and smiled.

She took the book and flipped to the last few portraits. "This is what I wanted you to see though. In all the later pictures, Cliff is leaning on that pedestal. After he made it, he insisted that it be in every portrait I took of him. How he must've laughed, posing with his stolen money, and all the while I had no idea."

Miles snapped the album closed. "He was a fool."

"His greed and arrogance cost him his life."

"That, too, but his biggest folly was in having you and letting you get away." He threw the photo album into the trash bin and reached for Addie. "I'd never let you get away from me."

Epilogue

The front bell chimed, and Addie wiped her hands on her apron and headed to the front of the studio.

Miles entered the reception area, shaking raindrops from his hat. He grinned and tossed her the newspaper. "Take a look at this."

She read the headline aloud. "Mystery solved. Missing money recovered." The article, two columns wide, outlined the returning of the railroad's property and hailed her as a heroine.

"How do you like that?" He read over her shoulder. "They even spelled your name right. And guess what? There's a reward."

"What?"

"The railroad is sending you a 10 percent reward for recovering their stolen loot. Just got the wire today." He patted his pocket. "Can't tell you how many people shook my hand and stopped to congratulate me on the way over here."

She shook her head. The entire town now knew the story, and to her surprise, no one held it against her that she'd been linked with Cliff Walker. The returning of the stolen property convinced everyone that she had nothing to do with the robberies. The fear that had held her hostage for such a long time seemed so puny and silly now, she wondered why she'd ever given it so much power.

Miles shrugged out of his coat and hung it and his hat on the rack. "Say, that turned out great." He moved to stand in front of the new photograph hanging on the wall.

Their wedding portrait. Addie hadn't wanted the typical stiff pose of the man seated and the wife standing behind with her hand on his shoulder. Instead, with a little help from Fran, they'd managed a portrait where Addie stood before Miles with his arms around her. She leaned back against his chest, and both of them appeared to be looking into the distance toward their future.

Free of the past, with their entire lives together before them.

Picture perfect.

A BRIDE'S SWEET SURPRISE IN SAUERS, INDIANA

by Ramona K. Cecil

Dedication

To my uncle, Wendell Lee Herekamp, whose stories of our family's history inspired *A Bride's Sweet Surprise in Sauers, Indiana*, and whose vast knowledge of the history of Sauers and the congregation of St. John's Lutheran Church was an invaluable resource in the writing of this book.

Special thanks to Melba Darlage and Melba Hoevener for their help with local insights, Bob and Tina Evans for their German translation of *A History of St. John's Parish*, and Rosalie Haines for her expert German language help.

Chapter 1

Have you lost your senses? My *Vater* will shoot you!" Fear for the young man standing before her bubbled up in Regina Seitz's chest.

A deep laugh rumbled from Eli Tanner, but the cacophony of his father's horse-powered gristmill behind them quickly swallowed the sound. The nonchalant grin stretching across his handsome face told her he did not share her concern. "Your pa is a reasonable man. He may run me off his farm and give me a tongue-lashing in German, but I doubt he would shoot me for taking you to a box supper at Dudleytown."

"He might if you take me without his consent and without a chaperone." With all her heart, Regina wished her words were not true. In her seventeen years, she couldn't remember a longer, colder winter than the one their little farming community had just endured. Now that the harsh weather had finally given way to a warm and glorious spring and with Lent and Easter behind them, she looked forward to occasions like this Saturday's gathering at the Dudleytown School to socialize with friends her age. And of all the boys in the county, she could think of no other she would rather have squire her to the event than Eli. But Eli hadn't seen the thundercloud form on Papa's face last September after her sister Elsie's marriage to her non-German husband, William. Eli hadn't heard Papa's booming voice ring like a death knell, proclaiming that he would never again sanction the marriage of a daughter to a non-German.

Eli took Regina's hands in his, sending a thrill through her. He drew her away from her pony cart and into a slice of shade closer to the mill's weathered gray walls. She still could hardly believe she had caught the eye of Eli Tanner. And she probably would not have if his previous sweetheart hadn't eloped with a young farmer from Driftwood— something she would never understand. For with his broad shoulders, thick shock of auburn hair, and green eyes that almost matched the spring's new growth all around them, the miller's son was, in Regina's estimation, the handsomest boy in all of Jackson County.

But he wasn't German, or even of German descent. And there lay the problem.

"I want to court you, Regina." At the passionate tone of Eli's voice, Regina's heart throbbed painfully. "Sooner or later, your pa must be told."

"He will not consent to it." Regina shook her head and hung it in despair. Tears welled in her eyes at the unjustness of it. "Papa is determined to have a German farmer for a son-in-law. Someone he can hand the farm down to." A cool breeze swept through their shady nook, and she shivered. But Eli's strong fingers wrapped warmly around hers, sending heat radiating up her arms and chasing the chill away.

Eli shrugged his shoulders. "Your pa will get over it. You said he was unhappy at first when your sister Sophie married that wheelwright and moved to Jennings County and again last fall when Elsie married the dry goods merchant from over in Washington County. But he never shot them." Chuckling, he bent and plucked a handful of blue violets from a lush patch of sweetgrass. "In fact, if memory serves," he said as he rose and tucked a couple of the flowers behind Regina's ear, his face so close to hers that his warm breath stirred her hair, "he threw both your sisters rip-roarin' weddings. He accepted their choices for husbands, so he should at least let me take you to a box social."

Regina hated the bitterness welling up inside her. She loved her sisters and was glad for their happiness. But it seemed so unfair that she should be punished because they hadn't chosen German farmers for husbands. She nodded, wanting to believe Eli. "It is true. Papa did give in to Sophie and Elsie. But I am his last chance to get a German son-in-law. I do not think he will give in so easily this time."

"Maybe not easily, but he will give in. You are his youngest and prettiest daughter." Grinning, Eli touched his finger to the end of her nose. "But unless he changes his mind by this Saturday, it will not help us for the box supper. So you must tell your folks that you are going with one of the girls you know, like Anna Rieckers or Louisa Stuckwisch."

Regina gasped. "Lie to Papa and Mama? You want me to break *Gott*'s commandments? I could never! My parents trust me. I would never go behind their backs. And even if I were foolish enough to try, someone would be sure to tell them I was there with you. Then Papa would never agree to let you court me and would probably lock me in the house until I am thirty!"

Eli's green eyes flashed, and for an instant a scowl furrowed his brow. But the stormy look passed as quickly as the clouds scooting across the midday sky, and his face brightened again. The lines of his features softened as he gazed at her. "You should always wear violets in your hair. They look good against your light hair and make your eyes look even bluer."

Regina's anger at his suggestion that she deceive her parents evaporated as she basked in his compliment.

"Eli!" Sam Tanner's stern voice barked from the mill door. "You got those bags of flour loaded?"

"Comin', Pa!" Eli called while keeping his gaze fixed firmly on Regina. He thrust the fistful of violets into her hand. "Just think about it, Regina. I'll be waitin' behind your barn at ten o'clock Saturday morning if you change your mind." He started toward the mill then turned back to her. "But I won't wait long."

Regina watched his broad back as he strode toward the mill's door. Something in the tone of his voice when he uttered those last words made her wonder if he intended a larger meaning than just the social event Saturday. She had no doubt Eli would not wait for her forever. And despite his optimism that Papa would change his mind, she doubted it. Not without strong convincing.

With a heavy heart, she climbed to the seat of the pony cart, flicked the reins down on the black and white mottled hindquarters of the little gypsy pony, and headed for home. Ever since January, when Eli began showing interest in Regina, she'd spent countless sleepless nights trying to think of ways to convince Papa to give up his obsession about marrying her off to a German farmer. But aside from simply rejecting every prospective suitor her parents suggested, Regina had yet to come up with any argument to dissuade Papa from his quest. And now with the coming of spring and Eli eager to declare his intentions, she could see her chances for happiness slipping away. On the bright side, Papa had at least stopped trying to push her toward every unmarried German farmer in the county between the ages of eighteen and fifty. But she couldn't believe he had given up entirely. He would likely begin again with his matchmaking when a new crop of German immigrants arrived.

That thought reminded her of the letter she'd picked up earlier at the schoolhouse where the community's mail was delivered. In her excitement to see Eli, she'd nearly forgotten about it. In the nearly eighteen years since her family had arrived in America, Papa and Mama had made it their life's mission to assist in the emigration of others from Venne, their old village in the kingdom of Hanover. So although it was common for Papa to receive letters from German families planning to immigrate to Sauers, he would doubtless be cross if she were to misplace or lose such a missive.

As the pony cart bounced along the rutted road to her family's farm, she gazed out over the countryside. Rolling fields of newly turned sod filled the April air with the earthy scent of spring, while milk cows grazed in verdant pastures spread over the landscape like acres of green velvet. She couldn't blame anyone for wanting to leave the cramped farms of Hanover for the abundance of fertile land here in Jackson County, Indiana.

She glanced down at the letter nestled in the basket on the seat beside her. It was postmarked Baltimore, Maryland, a regular port for immigrant ships from Bremen, Hanover. Picking it up, she examined the letter more closely. Scrawled in the top left-hand corner of the envelope was the name Georg Rothhaus. It sounded vaguely familiar. Most likely, Papa had mentioned the name in passing as a recent correspondent.

As she turned into the lane that led up to their two-story, hewn-log house, she stuffed the letter into her skirt pocket. Dismissing the letter, her mind raced. How might she best broach the subjects of the box supper and Eli to Mama and Papa?

Inside, her *Holzschuhe* clomped on the puncheon floor of the washroom that ran the length of the rear of the house.

"Is that you, *Tochter*?" Mama called from the kitchen a few steps away.

"*Ja*," Regina called back as she slipped off her wooden shoes. She smiled. Since Sophie and Elsie had married, Mama no longer had to specify *which* daughter.

The smell of simmering sausages and onions wafted through the kitchen doorway, making Regina's mouth water. Papa would be in soon for the midday meal. She padded into the kitchen in her stocking feet, praying God would give her the words to soften her parents' hearts toward Eli.

Mama glanced over her shoulder from her spot in front of the straddle-legged wood-box stove. "Did you get the flour?" With the back of her hand, Mama brushed from her face a few wisps of chestnut-colored hair that had pulled loose from the braids pinned to the top of her head. Regina had often wished that like Sophie and Elsie, she had inherited Mama's lovely brown hair instead of the pale locks more closely resembling Papa's.

"Ja, Mama. Two bags, like you asked. They are too heavy for me to lift, so I left them in the cart."

Regina heard the back door close then the sound of heavy steps on the washroom floor. Papa had come in for dinner. This was the perfect opportunity to present Eli in a good light. "Mr. Tanner's son, Eli, put the bags of flour in the cart for me, Mama. Wasn't that nice of him?"

Mama stopped pushing the meat and onions around in the skillet with a wooden spoon and grinned. "Ja, but that is his job, no?"

"Well, yes. I suppose." Regina's voice wilted. This was not going as well as she'd hoped.

"Do you mean these bags of flour?"

Regina turned to see Papa standing in the kitchen doorway, sock footed with a bag of flour on each of his broad shoulders.

He carried them to the pantry and plopped them on the floor, sending up plumes of pale dust. When he turned back to Regina and her mother, his smile had left, and his expression became stern. He rubbed the blond stubble along his jawline. "Ja, Regina, your *Mutti* is right. If Tanner or his *Sohn* had made you carry such heavy bags of flour, I would not be pleased. I would have to have words with them for sure."

With Papa getting his hackles up and talking of being displeased with the Tanners, Regina decided this might not be the best time to press her case about Eli. Thinking how she might change the subject, she remembered the letter.

She pulled the envelope from her skirt pocket and held it out to him. "Look, Papa, a letter came for you."

A look of anticipation came over Papa's broad face as he took the letter from her fingers. With impatient movements, he tore open the envelope. As he perused the pages, a smile appeared on his face and gradually grew wider until his wheat-colored whiskers bristled.

"Gott sei Dank!" His pale blue eyes glistened. Rushing to Mama, he hugged her and kissed her on the cheek. "Catharine, *meine Liebe.*" Then, turning to Regina, he hugged her so hard she could scarcely breathe, lifting her feet clear off the floor. Setting her back down, he kissed her on the forehead as if she were five years old. "Meine Regina. *Mein liebes Mädchen.*"

Stunned, Regina stood blinking at her usually undemonstrative father. Though she didn't know anyone with a deeper, more abiding faith in God, she couldn't remember hearing him actually shout out praises to the Lord. And he certainly wasn't one to openly show affection.

"Ernst, what has come over you?" Mama's brown eyes had grown to the size of buckeyes.

Still beaming, Papa gazed at the pages in his hand as if they were something extraordinary. "*Mutter*, you must prepare the house. We will be having very important guests soon."

"Who could be so important?" Mama gave a little chuckle and peered around Papa's shoulder at the missive. "Are we to host President Taylor or Governor Dunning?"

Papa shook his head. "*Nein.* Even more *wunderbar.*" Now he looked directly at Regina, a tender look bursting with fatherly affection. "Georg Rothhaus is coming and bringing his son Diedrich. Our Regina's intended."

Chapter 2

Diedrich faced the stagecoach, dread and excitement warring in his stomach. Shouldering the little trunk that held all of his and his father's worldly goods, he took a resolute step off the inn's porch.

He could hardly believe that their long journey was about to come to an end. But what end? His stomach churned, threatening to reject the fine breakfast the innkeeper had served them less than a half hour ago. According to the innkeeper, they were within a couple hours' drive of the little farming community of Sauers and Diedrich's prospective bride.

A firm hand clapped him on the shoulder. "Today we shall reach our new home, Sohn." Father's confident voice at his side did little to still the tumult raging inside Diedrich. Father was not the one facing matrimony to a girl he'd never met.

The thought made Diedrich want to turn around and go back into the inn. But he could not retrace the thousands of miles that lay between this Jackson County, Indiana, and his old home in Venne, Hanover. And even if he could, he'd only be returning to the same bleak choices that had prompted him to agree to the deal Father had made with Ernst Seitz—conscription into the army or sharing the meager acres of farmland that barely supported his brothers and their families.

Father's hand on Diedrich's back urged him toward the waiting stagecoach. Willing his feet to obey, Diedrich stepped toward the conveyance as if to the gallows. The gathering canopy of storm clouds above them seemed an ominous sign. In an attempt to quell the sick feeling roiling in his stomach, he reminded himself of his own secret scheme to avoid the matrimonial shackles *Fräulein* Seitz waited to clap on him.

In their two and a half months aboard the bark *Franziska*, Diedrich had spent many hours alone in his stinking, cramped bunk. Day and night the ship had pitched and rolled over the Atlantic, keeping Diedrich's head swimming and his stomach empty. During those agonizing hours, it wasn't thoughts of a bride he'd never met that had given him reason to endure the hardships, but thoughts of the California goldfields and the riches waiting there for him. Gold nuggets, the newspapers said, just lay on the ground waiting for anyone with an industrious nature and an appetite for adventure to claim their treasure and realize riches beyond their wildest imaginings. But Diedrich couldn't get to the gold in California without first getting to America. And it was Ernst Seitz's generous offer to pay Diedrich's and Father's passage in exchange for Diedrich marrying *Herr* Seitz's youngest daughter that had gotten them to America.

In all his twenty-one years, Diedrich had never prayed longer or more earnestly than he had during that sea voyage. As the apostle Paul had charged in his first letter to the Thessalonians, Diedrich had virtually prayed without ceasing. And many of his prayers were petitions for God to somehow release him from the bargain Father and Herr Seitz had struck without breaking the girl's heart or dishonoring Father.

Guilt smote his conscience. No virtue was more sacred to Father than honor. And Father was an honorable man. How many times had Diedrich heard his father say, "A man's word is his bond"? Scheming behind Father's back to figure a way to break the word bond he had made with their benefactor didn't sit well. But at the same time, Diedrich couldn't imagine God would bless the union of two people who had no love for each other.

The wind whipped up, snatching at the short bill of his wool cap and sending a shiver through him. He handed the trunk up to the driver to secure to the top of the coach while Father practiced his English, carrying on a halting conversation with their fellow travelers—a middle-aged couple and a dapperly dressed gentleman. Barbs of bright lightning lit up the pewter sky, followed by a deafening clap of thunder. All five travelers hurried to board in advance of the storm. They'd scarcely settled themselves in the coach when the heavens opened, pelting the conveyance with raindrops that quickly became a buffeting deluge.

Sitting next to the door and facing his father, Diedrich settled back against the seat. The next instant a whip cracked, the driver hollered a hearty "Heyaa!" and the coach jerked to a roll. The other passengers began to talk in English. Diedrich understood only an occasional word, but the conversation seemed mostly centered on the weather. The woman, especially, looked worried, and Diedrich shared her concern. Herr Seitz had written that the roads were particularly bad in the springtime and often impassable.

Father leaned forward and tapped Diedrich on the knee. A knowing grin began a slow march across his whiskered face. "Why so glum, mein Sohn? You look as if you are going to the executioner instead of into the embrace of a lovely young bride."

Diedrich tried to return Father's smile but couldn't sustain it.

Father's expression turned somber. "It was to save you from conscription that we came, remember? Who knows if King Ernest can keep Hanover out of the revolution." He shook his head. "I would not have you sacrificed in the ridiculous war with Denmark." Moisture appeared in Father's gray eyes, and Diedrich hoped their fellow travelers didn't understand German.

Leaning forward, he grasped his father's forearm. "I am grateful, Father." And he was. This time his smile held. Although for many years Father had shared Diedrich's dream to come to America, Diedrich knew the heartache leaving Venne had cost his parent. He would never forget how Father had hugged Diedrich's brothers, Johann and Frederic, as if he would never let them go. How the tears had flowed unashamed between the father and his grown sons and daughters-in-law at their parting. Hot tears stung the back of Diedrich's nose at the memory. But as hard as it had been to say those good-byes, he knew the hardest parting for Father was with the five little ones—knowing that he may never see his *liebe Enkelkinder* again this side of heaven.

Father shook his head. "Nein. It is not me to whom you should be grateful, mein Sohn. We both owe Herr Seitz our gratitude." A grin quirked up the corner of his mouth, and a teasing twinkle appeared in his eye. "Not only did he send us one hundred and fifty American dollars for our passage, but he will give you a good wife and me a fine Christian daughter-in-law."

The coach jostled as a wheel bounced in and out of a rut, and Diedrich pressed the soles of his boots harder against the floor to steady himself. Bitterness at what he was being forced to do welled up in him. And before he could stop the words, he blurted, "You do not know if she is a fine Christian woman or if she will make me a good wife, Father."

Father's face scrunched down in the kind of scowl that used to make Diedrich tremble as a child, though his father had never once lifted a hand against him in anger. "I may not know the daughter, but I know the Vater. Any daughter of Ernst's would be both a good wife and a fine Christian woman." Father's stormy expression cleared, and his smile returned. "And Ernst says she is pretty as well."

Diedrich crossed his arms over his chest and snorted. "Every father thinks his daughter is pretty."

Father yawned then grinned, obviously unfazed by Diedrich's surly mood. "You were too small, only a *kleines Kind* when the Seitz family left Venne for America. But I remember well Ernst's bride, Catharine, and she was *eine Schöne*. And their two little ones were like *Engelchen*. I have no doubt that your bride will be pretty as well."

Diedrich shrugged and turned toward the foggy window. Learning that Regina Seitz's mother was once a beauty and her sisters had looked like little angels as children did nothing to squelch his growing trepidation. But arguing with Father would not improve his mood. And that was just as well, for the sound of a muffled snore brought his attention back to Father, whose bearded chin had dropped to his chest and eyes had closed in slumber.

With Father dozing and the three other passengers engaged in a lively conversation in English, Diedrich turned his attention toward the window again. The rain had stopped. At least he didn't hear it pattering on the roof of the coach now. Peering through raindrops still snaking down the glass, he gazed at the green countryside speeding past them. If all went as he planned, it would matter little whether Regina Seitz was ugly, a beauty, or simply plain. By autumn, Diedrich should be on his way to California and the goldfields. But if things didn't go as he planned. . . No. He would not even consider the alternative. *Dear Lord, please do something to stop this marriage.*

Suddenly the coach came to a jarring halt, jolting him from his prayerful petition. Through the coach window, he could make out the front of a large white house. Apprehension knotted in his stomach. They had arrived. As he gazed at the building before him, he still could not help marveling at the size of the houses here in America. Though some were small and crudely made of logs, many others, like the one framed by the coach's window, were far larger and either made of brick or sided with thin planks of wood called clapboards. At least the Seitz home would have plenty of room for him and Father.

Sitting up straight, Father blinked and yawned. He stretched his arms as far as the coach's low ceiling allowed. "Why are we stopping?"

"I think we have come to the end of our journey." Diedrich had scarcely gotten the words out of his mouth when the coach driver opened the door at his elbow. Diedrich climbed out first, followed by Father, while their fellow passengers exited by the opposite door.

Back on the ground, Diedrich stretched his legs and arms. Though he did not look forward to the meeting that would soon take place inside the house before him, he was glad to leave the cramped quarters of the conveyance behind him. Coaches were clearly not built for the comfort of people Diedrich's height.

"Come on up to the porch, folks." The driver closed the coach door and ushered everyone up to the house's front porch. He balled his fist as if to rap on the door, but before he could, it opened, and Diedrich's jaw went slack.

A pleasant-faced young woman stood in the doorway. Though not stunning in looks, she was by no means ugly. In fact, the only remarkable thing about her was her distended middle, which clearly revealed she was in the family way.

Diedrich's heart plummeted. So it wasn't that Herr Seitz desired a German farmer for a son-in-law; he simply needed a husband for his daughter. Anger coiled in his midsection. Had he and Father endured an excruciating journey of two and a half months to now be played for fools?

He glanced at Father, whose wide-eyed expression reflected his own shock.

"*Guten Tag.*" The girl dipped her head in greeting then stepped back to allow her guests entrance. "Please come in." She ushered them into a spacious room furnished with several benches and chairs, some arranged on either side of a large fireplace.

Motioning for everyone to sit down, she began speaking rapidly in English. As he had in countless other such situations since his arrival in America, Diedrich caught only an occasional word. "Coffee" and "bread" suggested they would be offered food. The next moment a man of about thirty years entered the room from the house's interior.

The young woman smiled up at the man, who now stood beside her and rested his hand on her shoulder. Again the woman spoke and Diedrich understood only two of her words, but they were the most important ones: "Husband" and "Gerhart."

The coach driver spoke to the man and nodded toward Diedrich and Father, who sat together on one of the benches that flanked the fireplace. This time, the word "Deutsch" caught Diedrich's attention.

The man smiled and nodded. He stepped toward them, and Diedrich and his father rose. "Guten Tag," he said, reaching his hand out to each man in turn. "I am Gerhart Driehaus, and you have already met my wife, Maria." He cast a smile in the woman's direction as she waddled out of the room. "I understand you wish to go to the home of Herr Ernst Seitz."

"Ja," Diedrich and his father said in unison. As Father made the introductions, relief spilled through Diedrich, followed quickly by remorse for having mentally maligned their benefactor. Though he still planned to avoid marrying the man's daughter—or anyone else for that matter—he was glad to have no evidence that Herr Seitz had been dishonest with them.

Herr Driehaus cocked his head southward. "The Seitz farm is but two miles from here. Rest and enjoy some coffee and Maria's good bread and jelly while I hitch my team to the wagon. Then I will take you there."

Diedrich and his father uttered words of thanks. What a joy to converse again in their native tongue with someone besides each other—something they'd done little of since leaving the German community in Cincinnati.

Fifteen minutes later the coach departed the Driehaus home with the other passengers, leaving Diedrich and his father behind. Refreshed by steaming cups of coffee and light bread slathered with butter and grape jelly, Diedrich hoisted their little trunk into the back of Gerhart Driehaus's two-seater wagon. Father sat in front with Herr Driehaus while Diedrich took the backseat.

Soon they left the main thoroughfare and headed south down a hilly road. In places, the mud was so thick and the ruts so deep and filled with water that Diedrich feared the wagon would become bogged down. But the four sturdy Percherons plodded along, keeping them moving.

As they bounced along, splashing in and out of ruts, Herr Driehaus pointed out neighboring farms, and he and Father talked about crops and weather. The sun had come out again, causing the raindrops on tender new foliage to sparkle like diamonds. The clean scent of the rain-washed air held a tinge of perfume from various flowering bushes and trees. Suddenly the notion of living in this place didn't seem so bad to Diedrich, at least through the spring and summer. But if he didn't want to live here for the rest of his life, he would have to be as quick and agile as the little rust-breasted bird that just flew from a purple-blossomed tree along the roadway, showering Diedrich with raindrops.

"We have come to the home of Herr Seitz." With the announcement, Herr Driehaus turned the team down a narrow lane as muddy as the road they'd left. At the end of it stood a neat, two-story house with a barn and several other outbuildings surrounding it. Though just as large, this house, unlike the Driehaus home, was constructed of thick hewn logs, weathered to a silvery gray. A large weeping willow tree stood in the front yard. Bent branches sporting new pale green leaves swayed in the breeze, caressing the lush grass beneath.

Despite the serene beauty of the scene before him, a knot of trepidation tightened in Diedrich's gut. In a few moments, he would come face-to-face with the girl who expected to soon become his wife.

The lane wound between the house and the barn, and Herr Driehaus finally brought the wagon to a stop at the side of the house. They climbed to the ground, but as they stepped toward the house, a shrill scream from somewhere behind them shattered the tranquil silence.

They all turned at the sound. When Diedrich located the source of the noise, his eyes popped. A mud-covered figure emerged from the thick mire of the fenced-in barn lot. Only her mud-encased skirts identified her as female. She took a labored step forward, and her foot made a sucking sound as she pulled it out of the mud. But when she tried to take another step, she fell onto her knees again, back into the thick pool of muck. Emitting another strangled scream, she glanced over her shoulder. It was then that Diedrich noticed a large, dark bull not ten feet behind her. With his snout to the ground, the animal made huffing noises as he pawed the mire, sending showers of mud flying. The bull obviously didn't like anyone invading his domain.

Terror for the hapless female gripped Diedrich. In another moment, the great animal would be on her, butting and tramping her into the mud. Casting aside his coat and hat, he raced headlong toward the barn lot.

Chapter 3

H–help!" Regina struggled to pull her foot from the thick black mud. But the harder she tried, the deeper she sank. Her heart pounding in her ears, she glanced over her shoulder at Papa's bull, Stark. The huge dark beast had trotted to within feet of her. With his head lowered, he snorted and pawed at the sodden ground. His big eyes, dark and malicious, fixed her with an unwavering glare. What would it feel like when his head struck her like a giant boulder? Would she feel the pain when his horns pierced her body and his sharp hooves slashed at her flesh? Or would the first butt of his mighty head have already sent her to heaven where the scriptures told her there was no pain?

Determined not to learn the answers to the questions flashing in her mind, she managed to pull enough air into her fear-paralyzed lungs to let out another scream. Where was Eli? Couldn't he hear her? As perturbed as she had been that he'd surprised her in the barn after she had explicitly told him to stay away, the knowledge of his nearness helped to quell her growing panic. Surely he would hear her calls and come to her rescue.

The ground shook as Stark trotted closer. It almost seemed a game to the bull, like a cat that had cornered a mouse.

Finding strength she didn't know she had, Regina pulled one foot from the black ooze, but the other foot refused to budge, and she fell face forward again in the muck. Pushing herself up with her palms, she came up spitting unspeakable filth. If Eli had already left, maybe she could get Papa's attention. Mustering all her lung power, she let out another strangled scream.

Suddenly, she looked up to see a tall, broad-shouldered figure racing toward her. Clean shaven and lithe, the man was definitely not Papa. . .or Eli. Instead, she got the impression of gentle gray eyes that reminded her of soft, warm flannel, filled with concern. Straight brown hair fell across his broad forehead and his strong jaw was set in a look of determination.

Relief spilled through Regina as the stranger scooped her up in his arms. Murmuring reassurances, he ran with her toward the barn lot's open gate. The next several seconds passed in a series of sensory flashes. The clean scent of shaving soap filled her nose as she rested her face against his hard chest. Against her ear, she heard the deep, quick thumping of his heart like the muffled beats of a distant drum. The sound of his voice, rich and deep, uttered words of assurance as he strode toward the house, cradling her securely in his strong arms.

At the back door, he set her gently on her feet before Mama, whose face registered an ever-changing mixture of shock, fear, horror, and dismay. Gingerly grasping Regina's mud-drenched shoulders, Mama uttered unintelligible laments in tones that reflected the varied emotions flitting across her face.

Glancing over her shoulder, Regina managed to catch a parting glimpse of her rescuer before Mama whisked her into the house. Now covered in the mud she had deposited on him, he stood stock still, his kind gray eyes regarding her with wonder and concern.

A half hour later, Regina slid down in the copper tub and groaned. The clean, hot water into which Mama had shaved pieces of lye soap was now tepid and brown from mud and other unpleasant things on which Regina didn't care to speculate. If not for the grimy contents of the bathwater, she might be tempted to slip beneath the surface and not come up.

She shivered, remembering the angry look on the bull's face. Countless times she had taken that same shortcut from the barn to the house without any such mishap. But in her desperation to keep Papa from discovering her and Eli together in the barn, she hadn't considered that the rain had turned the barn lot into one huge mud puddle.

She scowled at a sliver of straw turning lazy circles atop the scummy surface of the water. It was all Papa's fault. If Eli were allowed to court her in the open instead of having to sneak around and surprise her in the barn like he did today, she wouldn't be sitting in the bathtub in the middle of the week washing off unspeakable filth. She wouldn't have had to disappoint Eli by missing the Dudleytown box supper last Saturday. She also wouldn't have had to tell him of Papa's plans to marry her off to a stranger. She had expected Eli to be unhappy and perhaps even angry at her news. But she hadn't expected him to demand she elope with him right away.

She sighed. For the past week, she had prayed for God to deliver her from the plans Papa and Herr Rothhaus were making for her future. And though a part of her longed to give in to Eli's demands, she couldn't believe God would want her to run away without a word to her parents. Such an impulsive action would doubtless break their hearts. Perhaps that was why God hadn't allowed her to give Eli an answer. For at that moment they'd heard the sound of a wagon approaching. Sure that Papa had returned from his trip to Dudleytown, she had instructed Eli to hide in the barn until the wagon was out of sight while she headed to the house through the barn lot.

She ran the glob of soap over her wet hair, working up a lather. On the other hand, by not leaving with Eli, she may have missed a window of escape God had opened for an instant. At least then she wouldn't be trapped in her upstairs bedroom, washing off barnyard muck in preparation for meeting the man Papa had chosen to be her future husband.

At the thought, her cheeks tingled with warmth. In truth, she may have already met him. *Diedrich Rothhaus.* Was it possible that the man with the strong arms and kind gray eyes was the one to whom Papa had promised her? Her heart did an odd hop. For days now, she had dreaded his coming. Nearly every night she drenched her pillow with her tears, praying that God would cause the man to decide to stay in Baltimore or Cincinnati—anywhere but here in Sauers.

The fractured memory of her rescuer flashed again in her mind. She tried to assemble the bits and pieces into a clear picture, but they refused to come into focus. Yet she knew without a doubt that the man she had left covered in mud at the back door did not fit the picture of the Diedrich Rothhaus she had conjured up in her apprehensive imaginings. But of one thing she was sure. The stranger who had carried her to the house spoke German.

"Du bist jetzt sicher." Yes. The words he had spoken so gently, assuring her of her safety, were not English words but German.

The door opened a crack and Mama slipped into the room with Regina's best dress draped over her arm. Her face, pruned up in a look of dismay, did not bode well for Regina. "I have brought your Sunday frock." Her voice held the stiff tone that always preceded a scolding.

Laying the dress and a bundle of small clothes on Regina's bed, she stepped to the side of the tub and shook her head. "I still cannot imagine what you were doing in that barn lot. You know how muddy it gets when it rains. And how many times has your Vater warned you to stay away from that bull? I cannot bear to think what might have happened if Stark had got to you." Her voice cracked with emotion, smiting Regina with remorse. "I thank Gott He sent that brave young man to save you." She pulled the ever-present handkerchief from her sleeve and dabbed at her watery eyes. "If not for Diedrich Rothhaus, we might be having a funeral instead of planning a wedding."

Regina groaned inwardly. So the man who rescued her *was* the man Papa had chosen for her husband. Her pulse quickened, but she forced her attention back to her mother, who, though stronger than most women Regina knew, did tend to be overemotional at times. "It is sorry I am, Mama. I did not think—"

"And you are usually such a thoughtful Mädchen." Shaking her head, Mama sniffed back tears, obviously not finished with her rant. "And as thankful as I am that young Rothhaus was there to get you away from the bull, how embarrassing that the first time your intended sets eyes on you, you are covered in mud!" She shook her head again and pressed her hand to her chest. "When I told your Vater what happened, I thought he would collapse right there in the kitchen. And he might have, but he did not wish to embarrass our family any further in front of Diedrich and Herr Rothhaus."

Diedrich. If only she could form a clear image of him in her mind. But it didn't matter what he looked like, or even that he had rescued her. The question remained—who would rescue her from him?

Mama helped Regina out of the tub and wrapped her in a cotton towel. "Poor Diedrich," her lamentations continued. "By the time he handed you to me, he was nearly as muddy as you were. Your Vater is helping him to wash and change into the spare set of clothes he brought with him." As Mama's voice grew more frustrated, she rubbed the towel over Regina's skin harder than necessary.

"Ouch!" Regina snatched the towel from her mother's grasp and stepped away. When would Mama and Papa stop treating her like a child? "I'm not a *Kind*, Mama. I can dry myself." At the hurt look on Mama's face, guilt nipped at Regina's conscience. Mama meant well, and besides embarrassing her and Papa in front of the Rothhauses, Regina *had* given her parents a terrible fright. She sighed, and her tone reflected her penance. "I am sorry I fell in the mud and what's-his-name had to pull me out." Though by now Regina knew the man's given name as well as her own, she couldn't bring herself to say it. "But I am not the one who asked him to come. And as I have been telling you and Papa for the past week, I do not want to get married! Especially to someone I have never met."

Mama cocked her head. Some of her earlier anger seemed to seep away, and she gave Regina a caring, indulgent smile. "I know this is happening very fast for you, Regina. But you know that your Vater and I want the best for you, and the Rothhauses are good people. Once you get used to the idea, I am sure you will be happy." Her smile turned to a teasing grin. "After all, you must marry someone, and Diedrich *is* very handsome. And he must have a brave and good heart to have gone in there with that bull to carry you to safety."

Or he is just very stupid. Regina decided to keep that thought to herself as she stepped into her bloomers and pulled her petticoats over her head.

Mama walked to the dresser and picked up Regina's hairbrush. "Do you want me to brush and plait your hair? We want to show your intended and his Vater how very pretty you are when you are clean."

Mama might as well have run her fingernails across a slate board for the way her comment sent irritation rasping down Regina's spine. The thought of parading in front of Diedrich Rothhaus like a mare he considered buying was beyond irksome. But at the same time, Mama's words planted the seed of a plan in Regina's mind. A plan that nurtured a tiny glimmer of hope inside her. Perhaps falling in the mud was not such a bad thing. Maybe it was part of God's plan to rescue her from a loveless marriage.

Regina put on her Sunday best dress of sky-blue linen and fastened the mother-of-pearl buttons that marched down its front. "*Danke*, Mama, but no." She gave her mother the sweetest smile she could muster. "I am sure you have things to do in the kitchen. I will be down to help you in a few minutes."

Tears glistened in Mama's eyes as she gazed at Regina. "What a beauty you are, liebes Mädchen." She hugged Regina and kissed her on top of her damp head, sending a squiggle of shame through Regina. "I would not be surprised if Diedrich Rothhaus insisted on setting the wedding date within the month."

Instead of bringing comfort, the compliment ignited a flash of panic in Regina. *Dear Lord, give me time to convince Diedrich Rothhaus that I am not someone he would want to marry.* As Mama left the room, closing the door behind her, Regina sent up her frantic prayer. Then she calmed herself with thoughts of her budding plan designed to thwart the life-changing one her parents had foisted on her.

Gazing into her dresser mirror, she watched her brows slip down into a determined frown. If Diedrich Rothhaus refused to marry her after all the money Papa had spent to bring him and Herr Rothhaus here from Venne, surely Papa would relent and let her marry Eli or whomever she chose. All she had to do was make herself repugnant to Diedrich Rothhaus.

She plaited her damp hair into two long braids. But as she brought them up to attach them to the top of her head as she normally did, she paused. Instead, she tied the ends of each with a blue ribbon as she used to do when a child, letting them dangle on her shoulders. She might as well put her plan into action immediately. Young Herr Rothhaus would doubtless find a girl who looked twelve far less appealing than one who looked Regina's age of seventeen.

Diedrich splashed tepid water from the tin dishpan onto his face, rinsing off the lye soap. Herr Seitz had brought him into this long narrow room between the back door and the kitchen to wash up before taking Father on a tour of the farm.

With his eyes scrunched shut against the stinging water and soap, he reached for the cotton towel *Frau* Seitz had left for him on the side of the washstand. He couldn't get his mind off the girl he'd carried to safety little more than a half hour earlier. Behind his closed eyelids, he saw again her big blue eyes wild with fear, shining from her mud-covered face. The face of his future wife? Though the image that lingered in his mind could not be called attractive, it was more than compelling. Something about the look in her eyes had made him want to protect her, reassure her.

Burying his face in the towel, he scrubbed, as if to scrub the image from his mind. He must be daft. Did he want to end up like his brothers, growing old before his time trying to eke out a living farming with too many hungry mouths to feed? No. He hadn't come all the way to America to become snared in the same trap into which his brothers had fallen before him. He must stick to his plan and let nothing—not even a pair of large, helpless blue eyes—distract him from reaching the California goldfields and the riches waiting there for him.

He dipped a scrap of cotton cloth into the tin basin of water and washed off the mud that still clung to his hands and arms. At the pressure of the cloth on his skin, he felt again the soft curves of the girl's body in his arms. She had fit as if she belonged there. Despite the cool spring air that prickled the skin of his bare torso, heat marched up his neck to suffuse his face.

At a creaking sound on the stairwell to his left, followed by what sounded like a sharp intake of air, Diedrich turned. What he saw snatched the breath from his lungs as if Alois, the strongest man in their village, had punched him in the stomach. The prettiest girl he'd ever seen stood as if frozen three steps from the landing. Her hair, the color of ripe wheat, hung in two braids on her shoulders. They made her look younger than her obvious years. But there was nothing child-like about her gently curved figure. Her blue frock matched her bright blue eyes, which were at least as big and round as Diedrich remembered from the barn lot and seemed to grow larger by the second. Her pink lips, which reminded him of a rosebud, formed an O.

It suddenly struck Diedrich that he was standing before her shirtless. Glancing down, he watched a bead of water meander down his bare chest to his stomach. He snatched his waiting clean shirt from a peg on the wall beside the washstand and held it against him to cover his bare chest. He opened his mouth to utter a greeting, but his throat had gone dry and nothing came out. He cleared his throat. Twice. Had he lost all his senses? She was just a girl. *Regina.* For months he had tried to fashion an image to attach to the name. But nothing he had ever envisioned approached the loveliness of the girl before him.

She remained still and mute. Fearing she might fly back up the stairs, he tried again to speak. This time he found his voice. "Are you all right?"

"Ja. Danke." She finally stepped down to the floor, though she stayed close to the stair rail as if to keep maximum distance between them. "Thank you for helping me. . .out of the mud." Though she spoke with a hint of an American accent, her German was flawless.

"*Bitte sehr.* I am glad you were not hurt. Forgive me." Turning away from her, he hurriedly shrugged on his shirt and began buttoning it up, praying she would still be there when he turned back around. She was.

"I am Regina." Unsmiling, she took a couple of halting steps toward him.

"I am Diedrich. Diedrich Rothhaus." Without thinking, he reached out his hand to her.

In a tentative movement, she reached out a delicate-looking hand that ended in long, tapered fingers and touched his palm, sending tingles up his arm to his shoulder. An instant later, she drew back her hand as if she'd touched a hot stove. Looking past his shoulder, she glanced out the open door behind him. "Papa and Herr Rothhaus are back from looking at the farm. You may join them outside until Mama and I call you for dinner."

She slipped past him and headed for the kitchen, leaving him feeling deflated. Not once had she smiled, and no hint of warmth had softened her icy tone. Instead, her stilted voice had felt like a glass of cold water thrown in his face.

Fully revived from the odd trance that had gripped him at first sight of her, Diedrich gazed at the spot where her appealing figure had disappeared. As beguiling as her face and form, Regina Seitz was an enchantress chiseled from ice. His resolve to find a way out of this arranged marriage solidified. And if his prospective bride's chilly reaction to him was any indication of her feelings in the matter, obtaining his goal might not be as difficult as he'd feared.

Stepping outside, Diedrich headed to the relatively dry spot in the lane where Father and Herr Seitz stood talking and laughing.

"Ah, there you are, mein *Junge*." Herr Seitz clapped Diedrich on the shoulder, his round face beaming. "I was telling your Vater, I have *wunderbare* news. On my way back from Dudleytown, I met Pastor Sauer on the road and told him about you and my Regina. He is looking forward to meeting you and Herr Rothhaus and will be happy to perform the marriage whenever we like."

Chapter 4

Regina looked down at her plate of fried rabbit, boiled potatoes, and dandelion greens and fought nausea. Not because of the food on her plate, which she normally loved, but from Papa's enthusiastic conversation with Herr Rothhaus speculating on the earliest possible date for her wedding.

"By the end of May, we should have the planting done." Papa wiped milk from his thick blond mustache that had lately begun to show touches of gray. "The first Sunday in June, I think, would be a fine time for the wedding."

June? Regina's stomach turned over. Unless she could think of a way out of it, in six weeks she would be marrying the stranger sitting across the table from her. She looked up at Diedrich, who sat toying with his food. Did the alarmed look that flashed in his eyes suggest he shared her feelings about their coming nuptials? Her budding hope withered. More likely he found the date disappointingly remote.

"Ja." Herr Rothhaus nodded from across the table, a boiled potato poised on the twin tines of his fork. His face turned somber and his gray eyes, so like his son's, took on a watery look. "Mein Sohn and I owe you and Frau Seitz much." His voice turned thick with emotion, and he popped the potato into his mouth.

Papa clapped the man on the shoulder. "Happy we are that you and your fine son are finally here, *mein Freund*. Over the last three months, I have said many prayers for your safe passage." He brightened. "And this Sunday, I shall ask Pastor Sauer to lead the whole congregation in a prayer of thanks for your safe arrival." Then he turned his attention to Regina, and his smile drooped into a disapproving frown—one of many he'd given her since they all sat down for supper. "Again, it is sorry I am that you came all the way across the ocean to see our Regina, and she is covered in mud."

Regina groaned inwardly. Did Papa have to keep bringing it up? And how many times did he expect her to apologize for embarrassing herself in front of the two men? Out of the corner of her eye, she thought she caught the hint of a grin on Diedrich's lips, but at that moment he lifted his cup to his mouth and took a sip of milk, covering his expression.

Mama turned to her, and in the same coaxing voice she used to speak to Regina's two-year-old nephew, Henry, said, "Regina, perhaps you would like to ask Diedrich about his voyage?" She rolled her eyes in Diedrich's direction, her expectant look conveying both a summons and a warning.

Regina sat in mute defiance. There may be nothing she could do to stop her parents from forcing her into a marriage with this Diedrich Rothhaus, but they couldn't make her like it. And they couldn't make her talk to him.

At her reticence, Papa leveled a stern look at her and in a lowered voice that held an ominous tone said, "Regina."

Diedrich's glance bounced between Papa and Mama, but then his gaze lit softly on Regina's face like a gray mourning dove on a delicate branch. "A rough winter crossing, it was. But thanks be to Gott, the *Franziska*, she is a sturdy bark with a crew brave and skilled."

Regina hated that Diedrich had come to her rescue once again. Even worse, she hated how her gaze refused to leave his. And how his deep, gentle voice soothed her like the caress of a velvet glove.

The three older people launched into a conversation about the Rothhauses' journey from Venne. Though he remained quiet, a pensive look wrinkled Diedrich's brow. Then in the midst of his father recounting an incident on the flatboat during their trip down the Ohio River from Pittsburg to Cincinnati, Diedrich broke in.

"Forgive me, Vater. Herr Seitz. Frau Seitz." He looked in turn at the three older people. "I have been thinking. You are right, Vater. We do owe Herr and Frau Seitz much, as well as Fräulein Regina." His tender gaze on Regina's face set her heart thumping in her chest. "The scriptures tell us to owe no man anything. And King Solomon tells us in Proverbs that the price of a virtuous woman is far above rubies." He turned to Herr Rothhaus. "Vater, I feel it is only right that before any marriage takes place, we should work the summer for Herr Seitz. With our labor, we can at least repay him our passage." His focus shifted to Regina. "And the extra months will allow time for Fräulein Seitz and I to get to know one another—which, I think, will make for a stronger union."

At his quiet suggestion a hush fell around the table. Then the elder Rothhaus began to nod. "Ja," he finally said. "What my son says makes much sense, I think. I am not a man who likes to feel beholden."

Looking down at his plate, Papa frowned. But at length he, too, bobbed his head in agreement, though Regina thought she detected a hint of disappointment in his eyes. "In my mind, you and your son owe me nothing, Herr Rothhaus. But I understand a man's need to feel free of obligation." Smiling, he turned to Regina and Mama. "And waiting until September will give you two more time to plan the wedding, hey, *mein Liebling?*"

During the exchange Regina sat agape, relief washing through her. Vaguely registering Mama's agreement, she could have almost bounded around the table and hugged Diedrich's neck. A reprieve! It did not entirely undo the deal, but it bought her some time to put her plan into action and a real chance of escaping this unwanted marriage. She glanced up at him engaged in conversation with Papa and couldn't stop a smirk from tugging up the corners of her lips. By the end of summer, Diedrich Rothhaus would beg to be let out of the agreement.

Over the next week Regina had managed, for the most part, to stay clear of Diedrich. Their only interaction was at mealtimes and after supper when everyone sat together in the front room listening to either Papa or Herr Rothhaus read from the Bible. To her parents' chagrin, Regina began taking less care with her appearance. Only on Sunday and when she took her pony cart past the mill on the road to Dudleytown did she make sure that her hair was neatly plaited and her dress clean and mended.

A smug grin lifted her lips as she fairly skipped through the chill dawn air to the barn, swinging her milk bucket. The sunrise painted streaks of red and gold in myriad hues across the blue gray of the eastern sky. The sight would normally be enough to brighten her mood, but this morning she had even more reason to smile. So far, her plan to turn Diedrich against her seemed to be working. Only rarely did she catch him looking her way, and she doubted the two of them had shared a dozen words since his arrival. On Sundays when the five of them all rode to and from St. John's Church together, Regina was careful to sit between Papa and Mama. And during the week, the men spent their days in the fields plowing and planting while Regina and her mother worked around the house.

Her grin widened. This morning she had taken her plan to discourage Diedrich even further. Time and again over the years, Mama had reminded Regina and her sisters that a man would often overlook appearance if his wife was a good cook. Regina had noticed that Diedrich and Herr Rothhaus were usually the first up and out of the house each morning, often putting in as much as an hour's work before returning for breakfast. So this morning, Regina had gotten up extra early and made two batches of biscuits, one the normal way and the other with twice the flour. It had taken some vigilance, but she made sure that Diedrich and his father got the rock-hard biscuits while she saved back the good, soft ones for her parents.

Remembering the look on Diedrich's face when he bit

into one of the hard biscuits, she laughed out loud. For a moment, she actually feared he had broken a tooth. But even more encouraging was the frown Herr Rothhaus had exchanged with his son when he tried unsuccessfully to take a bite of his own biscuit. Though the two men had smiled and thanked her, they were forced to finally abandon the biscuits. Somehow they'd managed to chew most of the eggs she'd fried to almost the consistency of rubber as well as the fried potatoes she'd carefully burnt.

As she neared the barn, she hummed a happy tune, trying to think of how she might destroy another meal for the Rothhauses. No man in his right mind would marry a woman who cooked like that, and no caring father would commit his son to a lifetime of dyspepsia.

In the barn, she made her way through the dim building to the stall where their milk cow stood munching on timothy hay. "Good morning, Ingwer." She pulled her milking stool near the big, gentle animal and patted her ginger-colored hide that had inspired the cow's name. "How are you this fine morning? Will you give me lots of good milk with thick, rich cream today?"

Settling herself on the stool, Regina giggled, the happy noise mingling with the cow's dispassionate moo. "I shall be careful not to startle you with cold hands so you will not kick over the bucket like yesterday," she said as she crossed her arms over her chest and warmed her hands in her armpits.

As she bent down and reached beneath the cow, a hard hand clamped down on her shoulder, and she jerked. Her head knocked into Ingwer's side, causing the cow to moo and kick the bucket over.

Whipping her head around, Regina met Eli's angry glower. She jumped to her feet. "Eli, you scared me! What are you doing here? You know my Vater will be very angry if he finds—"

"I thought you were my special girl. Now I hear you're gettin' married." Not a trace of sorrow or even disappointment touched his green eyes. The only emotion Regina could read in his twisted features was raw fury. For the first time, she felt fear in Eli's presence.

She shrugged her shoulder away from his grasp. If possible, his face turned even stormier. He stepped closer, and for an instant the urge to run from him gripped her. But that was silly. She'd known Eli since they were children. He would never hurt her.

His fists remained balled at his sides. The rays of the morning sun filtering between the timbers of the barn's wall fell across his thick, bare forearms. In the soft light, she could see the muscles flexing beneath his tanned skin like iron springs. He leaned forward until his face was within inches of hers. "So are you gettin' married or not?"

"No, of course not. I'm not marrying anyone." Regina prayed she could make her words come true. "And I *am* your special girl."

"Not what I heard." He eased back a few inches, but his face and voice remained taut with anger. "Heard you were marryin' some German right off the boat."

Regina waved her hand through a sunbeam that danced with dust mites. "Oh, it is all Papa's idea. I knew nothing about it." She didn't know who she was angrier with—Papa for making the deal with Herr Rothhaus without her knowledge, neighbors who had trafficked in gossip disguised as news, or Eli for questioning her interest in him. "Do not believe everything you hear, Eli. I have no intention of marrying anyone, including the man Papa chose for me."

Instead of diluting Eli's anger, Regina's words seemed to stoke it. Lurching forward, he grabbed her arms. His fingers bit into her skin as he glared into her face. "You'd better be telling me the truth. I let a man take a girl from me once. I won't make that mistake again."

Regina yelped at the pain his hands were inflicting on her arms and struggled to pull away. "Ouch! Stop it, Eli. You are hurting me!"

Ignoring her plea, he pulled her roughly to him, and a ripping sound filled her left ear. Glancing in the direction of the sound, she noticed with dismay that the right sleeve of her dress had torn away at the shoulder.

"Look, you tore my dress!" Furious, she wriggled in vain in Eli's iron grasp.

His only answer was a throaty chuckle as he tried to press his mouth down on hers. But she turned her head at the last instant, and his lips landed wetly below her right ear.

"Eli, please stop it!" Tears flooded down Regina's face. Vacillating between pain, fear, and anger at his bad manners, she fought to free herself.

"Let her go, friend." Like the sound of distant thunder, an ominous warning in German rumbled beneath the deep, placid voice to their right.

Chapter 5

Relief and shame warred in Regina's chest as she looked over to see Diedrich's tall, broad-shouldered form filling the barn's little side doorway less than five feet away. She had no idea how much German Eli knew. But whether or not he understood Diedrich's words, Eli could not mistake the threat in Diedrich's voice as well as his stony glower and clenched fists.

Eli took his hands from Regina and stepped back. The two men traded glares, and for a moment, Regina feared a fight might ensue. Instead, Eli visibly shrank back and turned to her.

"Call off your German dog, Regina." Though audibly subdued, his voice dripped with scorn as he shot Diedrich a withering glance. "And you tell *him* not to say a word to your pa about our. . .argument, or we are through." With one last caustic glance between Regina and Diedrich, Eli turned on his heel and stalked out of the barn.

Only when Eli had disappeared through the big open doors at the end of the barn did Diedrich cross to her. "Are you hurt?" His gray eyes full of concern roved her face then slid to her bare shoulder and the ripped calico fabric hanging from it.

"No, I am not hurt." Fumbling, Regina tried to fit the

torn sleeve back in place, but it wouldn't stay. She had done nothing wrong and should not feel embarrassed. Still, she did. But any embarrassment took second place to the anxiety filling her chest at Eli's parting warning. If Diedrich told Papa or Herr Rothhaus about what had just transpired between her and Eli, Papa would never allow Eli back on the farm. Stepping to Diedrich, she put her hand on his arm. "Please, do not tell Papa and Mama what you saw, or even that Eli was here. Eli is a. . .friend. We were just having an argument."

Diedrich's brow furrowed, and he glanced down at the straw-strewn dirt floor. After a long moment, he lifted a thoughtful but still troubled face to her. "To me, he did not look friendly. But unless I am asked, I will say nothing. And Herr Seitz knows he is here. The man you call Eli brought a bent driveshaft from the gristmill for your father to straighten at his forge."

Relief sluiced through Regina, washing the strength from her limbs. She grabbed the railing at the side of Ingwer's stall for support and blew out a long breath. "Gott sei Dank!" With the closest blacksmith shop at Dudleytown three miles away, it was not unusual for neighbors to bring their broken and bent iron pieces for Papa to fix at his little forge behind the barn.

"Thanks be to Gott that you were no more hurt." Only a hint of admonition touched Diedrich's voice as he bent and righted the milk bucket. When he straightened, his gaze strayed again to her bare shoulder. His face reddened, and he looked away. "You must mend your frock. I will milk the cow."

"Danke." At his kindness, Regina mumbled the word, emotion choking off her voice. *He is our guest. Of course he feels obliged to be kind.* But deep down, she knew his kindness did not spring entirely from a desire to be polite. She also knew intuitively that he would keep his word and not mention to her parents the incident between her and Eli. Turning to leave, she glanced back at his handsome profile and her pulse quickened, doubtless a reaction to her earlier fright with Eli and her embarrassment that Diedrich had witnessed the scene.

"Regina." His soft voice stopped her. "You do not want this marriage between us, do you?"

His blunt question caught her by surprise, and her heart raced as she turned around in the narrow doorway. Would Diedrich, like Eli, become enraged at her rejection? After all, he *had* sailed all the way from Venne to marry her. "No." The honest word popped out of her mouth, accompanied by an unexpected twinge of sadness.

To her confusion, instead of showing anger or disappointment, Diedrich's expression took on the same closed look she'd seen on Papa's face when he engaged in horse-trading. "Neither do I want it."

Regina's jaw sagged. "But—but Papa paid your way here so you would. . .so we would—"

"I know." He winced. "Why do you think I suggested that my Vater and I work here through the summer to pay off our passage?"

"You—you said so we could get to know each other better." Her face flamed, and her eyes fled his.

"May Gott forgive my lie." His deep voice sank even further with regret.

Amazed at his words, Regina took a couple of tentative steps toward him. So all her scheming to put him off had been unnecessary? "You do not want to marry me?"

At her breathless question the emotionless curtain that had veiled his eyes lifted and they shone with both sorrow and remorse. "Please, Regina, I mean you no insult. It is not my intention to hurt you. I mean, look at you. Any man would be pleased. . ." Reddening, he shook his head as if to bring his thoughts back into focus. He took her hands in his, and the gentle touch of his fingers curling around hers suffused her with warmth. "It is not that I do not want to marry you. I do not want to marry anyone. Not until I have made my fortune."

Regina slipped her hands from his and stifled the laugh threatening to burst from her lips. "Made your fortune?" She glanced through the open doors at the end of the barn. In the distance, the morning sunlight turned the acres of winter wheat to fields of emerald. From a fence post, a cardinal flew, the sunlight gilding the edges of the bird's ruby-red wing. This farm had been her home for the past ten years since her family moved here from Cincinnati, where they'd first settled after arriving in America. After their cramped quarters in the German part of the noisy city, this place had seemed like Eden to seven-year-old Regina. And she still loved the farm with all her heart, but there was no fortune to be made here, despite what Diedrich and his father might have been told. Shaking her head, she gave him a pitiful look. "I do not know what others have told you, but you will find no fortune here. Papa has one of the most prosperous farms in Sauers, and we are certainly not wealthy."

Diedrich nodded. "You have a beautiful farm. I have been plowing for days now, and never have I seen better, richer soil than what I have found here. But I do not mean to make my fortune in Indiana."

"Then where?" Intrigued, she barely breathed the query as she drew closer.

A spark of excitement lit his eyes and his expression grew distant. "By September I hope to have paid off my passage and earned enough money to make my way to the goldfields in California." He fished a tattered scrap of newspaper from his shirt pocket and handed it to her.

Regina could barely make out the faded German words, but what she could read had a distinctly familiar ring. Since last autumn when newspapers first heralded the discovery of gold in California, advertisements like this one—only in English—had peppered every newspaper in the country. Offering every kind of provision needed by the adventurous soul willing to make the trip west, such notices promised riches beyond all human imagination, with little more effort than to reach down and scoop up gold nuggets from California's streams and mountainsides. Many young men from all over the country, including Jackson County, had hearkened to the siren's song and braved myriad dangers to make their way to the continent's western coast. And though a goodly number had lost their lives in the effort, to Regina's knowledge, not one had "struck it rich" as the papers put it.

She handed Diedrich back the scrap of paper and experienced a flash of sorrow tinged with fear. Would he be among the number to forfeit his life in the quest of a golden dream?

Diedrich tucked the paper back into his shirt pocket. "You asked me to keep the secret of your *Liebchen* from your parents. I must ask you to keep from them my plans as well."

Heat flamed in Regina's cheeks that he had guessed Eli was her sweetheart. Then anger flared, stoking the fire in her face. Despite her relief in learning that Diedrich did not want to marry her any more than she wanted to marry him, it did not excuse the fact that the Rothhaus men had lied to Papa. They had taken advantage of his generosity and used his money to come to America under false pretenses. "And when do you and Herr Rothhaus plan to tell my parents that you lied to get money for your passage here? Or will we just wake up one morning to find you both gone?"

"Nein." He barked the word, and an angry frown creased his tanned forehead. He grasped her arm but not in a threatening manner as Eli had done; his fingers did not bite into her skin as Eli's had. "You do not understand. My Vater knows nothing of my plans. He is an honorable man. He made the agreement with your Vater in good faith." His chin dropped to his chest, and his voice turned penitent. "I have deceived my Vater as I have deceived yours." He let go of her arm, leaving her feeling oddly bereft. "I know it was wrong of me, but I had no other means to get to America." When he raised his face to hers again, his gray eyes pled for understanding. "For many months, both my Vater and I had prayed that Gott would find a way for me to leave Venne for

America before the army called me into service. So when the letter came from Herr Seitz offering us money for passage, it seemed an answer to our prayers." Diedrich's Adam's apple bobbed with his swallow. "My Vater was so happy that we were coming to America. I did not have the courage to tell him how I felt and to ask him to refuse your Vater's gift." He shook his head. "For months I have dreaded this moment, praying that Gott would find a way for me to get out of this marriage without disappointing both our Vaters." He swallowed again. His gray gaze turned so tender tears sprung to Regina's eyes. "But mostly, I prayed I would not break your heart."

Glancing away, Regina blinked the moisture from her eyes. So Diedrich Rothhaus was an honorable man. That was no reason for tears. And even if she wanted to marry him—which she did not—he did not want to marry her. At length, she lifted dry eyes to him. "So what do you suggest we do?"

He blew out a long breath and looked down at his boot tops, mired with the rich, dark soil of the back forty acres. When he lifted his face, a smile bloomed on his lips. Regina wondered why she had never noticed before the gentle curve of his mouth and the fine shape of his lips. "I think we should pray. I prayed I would not break your heart and Gott has answered my prayer. The harvest does not come immediately after the planting. Gott takes time to grow and ripen the grain. So maybe we should give Him time to work in this also. I am sure the answer to our prayers will come in His season."

Diedrich's notion seemed sound. If they rushed to Papa

and Herr Rothhaus now and confessed that they had no desire to marry, it would only bring discord and invite a barrage of opposition from their parents. Instead, the summer months would give Regina and Diedrich time to gradually convince their elders to dissolve their hastily cobbled plan to unite their children.

Regina nodded. "Ja. I think what you say is true. By harvesttime, the debt you and Herr Rothhaus owe to my Vater will be paid, and our Vaters will not feel so obliged to keep the agreement they made. Then when we tell them we do not think it is Gott's will that we marry, they will be more ready to accept our decision."

Diedrich stuck out his hand. "When we boarded the *Franziska*, my Vater said, 'We go to America where we can be free to live as we want.' If in this free land our Vaters can make a deal that we should marry, I see nothing wrong in the two of us making a deal that we should not."

With a halting motion, Regina placed her hand in his to seal their agreement. At his firm but gentle clasp, a sensation of comforting warmth like the morning sun's rays suffused her. Again she experienced regret when he drew his hand from hers.

He picked up the three-legged milking stool. "It is a deal, then. We shall work together to change our parents' minds and pray daily for their understanding." A whimsical grin quirked the corner of his mouth, and he winked, quickening Regina's heart. "I trust our agreement will now bring an improvement to my meals."

Regina's face flushed hotly. How transparent he must

have found her feeble attempts to dampen his ardor. And even more embarrassing was learning that her efforts were entirely unnecessary. But at least she would no longer have to come up with new ways to turn Diedrich against her. Knowing she'd gained an ally in her quest to avoid the marriage Papa and Herr Rothhaus had arranged for her should make her heart soar. So why did it droop with regret?

Chapter 6

There, *Alter*, does that feel better?" Diedrich lifted the last of the harness from the big draft horse's back. "At least you can shed your burden, mein Freund. I only wish mine came off so easily." What Diedrich had witnessed this morning had surely burdened his heart to a far greater extent than the leather harness and collar encumbered the big Clydesdale before him. He took the piece of burlap draped across the top beam of the horse's stall and began wiping the sweat from the animal's dark brown hide.

Anger, along with other emotions he didn't care to explore, raged in Diedrich's chest. A half day of plowing had not erased from his mind the scene he had come upon this morning in the barn. He hadn't felt such an urge to pummel someone to *Milchreis* since he was fourteen and found Wilhelm Kohl about to drown a sackful of kittens in the stream that separated their two farms. The sight of Regina struggling in the clutches of that rabid whelp she called "Eli" had made Diedrich want to take the boy's head off. At fourteen, Diedrich had plowed into eighteen-year-old Wilhelm without thought of the consequences, sending the bigger boy sprawling and the terrified cats scampering to the nearby woods. But when Wilhelm had righted himself and got the wind back into his lungs, he'd commenced to beat Diedrich until it was his face and not Wilhelm's that more closely resembled rice pudding.

Diedrich finished rubbing down the horse and tossed the piece of burlap over the stall's rail. If he had given in to his temper this morning as he had years ago with Wilhelm, the outcome would doubtless have been much different. Nearly a head taller than Eli and easily a stone heavier, he could have done serious damage to the boy if not taken his life altogether.

At the sobering thought, he blew out a long breath and shoved his fingers through his hair. Thanks be to Gott, over the past seven years he had grown not only in stature but also in self-control and forethought. Having declared his intentions, or rather the lack of them to Regina, Diedrich had no right to voice his opinion of her choice in a suitor, however brutish he considered the man. Still, for some reason, the girl to whom his father had promised him evoked in Diedrich a protective instinct he had rarely felt in his life. Twice since arriving in Sauers, he had seen fear shine from Regina's crystalline blue eyes, and twice he had felt compelled to vanquish it by coming between her and whatever threatened her.

He shook his head as if to dislodge from his mind the vision of Regina struggling in Eli's arms. A new burst of anger flared within him like bellows pumping air into a forge. In an attempt to calm his rising temper, he patted the horse's muscular neck. "What Fräulein Seitz does is not my concern, is it, mein Freund?" But saying it aloud did not make it so. The thought of Regina marrying that oaf Eli concerned Diedrich greatly. How could he leave for California with a clear conscience knowing he was likely opening the door for her to stroll into matrimony with the hot-tempered youth? Still, he could see no good way out of his conundrum. He hadn't come all this way to give up his dream of making his fortune in California. And even if he weren't planning to leave Sauers, he'd made an agreement with Regina. If he reneged on their agreement and forced her into an unwanted marriage, he'd likely consign them both to a miserable life. No, his best option was to simply stick to his plan—and their agreement—and pray she would have enough good sense not to run off with the scamp.

The large horse dashed his head up and down and emitted an impatient whinny, wresting Diedrich from his troubled reverie.

"Forgive me, Freund. Of course you are right. I must take care of what Gott has given me to do and leave the rest to Him." He crossed to a pile of hay and grasped the pitchfork sticking from it, then carried two large forkfuls of dried timothy hay to the waiting stallion.

As if to say thanks, the Clydesdale expelled a mighty breath through his flaring nostrils, his sleek sides heaving with the effort. The great puff of air sent hay dust flying, and Diedrich sneezed as it went up his nose.

"Ah, there you are, mein Sohn." Father's bright voice chimed behind Diedrich, turning him around. "I thought maybe you had already gone to the house for dinner."

"Nein, Vater. As you always say, the animals feed us, so we must feed them before we feed ourselves." Glancing over his shoulder, Diedrich sent his father a smile and was struck again by the marked change in his parent since their arrival in America. It was hard to believe that Father was the same brooding, work-worn man who had raised him. From the moment they stepped off the *Franziska* in Baltimore, Diedrich had witnessed a transformation in his normally sullen father. It was as if someone had lit a new flame behind his father's gray eyes. But it was more than that. Though half a head shorter than Diedrich, Father stood taller now, and there was a new lilt in his step that belied his fifty-six years. America was good for Father.

"Ja." Father bobbed his head as he dragged his hat from his still-thick shock of graying brown hair. A good-natured twinkle flickered in his eyes. "I do say that for sure. And it is true. But I wonder if after this morning's breakfast, you are not so eager to eat the food prepared by your intended?"

"Are you?" Sidestepping the question, Diedrich ignored his father's teasing tone and use of the word "intended." Turning to hide his fading smile, he forked more hay into the horse's manger.

Father chuckled and stepped nearer, his footfalls whispering through the straw strewn over the barn's dirt floor. "Herr Seitz assures me that this morning's breakfast must have been a mishap and that his Tochter is usually as good a cook as her Mutter."

"I'm sure it is so," Diedrich said, careful to keep his face averted. Though she'd made no such admission, Diedrich suspected that Regina had ruined the meal on purpose to discourage him from marrying her. But he could not share that suspicion with Father without betraying the secret agreement he and Regina had made.

"Spoken like a loyal husband-to-be." A smile lifted Father's voice. He clapped his hand on Diedrich's shoulder, sending a wave of guilt rippling through him. "You will see. By this time next year when she is no longer Fräulein Seitz, but Frau Rothhaus, *das* Mädchen will be making *köstlich* meals for us in our own home."

Diedrich tried to smile, but his lips would not hold it. He had no doubt that Regina would be making delicious meals for someone, but they would not be for him. It scraped his conscience raw to allow his father to fashion dreams of the three of them sharing a home in domestic tranquility, when Diedrich knew it was never to be.

Father slung his arm across Diedrich's shoulder. "Come, mein Sohn. The horse has had his feed. It is our turn now." He smacked his lips. "I can almost taste that *wunderbares Brot* Frau Seitz makes from cornmeal."

As they stepped from the barn, Father stopped. Turning, he faced Diedrich and grasped his shoulders. He shook his head, and his eyes glistened with moisture. "Mein *lieber* Sohn. Still sometimes I cannot believe it is true, that we are really here." He ran the cuff of his sleeve beneath his nose. "Since you were a kleines Kind, I have dreamed of coming to live in America. I gave up thinking it would ever happen. And now in the autumn of my life, Gott has resurrected my withered dream and made it bloom like the spring flowers." He waved toward a lilac bush laden with fragrant purple blossoms growing just outside the barn.

Diedrich groaned inwardly. He did not need any more

guilt rubbed like salt into his sore conscience. He forced a tiny smile. "I am glad you are happy here, Vater." He tried to turn back toward the barn's open doors, but Father held fast.

Father's throat moved with his swallow. "I am more than happy. Mein heart is full to overflowing. Soon I will have a new daughter-in-law, and in time, Gott willing, Enkelkinder to bounce on my knee. And it is you that I have to thank for making my dream come true." He gave Diedrich a quick hug and pat on the back. His voice thickened with emotion. "I do not know how I can ever thank you."

Later at the dinner table, Father's words still echoed in Diedrich's ears, smiting him with remorse. His appetite gone, he stared down at his untouched bowl of venison stew. Time and again on their walk to the house, he had been tempted to blurt out the truth. But doing so would not only humiliate Father and break his heart; it could render them both homeless as well.

He glanced across the table at Regina. In contrast to his sullenness, her mood had improved greatly. In fact, she looked happier than he had seen her. Her hair was neatly plaited and wound around her head like a halo of spun gold. Pink tinted her creamy cheeks, reminding him of the blossoms that now decorated the apple trees. Her lips, an even deeper rose color than her cheeks, looked soft as the petals of the flower they resembled. They parted slightly in laughter at a humorous comment by Frau Seitz. An unfamiliar ache throbbed deep in Diedrich's chest, and he experienced a sudden desire to know how Regina's lips would feel against his. Immediately, the memory of the miller's son trying to learn that very thing elbowed its way into his mind, filling him at once with rage and envy.

"Such a face, Diedrich. You do not like the stew?" Frau Seitz's voice invaded Diedrich's thoughts, bringing his head up with a jerk. "Regina made it herself."

He blinked at his hostess and reddened at Regina's giggle. "Yes. I mean no. *Es schmeckt sehr gut.*" A blast of heat suffused his face. As if to demonstrate his sincerity, he spooned some of the meat and vegetables swimming in dark gravy into his mouth. The stew was surprisingly tasty, but with Diedrich's worries twisting his gut into knots, it might as well have been sawdust.

"Danke." Regina gave him a sly smile as if to acknowledge their shared secret, sending his heart tumbling in his chest.

At the sensation, Diedrich sucked in air and almost choked on the chunk of venison in his mouth. If he'd found having Regina as an enemy uncomfortable, having her as an ally was proving no less disconcerting. He stifled a groan that bubbled up from his chest and threatened to push through his lips. Was there ever a more wretched soul than he? For the length of the spring and summer, he'd have to pretend to Father as well as Herr and Frau Seitz that he was happily betrothed to a girl whom he had secretly agreed not to marry. At the same time, he had to keep from Father his plans to leave for California until he earned enough money to pay back Herr Seitz for his passage to America. But most importantly, he needed to somehow find a way to convince Father and Herr Seitz that he and Regina should not marry while convincing Regina that she should not marry Eli. The last thing he needed was to lose his heart to this pretty Fräulein.

Chapter 7

Regina stood at the edge of the plowed and harrowed garden and inhaled the rich scent of the earth. How she loved the smell of newly turned sod in the spring. Each April for the past ten years, she, Mama, Sophie, and Elsie worked together to plant this little patch of ground behind the house with potatoes, cabbage, and string beans. What fun the three of them had as they talked, laughed, and sometimes even sang together while planting the garden.

Her heart wilted as she reached down to pick up her hoe and burlap sack of seed potatoes. With Sophie and Elsie miles away in their own homes and Mama busy ironing yesterday's laundry, Regina would plant the potatoes alone this year. She stepped from the thick grass into the soft, tilled ground, her wooden shoes sinking into the sandy soil. Instead of looking forward to spending a pleasant hour with her mother and sisters, today Regina saw nothing before her but a morning filled with lonely, monotonous, back-aching work.

Heaving a sigh, she looked toward the fields beyond the barn where Papa worked with the Rothhaus men tilling the fields for planting corn. A flash of resentment flared in her chest. While the arrival of Diedrich and Herr Rothhaus had greatly lightened Papa's work, it had increased hers and Mama's. With two extra people to feed and clothe, mother and daughter no longer had the luxury of working together on many of the daily household chores. Now they often needed to work separately in order to accomplish more in the same amount of time.

Continuing to gaze at the distant field, she could make out one man behind the cultivator and another with a strapped canvas sack slung across his shoulder, obviously planting corn. Was it Diedrich? She peered through squinted eyes, but at the extreme distance, she could not tell for sure. At the thought of him, an odd sensation of pulsating warmth filled her chest—a sensation for which she had no certain name. Relief? Yes, it must be relief. Learning last week that he, too, did not want the marriage their fathers had arranged for them allowed her to relax in his presence. Now she no longer avoided him. Indeed, she found it easier to converse with Diedrich than with Eli, who was usually more interested in trying to steal a kiss than talking.

Wielding the hoe, she gouged an indention in the soft dirt. Then, taking a piece of potato from the bag, she dropped it into the hole. Careful to keep the sprouting "eye" up, she covered it again with dirt, which she tamped down using the flat of the hoe blade. After repeating the process for the length of one row, boredom set in. With only the occasional chirping of birds for company, Regina began singing one of her favorite hymns to fill the silence. "Now thank we all our Gott, with heart and hands and voices—"

"Who wondrous things hath done, in whom His world rejoices." A deep, rich baritone voice responded, hushing Regina and yanking her upright.

Grinning, Diedrich strode toward her carrying what looked like a rolled-up newspaper. "Please do not stop singing. That is one of my favorite hymns."

The odd fluttering sensation in her chest returned. "I will if you will sing it with me."

"Who from our mothers' arms hath blessed us on our way," he sang. Regina lifted her soprano voice to join his baritone in singing, "With countless gifts of love, and still is ours today."

After jabbing a stick in the ground to mark the place where she'd planted her last potato, she trudged through the uneven dirt of the garden to where he stood.

Laughing, he clapped his hands together. "Well done, if I say so myself." His expression turned apologetic. "Forgive my intrusion on your work, but I would like to ask a favor."

Curious, Regina focused on the paper in his hand as she neared. From what she could tell, it looked to be the *Madison Courier* newspaper. "I was about to take a rest anyway." Though not entirely true, she liked that her reply erased the concerned lines from his handsome face.

Diedrich unrolled the paper. With a look of little-boy shyness that melted her heart, he held it out to her. "Will you read this to me, please? I cannot ask your parents or my Vater. And Vater knows less English than I do." He narrowed his gaze at a spot near the top right side of the paper. "I recognize only the word *California*."

Taking the paper from his hands, Regina followed his gaze and focused on an article beneath a heading that read Ho for California. Scanning the article, she saw it advertised a fort in Arkansas as a place for California gold seekers to gather. A feeling of apprehension gripped her, and for an instant, she was tempted to tell him the paper was simply reporting about gold having been found in California. But he'd be sure to find out the truth eventually. And besides, wasn't Pastor Sauer's sermon last Sunday on the evil of telling untruths?

"So what does it say?" Eagerness shone in Diedrich's gray eyes.

"It says gold seekers should go to a place called Fort Smith in Arkansas." Her drying throat tightened, forcing her to swallow. "It lists all the items someone going to the goldfields will need and claims they have those things for sale. It also says the government is building a road called the Fort Smith–Santa Fe Trail to the goldfields."

"Then this Fort Smith, Arkansas, is where I should go?" His eyes sparking with interest, he took the paper from her limp hands.

Regina fought the urge to tell him no, that he shouldn't go there. Instead, she mustered a tepid smile and with a weak voice said, "Yes, I suppose it is."

Anticipation bloomed on his face, and he rolled the paper back up and stuffed it inside the waistband of his trousers at the hip. He took her hands into his, and his flannel-soft eyes filled with gratitude. "Danke, Regina." His calloused thumbs caressed the backs of her hands, and her heart took flight like a gaggle of geese. He dropped her hands, and she experienced a sense of loss.

She turned and faced the garden again. "Well, I must get

back to my planting, or we will not have potatoes this year." Despite an effort to lighten her voice, it sounded strained.

"I am done with the plowing, and Vater and Herr Seitz are finishing the corn planting." He looked over the little garden patch. "I would be happy to help you finish planting the potatoes."

With her heart slamming against her ribs, her first inclination was to decline his offer. What was the matter with her? Eli was her sweetheart, not Diedrich. Besides, by the end of harvest, Diedrich would be heading for California. She looked at the hoe and the nearly full sack of seed potatoes lying in the dirt. Diedrich and his father caused her enough extra work, so why not accept his help? She nodded and smiled. "Danke. I would much appreciate that."

For the next hour, they worked together with him digging the holes and her dropping in the pieces of cut potato. As they worked, they sang hymns, and Regina marveled at how well their voices blended. When not singing, they swapped anecdotes about tending gardens as children with their siblings.

"Do you miss your brothers?" Regina asked as she placed the last piece of potato in the little gully Diedrich had just dug.

His face took on a pensive expression, and he rested his chin on the back of his hands, which covered the knob of the hoe's handle. "Ja. I do miss them."

Regina stood and brushed her palms together, dusting the soil from them. "Your brothers did not want to come here?" Herr Rothhaus had mentioned his older sons and their families on several occasions but had never said if they, too, would like to come to America.

Diedrich shook his head. "Johann, no. He is the oldest and is attached to the farm in Venne. Frederic, I think, would come, but his wife, Hilde, is with child again. Even if they had money for the passage—which they do not—she was not willing to risk it."

His comment struck home for Regina. "I was born on ship during Mama and Papa's voyage here." Her gaze panned the surrounding farm. "I am glad Mama was courageous." For a moment they shared a smile, and warmth that had nothing to do with the midday sun rushed through her.

Diedrich jammed a maple stick into the ground at the end of their last row of potatoes to mark it, then glanced up at the sky. "Now all we have to do is pray for Gott to send the sun and the rain." Grinning, he nodded toward the split log bench near the house. "I think we have earned a rest."

"So do I." Regina followed him out of the patch of tilled ground, unable to remember a more enjoyable experience planting potatoes. As she stepped from the loose soil of the garden, one of her wooden shoes sank deep into a furrow, and when she lifted her foot, the shoe stayed behind. Not wanting to get her sock dirty, she balanced on one foot and bent the shoeless one back beneath her.

At her grunt of dismay, Diedrich turned around. Seeing her plight, he hurried to her. "Here, hold on to me." He reached down to retrieve her shoe. Obeying, she slipped her arm around his waist and felt the hard muscles of his torso stretch with his movement. Her heart quickened at their nearness as he held her against him with one hand while placing the Holzschuh on her stockinged foot.

With her shoe back in place, she mumbled her thanks and stepped away from him as quickly as possible, hurrying to the bench in an effort to hide her blazing face. She tried to think of an instance when Eli had kindled an equally pleasant yet unsettling reaction in her but couldn't.

They perched at opposite ends of the bench, leaving a good foot of space between them. For a long moment, they sat in silence. The gusting breeze, laden with the perfume of lilac blossoms, dried the perspiration beading on Regina's brow.

At length, Diedrich reached behind him and pulled the newspaper from the waistband of his trousers. He looked at it for a moment then turned to Regina. "I have another favor to ask. I would like for you to teach me to read the English. I will never make it to California if I cannot speak or read the language of America."

Like all the local young people of German heritage, Regina was fluent in both German and English, having learned English in school. Switching between the two languages felt as natural to her as breathing. With German spoken exclusively at home, it hadn't occurred to her that Diedrich lacked that advantage.

She smiled. "I'm not sure how good a teacher I will be, but I will try."

She scooted closer and, bending toward him until their shoulders touched, began to point out some of the simpler words on the pages of the open newspaper. "*And.*" Dragging out the enunciation, she pronounced the word above her index finger then had him repeat it.

An obviously quick learner, he mastered the one-, two-, and three-letter words by the first or second try. So Regina moved on to some larger words but with decidedly less success, making for humorous results.

After butchering the word *prospectors* for the third time, he began guessing at its pronunciation, making the word sound sillier with each try and sending Regina into fits of laughter so hard that tears rolled down her cheeks. "Nein, nein, nein!" she gasped between guffaws, her head lolling against his shoulder.

"Regina."

At the sound of her name, she looked up to see Eli standing a few feet away and eyeing her and Diedrich with an angry glare.

Chapter 8

I thought you said you weren't interested in him." Despite his earlier fierce look, Eli's voice sounded more hurt than angry as he cast a narrowed glance over Regina's shoulder toward the bench she'd sprung from seconds ago.

"Diedrich asked me to teach him English, that is all." She shrugged, trying to force a light tone.

"Diedrich, huh?" Eli shot another glare past her, his voice hardening and his brow slipping into an angry V.

Despite the dozen or so feet between them, Regina could feel Diedrich's eyes on her back. Thankfully, he had not followed her across the yard to where she and Eli now stood beneath the white-blossomed dogwood tree. She desperately wished he would discreetly leave her and Eli alone, but after the two men's confrontation in the barn last week, she doubted he would. Why did Eli have to come at this very moment?

Sighing, she put her hand on Eli's arm. His tensed muscles reminded her of a cat about to pounce. Though admittedly flattering, Eli's jealousy was growing tiresome. As much as she tried to make her voice sound conciliatory, she couldn't keep a frustrated tone from creeping in. "What I told you is true." The temptation to tell him about the agreement she and Diedrich had made tugged hard. But she couldn't risk him blurting it out in an unguarded moment. "You will just have to believe me."

Eli groped for her hand, but for reasons she couldn't explain, she drew it back and crossed her arms over her middle, tucking her hands protectively beneath them. "Why are you here?"

"My uncle's barn burned near Dudleytown last night."

A wave of concern and sorrow swept away her defenses, and she reached out to touch his arm again. "Oh Eli, I am sorry to hear that. I hope your uncle and his family were not hurt."

He gave an unconcerned shrug. "Na. They're all right. Lost a couple of pigs, but they got the horses and cows out." A grin crept across his handsome face. "Thing is, Pa and some of my uncle's neighbors are plannin' a barn raisin' soon as Pa can get enough lumber sawed at the mill. He's invitin' everybody in Sauers to come." Fun danced in his green eyes, and he grasped her hands. "Your pa's already agreed to come and bring you and your ma." His smile faded briefly as he glanced behind her. "And them two fellers stayin' here with you." He focused on her face again, and his smile returned with a roguish quirk. "We can see each other all day durin' the barn raisin'. And with so many people about, I'd wager we could prob'ly slip off and get some time to ourselves and nobody would even notice."

Drawing her hands from his, she stepped back and thought she heard a stirring sound behind her. She prayed Diedrich would not feel compelled to save her from Eli's exuberance. The prospect of having to step between the two men to prevent them from coming to blows did not appeal to her. Nor did she relish the notion of explaining to Papa and Herr Rothhaus what had prompted the fisticuffs.

Thankfully, Eli made no move to recapture her hands or, worse, try to steal a kiss, which would doubtless bring Diedrich sprinting to her side.

Eli's gaze, focused behind her, tracked to the right as if following a moving object. Was Diedrich, after all, deciding to intrude on her and Eli's conversation? Or had he gone, leaving the two of them alone? Oddly, she found the second notion more disconcerting than the first.

Eli's expression sobered, and he took a couple of steps backward. "I just wanted to let you know about the barn raisin'. An' if you *are* my special girl, you can prove it by sneakin' off and spendin' some time alone with me durin' the meal." Reaching up, he plucked a blossom from the boughs above them and pressed it into her hand.

Before Regina could tell him that her parents would never allow her to do such a thing, he turned and took off at a quick trot, disappearing around the corner of the house. Opening her palm, she stared at the ivory-colored flower with its spiky crownlike center and jagged, rust-stained tips that edged its four petals. Three weeks ago on Easter Sunday morning, Pastor Sauer had suggested that the appearance of the blossoms should be a reminder of Christ's sacrifice for man's sins. Guilt pricked like a thorn at her heart. She doubted Christ, or her parents, would approve of what Eli had asked her to do.

Had Diedrich heard? Though he couldn't read English,

both he and his father had displayed an ability to understand some of the spoken words. At the thought of his having overheard Eli's demand, a flash of panic leapt in her chest. She spun around to look for him, but he had gone. Instead of bringing her relief, the sight of the empty bench brought a strange forlornness.

Thunder boomed, shaking the bed Diedrich shared with his father and rattling the window glass across the dark room. Wide awake, he rolled onto his side, searching in vain for a more comfortable, sleep-inducing position. The ropes supporting the feather tick mattress groaned in protest with his movements, while a white flash of lightning cast an eerie glow over the room.

Through the tumult Father slept, his snores and snorts adding to the cacophony of the storm outside. Diedrich rolled onto his back again and closed his eyes, but still sleep eluded him.

Sighing, he sat up in surrender. He swung his legs over the side of the bed and pressed his bare feet to the nubby surface of the rag rug that covered much of the puncheon floor. At supper, his concerns about Regina and her attachment to the boy called Eli had robbed him of his appetite. But now, his stomach rumbled in protest of its emptiness. In truth, it was not the raging storm but thoughts of Regina and Eli that had kept sleep just beyond Diedrich's grasp.

As quietly as possible he pulled on his trousers and shirt

and padded barefoot across the room, hopeful that the sounds of the storm would cover any creaking noises his movements might evoke from the wood floor. He would rather Herr or Frau Seitz not discover him wandering about their home in the middle of the night.

Intermittent flashes of lightning guided him to the kitchen at the back of the house. But upon reaching the room, he realized he would need a more constant light in his quest for food or risk knocking something over and waking everyone in the house.

He lit the tin lamp on the kitchen table, suffusing the space with a warm, golden glow. In search of the remnants of last night's venison supper, he stepped to the black walnut cabinet where he had seen Frau Seitz and Regina store left-over food from meals. As he reached up to grasp the knob of the cabinet door, he caught a flicker of movement out of the corner of his right eye.

Freezing in place, he peered intently through the kitchen doorway that opened to the washroom. A creaking sound emanated from the enclosed stairway that led up to Regina's bedroom. For a heart-stopping moment, Diedrich contemplated blowing out the lamp and bolting to the interior of the house and his own bedroom. But before he could move, a small dancing light appeared on the back door and a shadowy figure emerged from the stairwell.

A small gasp sounded from the washroom. Unable to speak or move, he gazed unblinking at the vision before him. Fully dressed, but barefoot and with her unplaited hair cascading around her shoulders, Regina stood motionless in the threshold between the washroom and kitchen. Light from the amber finger lamp in her hand burnished her loosed tresses, making them appear as a cloud of gold around her face.

"Verzeihst du mir." Finding his tongue at last, Diedrich murmured his apology. "Forgive me for waking you." He glanced at the cabinet. "I woke up hungry and thought. . ."

To his surprise, she smiled and walked to him. "It was the storm that woke me, not you." She glanced upward. "The sounds are more frightening to me upstairs with the big cottonwood tree swaying just outside the window beside my bed. So during storms, I often come down and sit near the bottom of the stairs. I was on my way down when I saw your light in the kitchen." As if to lend validity to her words, an explosion of thunder shook the house. She jerked, and for a moment, Diedrich feared she would drop the glass lamp. He eased it from her fingers and set it beside the tin one on the kitchen table.

The look of fear on her face made him want to comfort her. Protect her. Instead, he said the stupidest thing that could come out of his mouth. "It is just noise. It cannot hurt you."

Giving him a sheepish smile, she opened the cabinet, releasing the welcome aroma of roasted venison. "I know it is silly of me, but I have always been afraid of storms. Mama says I was born during a storm at sea on their journey from Bremen to Baltimore." She handed him a platter covered with a cotton towel. "My fear of storms wasn't so bad when my sisters were here and shared my room, but now that I am alone in my bed. . ." Her words trailed off as if she realized she'd said too much, embarrassing herself.

"This venison smells *wunderbar.*" Rushing to her rescue, Diedrich hastened to change the subject. Why did he always feel compelled to protect her, even from herself?

She took down another plate from the pantry cabinet, and Diedrich inhaled a whiff of sourdough bread. "If you will slice the meat and Mama's good *Bauernbrot,*" she said, "I will dip us each a *Becher* of milk." Darting about the kitchen, she produced two plates and a large knife then headed toward the crock of milk beside the sink.

When they finally sat together at the table with the ingredients for their middle-of-the-night repast, Diedrich propped his elbows on the tabletop and bowed his head over his folded hands as Regina did the same. Diedrich's whispered prayer of thanks was swallowed up by a violent crash of thunder. Regina gasped and jumped then visibly trembled as the sound continued to roll and reverberate around the little kitchen.

Diedrich's heart went out to her. Remembering his trepidation during an especially rough storm at sea, he understood some of her fear. He reached across the table and gripped her hand, warm and small, trembling in his. The urge to round the table and take her into his arms and hold her close to him became almost suffocating.

"You are safe." The words seemed simplistic and woefully inadequate, but they were all he could think to say. Yet despite how feckless they sounded, those three words appeared sufficient. For as the sound subsided, rolling off into the distance, a measure of fear left her eyes.

"Danke." Drawing her hand from his, she glanced down, a self-conscious smile quivering on her lips.

For several minutes, they ate in silence. When a bright flash of lightning that Diedrich knew would precede another clap of thunder lit the kitchen, he tried to think of something that would distract her from the coming noise. An idea struck, and he hurried to wash down his bite of venison and bread with a gulp of milk. "How do you say *Blitz* in English?"

"Lightning," she said around a bite of bread.

"Lightning," he repeated, and she nodded.

Thunder rumbled, and she appeared to stiffen. She gripped her mug of milk so hard her fingers turned as white as its contents.

Diedrich covered her hand with his to draw her attention back to him. "*Donner.* How do you say Donner?" If he could keep her distracted, maybe she would forget to be frightened.

"Thunder." Her voice trembled slightly, mimicking the sound outside as it dissipated and rolled away.

"Thun–er." Diedrich dragged out the enunciation, intentionally leaving out the *d* to keep her focused on teaching him the word.

She smiled and giggled, a bright, almost musical sound. His heart bucked like Father's prize bull the time Frederic was fool enough to climb on the animal's back. "Nein." She shook her head. "Thun–*der.*"

"Thunder," he managed to whisper, his racing heart robbing him of breath.

The wind howled and assailed the kitchen window a blast of rain.

Regina glanced at the window. "Rain," she said. "*Regen* is rain."

"Rain," he repeated, glad to see that the fear had left her blue eyes.

For the next several minutes they ate while taking turns coming up with words for her to translate into English. Lightning flashed and thunder rumbled, but as they finished their food, she no longer seemed affected by the noise. Now fully engaged in the game, she appeared completely relaxed.

"*Scheune.*" Her voice held a challenge as she leaned back in her chair and crossed her arms over her chest.

A desire to show off sparked in Diedrich. This was one of the few English words he had learned from Herr Seitz. Answering her smug look with one of his own, he locked his gaze with hers and said, "Barn. *Scheune* in English is barn."

"Ja!" The word burst from her mouth on a note of glee loud enough to rival the storm's noise. Immediately, she clasped her hand over her mouth and cast a wide-eyed glance toward the doorway that led to the inner part of the house as if afraid she had woken their parents. When several seconds passed and no one appeared, a nervous-sounding little giggle erupted from behind her fingers. Rising, she gave ~~h~~im a self-conscious grin and gathered up their plates and ~~said,~~ "I think we should go back to our beds now before we ~~wake~~ ~~them~~ *rn*," she whispered.

~~Diedrich watc~~hed her move about the kitchen and his ~~conscience warned, *I dare not l~~*ose my heart to this girl. I cannot!* But ~~his heart forged~~ on, scorning his censure. If only he ~~knew the truth, the~~n maybe when autumn came he could leave for California with an unshackled heart. But that could not happen as long as Regina continued to court that brutish fellow, Eli. The concerns that had kept Diedrich awake rose up in his chest, demanding release. Somehow he must find the words to dissuade her from considering the scoundrel for a husband. *Dear Lord, give me the words that would convince her to turn away from Eli Tanner.*

When she had returned the meat and bread to the pantry cabinet and closed the doors, Diedrich walked to her and took her hand in his. He chose his words with care, as if he were picking fruit for a queen.

"Regina." He gazed into her eyes, which sparkled like blue stars in the lamplight. At her expression of questioning trust, he nearly lost his nerve. His arms ached to hold her, but that wouldn't do. Instead, he caressed the back of her hand with his thumb and swallowed to moisten his drying throat. "Regina," he began again. "I do not know how well you know this fellow, Eli. But I do not think he is a good man. It is my opinion that you would be wise to consider—"

"I did not ask for your opinion." She yanked her hand from his grasp. "You know nothing of Eli or of me." Her expression turned as stormy as the weather outside. "Just because your Vater and mine made a deal does not give you the right to tell me what I should do!"

Chapter 9

Regina stood in front of the dresser mirror and slipped another pin into the braid that crowned her head. A bright ray of morning sun dappled by the new leaves of the cottonwood tree outside her window speckled her hair with its light. Though vanity was a sin, she always liked to look her best for church. She fingered the snowy tatting that edged the collar of her blue frock. For reasons she couldn't explain, she wanted to look especially nice today. Inspecting her reflection, she smoothed down all hints of wrinkles in her freshly washed and ironed Sunday frock. She couldn't help thinking of Diedrich's comment last Sunday when he helped her onto the family's wagon for the trip to church. "With your golden hair and blue frock, you remind me of a summer sky."

Diedrich. There he was again. Always loitering on the fringes of her mind. More and more, she found herself thinking of him. Since the storm two nights ago, they hadn't spoken again at length. At the realization, regret smote her heart. Many times she had wanted to apologize for lashing out at him, but somehow she had not found the right moment. He had obviously gotten the wrong impression of Eli when he saw them arguing in the barn and was just trying to protect her. But his words of caution, however carefully delivered, had touched the one nerve in Regina that everyone, including Eli, had lately rubbed raw. With the exception of her eldest sister, Sophie, who had always delighted in bossing her around, Regina had been allowed the freedom to make most of her own decisions in life. Now, suddenly, everyone seemed determined to wrest that control away from her. Papa, Mama, Herr Rothhaus, and even Eli, with his demands that she spend time alone with him at the coming barn raising, all wanted to tell her what to do. She had appreciated the fact that Diedrich had not treated her in a dictatorial manner but had shown her the respect due a friend and equal. So when he voiced his opinion of Eli, it was, as Mama often said, "the drop that makes the barrel overflow."

As she remembered how she had angrily stalked away from him after he had tried so hard to quell her fear during the storm, guilt gnawed at her conscience. Her mouth turned down in a frown. Ironically, their secret pact to not get married had formed a bond between them that never could have occurred had they agreed to their parents' bargain. And now she feared she had broken that bond. She missed the easy friendliness she and Diedrich had enjoyed before she'd allowed her temper to shatter it. Oddly, her arguments with Eli had never bothered her as much as this one rift with Diedrich, possibly because she felt at fault. Though she instinctively sensed that Diedrich was not one to hold a grudge, she knew she would not be easy again until she had made amends with him. Still, she dreaded the encounter, which was sure to be awkward.

So despite the sunny day, her mood remained clouded.

She usually looked forward to attending Sunday morning church service and enjoyed Pastor Sauer's sermons. But this morning she had to force her feet toward the stairs. Even anticipation of seeing friends like Anna Rieckers and Louisa Stuckwisch had not spurred her to dress more quickly. But Mama had already called up twice, warning Regina she'd be left behind if she didn't come down soon, so she could delay no longer.

When she reached the bottom step, her heart catapulted to her throat and she froze. Dressed in his best with hat in hand, Diedrich stood near the back door. She hadn't expected him to be waiting for her. Before she could say anything, he spoke.

"*Guten Morgen*, Regina." Though his lips remained unsmiling, his gentle gray gaze held no speck of grudge. If anything, his expression suggested apology. "The others have all gone out to the wagon, but I hoped we might speak alone."

"Guten Morgen, Diedrich." Her throat went dry, making her words come out in a squeak. If she was going to make amends, now was the time. She opened her mouth.

"Diedrich."

"Regina."

They spoke in near unison, and he smiled, dimpling the corner of his well-shaped mouth. "*Bitte*, you speak."

Shame drove her gaze from his face to the floor. "Verzehst du mir. I should not have acted so rudely the other night."

"Nein." Wonder edged his voice, and he took her hands in his. "It is I who should ask your forgiveness." His thumbs caressed the backs of her hands as they had done during the storm, sending the same warm tingles up her arms. "You were right. It is not my place to say whom you should choose for friends." He grinned. "I only hope you still count me among them."

Regina wanted to laugh with glee. She wanted to jump up and down and clap her hands like when she was small and Papa bought her a candy stick at the Dudleytown mercantile. She couldn't say why, but knowing the friendship that had sprung up between her and Diedrich was still intact made her happy. But instead of embarrassing herself with childish antics, she smiled demurely and murmured, "Of course you are my friend." Turning her face to hide her smile, she focused on reaching for her bonnet on a peg by the back door.

He blew out a long breath as if he had been holding it. *"Ich bin froh."*

Glad. Yes, glad fit how Regina felt, too. She basked in his smile as he escorted her to the wagon where her parents and Herr Rothhaus sat waiting.

And the gladness stayed with her throughout the church service. From time to time, she found her gaze straying to the men's side of the church. With his Bible—one of the few things he'd brought from Venne—open on his lap, Diedrich sat beside his father, his rapt attention directed toward the front of the church and Pastor Sauer. His straight brown hair lay at an angle across his broad forehead and his clean-shaven jaw in profile looked strong, as if chiseled from stone. Regina wondered why she had never noticed how very handsome he was.

An odd ache burrowed deep into her chest. Perhaps it

would not have been the worst thing in the world if Papa and Herr Rothhaus had gotten their way and she had ended up with Diedrich for a husband.

" 'And be ye kind one to another, tenderhearted, forgiving one another, even as God for Christ's sake hath forgiven you.' " Pastor Sauer's compelling voice drew Regina's attention back up to him. He paused and stroked the considerable length of his salt-and-pepper beard as if allowing time for the scripture to soak into his congregants' brains. The subject of his sermon had been directed particularly toward married couples. But the words of the scripture drew in Regina's mind a stark contrast between how Diedrich and Eli treated her.

She glanced over at Diedrich again, and the ache in her chest deepened. It didn't matter how sweet, caring, or handsome Diedrich was. Eli was handsome, too. And he wanted to marry her. Diedrich wanted to hunt for gold in California.

Diedrich pumped the pastor's hand. "It was a fine sermon, Pastor Sauer."

Pastor Sauer gave a little chuckle and clapped him on the shoulder. "Danke, Sohn." Then, leaning in, he added, "And one you should remember, maybe, hey?" With a twinkle in his eye, he shot a glance across the churchyard to where Regina stood talking and giggling with two other young women. "Herr Seitz tells me you and Fräulein Seitz have decided to wait until after the harvest to wed." He nodded his head in approval. "That is *gut*. Learn your bride's heart before you wed. It will make for a more harmonious home."

Diedrich quirked a weak smile that his mouth refused to support for more than a second. He felt like a liar and a fraud. But he couldn't share his true plans with Pastor Sauer any more than he could share them with Father or Herr and Frau Seitz.

Giving the pastor's hand a final shake, he headed for the patch of shade where the Seitz wagon stood. *"Learn your bride's heart."* The pastor's words echoed in his ears.

It almost made him wish Regina *was* his bride-to-be, as everyone thought. For every day, he learned something new and wonderful about her. This morning he had learned she had a sweet heart, full of forgiveness. And if not for the beckoning goldfields of California, a life here with Regina on this fertile land would be more than enticing.

It had troubled him that yesterday she seemed to make a concerted effort to keep her distance from him, finding reasons to stay near her mother. He had surmised she was still angry with him over his comment about Eli, and didn't blame her. Of course she would have viewed his words as meddling in her personal business, and rightly so. But what had troubled him more was the look on her face this morning when she came downstairs. For one awful moment, he had seen something akin to fear flicker in her eyes. Had she stayed away from him because she thought that, like Eli, he might respond to her earlier righteous indignation with anger? The thought both sickened and angered him. He hardened his resolve to do everything in his power over the summer to open her eyes to the dangers the Tanner boy presented.

At the wagon, he turned and looked back in her direction,

and his heart quickened. A wide smile graced her lovely face as she carried on an animated conversation with her friends. The morning sun turned the braids that circled her head to ropes of gold, while her calico bonnet dangled negligently from her wrist, brushing her sky-blue skirt with her every gesture. She laughed, a bright, musical sound that always reminded him of a brook tripping over stones.

"Diedrich. I was looking for you." Herr Seitz put his hand on Diedrich's shoulder, jerking him from his musings. "I hope you are not so much in a hurry for dinner." He glanced over his shoulder at Father, who was sauntering toward them with Frau Seitz on one arm and Regina on the other. "Your Vater and I have agreed it is a nice morning for a drive."

As was their usual custom on Sundays, they had forgone breakfast this morning, opting instead for a larger meal after church. And though Diedrich's stomach gnawed with emptiness, his curiosity was piqued. "Ja, it is a gut day for a drive. I can wait to eat." Since their arrival nearly a month ago, Diedrich had rarely left the Seitz farm. And though his stomach might protest, he was eager to see more of the countryside.

Herr Seitz turned to his wife. "Come, Mutti. We are going to take a drive." He helped Frau Seitz to the front seat of the wagon, while Diedrich helped Regina up to the seat behind it. Diedrich and his father would sit in the last of the three seats in the spring wagon.

Frau Seitz huffed. "I know it is a nice day, but could we not take our drive after dinner? Regina and I have *Kaninchen* to fry and *Brötchen* to bake."

"The rabbit and the rolls will wait." Herr Seitz shook

his head as he settled beside his wife and unwound the reins from the brake handle. "This drive is *wichtig*."

Regina gave a little laugh as she adjusted her skirts. "You are acting very peculiar, Papa. I do not see what could be important about a Sunday drive around Sauers. But if we must go, could we take the road past Tanners' mill? It has fewer ruts than some of the other roads." Though her voice sounded nonchalant, Diedrich detected a note of stiffness about it. From his experience, her opinion of the road's surface was correct. But he doubted it was the true reason she wanted to go in that direction. Instead, he suspected she hoped to glimpse her sweetheart as they passed the mill. At that thought, he experienced a painful prick near his heart.

Herr Seitz shook his head. "We will not be going past the mill, Tochter. What I want to show you is at the west boundary of our land."

Her hopeful expression dissolved into a glum look that saddened Diedrich. Why could she not see that Tanner did not truly care for her—that no man who loved her would treat her so roughly.

When Diedrich had settled beside his father in the seat behind Regina, Herr Seitz looked over his shoulder as if to assure himself everyone was settled. Focusing his gaze on Diedrich, he grinned. "Diedrich, you should sit with Regina. I do not think your Vater will mind to have a seat to himself." Did the man have a twinkle in his eye? Herr Seitz turned back around before Diedrich could be sure.

"Ja, Diedrich. You should sit with your intended for this ride." Father gave Diedrich's arm a nudge.

Rising obediently, Diedrich made his way up to the seat Regina occupied. "Of course. It would be my pleasure." And though his words could not have been truer, he was not at all sure Regina felt the same. But to his surprise, she offered him a bright smile when he sat down beside her. And as they bounced over a rutted road that was little more than a cow path, they fell into easy conversation. Regina gleefully pointed out to him the homes of her friends, adding interesting tidbits about the families and their farms.

"Anna's family has six milk cows," she said, indicating a neat white clapboard house nestled among a stand of trees. "And since she is the only girl and her brothers hate to milk, she must help her Mutter milk all six cows every morning and every evening."

As she talked, Diedrich nodded and offered an occasional comment, but mostly he simply enjoyed watching her smiling face and the light in her eyes as she spoke about the area. Clearly, she loved this place.

After passing acres of neatly tilled fields, the wagon turned down the narrow. path that marked the boundary between Herr Seitz's cornfield, which Diedrich had recently helped to plant, and a neighboring forest. At last, Herr Seitz reined in the team of horses, bringing the wagon to a stop.

"We are here." He turned a beaming face to Diedrich and Regina.

Perplexed, Diedrich sat mute, unsure what "here" meant.

Regina's tongue loosened quicker. "Papa, why have you brought us to the back end of the cornfield and Herr Driehaus's woods?"

Herr Seitz's smile turned smug, as if he knew a great secret. "These are not Herr Driehaus's woods any longer. He sold them to me last week, all twenty acres. It is on this land we will build a home for you and Diedrich and Georg."

Chapter 10

Stunned to silence, Regina could only look helplessly at Papa. She turned to Diedrich, but his blanched face reflected the same shocked surprise that had struck her mute.

A sick feeling settled in her stomach. She had completely forgotten that Papa had talked of purchasing this land back when Elsie was courting Ludwig Schmersal, before she became betrothed to her husband, William.

"Well, have you nothing to say?" Papa eyed her and Diedrich with a look of expectation. The whiskers on his cheeks bristled with his wide grin.

Mama saved them both. Turning to Papa, she clasped her hand to her chest and said in a breathless whisper, "Twenty acres? Can we afford this, Ernst?"

Papa waved off her concern. "Do not worry, wife. With Georg and Diedrich helping with the farm this summer, I expect the profits from the corn and wheat crop to more than cover the cost of the land." He shrugged. "Besides, since the land has not been improved and adjoins our farm, Herr Driehaus gave me and Georg a very good price: one dollar and seventy-five cents an acre."

Diedrich swiveled in his seat and gaped at his father. "You knew of this, Vater?"

Herr Rothhaus nodded, and the same smile Regina had

seen so many times on Diedrich's face appeared on the older man's—except on Herr Rothhaus's face, graying whiskers wreathed the smile. "Of course. It is a fine surprise, is it not, Sohn?"

"Ja, a fine surprise, Vater." Diedrich gazed at the woods as if in doing so he could make them vanish. "But you should not have agreed to such an extravagant gift."

Herr Rothhaus shook his head. "Of course I did not agree to accept the land as a gift. I have promised Ernst that we will pay him back for the land as soon as our first crop is sold. But we cannot take advantage of the Seitzes' hospitality forever. We need a house built and ready for us when you and Regina wed this autumn."

What blood was left in Diedrich's face seemed to drain away. Regina had to fight the urge to confess all to their parents. But what good would that do? The deal had been made. The money had been spent.

To his credit, Diedrich turned back and sent a heroic if somewhat taut smile in Papa's direction. Some of the color returned to his face, and he said in a voice that belied the tumult Regina knew must be raging within him, "Danke, Herr Seitz. This will be a gut spot for a home. And as my Vater said, you will be paid back in full. I promise."

Was he thinking that he would find enough gold in California to pay Papa back? Regina could imagine Papa's face in the fall when Diedrich revealed his plans to head to the goldfields. She was glad she hadn't eaten anything this morning, for if she had she would have lost it for sure.

The ride home was accomplished in silence except for

Papa and Herr Rothhaus carrying on a rather lively conversation across the length of the wagon, discussing plans about how the new house should be built.

Panic gripped Regina. Struggling for breath, she looked helplessly at Diedrich. Oddly, his expression had turned placid. Smiling, he patted her hand as if to assure her all would be well.

Regina tried to return his smile, but her lips refused to form one. She had learned enough about Diedrich to know he would pay Papa back or die trying. And that terrified her.

The next day, as she worked with her mother in the kitchen, Regina's mind continued to wrestle with the thorny problem Papa had presented to her and Diedrich.

Smiling, Mama glanced up from peeling potatoes. "You are very quiet today, Tochter. I wonder, are you thinking of your new home the men will be building soon?" As she talked, she worked the knife around a wrinkled potato covered in white sprouts, divesting it of its skin in one spiral paring. The vegetable was among the few remaining edible potatoes from last year's crop Regina had managed to find in the root cellar. She was eager to harvest the first batch of new potatoes from the crop she and Diedrich had planted, but that wouldn't be until at least July. It saddened her to think that shortly after the first potato harvest, Diedrich would be leaving for Arkansas to be outfitted for his journey to California.

"Ja, Mama. I was thinking of the house." At the stove, she

offered her mother a tepid smile and lifted the lid on the pot of dandelion greens to check if it needed more water. If only she could share her concerns with Mama. But she couldn't, so better to steer the conversation in another direction. "I was thinking, too, about Pastor Sauer's message yesterday." That wasn't a complete lie. The pastor's message *was* one of the many thoughts swirling around in Regina's head as if caught up in a cyclone.

Mama dipped water from the bucket beside the sink and poured it into the pot of peeled potatoes, which she then carried to the stove. "And what about the pastor's sermon were you thinking?"

Regina gave the steaming greens a quick stir with a long wooden spoon. Assured they had sufficient water, she returned the lid to the pot. "I was thinking of the verse Pastor read from Colossians." Surely sometime in her life she had read the verse before, but it had obviously never struck her as it did yesterday.

Mama nodded. "'Husbands, love your wives, and be not bitter against them,'" she recited. Turning from the stove, she cocked her head at Regina and crossed her arms over her chest. "So what about the verse do you not understand?"

In an effort to hide her expression, Regina walked to the sink and began dumping the potato peelings by handfuls into the slop bucket, careful to keep her back to her mother. "Pastor said it meant that a husband should always treat his wife with kindness." She couldn't help thinking of Eli's angry outburst in the barn and how he had torn her dress when she tried to pull away from him. And how his demeanor and actions had frightened her. "But surely husbands get angry at their wives sometimes."

Mama's laugh surprised Regina. "Of course they get angry. Just as wives get angry at their husbands. But husbands and wives can be angry at one another and still be kind." She crossed the kitchen to Regina and gently took her arm, turning her around. "Regina, you have seen your Vater angry with me many times, but did you ever see him raise his voice to me or his hand against me?"

Regina shook her head. "Nein, never." Such a thing was unimaginable. And neither had Papa treated her or her sisters in that manner. *So why did I allow Eli to treat me so roughly?* The question that popped into Regina's mind begged an answer or at least some justification. Regina and Eli were not married. Surely he would treat her differently if she were his wife.

Mama walked to the table where the two skinned squirrels Father had shot this morning lay soaking in brine. Taking up the butcher knife, she began cutting the meat into pieces for frying. "It is only natural for you to be thinking of these things with your wedding day coming in September. Your sisters, too, were full of questions before they wed." She sent Regina an indulgent smile. "But I am confident you will have no concerns with how Diedrich will treat you. Besides being a good Christian young man, he does not seem to be one who is quick to anger. And I have seen nothing but consideration and kindness from him."

Regina agreed. Her heart throbbed with a dull ache. Everything Mama said about Diedrich was true. One day he would make someone a kind and sweet husband. But not Regina. Suddenly, the image of Diedrich exchanging wedding vows with some anonymous, faceless woman drove the ache deeper into Regina's chest.

Mama held out a crockery bowl. "Here, fetch some flour for coating the meat." She glanced out the window as Regina took the bowl. "In an hour the men will be in from the fields and expecting their dinner. So we must get this *Eiken* browned and into the oven."

In the pantry, Regina scooped flour into the bowl from one of the sacks on the floor. Her mind flew back to the day when she had fetched the flour from the mill. So much had changed in her life—and her heart—since that day. Was it only a month ago? It seemed so much longer. That day, her mind and heart had brimmed with thoughts of Eli. She remembered how her heart had pranced with Gypsy's feet as the pony bore her ever nearer to the gristmill and her sweetheart. She thought of how she had reveled in Eli's every touch and how her heart had hung on his every word. But lately, thoughts of him no longer caused joy to bubble up in her or sent pleasant tingles over her skin.

Yet she still experienced those feelings. But now the man who sparked them spoke German and had not green but gray eyes. Had Diedrich indeed replaced Eli in Regina's heart? It was true that Diedrich was kind and sweet. But he was also leaving Sauers in the fall. To allow her heart to nurture affection for him would be beyond foolish. Most likely, her waning interest in Eli was caused by her seeing him so infrequently. And that wasn't Eli's fault. Yesterday she had asked

Papa to drive by the mill, hoping to catch a glance of Eli. She needed to know if the sight of him still made her heart leap when he wasn't surprising her by coming up behind her unexpectedly. And though mildly disappointed she didn't get the chance to test her reaction at seeing Eli, missing an opportunity to see him hadn't made her especially sad.

An hour later with the squirrel golden brown in the frying pan, Mama took the corn bread from the oven and plopped it on top of the stove. She glanced out the kitchen window and gave a frustrated huff. "The meal is cooked and ready for the table. I hope the men come in soon." Shaking her head, she clucked her tongue. "With the planting done, they may have time to dawdle, but we have a day's work to do before the sun goes down."

Regina looked up from the table where she worked placing the stoneware plates and eating utensils. She agreed. Not only would she and Mama need time to clean up the kitchen after the meal, but this was wash day. Outside, they had two lines of laundry drying in the sun and wind that would need to be taken down before time to begin preparing supper. "Do you want me to go call them in?"

Mama shook her head. "Your Vater and Herr Rothhaus have gone to look at the new piece of land. You would have to hitch Gypsy to the cart or ride one of the horses, and that would take too long. I am sure they are already on their way home. But Diedrich is here on the farm, fixing the lean-to behind the barn that was damaged in the storm. It would be gut if he came on in and washed up before the others arrive."

Nodding her acquiescence, Regina headed out of the

house. She hadn't had a chance to talk to Diedrich in private since they learned about Papa buying the land. This would give her the perfect opportunity to find out his thoughts on the situation. The placid look that had come over his face after the initial shock of Papa's announcement still puzzled her. She couldn't imagine him heading to California in the fall and leaving his father alone with the debt. A tiny glimmer of hope flickered in her chest. Was it possible he might actually give up his dream of California gold and stay in Sauers? She wished her heart didn't skip so at the thought. Diedrich was a friend, nothing more. But her rebellious heart paid no attention to the reprimand, dancing ever quicker as she neared the barn.

Skirting the barn lot, she approached the end of the barn where the lean-to that sheltered the plow, cultivator, and other farming tools jutted out from the back of the building. As she rounded the corner of the barn, a sudden, deafening crash shattered the calm. Her heart catapulted to her throat, and she jumped back. Stunned, she stood frozen in place as her mind tried to grasp what had just happened. Slowly, a sick feeling began to settle in the pit of her stomach. Then panic, like a burst of heat, thawed her frozen limbs. As if her feet had grown wings, she rushed toward the source of the din, now quiet.

When she reached the back of the barn, her mind refused to accept what her eyes saw. The entire roof of the lean-to lay in a heap of hewn logs and lumber.

Chapter 11

Regina felt as if someone had squeezed all the breath out of her lungs. Heaving, she managed to pull in enough air to scream one word. "Diedrich!"

Scrambling to the debris pile, she began frantically pitching pieces of wood from the rubble. Splinters became imbedded in her hands. She didn't care. "Diedrich, where are you? Can you hear me? Are you hurt?" Sobs tore from her throat and tears flooded down her cheeks. She had to get to him. She *had* to! Scratching and clawing, she worked her way through the seemingly endless mountain of rubble, all the while calling his name over and over. Somewhere under the pile of wood he lay injured and unconscious. . .or worse. No! Her mind wouldn't accept that. Her *heart* wouldn't accept that.

"Diedrich! Tell me where you are." Somehow she lifted beams she never would have imagined she could move. Her arms burned, and her chest felt as if Papa's forge burned inside it, her heaving lungs the bellows feeding the flames.

Her mind told her she could not do this. She needed to get Papa and Herr Rothhaus to help. But her heart kept her tethered to the spot. She couldn't leave Diedrich alone. "Hold on, Diedrich. I will get you out. I will. I will!" Squeezing her words between labored breaths and ragged sobs, she tugged on a giant beam, but it wouldn't budge. The rough wood tore at her palms. She didn't care. "Dear Lord, help me to get him out. Just let him be alive." Grunting, she shoved her desperate prayer through gritted teeth as she wrapped her bruised arms around the enormous log. Clutching it in a death grip, she gave a mighty pull. But the timber refused to move more than a few inches. Her burning muscles trembled and convulsed with the effort. At last, her strength depleted, she could hold it no more and the beam settled back onto the pile of wood with a thud, taking her down with it. Gasping for breath and praying for strength, she tried again, but her muscles refused to respond. The dark shadow of defeat enveloped her, leaving her body limp and her eyes blinded with tears.

An agony Regina had never known rent her heart like a jagged knife. She would never see Diedrich's smile again or hear his voice or feel his touch. She sank to her knees on the heap of wood. Somewhere from deep within her, a tortured wail tore free. She raised her face to the sky and screamed the name of the man she realized, too late, owned her heart. "Died-rich!"

"Regina."

For a moment Regina thought she had imagined his voice. In an instant, her spirits shot from the pits of grief to the heights of joy. Diedrich was alive! But how could his voice sound so strong, so calm and unaffected from beneath the pile of wood? "Diedrich." Her heart thumping out a tattoo of hope, she peered breathlessly into a gap between the planks that she'd opened with her digging, but she could see nothing in the dark abyss.

"Regina. What has happened? What are you doing?" Suddenly, she realized the voice did not come from within the mountain of lumber but from a spot beyond her left shoulder. Jerking her head around, she saw what she'd thought to never see again—Diedrich alive and safe striding toward her.

"Diedrich." Since she'd found the dilapidated lean-to, she'd called his name with nearly every breath she'd drawn into her lungs. She'd uttered it through her sobs and screamed till her throat was raw. But this time it came out in a breathless whisper. She pushed to her feet as disbelief gave way to unmitigated elation that surged through her, renewing her limbs with strength. With fresh tears cascading down her cheeks, she ran to him. Blindly she ran, sobbing her joy, sobbing her relief. "Diedrich. Dank sei Gott." This time she breathed his name with her prayer of thanks like a benediction an instant before he caught her to him.

His strong arms engulfed her, holding her close to his heart. Clinging to him as if he might vanish were she to let go, she wept her relief against his shirtfront until it was sodden with her tears. "I thought—you were under—there. I—I thought—you were—dead." Her words limped out through halting hiccups.

"Oh Regina." His voice sounded thick with emotion. His breath felt warm against her head. She reveled in the sensation of. . .Diedrich. Still holding her securely, he pushed away from her enough to look in her face. His unshaven jaw prickled against her chin as he gently nudged her head back. For the space of a heartbeat, his soft gray eyes gazed lovingly into hers. Then slowly, as if in a dream, his eyes closed, his face lowered, and his lips found hers.

Closing her eyes, Regina welcomed his kiss. For one blissful moment, time was suspended. There was no sky, no earth. Only a sweet sensation of happiness swirling around the two of them in a world of their own as Diedrich's lips lingered on hers. Where Eli's kisses had been rough and taking, Diedrich's were tender and giving. Eli's embraces had felt confining, but Diedrich's arms were a sanctuary.

Too soon his face lifted and his lips abandoned hers. Slowly, Regina's eyes opened as if reluctantly rousing from a beautiful dream. The wonder on his face mimicked the emotion filling her chest. But then, as if he suddenly became aware of what had happened, his brows pinched together in a look of pained remorse. Releasing her, he dropped his arms to his sides and stepped back. "Regina. Forgive me. I should not have. . ." He seemed at a loss for words as his gaze turned penitent.

Of all the emotions Regina imagined he might express at this moment, regret was not among them. Anger and hurt chased away all remnants of the bliss she had felt seconds earlier, and the last drop of mercy seeped from her broken heart. Forgive him? He releases an emotion within her so powerful that it shakes her to the core then asks her to forgive him as if he had simply trod on her toes? No, sir! Let him wallow in his guilt. She obviously meant nothing to him. Like Eli, Diedrich simply enjoyed kissing girls. At least Eli wanted to marry her someday.

Clutching her crossed arms over her chest to quell her

trembling, she glared at him. "Mama would like you to come and wash up for dinner." Her flat tone reflected her deflated spirit. Whirling away from him to hide the tears welling in her eyes, she ran toward the house, ignoring the words of apology he flung in her wake.

Dinner passed in torturous slowness with Regina focused on her nearly untouched plate, careful to avoid looking at Diedrich. He, too, said little, speaking directly to her only once when he inquired about the condition of her now bandaged hands. Shrugging off his concern, she'd mumbled that her injuries were of no consequence, though Mama had pulled four large splinters and several small ones from Regina's palms before washing the wounds with stinging lye soap and wrapping them with strips of clean cotton. Yet in truth, she had not lied. The soreness in her hands was miniscule compared with the pain Diedrich's nearness inflicted on her heart.

Thankfully Regina's and Diedrich's reticence seemed to go unnoticed by their parents, who filled the void with praises to God for delivering Diedrich from certain death or injury and discussions of how the lean-to might be more securely rebuilt. When Regina could no longer bear their conversation, which revived the agonizing moments she'd experienced atop the ruined shed, she made her excuses and fled to the clothesline behind the house.

Her bandaged hands hampered her movements as she worked her way down the clothesline, snatching the wooden pins that secured the laundry to the twine. If she worked fast enough, maybe she could ignore the tempest raging inside her that Diedrich's kiss had loosed. But no matter how fast she worked, she couldn't escape the heart-jolting truth she could no longer deny. She loved Diedrich. With all her heart. With every ounce of her being, she loved him. Somewhere deep inside, she'd known it even before she thought she had lost him beneath the collapsed roof of the lean-to. Yet knowing that loving Diedrich was futile, she'd lied to herself, pretending her feelings for him didn't exist. But that pretense had crumbled beneath the soft touch of his lips on hers.

Anger shot a burst of energy through her arms, and she whipped a bedsheet from the line with unnecessary ferocity. What good did it do to love him when he didn't love her back and didn't even plan to stay in Sauers? Gripping both ends of the material, she gave it such a sharp snap that it cracked like a gunshot. And though the action undoubtedly sent any insects that might cling to the sheet flying, it did nothing to relieve Regina's pain and frustration.

Why, Lord, why did You allow Diedrich to come here in the first place? Most likely, Papa would have eventually relented and allowed her to marry Eli. And until today, she could have married him and lived happily. But no longer. Now she could not imagine marrying anyone but Diedrich.

Once she had thought she loved Eli. Unpinning a shirt from the line, she gave a sarcastic snort. The infatuation she'd felt for Eli compared to her love for Diedrich was like the difference between the light from her little finger lamp and the brightest sunlight. It was as if she had lived her whole life with all her senses dulled, and now they were suddenly awakened, keen and sharp.

As she folded the shirt, she realized it belonged to

Diedrich. It was the shirt he had worn when he first arrived. The shirt she had pressed her face against when he carried her from the barn lot. Another stab of pain assaulted her heart, followed by a flash of bitterness. Whenever disappointments had come in life for her or her sisters, Mama would always quote the verse from Romans: "And we know that all things work together for good to them that love God, to them who are the called according to his purpose."

Regina's lips twisted in a sneer. She dropped the shirt into the basket then finished taking down the rest of the laundry. Well, she *did* love God. She loved Him with all her heart and had trusted Him all her life. And what did He do? He allowed her to fall desperately and completely in love with a man who said he didn't want to marry her. She could almost imagine God looking down on her and mocking her from heaven.

Blinking back tears, she headed for the house. As she walked, a thought struck, igniting a tiny glimmer of hope. Diedrich *had* kissed her, so he must hold some degree of affection for her. It was at Elsie's wedding last fall that she'd first set her cap for Eli. And though it had taken a few months to catch his eye, she had eventually succeeded. Perhaps, if Regina tried, she could win Diedrich's heart before harvest. With that glimmer of hope to dispel her dark mood, she stepped into the house.

In the kitchen, Mama turned from the ironing board, where she stood flicking water from a bowl onto Papa's good shirt. She rolled up the shirt and crossed to Regina, a look of concern furrowing her brow. "Ah, my poor liebes

Mädchen." She patted Regina's cheek. "Your face tells me you are in pain. Are your hands hurting you so much?"

"Nein." Forcing a smile, Regina shook her head. "They are only a little sore." How she longed to tell her mother it was not her hands that pained her most but her heart.

Mama took the basket of clothes from Regina and set it on the floor then gently turned her bandaged hands palms up. "I do see two specks of blood. You should have told me that the work pained you. I could have brought in the rest of the wash."

Regina drew her hands from her mother's grasp. Though tempted to blame her sour expression on her superficial wounds, she did not care to add a bruised conscience to her emotional and physical injuries. "Truly, my hands hurt only a little. The accident upset me, that is all." Mama—always wanting to fix things. But for once, Mama couldn't fix what troubled Regina. And the less Regina talked about it, the better.

"Hmm," Mama murmured. "I still think it is best if tonight I make a raw potato and milk poultice for your hands. That should take out the soreness." Then a smile replaced her serious expression. "It was a brave and good thing you did, Tochter—trying so hard to move that wood when you thought Diedrich was underneath it. After you left the table, he asked me about your hands. He said he was *sehr* sorry you were hurt and hoped your injuries were not severe."

Regina stifled the sarcastic laugh that bubbled up into her throat. Diedrich broke her heart by saying in as many words he wished he hadn't kissed her, then worried about a couple of splinters in her hand? "I hope you eased his mind about my injuries."

Grinning, Mama gave her a hug. "I did. I also told him he is a fortunate young man to be marrying a girl who would do such a thing for him."

How Regina would have loved to see Diedrich's face when Mama said that! With great effort she reined in the cackle of mirth threatening to explode from her lips but allowed herself a wry grin. "I'm glad you did, Mama." Diedrich deserved to feel a little guilty.

Mama went back to dampening pieces of clothing in preparation for tomorrow's ironing.

"Do your hands feel well enough to put clean sheets on the beds, then?"

"Ja, Mama." Regina gathered the sheets from the basket and headed for the interior of the house and the downstairs bedrooms. The first bedroom she came to was the one Diedrich shared with his father.

As she stepped through the doorway, her heart throbbed painfully. Though the two had been here a scarce month, this room had become very much theirs. She couldn't imagine them not being here. She couldn't imagine *Diedrich* not being here. Once he left, would she ever be able to walk into this room without thinking of him? The thought drove the ache in her heart deeper.

Her gaze went to the small hobnailed trunk at the foot of the bed. What must it be like to have to fit a few precious pieces of your life into something so small then take it across the ocean to begin a new life in a strange land? One of those precious items—the little black Bible father and son had brought from Venne—lay atop the trunk. Suddenly the need to touch something that belonged to Diedrich filled her, and she picked it up. With her finger, she traced the raised lettering embossed in the black grain of the leather. So much of the gold had worn away she could barely make out the words *Heilige Schrift*.

Gold. It was what Diedrich wanted, what he dreamed of.

Her eyes misted, so she closed them. Again she felt his lips on hers and his arms holding her close against him. His words may have suggested that the kiss they shared meant nothing to him. But his caresses had told her something very different. Could she convince him to give up his dream for her? Somehow she must, or live the rest of her life with a Diedrich-shaped hole in her heart.

Heaving a sigh, she started to lay the Bible back onto the trunk when she noticed a folded piece of paper sticking up from inside the back cover. Curious, she slipped it out. Unfolding it, she saw that it was part of a map. Two circled words on the map drew her gaze. "Fort Smith." She remembered the article about the place in the *Madison Courier*. She glanced at something scribbled along the edge of the map. The words she saw penciled in the margin of the page smote her heart with another bruising blow. "California or bust."

Chapter 12

Diedrich swung the broadax above his head then, with a savage blow, brought the blade down on the poplar log, sending wood chips flying. A few more blows and he would have another log cut in two. After rebuilding the demolished lean-to behind the barn, he, along with Father and Herr Seitz, had worked for the past three days felling trees on this wooded land Herr Seitz had bought from Herr Driehaus. By the end of the week, they hoped to have enough timber cut to begin construction on a log house.

Though used to strenuous farmwork, Diedrich couldn't remember feeling more exhausted after a day's work than he had these past three days of cutting trees. Every muscle in his body ached, and he marveled at the stamina of the two older men who worked a few yards away, cutting branches from felled trees.

Despite the hard work and the long hours, Diedrich relished the labor. Anything to keep his mind off Regina. Yet however hard he worked, he couldn't get out of his head the image of her kneeling on that pile of lumber, sobbing his name, and tugging on a beam so large it would challenge even his strength, let alone hers. And at night, as tired as he was, the memory of her tear-drenched face as she ran toward him robbed him of sleep. He could still feel her body trembling against him. She fit in his arms as if God had made her for them, and he ached to hold her again.

But the memory that most tortured him day and night was of the kiss they had shared. In that one moment—at once wonderful and terrible—his life had changed forever. In an instant, the feelings he had tried to fend off for weeks had crashed down upon him with as much force as if he *had* been beneath the shed when it collapsed. He could no longer deny his love for Regina. But what he should do about those feelings, his mind and heart could not agree. So he worked. He worked until the blisters forming on his hands turned to calluses. He worked until his mind was too tired to think and his body too numb to feel. . .anything.

Wielding the ax, he slammed the broad blade into the log again with a mighty force, this time severing it. The two pieces of the log now joined a dozen of their fellows, each eighteen feet in length and ready to be hewn into squared beams for construction of the house's walls. The house in which he and Regina were supposed to live together as husband and wife. If only he could believe that was a possibility. He shook his head as if he could sling from his mind the images that notion formed there—tender, sweet images that gouged at his throbbing heart. He needed to keep working.

Swiping his forearm across his sweaty brow, he turned to find another suitable poplar. But then he stopped, pressed the ax head against the log, and leaned on the tool's handle. Gazing at the forest before him, he huffed out a frustrated breath. He could single-handedly cut down all twenty acres of trees and still not calm the tumult inside him.

He scrubbed his sweat-drenched face with his hand. The question that had haunted him for three days echoed again in his mind. Was it possible Regina loved him, too? Her tears and her kisses said yes. But when he had let her go, her expression had reflected very different emotions. What had he seen there? Shock? Anger? Disgust? Pain slashed at his heart. Surely she could not think he would take advantage of her fear that he'd been injured in order to steal a kiss from her. No, he couldn't believe that. He had seen her eyes close and her lips part invitingly. He had felt how sweetly, how eagerly she returned his kiss. So why had she run away from him, especially when he'd been quick to apologize for his impulsive actions? The only answer that made any sense ripped at his battered heart. She had simply gotten caught up in the moment and immediately regretted what had happened.

If only he knew for certain she felt about him the same way he felt about her, he would give up his dreams of adventure and riches in an instant. Without regret or a backward glance, he would trade all the gold in California for Regina's love. But so far, he had not mustered the courage to confront her—to demand she tell him her feelings one way or the other and put him out of his misery. For until he knew for sure, he could still nurture hope. And despite their secret bargain not to marry in the fall, maybe, just maybe, he could change her mind and win her heart away from Eli Tanner.

"You are working too hard, Sohn." Diedrich hadn't noticed his father walk up. "I know you are eager to build our home, but you must be alive to enjoy it, hey?" Chuckling, he clapped Diedrich on the shoulder.

Diedrich answered with a wry smile. If Father knew the real reason he was working so hard, Diedrich doubted he'd be laughing.

Father walked to a log that lay in a slice of shade. Sitting, he motioned for Diedrich to join him. "Ernst says his ax is getting dull and he forgot to bring a pumice stone." He waved at Herr Seitz, who waved back from across the clearing as he walked, ax in hand, toward the wagon. "He said we should take a rest while he sharpens his ax."

Sending a wave toward Herr Seitz, Diedrich sat on the log. Father leaned back against the smooth bark of a beech tree, his arms crossed over his chest and his legs stretched out in front of him with his feet crossed at the ankles. Diedrich hunched forward, his arms on his knees. For a moment, they sat quietly, enjoying the cool breezes that rustled the canopy of leaves above them and dried the sweat from their faces. Only the chattering and squawking of birds in the trees and the occasional beating of wings as the fowl took flight disturbed the silence.

At length Father angled his head toward Diedrich. "So tell me, Sohn, what is it that has been troubling you?"

Diedrich gave a short, sardonic laugh. Of course Father would have sensed his discontent. Pausing, he contemplated how best to answer. In the end, he decided to ask a question of his own instead. "Did Mama love you when you married?" Diedrich remembered Mama saying that though she and Father had known each other all their lives, their marriage was arranged by their parents.

A surprised look crossed Father's face, followed by a wince that made Diedrich regret the question. In the five years since Mama's death, Father had rarely mentioned her. He had cared for Mama deeply. Diedrich had never questioned that. And he sensed Father's silence on the subject was not due to lack of affection, but on the contrary, because he still found it too painful to touch with words. Diedrich was about to apologize for asking when Father's lips turned up in a gentle smile. Resting his head back against the tree, Father ran his curled knuckles along his whiskered jaw, a sure sign he was giving the question consideration. Finally, he said, "I don't think so, not at first."

"But she did. . .later?" Hoping he had not overstepped his bounds, Diedrich turned his gaze from Father's face and focused instead on a colony of ants marching in a line along a twig.

A deep chortle rumbled from Father, surprising Diedrich. "Oh yes. Later she did."

Emboldened by the lilt in Father's voice, Diedrich pressed on. "So what did you do to win her love?"

Another soft chuckle. "I just loved her, Sohn, as the scriptures tell us in Ephesians. 'Husbands, love your wives, even as Christ also loved the church, and gave himself for it.' Were you not listening to Pastor Sauer's sermon last Lord's day?"

"Of course I was listening. I just thought maybe you would know something I could do. . . ." Diedrich let the thought dangle. He never should have broached the subject in the first place. How could Father give him any useful advice when he had no idea Regina had already situated her affection on another?

Drawing his knees up, Father leaned forward and put his hand on Diedrich's shoulder. "I know it was a difficult thing, asking you to marry someone you had never met, Sohn, but Regina seems to be a very caring, God-fearing girl. She treats her parents with affection and respect, and I am sure she will treat you in the same manner." He grinned. "And she is very pretty, too. I do not know what more you could want."

Diedrich nodded mutely, though he wanted to say that what he wanted was Regina's full heart—that he wanted to know if by some miracle he'd been blessed to win her love, she would not look at him one day and wish she had married Eli Tanner. "Everything you say is true, but I just thought perhaps you could tell me what I might do to grow her affection for me."

Father sighed. "Do not concern yourself, Diedrich. I have seen Regina look at you with affection. In time, I am sure her feelings for you will grow to a deeper love." Then as he gazed across the clearing to the cornfield, his eyes turned distant and his voice wistful. "Just love her, Sohn. Love begets love."

Diedrich ventured a glance at Father's face and, noticing a glistening in his eyes, decided he should not pursue the conversation further. Bringing up painful memories would not help Diedrich win Regina's heart. Father said he had seen Regina look at Diedrich with affection. With that to give him courage, he would pray for God's guidance and confront Regina. At the very next opportunity to speak with her alone, he would bare his heart to her and accept whatever happened.

Perched on a three-legged stool, Regina hunched over the butter churn. Gripping the handle of the dasher, she began pounding it up and down. She'd decided that the shade of the big willow in the side yard would be a pleasant spot to churn the butter. It also provided a good view of the lane.

Since the devastating kiss she had shared with Diedrich, she'd had few opportunities to encourage his attention. It hurt to realize that, if anything, he seemed to avoid her. But she couldn't really blame him. He along with Father and Herr Rothhaus had been working so hard on clearing the new land that they hardly had energy to eat, let alone make conversation. But this morning at breakfast, Papa had said by noon today they might have enough logs cut to begin work on the house. And if so, they would likely come in early for dinner. Since Regina and her sisters were little, Mama had preached that a man found nothing more captivating than an industrious girl. So at every opportunity, she wanted Diedrich to find her engaged in some kind of domestic occupation. And if they were to come home early, Diedrich was sure to see her here hard at work, making the butter he so loved to slather on corn bread.

With the willow's supple branches draping over her shoulder like a green ribbon, she hoped to present a fetching picture. A few coy smiles and the batting of her eyes had proved sufficient to catch Eli's attention. But Diedrich was a far more serious person and would likely find such antics silly and juvenile.

She sighed. If only she could talk with Elsie. Scarcely two years Regina's senior, Elsie had, until her marriage to William last September, been Regina's lifelong confidant. While Regina had never been especially close to her more staid and proper eldest sister, Sophie, Regina and Elsie had grown up playing and giggling together. Unlike Sophie, who would most likely ridicule Regina's heartache, Elsie would sympathize and know exactly what Regina should do to win Diedrich's heart.

At the distant sound of a wagon rumbling down the lane, Regina's heart hopped like a frightened rabbit. The men must have met their day's goal of felled trees. Rising slightly, she repositioned her stool so she could angle her profile for a more flattering effect.

But as the wagon neared, her heart dipped. It was definitely not their wagon or team of horses. Butter churn forgotten, Regina walked toward the lane to see who might be visiting. When the wagon came to a stop between the house and the barn, she finally recognized Elsie's husband, William. Her heart skipped with her feet as she hurried toward the wagon. She hadn't seen Elsie since Easter. It was as if God had answered her prayer before she prayed it.

Bouncing up to the wagon, she peered around William but could not see Elsie. Shading her eyes from the sun with her flattened hand, she tipped her face up to her brother-in-law. "Guten Tag, William. Where is Elsie?"

Only now did she notice the somber expression on William's face. Since he was naturally jovial, his glum look curled her heart in on itself. Regina's smile wilted. "William, what is wrong?" Fear tightened her chest and filled her mouth with a bad taste. As William climbed down, she gripped the wagon wheel to support her legs, which had gone wobbly. Once he reached the ground, the gray pallor on his drawn face was visible beneath at least two days' growth of straw-colored beard.

The quick *clop-clop* of wooden shoes sounded behind Regina, and before she could ask anything more about Elsie, Mama's stern voice at her left shoulder demanded, "Where is my Elsie? Is she all right?"

William's blue eyes brimmed with tears and sorrow. Torturing his battered brown hat in his hands, he shook his head mutely.

Chapter 13

William." Mama gripped William's shoulders and leveled a no-nonsense gaze into his eyes. "You tell me now—what has happened to my Elsie?"

William sniffed and ran his sleeve beneath his nose. Even as terror clutched at Regina's throat, her heart hurt for William, who looked suddenly older than his twenty-one years. "Doc Randolph says she was with child, but. . ." He shook his head again. A tear coursed down his scraggly cheek and disappeared into the bristle of pale whiskers. He paid it no mind. "She is restin'. Doc says she is out of danger and should be up on her feet again in a few days." His sad gaze shifted between Mama and Regina. The semblance of a smile quavered on his lips. "She was so lookin' forward to tellin' ya about the babe."

Mama pulled him into her arms as if he were Sophie's two-year-old, Henry, and had just fallen and skinned his knee. "It is sorry I am, lieber Sohn. Sometimes it is hard, but we must trust Gott. I know my liebes Enkelkind is in His arms." Letting William go, she brushed the wetness from her cheeks and offered him a brave smile. "These things, they happen. There will be more *Kinder*." Mama squared her shoulders. "I must go to her."

Regina blinked away the tears welling in her own eyes

and gripped her mother's arm. "I know you want to go to Elsie, Mama, but I am not sure I am ready to take care of everything here alone. And think, is it proper for me to be here without you while Diedrich is. . ." Her face heating, she abandoned the thought. As much as she hoped to win Diedrich's affection, the last thing she wanted was to force him into a marriage because people in the community thought something improper had occurred.

Mama sighed, and her brow wrinkled in thought. "Of course you are right, Tochter. Such a thing would not be *korrekt*. I would not have your wedding day tarnished with talk of impropriety."

William shook his head. "My ma was seein' to Elsie, but then my sister's kids got sick, and she had to go help with them." He scrubbed his face with his hand. "Doc said Elsie has to stay in bed for the next several days, so I've been tryin' to take care of her and the store at the same time. It's 'bout got me frazzled. I closed the store and found a neighbor lady willin' to sit with Elsie until I can get back tomorrow evenin'. But with the doctor bills, we cain't afford to close down anymore."

"Why don't I go?" As sad as Regina was about William and Elsie's loss, she wondered if something good might come of this unfortunate situation. She had just been thinking how she would like to talk to Elsie, and this was her chance.

William nodded at Regina. "Elsie would like that. She's been pinin' for you. I think you just might be the medicine she needs to lift her spirits."

Mama bobbed her head in agreement. "Ja. You should

go, Regina, and see to your *Schwester*." She smiled at William and, putting her hand on his back, guided him toward the back door. "But now we must feed you before a big wind comes and blows you away."

A half hour later, between helping Mama with dinner and making a mental list of what she'd need to take with her to Salem, Regina scarcely noticed when Diedrich, Papa, and Herr Rothhaus returned to the house. The conversation at the meal was focused on the sad news and comforting William. More than a few tears were shed around the table and many prayers went up, asking God to comfort the grieving young couple and restore Elsie to full health.

His eyes glistening, Papa paused in slicing a piece of roast pork. "We know what you are feeling, William. Do we not, Mutti?" He sent Mama a sad smile. An odd look crossed Mama's face, and though she nodded, she quickly changed the subject to what foods Regina should make for Elsie that might help to build back her strength.

Though Regina wondered about Papa's comment and Mama's reaction to it, she had more pressing concerns to occupy her mind. And one of them sat across the table from her. Diedrich had said little aside from joining his father in offering his sympathy and prayers. But several times during the meal, she thought she noticed disappointment as well as sorrow on his face when he looked at her. Most likely, he was simply sad about the news William had brought them. But Regina couldn't help hoping his glum look had something to do with his learning that she would be leaving the farm for several days.

The next morning after breakfast, when Regina came down from her bedroom with a calico sack full of necessities for her stay at William and Elsie's home, she found Diedrich waiting at the bottom of the stairs.

"Regina." His gray eyes held hers tenderly, snatching her breath away and sending her heart crashing against her ribs. For the space of a heartbeat, she thought—hoped—he might actually kiss her. Instead, he simply took the sack from her hands. Deep furrows appeared on his broad forehead. "There is something—something I have wanted to say. Needed to say. . ."

"Are you ready to go, Regina?" William came through the kitchen door into the washroom, with Papa and Mama trailing behind him.

Diedrich looked down at the floor. When he looked up, he gave her a sad smile. "Tell Elsie I am praying for her and William."

"Danke." Regina managed the breathless word as William took her calico sack from Diedrich's hands and ushered her outside.

With a thirty-mile trip ahead of them, they would need to head out as soon as possible to make it to Salem before sunset. So good-byes were quickly said all around, with Papa promising to fetch her home five days hence. Regina hugged Mama and Papa, and even Herr Rothhaus gave her a hug and a quick kiss on the cheek. But Diedrich only took her hand and, in a voice scarcely above a whisper, murmured, "*Gott segne und halte dich*, Regina," before helping her up to the wagon seat beside William. His gaze never left hers, and her heart throbbed painfully at the tender look in his eyes.

"God bless and hold you, too, Diedrich." Somehow she managed to utter the sentiment around the lump in her throat. A moment later William snapped the reins down on the horse's rumps, and with a jerk, the wagon began to roll down the lane. Away from home. Away from Diedrich. What had he been about to say before William cut him short at the back door? That question would doubtless haunt her until she returned home and got the chance to ask him.

But over the next few days, all other thoughts faded as Regina's concern for Elsie demanded first place in her mind and heart. How it had ripped at Regina's heart to see her beautiful, vibrant sister lying abed, gaunt and melancholy. That first evening, they spoke little. For a long while, they had simply held each other and cried. And when they finally did speak, the words were tearful prayers directed heavenward for the little one they would never hold.

William had made up a little straw tick pallet for Regina in the kitchen, and the next morning at the break of dawn, she was awakened by a knock at the kitchen door. A large, rawboned woman who introduced herself as Dorcas Spray, the neighbor lady who had sat with Elsie the day before, presented Regina with a fat, rust-colored rooster she'd just killed. "A good dose of chicken broth will set Elsie right," she said. Then, lamenting that she could stay only a moment, she thrust the fowl's scaly yellow feet trussed up with twine into Regina's hands, its broken neck dangling at her knees. Trying to sound appreciative, Regina had thanked the woman then spent the rest of the morning plucking, butchering, and stewing the rooster. But at noon, when she finally handed Elsie a large cup of the meat broth, her sister's smile was more than sufficient payment for her work. According to William, Elsie had scarcely eaten anything since losing the baby, so it heartened Regina to see her sipping the hot chicken broth with gusto.

"Mmm, what did you put in this, Regina? It tastes even better than Mama's." With eyes half-closed, Elsie inhaled the fragrant steam curling up from the stoneware cup she cradled in both hands. The sight filled Regina with gladness. It was the first time since her arrival she had seen her sister smile. Some of the pink had begun to return to Elsie's cheeks as well, and Regina's concern for her sister's health began to abate.

"Thyme." Regina picked up the tortoiseshell comb from the dresser across the room then pulled a chair up beside the bed where Elsie sat propped up with pillows. "Mama only puts in salt, pepper, and sage, but I like the taste of thyme," she said as she combed her sister's nut-brown hair.

"Me, too." Elsie grinned and took another noisy sip. Then her grin faded, and the sad frown returned. "Gunther," she uttered softly, her cinnamon-brown eyes filling with tears. "If the baby was a boy, I was going to call him Gunther, after Mama's papa—our grandpapa. And if it was a girl, Catharine after Mama." Her voice broke on a sob, and Regina dropped the comb to the bed and wrapped her arms around her sister.

"And you will use those names one day," she murmured as she rocked Elsie in her arms and kissed her head. "Gott has named this one, and one day you will know the name."

Elsie sniffed and, with teardrops still shimmering on her lashes, offered Regina a brave smile and nod. She drained the rest of her broth, and Regina went back to combing her sister's hair. Though she rejoiced to see Elsie emerging from the heartrending ordeal, she suspected her sister would continue to suffer moments of sadness like the one she just experienced. She prayed that with time those painful moments would become rare and blunted.

"William has been wonderful through it all." Though still tremulous, Elsie's voice lifted bravely as Regina braided her hair. "I love him even more now, I think, than I did the day we married." Then her wistful tone turned almost playful. "And what of you and Eli Tanner? At Easter, you told me he wanted to court you."

Regina paused in tying her sister's braids with lengths of thin red ribbon. She suddenly remembered that Elsie knew nothing of Diedrich. Trying to keep her voice unaffected, she simply said, "Papa has chosen someone else for me."

Elsie sat up straighter. Her eyes grew round, and she put her hand on Regina's shoulder. "Who?" she whispered in breathless interest.

"His name is Diedrich Rothhaus. He and his father arrived from Venne last month." She told Elsie about the deal Papa and Herr Rothhaus had made, agreeing that Regina and Diedrich would marry.

Elsie hunched forward. "So tell me, what is he like? Do you like him?"

The memory of the kiss she and Diedrich had shared returned with a bittersweet pang. How could she put her feelings into words when she felt as if a cyclone were swirling in her chest? Her eyes filled with tears.

"Oh Regina. Is he that awful?" Elsie hugged her. Sighing, she sank back onto the pillows, and dismay filled her voice. "I was afraid Papa would do something like that. He was so disappointed when I refused to marry Ludwig Schmersal and later fell in love with William."

Before she thought, Regina said, "But you didn't reject Ludwig until he decided to join the army and go fight in Texas." Smote with remorse for her thoughtless comment, she cringed inwardly. This was not a time to remind Elsie that her first love had died in the war with Mexico.

Elsie smiled. "And Gott sent William to help soften that heartache for me." Her brows pinched together in a thin, inverted V. "Surely if we try, we can think of a way to change Papa's mind and get you out of this marriage."

"But I don't want out of it!" Regina blurted, eliciting a puzzled look from Elsie. Suddenly, tears rained down Regina's cheeks, and the whole tangled mess tumbled from her lips like apples from a torn sack.

At length Elsie gave a huff. "Let me get this straight. You liked Eli, but now you like Diedrich. But Diedrich wants to go to California, and Eli still wants to marry you?"

Regina nodded.

Emitting a soft sigh, Elsie reached over and took Regina's hands she had nestled in her lap. "My liebe Schwester. I can see why you are confused. But that is why Gott has given you a head to think with as well as a heart to feel with." She tapped Regina gently on the head. "I thought I loved

Ludwig, too. But when he told me he was going to the war, I knew I did not want to become a widow at eighteen." She sighed. "As it turned out, I was right. And by the time we got the sad news about Ludwig, I was already in love with William." She pressed a hand to her chest and, glancing at the bedroom doorway as if to assure herself her husband was not within earshot, said, "My heart hurt when I learned of Ludwig's death, and there are times when I still think of him fondly. But if Ludwig had truly loved me, he would not have left for the army. And unless Diedrich changes his mind about going to California, I think you should forget about him and remember why you liked Eli in the first place. At least *he* will likely stay in Jackson County."

The next day Elsie's advice was still echoing in Regina's mind as she rearranged lanterns on a shelf behind the store's counter. She had offered to watch the store while William rested and spent some time with Elsie, who was feeling much better.

Though fun loving and possessing a decidedly romantic streak, Elsie also had a good, reasonable head on her shoulders. As tightly as Regina's heart twined around Diedrich, she had to admit that her sister's logic made good sense. One kiss did not mean Diedrich loved her and wanted to marry her. If he remained steadfast in his plans to head for California in the fall, then she would know she should steer her heart back to Eli.

The little bell William had fixed to the front door jingled, and Regina abandoned her musing. William had warned that, being Saturday, the store might become busy. His prediction had proved accurate. Regina had already waited on several customers this morning and enjoyed the experience. Wondering whether she would be met by a housewife needing food staples or dry goods or a farmer needing a tool or ammunition for his rifle, she turned around and her heart hopped to her throat. Eli stood in the doorway, looking as handsome as she had ever seen him.

He sauntered toward the counter, no hint of surprise touching his roguish smile. "Heard you were here seein' to your sister." The swagger in his voice matched his gait.

"Yes. Elsie is. . .feeling much better." Regina didn't even care how he had learned she was here. Such news would undoubtedly spread quickly. She sensed, however, that he was not here out of concern for Elsie or William.

"That's good. Glad to hear it." His stilted tone held more duty than genuine concern. With an air of negligence, he picked up a pewter candleholder on the counter and studied it.

"Is there something I can help you with?" His cavalier attitude raked her nerves like a wool carder. She had to force herself not to snatch the pewter piece from his hands as if he were her toddler nephew.

"Came to Salem to get a gear wheel for the mill, so I thought I'd stop by to let you know that the barn raisin' for my uncle will be this comin' Friday. I wanted to know if you planned to be back home by then." He wandered over to a display of men's felt hats on a hat tree and began trying them on for size. He positioned a wide-brimmed black hat at a jaunty angle atop his auburn curls and shot her a devastating smile. "How do I look?"

Warmth spread over Regina's face, and her heart fluttered like it used to when she looked at him. She wanted to tell him he looked better than any man had a right to, but she suspected he already knew that. Pretending interest in the copper scales on the counter, she ignored the question about his appearance and forced a nonchalant tone. "Papa will fetch me home Monday."

He took off the hat and put it back on the tree then moseyed over to her. Easing behind the counter, he came up close to her and slipped his arms around her waist. Her first instinct was to pull away and tell him he shouldn't be behind the counter. But with many breakable items on the shelves behind them, she didn't want a tussle. "That's good, 'cause I'm plannin' a surprise for you." Without warning he pressed a hard, wet kiss on her lips then turned and strode out of the store before she could utter a reproach.

Stunned, Regina gazed at his retreating figure and absently touched the back of her hand to her mouth, which felt bruised. She couldn't guess what surprise Eli had planned for her, but instead of igniting eagerness, the prospect of discovering what it might be filled her with consternation.

Diedrich followed Herr Seitz into the Dudleytown store. A barrage of sights and smells assailed his senses. This was his first time to visit the store. Normally, seeing such a huge collection of disparate items all crammed into such a small space would have captured his full attention. But it only reminded him of Regina, and he found himself wishing he were in the Salem mercantile instead of the little Dudleytown general store.

In the two days since Regina left with William McCrea, she'd reigned over Diedrich's thoughts like a queen. The longing to see her again had become like a physical ache, throbbing day and night beneath his breastbone. Thanks be to God, Herr Seitz would travel to Salem Monday and bring her home. *Home.* When had the Seitz farm become home to him? He knew the answer. The moment Regina had claimed his heart. But when she did return and he managed to find a private moment with her to tell her his feelings, what if she rejected his love? Where then would he find a home? He recoiled from the thought, but forcing himself to face the possibility, he knew his only option was to stick to his original plan and head west as soon after harvest as possible.

"She is what you need, do you not think?" Herr Seitz's words jarred Diedrich from his melancholy thoughts.

Diedrich's heart raced and his eyes widened as he turned to the older man. "W–what?" Had he murmured Regina's name aloud unknowingly?

Herr Seitz held up a hammer. "You will need your own hammer for the barn raising this Friday, as well as later, building the new house, *nicht wahr?*"

"Ja." Nodding, Diedrich turned away, pretending to examine a piece of harness as heat marched up his neck to his face. Though Herr Seitz expected Diedrich to marry Regina, he was glad the man could not read his thoughts.

Smiling, Herr Seitz clapped him on the back. "Take your time and look around while I have Herr Cole gather the items on Frau Seitz's list as well as the nails we will need for our work on the house."

Returning the man's smile, Diedrich nodded. As he strolled about the store, his mind wandered back to Regina. Finding an array of iron skillets displayed on the wall, he couldn't help wondering which one she would prefer if she were choosing for their home.

"Diedrich." Herr Seitz appeared again at his shoulder, a frown dragging down the corners of his mouth. "Herr Cole does not have the nails we need, but I still must purchase from him the other items Frau Seitz wants. So if we want to get home in time to get any work done today, I will need you to go to the blacksmith shop down the street for the nails."

Sehr gut. Diedrich nodded. He had noticed the blacksmith shop when they passed it on the way to the general store.

Herr Seitz shrugged and his tone turned grudging. "Herr Rogers asks more money for his nails, but he usually has a large amount to sell." Herr Seitz pressed several coins into Diedrich's hand, and an unpleasant feeling curled in his stomach. Suddenly, he was glad Regina was not here to see her father dole out money to him as if he were a child. Since he and Father had left Venne, they'd been living off the generosity of Herr Seitz. Diedrich longed to have his own money. Money he had earned with his own two hands.

As he walked down the street, thoughts of the California goldfields once again fired his imagination. How he would love to have his own money, his own gold. But sadly, if he left Sauers for the goldfields, it would mean he had lost all hope of winning Regina's love. And no amount of gold would compensate him for such a loss.

Diedrich stopped in front of a weathered gray building. Its yawning doors beckoned, and he didn't need to read the brick-colored lettering above them to tell him he'd found the blacksmith shop. The *clang, clang, clang* of iron on iron as well as the blast of heat radiating from within the establishment told him he could be nowhere else.

As Diedrich stepped into the building's dim interior, a giant of a man with a chest like a barrel and sweat dripping from his flame-red hair glanced up from his work at an anvil. Fixing his gaze on Diedrich, he said something in English, of which Diedrich understood only "friend" and "seat." But as the blacksmith accompanied his comment with a nod toward an upturned keg, Diedrich understood him to mean he should sit and wait.

He situated himself on the barrelhead the blacksmith had indicated, next to another man who also waited on an upturned box. The man beside him, dressed in buckskin and wearing a battered felt hat pulled low over his face, stopped whittling the piece of wood in his hands. Turning, he lifted a smiling, if somewhat scraggly, bearded face to Diedrich and stuck out his hand. "Zeke Roberts." His friendly grin revealed a mouth full of blackened teeth and spaces where several were missing.

Diedrich grasped his hand. "Diedrich Rothhaus." He hoped the man didn't expect to engage in conversation and wished he'd learned more English from Regina.

The man cocked his head and in flawless German said, "I detect a German accent. Do you speak English?"

Relieved not to have to scour his brain for the right English words, Diedrich held up his index finger and thumb, leaving only a small space between.

Zeke nodded. "Ah, you haven't been here long, then?"

Diedrich shook his head. "My Vater and I arrived last month. For now, we are living in Sauers with the Seitz family." Unsure about Regina's feelings, he was not inclined to enlighten Herr Roberts on the reason he and Father were brought here.

Zeke went back to his whittling. "Then I doubt you would be interested in going to California?"

The word caught Diedrich by surprise. He jerked to attention, his spine stiffening. "California?"

"Ja. Next spring, I plan to leave for the California goldfields. That is, if I can sell my house in Salem and find a couple of adventurous fellows willing to partner with me in the venture." He shot Diedrich a grin. "When I saw you walk in here, I thought to myself, now there's just the kind of young fellow I'm looking for." Then, pausing in his work with the knife, he shrugged. "But if you are settled here, I doubt you would be interested in such an arrangement." He puffed a breath, blowing shavings from the piece of wood, which was beginning to take the shape of a bird in flight.

Diedrich's heart galloped then slowed to a trot and finally limped. Mama always told him God never closed one door without opening another. Did his meeting Zeke Roberts mean Regina would reject his love and God had sent this man to provide him a way to California? Though the notion pained him, he could not dismiss it out of hand.

"So would you be interested?" Zeke gave him a gap-toothed grin.

Diedrich swallowed to wet his drying throat. Somehow he forced out the word "Possibly."

Chapter 14

Kneeling over the auger, Diedrich twisted the tool's handle and grunted with the effort of driving the spiral iron bit deep into the eight-by-eight support beam. But no amount of exertion could numb the pain in his heart. Sadly, it appeared he had been right about his meeting with Zeke Roberts. God was obviously preparing him for Regina's inevitable rejection. Since her return from Salem, he had noticed a decided coolness in her attitude toward him.

Several times he had tried to talk with her privately, but each time she had shied away, citing varying excuses for avoiding a conversation with him, including having to help her mother with food preparations for today's barn raising. And in the nearly six hours since Diedrich and his father had arrived here in Dudleytown with the Seitzes to help built Herr Tanner's new barn, he still had found no opportunity to speak to Regina alone.

Pausing in his work with the auger, he leaned back, resting on his heels. The sights, sounds, and smells of the construction site swirled around him, lending a festive air to the proceedings. The sounds of hammering and sawing mixed with the constant buzzing of myriad voices generated by the milling crowd. A westerly breeze brought tempting aromas from the food tables to mingle with the scents of freshly cut lumber as well as the still-lingering smell of the old, burnt barn. But despite the joyful atmosphere, Diedrich's aching heart robbed him of all celebratory feelings. And the happy cacophony around him could not drown out the incessant refrain ringing in his ears. Regina didn't love him.

Pivoting on his knees, he glanced across the barn lot to the long trestle tables covered with dishes of food. Seeking Regina, his gaze roamed the large group of women swarming around the tables. When he finally found her, a sweet ache throbbed in his chest. She threw back her head in mirth as if in response to someone's humorous comment, and his heart pinched. He had allowed himself to hope he might enjoy her smiles and hear her laughter every day for the rest of his life. But with each passing moment, that hope grew dimmer.

At least for once, he didn't see Eli Tanner anywhere near her. So far, the boy appeared to spend more time talking to Regina than helping to build his uncle's new barn. An ugly emotion Diedrich didn't care to name filled his mouth with a bad taste. If Regina was determined to marry the cur, there was little he could do about it. Still, as long as Diedrich remained here in Jackson County, he would keep a close eye on the Tanner boy, especially when he was near Regina.

"*Pass auf*, Sohn!" Father's warning to look out scarcely registered in Diedrich's brain before he found himself slammed to the ground. The next instant he felt a stiff breeze as something whizzed past his head.

When Father's weight finally lifted off him, Diedrich pushed up to all fours, spitting bits of grass from his mouth. Out of the corner of his eye, he saw Eli Tanner and another youth carrying a ten-foot-long plank—obviously the object that had nearly hit him and Father. The smirk on Eli's face made Diedrich wonder if the close call was entirely an accident.

Father, already on his feet, reached down and grabbed Diedrich's arm, helping him up. "Sorry I am to knock you down, Sohn. But when the *Jungen* came through here and began to swing that board around, I saw that your head was in the way of it. I do not want to think what might have happened if it had hit you. Only Gott's mercy saved you."

Feeling more than a little foolish, Diedrich gave his father a pat on the back. "Ja. Gott's mercy and a Vater with a sharp eye," he said with a sheepish grin.

Walt Tanner, the man whose barn they were building, rushed up and began speaking rapidly in English. Though Diedrich understood few of his words, he clearly read regret and apology in the man's face.

Herr Seitz came striding up, concern lining his face as well. Once he had assured himself Diedrich and his father were unhurt, he engaged in a quick exchange with Walt Tanner in English then turned back to Diedrich. "Herr Tanner wants to know is everyone all right? He wants me to tell you that before the Jungen brought the board through this place, he called for everyone to get out of the way. It did not occur to him you would not understand his words."

The look of sincere remorse on Tanner's face evoked sympathy in Diedrich. It was not the man's fault that his nephew and the other boy had acted carelessly. He reached his hand out to Walt Tanner, who accepted it. "Danke, Herr Tanner.

My Vater and I appreciate your concern, but we are unhurt." He grinned. "Only my pride is bruised a little, perhaps."

Herr Seitz translated Diedrich's words and Tanner nodded, while a look of relief smoothed the worry lines from his face. After shaking hands again with Diedrich and his father, Walt Tanner went back to his work.

When everyone had gone back to what they were doing before the near accident, Father gripped Diedrich's arm. He glanced across the barnyard to the food tables where Regina and the other women continued to work and visit, apparently oblivious to the subsiding commotion at the building site. A teasing grin quirked up the corner of Father's mouth. "I do not know if it was your stomach or your heart that drew your attention away from the work happening around you, but you must be more watchful, Sohn." He gave Diedrich a wink. "You will have many opportunities to look at your intended in safety," he added with a chuckle.

Diedrich tried to smile, but as his gaze returned to Regina, his smile evaporated. She was laughing and talking to Eli again. Seeing her playfully bat his hand away from the food, Diedrich almost wished Father had let the board hit him and put him out of his misery. It couldn't have hurt any worse than the pain he was feeling now.

"Eli, I told you not to touch the food!" Regina smacked Eli's hand as he reached for a slice of Mama's raisin and dried apple *Stollen*. He seemed to have spent more time talking to her and sneaking bits of food than helping with the barn building. So far, she had seen no hint of the surprise he had promised, just his hovering presence, which was becoming increasingly aggravating.

"I'm hungry." With a lightning-fast motion, he snatched a pickled beet from the top of an open jar and popped it into his mouth. "Besides," he said around chewing the beet, "you and your ma always bring the best food." The whine in his voice turned wistful, and pity scratched at Regina's heart. Having lost his mother nine years ago, Eli probably did look forward to the varied dishes offered at occasions like this barn raising.

Regina placed a linen towel over the open jar of beets. "We will ring the dinner bell in a few minutes." She glanced across the barn lot to the spot where the skeleton of the new building was beginning to take shape. The blackened earth around the site served as a reminder of why a large part of Dudleytown as well as Sauers was gathered here.

Unbidden, her gaze sought out Diedrich. Though standing with his back to her and amid at least a dozen other men, Regina had no trouble finding him. His broad back and exceptionally tall figure made him easy to recognize. Even from this distance, she could see the muscles across his back and shoulders move beneath his white cotton shirt as he worked with the other men to stand up a section of wall. Her heart sped to a gallop. Since her return from Salem, she had tried to take Elsie's advice and shut Diedrich out of her mind and heart, but he kept nudging his way back in. She had prayed that at her first sight of Eli this morning, her heart would jump like it had when he entered William and Elsie's store. But it hadn't. In fact, compared to Diedrich, Eli appeared juvenile and almost silly. And for the past several minutes, all she'd wanted to do was find an excuse to get away from Eli. She was about to tell him she needed to go help her mother with something when Mama appeared at her elbow.

"Eli is your name, is it not?" At his nod, Mama maneuvered between him and Regina to set a towel-swathed pan of corn bread on the table. "Your *Onkel* will have a fine new barn soon, ja?"

"Yeah." He chuckled. "It will almost be worth havin' the old one burn down."

Mama frowned, and Regina had to suppress a giggle. If Eli wanted to make a good impression on her mother, he was doing a very poor job of it. Mama glanced toward the construction site, and her frown deepened. "My Ernst tells me there was almost an accident with Diedrich Rothhaus earlier. That he was nearly hit by a beam."

Regina gasped, her throat tightening. The same flash of fear she had felt when she thought the lean-to had fallen on Diedrich sparked in her chest. "Was he hurt?" Breathless, she glanced across the barn lot at Diedrich in search of any sign of injury.

Eli gave an unconcerned chuckle, and anger flared in Regina's chest. "Nah." He negligently reached over, broke off a piece of Stollen, and began nibbling on it. "His pa pushed him out of the way." He shrugged. "Uncle Walt hollered for him to move, but I reckon he didn't get it through his thick skull." He snorted, and Regina wondered why she had ever thought him handsome. "I doubt he would have even felt it if it had hit him."

Mama's look of disapproval mirrored the disgust rising in Regina. She understood that Eli viewed Diedrich as a rival for her affection. *If only that were so.* But it did not excuse his callous attitude, and Regina had no interest in making excuses for him to Mama.

Mama opened her mouth as if about to say something, but another woman pulled her away with a question about the food.

When Mama left, Eli grasped Regina's hand. "After the dinner break, come to the west side of the barn. I have somethin' I want to show you."

Regina yanked her hand from his. She wanted to tell him she had no interest in anything he had to show her. Instead, she bit her bottom lip and groped for a more diplomatic excuse to decline his invitation. The dinner bell began to ring. She cocked her head to the right where she expected the serving line to form. "You'd better get in line." She would make no promises. And after dinner, there would be enough work with the cleanup to provide ample excuse for her to avoid Eli.

"The west side of the barn," Eli reiterated. Then with a parting wink and grin, he trotted off to join the crowd of men advancing toward the food tables.

Regina's gaze scoured the group in search of Diedrich, but she didn't see him.

When all had assembled, Pastor Sauer's booming voice bade everyone pause and give thanks for the repast set before them. After the prayer was finished and the last amen faded away, Regina moved to a spot behind the serving table. The men, who had worked hard all morning constructing the barn, would eat first.

While serving the dishes before her, Regina occasionally glanced down the line of male faces, looking for Diedrich. She scarcely noticed when Eli passed in front of her, absently plopping chicken and noodles on his plate and ignoring his reminder to join him later. At last, her gaze lit on Diedrich's face, and her heart danced. Sadly, she realized Elsie's advice would do her no good. It was useless to continue trying to veer her heart away from Diedrich. It belonged to him now, and she could not call it back. And unless she could change his mind about going to California, her heart was destined to be broken.

As Diedrich neared, her pulse quickened. She caught his eye, and they exchanged a smile. For an instant, she got the fleeting impression he was seeking her out as well. But even if he was, she was sure it was only because of the friendship they had built over the past month. *A friendship built on the understanding that we will not marry.*

"Hey, gal, I'd like some of them chicken and dumplin's, if ya don't mind." The gruff voice pulled Regina's attention from Diedrich to the burly man in front of her. Her cheeks burning, she mumbled her apologies and dipped a generous portion of the food onto the man's plate. Did Diedrich notice her blush, and if so, did he guess her preoccupation with him had caused her discomposure? She prayed not. Somehow she must learn to control her responses to his smiles—his nearness. Until such a time as she won his heart, she must hide her feelings from him at all cost. If he ever did choose her over his dream of California gold, she needed to know he did it with a free and willing heart—not out of some dogged sense of duty.

Reclaiming a tight rein on her composure, she forced her attention back to serving food to the workmen filing along the opposite side of the table. So when she looked up to find Diedrich standing before her, her heart did a somersault. Flustered, she blurted, "I heard about the accident with the beam. I am glad you were not hurt." His face reddened, and she groaned inwardly. Clamping her mouth shut, she dipped him some of the chicken and dumplings. Embarrassing him was not a good strategy for winning his heart.

He grinned. "I was hoping you did not see that. It is clear, I think, that I need more of your English lessons." His grin disappeared, and his gray eyes searched hers. His Adam's apple moved with his swallow. "Regina, I need to speak with you privately. Perhaps when you get your food, we can sit together and talk?"

"Come on, man. The rest of us want to finish gettin' our vittles, too." A bearded man behind Diedrich shifted impatiently. Though Regina doubted Diedrich understood all of the man's words, his embarrassed expression clearly showed he comprehended the fellow's meaning.

"Ja," she managed to murmur before Diedrich moved on. Had Diedrich read the longing in her face and wanted to remind her of their bargain?

At the thought, her stomach knotted. The moment the

last man was served, she abandoned the food table. She couldn't even think of eating until she found Diedrich and learned what was on his mind.

Making her way through the milling and shifting crowd, she glanced about. Diedrich hadn't mentioned where she should look for him. Suddenly, someone grabbed her hand. Looking up, she met Eli's eager expression with one of dismay. Impatience and aggravation twined in her chest. She tried to pull her hand free, but he held tight. "Let go of me, Eli! I'm looking for someone."

His forehead furrowed angrily. "You're supposed to be looking for *me*. You promised me you would spend some time with me, remember?"

She groaned. She had promised him. At the very least, she had allowed him to believe she would spend time with him. And if what he told her in the store was true, he had gone to some trouble to concoct a surprise for her. Mustering patience, she heaved a sigh. "All right. Show me your surprise." The sooner she humored him, the sooner she could search for Diedrich.

Gripping her hand so hard it hurt, Eli towed her toward a thicket that edged the woods surrounding his uncle's farm. "Let me go, Eli! That hurts." Dodging branches and prickly briars, she stumbled through the wooded undergrowth. But despite her complaints, Eli kept a tight grip on her hand. Finally, they reached a clearing, and he stopped and let go of her hand. There, across the little creek that ran through the clearing, stood a tethered horse hitched to an open surrey.

Confused, Regina turned to him. Had he bought a surrey

and wanted her opinion of it? "Is this yours?"

He shrugged. "Nah. I borrowed it from my uncle."

Regina huffed her impatience. She was not about to go gallivanting around Dudleytown with Eli. "You know I can't go riding with you without Papa's permission."

Grinning, Eli took her hand again and towed her closer to the creek. "We won't need anybody's permission to ride together after today. Two miles away, there's a preacher waitin' to marry us."

Chapter 15

Regina's eyes popped, and her jaw sagged. Yanking her hand from his, she took two steps backward. "Have you lost all reason?"

Eli's face transformed into an angry mask. His green eyes turned stormy, reminding her of how the sky looked once when a cyclone came through Sauers. He grabbed at her hand again, but she pulled it away. "I'm tired of waitin'. We're gettin' married this afternoon, and that's the end of it!"

Raw fear leapt like a hot flame in her chest. She struggled to breathe. Surely he wouldn't force her to go with him. Then slowly, cool reason flooded back, extinguishing her fear. Even if Eli did force her to go stand with him before a preacher, no preacher she knew would perform such nuptials against her wishes.

Drawing in a deep, calming breath, she turned to him. "Eli, I cannot marry you—ever."

Hurt and anger twisted his handsome features. "You like me. I know you do. You said so."

Sadly, Regina knew he was right. She bore at least part of the blame for the predicament in which she found herself. For months she had encouraged Eli, even pursued him. Tears sprang to her eyes, and she hung her head in shame. "I am sorry I let you think I wanted. . . It was wrong of me. But I

454

know now I cannot marry you, Eli."

He cursed, shocking her. Fear flared again. She had seen him angry before, but even the time they had argued in the barn, he hadn't cursed at her. "Quit worryin' about what your folks think, Regina. I wager they won't like it much at first, but they'll get used to the idea in time."

He stepped toward her, and she took another step back. The time had come to share with Eli what she now realized. "I have told you before I would never marry without my parents' blessing, and that is true. But it is not the only reason I cannot marry you."

Stepping closer, he held out his hands palms up. "What other reason is there?"

Unsure how he would react to her next words, Regina prepared to bolt, praying she could find her way back to the barn lot. "I cannot marry you because I do not love you. I love someone else."

Eli's face scrunched up, and his eyes narrowed to angry green slits. "And who *do* you love—Rothhaus?" He nearly spat Diedrich's surname.

"Yes," she blurted. It felt good to say it. And now that she had, she wanted to scream it. "I love Diedrich Rothhaus."

A rustling sounded a few feet behind her. She spun around, and for an instant, her heart jolted to a dead stop in her chest. Diedrich stood less than two yards away, his eyes wide and his mouth agape.

For an excruciatingly long moment, they both stood stock still, exchanging a look of stunned incredulity. The awareness in his eyes confirmed he had both heard and understood her declaration of love for him. A wave of humiliation washed through her. Her feet, which seemed to have taken root in the woods' decaying underbrush, sprang to life again. Spurred by her embarassment, they now seemed to have sprouted wings, and she ran. As she sped past Diedrich, she thought she heard him utter her name, but the ringing in her ears drowned it out. Dead leaves moist from recent rains slipped beneath her feet. Brambles clutched at her clothes. Branches stung her face and arms. She ignored it all. She didn't even care where she ended up as long as she didn't have to face Diedrich. What did he think? What did he feel? Sadness? Pity? Or worse—fear that she would break their secret agreement and force him into the marriage their fathers had bargained?

By the grace of God, she suddenly emerged from the wood into a clearing behind the building site of the new barn. Gasping for breath, she finally stopped. With her whole body trembling and her heart slamming against her ribs, she clutched a poplar sapling for support. She feared if she let go of the tree, she might crumple in a heap. But knowing Diedrich was doubtless only steps behind her lent strength to her shaky limbs. She couldn't let him find her in this state. She had to have time to compose herself and gather her thoughts before allowing him to confront her with what he had heard her say.

Drawing a deep, tremulous breath, she somehow made her way to the food tables. There she noticed Anna Rieckers wrapping a cotton towel around a large crockery bowl. Glancing up, her friend caught sight of Regina and halted in her work. A look of concern etched on her face, she stepped toward her.

"Regina, are you sick? You do not look well." She grasped Regina's arms, and Regina slumped against her, glad for the support.

"I—I don't feel well." It was not a lie. Between the shock of Eli trying to force her to elope with him and Diedrich learning that she loved him, Regina felt physically ill. She was glad she hadn't eaten anything before leaving the food tables—for if she had, she surely would have lost it back in the woods.

Anna's pale blue eyes shone with compassion. "Come. You need to sit down. Let me help you to the quilts Mama and I spread in the shade." Slipping her arm around Regina, Anna gently steered her toward a giant catalpa tree. "We are about ready to leave for home, but you can rest on the quilts until we get the wagon loaded."

Regina stopped. "You are going home?" The Rieckers would need to pass by Regina's house. Perhaps they would be willing to take her home.

Anna nodded, and a look of disappointment pulled her lips into a frown. "Ja. Papa and my brothers will stay for a while, but Mama and I need to get home and start the milking." Swiping at a strand of blond hair blown across her face by a passing breeze, she cast a longing glance toward the skeletal framework of the new barn. "I was hoping to spend more time with August, but Papa won't let him bring me home until we are formally promised."

Regina had known for months that Anna and August

Entebrock were keeping company. August's name was one Papa had mentioned last fall as a possible suitor for Regina. She remembered being happy to report to Papa that the twenty-year-old farmer was courting her best friend and thus unavailable.

Anna's narrow shoulders rose and fell with a deep sigh. "You are so fortunate that your intended lives with your family. You get to see him every day."

Regina wished she could confide in Anna that seeing Diedrich every day felt at times more like a curse than a blessing. Best friends since childhood, she and Anna had long dreamed of marrying the same year and raising their families next to one another. Except for Papa, no one had been more excited than Anna to learn of Regina and Diedrich's pending engagement. It had taken all of Regina's fortitude not to share with Anna her earlier feelings for Eli and the deal she had made with Diedrich. And while she could trust her sister Elsie to keep her secret, Anna's exuberance sometimes caused her to blurt things without thinking. Regina couldn't risk the truth getting back to Papa.

Scanning the building site, Anna gave a little gasp. "Oh, there is your handsome *Verlobter*. Perhaps I should tell him you are not feeling well. He may want to take you home." She turned as if to go fetch Diedrich, but Regina clutched her arm, restraining her.

"Nein!" The word exploded from Regina's lips. At the stunned expression on Anna's face, Regina tempered her voice. "Of course Diedrich cannot take me home, Anna. That would not be korrekt unless Mama and Papa came, too."

Anna reddened, and she shook her head. "Nein, nein. Of course I did not mean that the two of you should go home alone. I was thinking that his Vater would go, too."

"There you are, Regina. I have been looking everywhere for you." Mama strode toward them, a less-than-pleased expression on her face. Despite the stern look and the censure in her voice, Regina couldn't remember being happier to see her mother. But before she could say anything, Anna piped up.

"Frau Seitz, Regina is not feeling well."

"Oh?" Mama's perturbed expression melted into one of concern. She pressed the back of her hand against Regina's forehead and then her cheeks. "You do look flushed. Perhaps you should lie down in the back of the wagon for a while."

Regina cast a hopeful look at Anna then back to Mama. "Anna and her Mutter are leaving soon. I was thinking maybe they could take me home." She turned imploring eyes back to Anna.

Anna smiled. "I will go ask Mama, but I know she would be happy to take you home."

Mama nodded, and Regina felt some of the tension drain from her body. "That would be gut, I think." Mama smiled and patted Regina's cheek. "You probably ate something that did not sit well. You should go home and rest now, and tomorrow I will give you a good dose of castor oil."

Regina shivered at the thought of the castor oil but managed a weak smile. She would drink a whole bottle of the stuff if it kept her from having to face Diedrich.

A half hour later, feeling at once foolish and deceptive,

Regina stood in her own yard and waved good-bye to Anna and her mother. Eventually she would have to face Diedrich, but at least their confrontation would not be witnessed by dozens of curious onlookers.

Turning, she stepped toward the house then stopped. Though still a bit shaky from this afternoon's occurrences, the last thing she felt like doing was taking a nap. She needed to keep both her mind and body busy. Tipping her head up, she shaded her eyes with her flattened hand and squinted at the sun riding high in the sky. It was still early afternoon. She should be able to get most of her chores done before everyone came home in an hour or so.

She slipped into the washroom and exchanged her leather shoes for her Holzschuhe then grabbed the egg basket. Over the course of the next hour, she gathered the eggs, hoed the garden, and picked a mess of dandelion greens for supper. But as she headed to the barn to feed the horses and milk the cow, the tension knotting her stomach had not loosened, and she knew why. Though she'd rolled the question around in her head all afternoon, she still hadn't decided what she would say when Diedrich confronted her about her feelings for him. Clearly, she had two choices—tell him the truth and burden him with guilt or deny her feelings and lie. Her conscience recoiled from both options.

Inside the barn, she was met by the familiar and somehow calming smells of hay, manure, leather, and animals. As she approached the stall, Ingwer greeted her with a friendly moo. Bobbing her head, the cow eyed her with a quizzical look as if to ask why she was being milked so early. Grinning,

Regina pulled the three-legged stool from the corner of the stall and situated it at the cow's right side. She positioned the bucket beneath the udders and settled herself on the stool. "I know it is early, *meine Alte*," she said as she patted the cow's ginger-colored side, "but milking you calms me, and I need to think clearly."

The first splat of milk had scarcely hit the bucket when Regina heard the distant jangling of a wagon and team coming down the lane. For an instant, her chest constricted then eased. Even if Diedrich wanted to talk with her alone, finding a private moment would be difficult. She went back to milking, confident she could avoid spending any time alone with him at least for the rest of the day.

"Regina." Though quiet, the sound of Diedrich's voice brought Regina upright. She slowly turned on the stool, her face blazing and her heart pounding so hard she feared it might burst from her chest. She glanced behind him, praying she would see either Papa or Herr Rothhaus. She didn't.

No smile touched his lips as he walked toward her. His soft gray eyes held an intense look she had never seen in them before. Rising on wobbly legs, she leaned her shoulder against Ingwer for support. She had no idea what to say, so she was glad when he spoke first.

"Frau Seitz said you were feeling sick. Are you better, then?"

"Ja," Regina managed to croak, her back pressed against Ingwer's warm side.

He stepped closer, his gaze never veering from her face. "I do not know much English." As he neared, he reached out and took her hands in his. At the touch of his strong, calloused hands on hers, her throat dried and her insides turned to jelly. "But I know the word *yes*, and I know the word *love*." His thumbs gently caressed the backs of her hands. "I need to know if what you told Tanner is true. Do you love me?"

Regina swallowed hard. Her mind raced with her heart. What should she say? She knew Diedrich. The memory of the words he had spoken to her weeks ago came flooding back. *"I prayed I would not break your heart."* If he even suspected he would break her heart by going to California, he would forfeit his dream. And in September, as their fathers had agreed, she would marry the man standing before her— the man she now loved. But she would not have his heart. No. She would not wake each morning with the fear of finding regret in her husband's eyes and have her heart broken anew every day for the rest of her life.

"Regina." His gentle grip on her hands tightened, and his throat moved with his swallow. "Tell me. Did you mean the words you said to Tanner?"

Her heart felt as if it was being squeezed by an iron fist, and she winced with the pain. Hot tears stung the back of her nose and flooded her eyes. Unable to hold his gaze, hers dropped to the pointy toes of her wooden shoes. *Dear Lord, forgive my lie.* She shook her head. "I just told Eli that so he would leave me alone."

He let go of her hands, and she fought to suppress the sob rising up from the center of her being. But then she felt his hands slowly, gently slip around her waist, drawing her to him. His head lowered, and his lips found hers. Reason unhitched. Her heart took control, and she welcomed his kiss. She felt as if she were floating. Were her feet still on the ground? It didn't matter. Nothing mattered but the sweet sensation of Diedrich's lips caressing hers. She slid her arms around his neck and clung to him, returning the tender pressure of his kiss with matching urgency. Then suddenly it was over. He raised his head, freeing her lips.

With all her senses still firing, Regina slammed back to reality with a jarring jolt. Feeling as limp as a rag doll, she stepped back out of his embrace and leaned against the cow, which shifted and mooed.

A smile crawled across Diedrich's lips until it stretched his face wide. "You can lie to me with your words, mein Liebchen, but your kiss, I think, tells me the truth." Still smiling, he turned and walked out of the barn.

Somehow Regina managed to finish the milking. Her mind and heart still spinning, she said little as she later helped Mama with supper. Occasionally Mama would press the back of her hand to Regina's forehead and cheeks, then, clucking her tongue, vowed to dose her with any number of herbal concoctions. Supper passed in a fog with Regina tasting nothing she ate. Diedrich, on the other hand, seemed especially cheerful and animated. She tried not to look at him during the meal, but several times he caught her eye and gave her a sweet, knowing smile that sent her heart bounding like a rabbit chased by a fox.

When everyone had finished and the older men pushed back from the table, Mama glanced at Regina's half-eaten plate of food. "I think for sure you are not well, liebes

Mädchen. It is best, I think, that you go on up to bed."

Desiring time alone to ponder the many emotions raging inside her, Regina was about to agree. But before she could speak, Diedrich piped up.

"Please, Frau Seitz, if Regina feels well enough at all, I would especially like for her to join us in our evening Bible reading." The glint in his eye told Regina he knew she was not really sick—at least not sick in the way Mama thought.

Regina offered a tepid smile. "Ja. I feel well enough." She couldn't begin to guess why he might want her present for the Bible reading. Earlier in the barn, he had seen through her lie. Was he or his father planning to read scripture admonishing liars? As strange as this day had been, she was prepared to believe anything might happen.

A few minutes later, as they did each evening after supper, everyone gathered in the front room. Regina sat in her normal place on a short bench beside the hearth. Mama, as usual, settled in her sewing rocker situated on the opposite side of the fireplace. The three men pulled up chairs in a half circle facing the fireplace. Usually, either Papa or Herr Rothhaus would read a scripture, followed by a few minutes of discussion about the verses, after which one of the men would offer prayer. Then for an hour or so, everyone would discuss the day's events until daylight slipped away and yawning broke out around the group. As soon as the prayer was finished, Regina planned to make her excuses and head upstairs.

Diedrich took a chair facing Regina. Her disconcertment growing, she studiously kept her gaze focused on her hands folded in her lap. Was he, too, thinking of the sweet kiss they had shared in the barn? And why was his mood so cheerful if he thought she was in love with him?

"Vater." Diedrich turned to his father seated to his left between him and Papa. "If you and Herr Seitz do not mind, I would like to read the scripture this evening."

"Sehr gut, Sohn." Herr Rothhaus looked a bit surprised but handed Diedrich the Bible. Sensing something momentous was about to occur, Regina held her breath and braced for whatever might happen.

Diedrich opened the Bible at a spot marked by a small slip of paper. Regina noticed two other such markers protruding from the book's pages. The sight did nothing to ease her building trepidation.

Diedrich cleared his throat, and everyone became quiet. Then in a clear voice he read—or more accurately recited—from the fourth chapter of Lamentations. All the while, his eyes never left Regina. " 'How is the gold become dim! how is the most fine gold changed!' "

Regina's heart began to pound in her ears and tears misted her eyes.

He turned to another marked page. "Proverbs 18:22," he announced then read, " 'Whoso findeth a wife findeth a good thing, and obtaineth favour of the Lord.' " His voice softened as his gaze melted into hers. Now tears began to course in earnest down Regina's cheeks. But he was not finished. He flipped the pages to yet another marker and said, "Proverbs 31:10." Then, closing the book he rose, set the Bible on the chair, and walked to Regina. With his eyes firmly fixed on hers, he recited, "'Who can find a virtuous woman? for her price is far above rubies.' Or gold."

Herr Rothhaus shook his head, bewildered. "Sohn, I do not think it says the part about gold."

"I know, Vater, but I am saying what is in my heart." Diedrich took Regina's hands in his and knelt before her. Her tears became a torrent. "Regina, mein Liebchen," he murmured. "You are mein Liebling, mein *Schätzchen*."

Regina could hardly believe her ears. Her heart sang as he declared her his sweetheart, his darling. . .his treasure.

From her seat on the other side of the hearth, Mama sniffed and dabbed her eyes with the hem of her apron. Papa and Herr Rothhaus exchanged grins while nodding their approval.

"*Ich liebe dich*, Regina," Diedrich said, his eyes shining with unvarnished adoration. "I know we have been promised for many months, but my heart needs to ask you here, in front of our parents, do you love me, too? And if we were not promised, would you still want to be my wife?"

Her heart full to bursting, Regina nodded. "Ja." The word came out on a happy sob. Still holding her hands, Diedrich stood, bringing her up with him. Taking her in his arms, he placed a chaste kiss on her cheek; then, lifting his lips to her ear, he whispered softly so only she could hear. "I love you, my darling. You are worth more to me than all the world's gold."

Mama wept openly, the sound blending with the creaking of her rocking chair. Papa cleared his throat and in a voice thick with emotion said, "I think we should hurry to finish that new house, hey, Georg?" Herr Rothhaus agreed with a hearty laugh.

All of this filtered vaguely into Regina's brain. The amazing miracle unfolding before her dominated her mind, heart, and senses, as did the man she loved—the man in whose arms she rested.

For Regina, the next four weeks would pass in a blissful blur. The men hurried to finish the house before threshing time began in early July. Mama and Regina spent their days planning the coming wedding, making strawberry and cherry preserves, and tending the garden. The moments Regina and Diedrich enjoyed alone were few and precious—a tender glance or touch of their hands in passing, a stolen kiss in the washroom or behind a piece of laundry drying on the line when Regina hung out the wash. As the idyllic summer days drifted by, Regina lived for the day she would become Frau Rothhaus.

By mid-June, Mama decided it was time to begin piecing together the squares of cloth that would become Regina and Diedrich's wedding quilt. Over the years, Mama had kept in a cedar box precious squares of cloth that held sentimental significance to the family.

This morning with the men gone again to work on the house, Regina and her mother sat together in the front room, the basket of quilting squares on the floor between them.

A gentle breeze wafted through the open front door, bringing with it the fragrance of roses and honeysuckle as well as the lulling hum of the bees that hovered around the blossoms. Working her needle along a square of cloth, Mama pressed her foot to the puncheon floor, setting the rocker creaking as it moved in a gentle motion. "I am hoping we can find a day soon when your sisters can come and we can all work together on this quilt as we did for each of theirs."

Regina looked up from the needlework in her own hands. "That might be hard to do. Elsie is always busy helping William with the store. And with baby Henry walking now, Sophie has her hands full, especially since she and Ezra moved into that big house in Vernon."

Mama frowned. "Sometimes I wish your sister did not have such grand tastes. I worry how they can afford such a nice home. The smaller house they had before would have served them well until Ezra and his brother built up their wheelwright shop, I think."

Regina agreed. She'd never understood Sophie's appetite for extravagance. To Regina, the notion of having her own home, however humble, was in itself heady. In truth, she would happily live in a mud hut as long as she was with Diedrich. But she was genuinely proud of the two-story log home he and his father were building for her. And eventually, as they gradually built on to it, her house would rival this home she had grown up in. Yet she knew her eldest sister would likely scoff at it. She remembered how Sophie had gasped in horror when she learned Elsie and William would be living in three small rooms attached to the back of their store.

Not wanting to hear another of Mama's rants about

Sophie's spendthrift ways, Regina decided to steer the conversation to the quilt pieces.

She reached into the basket and brought up a bright blue square of cloth. "This was from your wedding dress, am I correct?"

Smiling, Mama nodded. "Ja, you remember well from when we made your sisters' quilts, I think."

Next, Regina held up a scrap of faded yellow material. This one, she couldn't guess. It didn't look like material from any of the dresses she or her sisters had worn as youngsters. "And what is this from, Mama? I do not recognize it."

Mama looked up, and the smile on her face vanished. Her complexion blanched, frightening Regina. She looked as if she had seen a ghost. Her shoulders sagged, and before Regina's eyes, her mother seemed to age ten years. Her brown eyes, welling with tears, held both sorrow and resignation. "I had completely forgotten I'd saved that." She exhaled a deep breath as if gathering strength. "Regina, there is something you need to know. Something your Vater and I should have told you long ago."

Regina's scalp tingled in the ominous way it often did before a storm. With fright building in her chest, she held out the square of cloth that trembled in her shaking fingers. "Mama, what is this cloth?"

A tear slipped down Mama's cheek. "It is from the swaddling blanket you were wrapped in when your mother gave you to me."

Chapter 16

W ell Sohn, we shall have a nice warm home, I think."
Smiling, Father turned a slow circle in the center of
the house's main room and eyed their handiwork.

Diedrich tugged on the ladder he'd just nailed against
the loft to test its sturdiness and gave a solemn nod. In a
little over a month, they had cleared an acre of land and built
on it a twenty-two-by-thirty-foot log home with a full loft.
Though his head told him that what he, Father, and Herr
Seitz had accomplished on the house in six weeks' time was
more than impressive, he still wished he could present Regina with something grander.

Father ambled to the east end of the room. There, he cast
a studious gaze at the rough-hewn wall and stroked the graying whiskers that covered his chin. "Now, I think, we should
begin work on furniture for our home. Ernst explained how
is made the beds called *wall peg* that are built against the
wall." He sent Diedrich a sly grin accompanied by a wink.
"You and your bride will need a good strong bed for sure,
hey?"

Heat shot up Diedrich's neck and suffused his face.
"Vater!" Since that blessed evening when he and Regina
had declared their love for each other, his intended had set
up court in his mind and heart. Waking or sleeping, not a

moment passed that he didn't find her lingering sweetly on his mind. He had enough trouble keeping his thoughts from straying beyond korrekt boundaries. He did not need Father's teasing comments making the task more difficult.

Father leaned his head back and roared in mirth. "It is only the truth I am saying."

He crossed to Diedrich and gave him a good-natured clap on the shoulder. "Your bride, too, will want *stark* furniture. After dinner, I think, we will begin to build the bed."

Diedrich glanced at the wedge of sunlight angled across the puncheon floor through the open southerly door. He nodded. "Sehr gut, Vater. My stomach as well as the sun tells me it is time we should head back to the Seitzes' kitchen for dinner." The instant the words were out of his mouth, Diedrich groaned under his breath. The way Father liked to tease him about Regina, he was liable to ask if Diedrich's stomach was the only part of him nudging him back to Regina's home. But Father only grinned and followed Diedrich out of the house, keeping all other thoughts on the subject to himself.

Outside, Diedrich closed the front door to keep out any small animals that might be enticed by the shade to amble in while he and Father were gone. Then, stepping back away from the building, he allowed himself a parting look at the house. His and Regina's home. The thought filled him with joy and a yearning for the day he would carry his love into their new home. His gaze roved over the two-story building. The front door, situated exactly in the center of the south wall, was flanked by a window on each side. One let light into the large room that would serve as their front room and bedroom. The other brought light into the kitchen. Directly above those were two more windows cut under the eaves, allowing daylight into the loft. Eventually, he would build a proper staircase up to the second story. There, God willing, he would have need to fashion bedrooms for his and Regina's sons and daughters. His gaze slid down the house's plain front facade. He also would build a long porch with a roof above it so that Regina could sit in the shade and sew, shell peas from her garden, or pare apples from the trees he would plant. Then another, even sweeter image assembled itself in his mind, and his heart throbbed with longing. How clearly he could see her sitting there on the front porch, rocking their first child against her breast while a summer zephyr played with a strand of her golden hair and ruffled the soft, pale fuzz of their babe's head.

Yes, Father was right. It was a good, sturdy house—a house he could be proud of.

At that moment, Herr Seitz appeared from the cornfield that faced the house. He had spent the morning cultivating the green stalks now chest high. Unfamiliar with the crop in his old home of Venne, Diedrich liked the plants with their feathery tassels and long, drooping tapered leaves that whispered softly as the summer breeze rustled through them. Even more, he liked the prospect of the grain that would provide them with cornmeal to make the tasty yellow bread Regina and her mother served at nearly every meal.

As Diedrich bounced along in the back of the wagon, anticipation built in both his stomach and his heart. He could scarcely wait to see Regina again. Her sweet smiles fed his spirit like her good cooking fed his stomach.

But when they finally arrived at the house, he was surprised when she didn't meet him at the back door as she often did. As he waited his turn at the washstand inside the back door, he inclined his ear, listening for her voice. But instead of hearing her normally cheerful tone as she conversed with her mother, he caught only an occasional unintelligible word mumbled in a flat monotone. At the sound, a grain of concern planted itself in his chest and quickly grew to a niggling worry. Back in April, Pastor Sauer had advised Diedrich to learn Regina's heart. This he had done. He had come to know Regina's heart well enough for him to sense when something was not right with her. When he finally entered the kitchen, her downcast expression confirmed his suspicions. Frau Seitz also seemed distant and somewhat glum. Had mother and daughter had some kind of an argument? Diedrich could hardly imagine it. Even when Regina had initially rejected her parents' plans for her and Diedrich to marry, she had never, to Diedrich's knowledge, dishonored them with a cross word.

At the table, he tried to engage her in conversation about the progress he and Father had made on the house this morning. But despite his best efforts, he could scarcely evoke the smallest smile from her. And even when she did smile, it didn't reach her lovely blue eyes, which today reminded him more of a faded chambray shirt than a cloudless summer sky. Clearly something troubled her. And though he sensed he was not the cause of her melancholy mood, the thought brought him only a measure of relief. He was gripped by a profound need to know what had stolen her joy and a strong determination to do whatever was in his power to restore her happiness. He would not go back to work on their new home until he'd seen things set right with Regina.

After the meal, Father and Herr Seitz went to the front room to let their meals settle and discuss the work on the log house. Diedrich stayed in the kitchen, quietly watching Regina and her mother tidy up after the meal. Watching them work together, Diedrich grew more bewildered over Regina's odd demeanor. He could detect no anger or tension between Regina and her mother.

When the last dish had been washed, dried, and put away, Diedrich rose. Stepping toward the two women, he held his hand out to Regina while addressing her mother. "Frau Seitz, may I have your permission to take Regina for a walk?" Frau nodded. "Ja, it is sehr gut that you talk." Regina took his hand, and for the first time since he came in for dinner, she gave him the sweet smile he'd come to expect—the smile that felt like a caress.

Her face a somber mask, the usually undemonstrative Frau Seitz gave Regina a quick hug. She and Regina exchanged a look Diedrich couldn't decipher. Then she said something very odd. "You are my daughter, liebes Mädchen. Do not forget that."

Regina's eyes welled with tears that gouged at Diedrich's heart. She gave her mother a brave smile and whispered, "I know, Mama."

At once, curiosity and concern twined around Diedrich's

heart like the wild vines that sprang up among the corn-stalks. The moment he and Regina stepped outside, he was tempted to stop and insist she tell him what was the matter. But better judgment counseled him to wait. To his surprise, she spoke first.

"Diedrich, let us go see the garden. Our potato plants are flowering now. We should have new potatoes to fry soon." Her voice still sounded sad and distant. Taking his hand, she led him to the bench beside the house that overlooked the garden. Regina was right. The plants looked robust and healthy. The memory of the day they had planted the potato crop together came back to Diedrich and in an odd way re-inforced the bond he felt with her.

When they had settled themselves on the bench, a large tear escaped her left eye. For a moment it clung to the golden fringe of her lower lashes, glistening in the sunlight like a dewdrop. Then a blink dislodged it, sending it to the rose-pink apple of her cheek to meander down her face.

Diedrich could bear it no longer. Placing his finger be-neath her chin, he gently turned her face to his. "Regina, please tell me, what is the matter? Have I done something to upset you?"

Her wide-eyed look of surprise washed him with relief. "No, mein Liebling, it is not you." Then, turning away from him again, she hung her head and focused on her hands clasped in her lap. "I—I am not who you think I am. I am not who *I* thought I was."

The last strands of Diedrich's patience frayed. He had no more interest in puzzles or guessing games. Gently grasping her shoulders, he turned her to him. "Regina, what is this nonsense you are saying? In less than three months we shall be married. You must tell me now what is troubling you."

Her chin quivered, smiting him with regret. "This morning Mama told me that she did not give birth to me."

"What?" Diedrich had never met a kinder, more caring Christian woman than Frau Seitz. He couldn't imagine her saying something so hurtful to her child. . .unless it was true. And if it was, why had she waited until now to tell Regina? But if it were true, Frau Seitz's odd comment earlier asking Regina not to forget that she was her daughter began to make sense.

Regina sniffed and drew in a ragged breath. "We were piecing together my wedding quilt." Quirking a smile, she blushed prettily, making his heart canter. "When I found a piece of material I didn't recognize, Mama's face looked so terrible I thought she was having an attack of apoplexy." Her voice turned breathless at her remembered alarm. She went on to tell him how her mother claimed it was from the blanket Regina was wrapped in when her birth mother gave her away.

"But who was your real mother, and why would she give you away?" Now Diedrich fully understood Regina's discomposure. He, too, struggled to assimilate the revelation. His heart broke for his beloved. He couldn't imagine how it must feel to learn something so shocking.

Regina sniffed again, and Diedrich had to force himself not to pull her into his arms and comfort her against him. But he sensed that she needed to tell this, and he needed to hear it. "Mama said I was born on the boat from Bremen to Baltimore to a couple named Eva and Hermann Zichwolff."

"But they didn't want you?" The thought, which seemed incredible to Diedrich, angered him.

Another tear tracked down Regina's face. "Mama said there was much sickness on the ship. Not everyone who left Bremen lived to see America."

Diedrich nodded. He knew he and Father were very fortunate that during their voyage to America the *Franziska* had experienced no losses.

Regina kept her gaze fixed on her hands, which she wrung in her lap. "My Vater. . .my natural Vater." She stumbled on the words as if she couldn't believe she was saying them. "He died two weeks before I was born and they buried him at sea. A few days after I was born, Mama also gave birth to a baby girl." She shook her head sadly, and her voice took a somber dip. "But her baby lived only a few hours." After pausing to draw in a fortifying breath, Regina continued. "When they docked in Baltimore, many of the German immigrants were taken into homes of German-speaking people there. Eva, the woman who gave birth to me, spoke passable English. Not having a husband to take care of her and. . .me, she began looking for domestic work. Mama said Eva was given the opportunity to work for a very wealthy Baltimore family. But the family said she could not bring me." Regina shrugged. "Eva remembered that Mama had lost her child and would be able to provide me with nourishment, so she took me to her."

Smiling bravely through her tears, Regina patted her chest. "Mama's heart still hurt very much after losing her baby girl. She told me that when she took me as her own, it helped to soothe that hurt." She dabbed at her tear-drenched face with her apron hem. "Mama did say Eva cried when she gave me away."

Diedrich's heart bled for everyone involved, but mostly for Regina. He grappled for words that might bring her comfort. Gently stroking her arms from shoulder to elbow, he finally said, "I would say Gott has blessed you doubly. He gave you to a birth mother who cared enough to find you good, loving parents when she couldn't keep you. Then He not only gave you a wonderful mama and papa but two sisters as well."

More tears flooded down Regina's face. "You do not mind, then, that I was born Regina Zichwolff?"

Diedrich grinned. "Your name could be Regina *Schlammpfütze* and I would love you just the same." Giving her the surname of Mudpuddle reminded him of the first time he set eyes on her, and he couldn't help a chuckle. She giggled through her tears, making him wonder if perhaps they were sharing the same memory.

Then, turning serious, he cupped her face in his hands and gazed deeply into her lovely cerulean eyes. "It is sorry I am, mein Liebchen, that you have had such a shock today." He brushed away her newest tears with his thumbs. "But it makes no difference to me or the life we will soon have together." Then he smiled as another revelation struck. "Except that if your life had not happened as it did, I would not have you here in my arms. I think, even then, while Gott was taking care of you, He was also thinking of a four-year-old boy named Diedrich in Venne, Hanover."

This brought a smile to her lips, and he had to kiss them, lingering perhaps a moment or two longer than might be considered proper. When he finally forced himself to let her go, she smiled, and her eyes opened slowly as if from a pleasant dream. "I do love you, Diedrich," she murmured.

He had to kiss her again. He finally left her humming happily in the garden as she checked for potatoes big enough to harvest. Though he was stunned by what he had learned, Diedrich's heart was full. He prayed that his love would always be sufficient to vanquish every sadness in Regina's life as well as nurture her every joy.

When he stepped into the house in search of Father and Herr Seitz, Frau Seitz informed him that Father had already headed back to the new house and Herr Seitz had gone to check the maturity of the wheat crop. She grinned. "They did not want to disturb your talk with Regina."

With a quick word of thanks he turned to leave, but Frau Seitz took hold of his arm, halting him. "How—how is Regina?" Concern dulled her brown eyes and etched her forehead.

Diedrich smiled and squeezed her hand. Thinking of what this woman had meant to Regina and all she had done for her over the years, he wanted to thank her. Instead, he said, "Regina is happy that Gott has blessed her with a wonderful Mutter and Vater."

Frau Seitz's eyes glistened with unshed tears. She patted his hand. "And Gott will bless her soon with a wonderful husband."

Giving Frau Seitz an appreciative nod, he headed for the back forty acres and the new house. Father had taken the wagon and team, so Diedrich would have to either hitch the little gypsy pony to its cart or walk. Since it was a pleasant day and his spirits were high, he decided to make the nearly two-mile trek on foot.

As he walked, he remembered the name of Regina's birth parents. Herr Seitz had said many of their fellow passengers on the boat they had taken to America were also from Venne. He must ask Father if he knew of the name Hermann Zichwolff.

When he stepped into the house, Father turned from pounding a peg into the narrow gap between two logs on the east wall. He angled a grin toward Diedrich. "I was wondering if you would come back to help me with this bed, or if you had decided to spend the rest of the day holding hands with your Liebchen."

At his father's glib comment, Diedrich experienced a flash of anger. But Father had no knowledge of the emotional turmoil Regina had endured today.

Diedrich walked to his father. "Regina learned something upsetting today. I did not wish to leave her until her heart had calmed." He then shared with his father what Regina had told him.

An odd, almost wary look crossed Father's face. "So of whose blood is she?"

Diedrich couldn't imagine why Father would care. "Do you know the name Hermann Zichwolff? He and his wife, Eva, were Regina's natural parents."

Father's face blanched so pale it looked as if it were covered in flour. Then his face turned to a shade of red so deep it became almost purple. In all his life, Diedrich had never seen his father in a rage. But no other word fit the look of fury that twisted his father's features into someone Diedrich didn't recognize.

Balling his fists, Father fixed Diedrich with a murderous glare, his eyes nearly popping out of his head. "I forbid you to marry that girl! As long as I am alive, I swear it will not happen!"

Chapter 17

Disbelief, confusion, and pain swirled in Diedrich's chest like a cyclone. In all his twenty-one years, he had never raised his voice to his father in anger or spoken an insolent word to him. But at this moment, it took all his strength of will not to do both. He strained to hold his raging temper in check, his tense muscles twitching with the effort.

Three stilted strides brought him to his father. He held out his hands palms up in a helpless gesture. "Why, Vater? Why would you say such a thing? Was it not for me to marry Regina that we came across the ocean to America?"

Some of the anger seemed to drain from Father's face, and a glimmer of regret flashed in his eyes. He blew out a long breath as if to regain control of his emotions. His expression begged understanding. In a measured voice he said, "I know you have grown fond of the Mädchen, Sohn, but—"

"Fond?" Diedrich almost spat the word then chased it with a mirthless laugh. "Fond, Father?" He tapped his chest so hard he expected to later find it bruised. "I love Regina with all my heart. You yourself heard me declare it, did you not?"

A stubborn frown etched wavy lines across Father's broad forehead. "But that was before we knew Ernst had tricked us."

Diedrich fought the urge to scream. Had Father gone

mad, or had he? Or had they both lost their senses? He struggled to understand. "Please, Vater, tell me how you think Herr Seitz has tricked us."

Another fierce look of anger flashed in Father's eyes like jagged lightning. "He lied to us, Sohn! He told us she was his daughter. And now I find that she is the daughter of. . ." He abandoned the thought as if it were too abhorrent to put to voice, and his face screwed up like he smelled something fetid.

Clearly, for some unknown reason, Father held hard feelings against Regina's birth father. But the man was dead and had been for nearly eighteen years. Nothing would change Diedrich's love for Regina or budge his determination to make her his wife. But for him to convince Father that Regina's parentage made no difference, he needed to understand why Father felt as he did. "Father, who was Hermann Zichwolff?"

Father winced and jerked as if he'd been physically struck. Then his shoulders slumped, and he trudged over to the pair of three-legged stools beside the fireplace. Perching himself on one, he motioned for Diedrich to take the other.

Diedrich obeyed, praying that with the telling, Father might rid himself of the ill feelings he'd evidently held against the man for years.

Father leaned forward, his clasped hands resting on his knees. "Do you remember hearing me speak of your Onkel Jakob?"

"Ja." Diedrich remembered Father mentioning his brother, Jakob, only a handful of times. But by the glowing tones Father had used, Diedrich had surmised that Father had idolized his older brother. Beyond that, Diedrich knew little about his late uncle except that he had died young, fighting in the army of the emperor Napoleon.

Father angled a glance up at Diedrich. "You know that Jakob died in the battle of Wagram in 1809." Diedrich nodded. "But what you do not know is that he should not have been there."

Though curious at Father's comment, Diedrich said nothing, respectfully waiting for Father's tale to unfold.

Father rubbed his palms along the tops of his thighs. "When I was but twelve, my Vater—your *Großvater*—wanted to buy twelve milk cows." He gave a sardonic snort. "He said we would become wealthy dairymen. But he had no money to buy the cows, so he went to the local moneylender, Herr Wilhelm Zichwolff, and asked if he would loan him the money. Herr Zichwolff agreed to loan Vater the money but insisted he put up our farm as collateral."

Father paused and cleared his throat, and Diedrich sensed he had come to a painful part of the story. "Within six months," Father continued, "half of Vater's new cows sickened and died, and when the time came to pay Herr Zichwolff, he could not. Vater begged Herr Zichwolff to give him more time so his remaining cows would have time to produce, but Herr Zichwolff would not." Remembered anger hardened Father's tone. "Then, like now, young men were being forced into the army. But at that time, it was Napoleon's army." Father cocked a sad smile toward Diedrich. "Jakob was eighteen and the right age to go to the army, but since farmers produced food for the army, the boys from farms did not have to go." His lips twisted in a sneer. "But the sons of moneylenders were not exempt, and Wilhelm's son, Hermann, was ordered to go fight for Napoleon." Father's body seemed to stiffen as he pressed his hands against his knees. Diedrich knew that if a man of means was called to serve in the army and didn't wish to go, he could pay someone else to serve in his stead. Sensing what was coming next, he swallowed hard and waited for Father to continue.

Father rose and walked to the open front door and gazed out over the cornfield as if he could see all the way back to Venne. For a long moment, silence reigned, interrupted only by the happy chirping of birds and the soothing drone of bees. At length, Father spoke. "Herr Zichwolff told Vater his debt would be forgiven if Jakob went to fight in Hermann's place." Father sniffed, and his voice broke with emotion. "Vater had no choice. If Jakob refused to go to the army, Herr Zichwolff would take our farm, and we would be left homeless. So Jakob went." His voice sagged with his shoulders. "And three years later, Jakob died fighting in the battle of Wagram."

Imagining how he might feel if someone had done to Johann or Frederic what the Zichwolffs had done to Uncle Jakob, Diedrich could understand some of Father's anger and grief.

Now an angry growl crept into Father's voice. "For many years, Hermann lived free and like a king on his Vater's money. Finally, at the age of forty, after he had squandered much of his family's wealth, he took a wife." Father shook his head. "You cannot know the relief, the joy I felt when I learned that the reprobate and his Frau were leaving Venne for America. I could shut the Zichwolffs from my mind forever and never have to think of them again."

Father slowly turned away from the open door and stepped back into the room. He suddenly looked far older than his fifty-six years.

Diedrich slid from the stool and crossed to his father. "But why did you never tell me this story before?"

Father shuffled back over to the east wall and picked up the stout hammer. "When Jakob was killed, I vowed never to speak the name Zichwolff again. And until today, I had kept that vow."

Somehow Diedrich needed to make Father understand that the despicable actions of Wilhelm and Hermann Zichwolff had nothing to do with Regina.

He stepped toward Father. "Father, I know how you must feel. It was a hateful and cowardly thing that Herr Zichwolff did to our family, but it was not Regina's fault. It happened long before she was born."

When Father spoke, his voice drooped with his countenance. "I know, Sohn. But that does not change the blood that runs through her veins or my feelings about it. I wish it were not so, but I cannot change how things are." Picking up one of the stubby pegs he had fashioned earlier from an oak branch, he placed the sharpened end at a chink between the logs and gave it a mighty pound, driving it into the crevice.

"But, Vater. . ." Pain and frustration hardened Diedrich's voice. His heart writhed at the thought of having to choose between Father and Regina. "You know Regina. Not so long ago, you were telling me what a good Christian girl she is. She is the same girl today as she was then."

Father shot him a fierce glance. "To me, she is not the same. And you will *not* mingle our family's blood with the blood of Hermann Zichwolff. I will not have it!"

All his life, Diedrich had loved and admired his father. He never knew a kinder, more God-fearing or honorable man. And until this moment, he would not have imagined he could feel the kind of disdain for his parent now souring in the pit of his stomach. Watching Father nonchalantly return to his work after declaring Regina unfit to be his daughter-in-law and the mother of his grandchildren fed the rage boiling in Diedrich's belly. To his horror, he had to suppress the urge to pummel his sire.

He thought of every scripture about forgiveness Father had taught him over the years. Though mightily tempted to throw them back into his father's face, he resisted, not wanting to sin himself by breaking the commandment that bade him honor his father and mother. Instead, he decided a more prudent and less confrontational tack might be to remind Father of his obligation to Herr Seitz. He had never known Father to let a debt go unpaid.

Diedrich grasped his father's shoulder, turning him to face him. "But what of the debt we owe Herr Seitz? We still owe for our passage." He waved his hand to indicate the building around them. "And now we also owe him for this house and this land."

Father slammed the hammer to the floor with a clunk and gave a derisive snort. "Ernst Seitz lied to us. To my mind, our bargain is void, and I owe him nothing!"

Diedrich noted that Father had chosen to omit the prefix Herr when he mentioned their benefactor's name—a definite insult. "You may not feel you owe him, Father, but I do. I owe him much." He raised his voice, no longer concerned about keeping a civil tone. "And what about the food you eat and the bed you sleep on? Are they not the charity of Herr Seitz?"

His father shoved past him and stalked to the open front door. "Do you not think I would return to Venne this moment if I could? At least there I have sons who honor me. And I have my own land." He narrowed a glare at Diedrich. "The land Jakob died to keep in our family's hands and out of the hands of Wilhelm and Hermann Zichwolff." The instant he uttered the name, he spat into the dirt outside the front door.

"But you cannot go back, Father." Now Diedrich's voice dripped with insolence and he didn't care. "So you will sleep in Herr Seitz's bed and eat Herr Seitz's food until I have worked enough to earn back our passage and the cost of this land."

Father swung back to Diedrich, his face an ugly mask of fury. "I will not set foot in his house again! I will live here, in this house we have built with our own hands." He held out his hands, his curled fingers calloused and gnarled with years of work. "And to pay for my food, I will find other work here in Sauers. Surely one of our neighbors could use an extra pair of hands."

Tears stung the back of Diedrich's nose, and he

swallowed the lump that rose in his throat. "You can do whatever you want, Father, but I will not forsake Regina. Not for you, not for anyone."

Father's eyes glistened with unshed tears, and he stared at Diedrich as if he had never seen him before. "Then I shall have but two sons, for you shall be dead to me."

Chapter 18

Warring emotions clashed in Regina's chest as she led Gypsy from the barn. The shaggy pony almost pranced as she stepped into the sunlight pulling the little cart behind her.

Regina paused to rub the pony's velvety nose. "I am excited about going to see Anna, too, Gypsy, but I wish I could have seen Diedrich before I left." Twenty minutes earlier, Anna's brother Peter had appeared at the back door with news that his mother was ill. As each other's closest neighbors, it was common practice for Regina's family and the Rieckers to call on one another for help. Peter had assured Regina that his mother wasn't seriously ill, just down with a touch of ague. But since he and his brothers were busy helping their father put up hay, Anna would need help with the milking.

Normally Regina would have jumped at the chance to visit Anna. But Mama's stunning news this morning had shaken her to the core. Mama, too, had broken down and wept bitterly, begging Regina to forgive her for keeping the circumstances of her birth secret for so many years. At that moment, Regina's only focus had been to comfort her mother, assuring her that she forgave her and loved her and Papa very much.

But later, the realization that she had been born to someone else—that a woman she never knew had given birth to her and named her Regina—came crashing down on her like a building. Somehow she had managed to hold her tears through the noon meal. From his concerned glances, she knew Diedrich had sensed something was amiss. So she hadn't found it surprising when he lingered in the kitchen and asked her to walk with him. Not only had she felt it her duty to tell him what she had learned; she had also felt the need to share her burden with him. Yet her whole body had tensed and trembled as she wondered how he would take the news. She felt silly now, thinking of her unfounded worries. She should have known such news would make no difference to him or budge his love for her.

Smiling, she remembered how he had tenderly slipped his arm around her waist and how her tension had drained away at his touch as he guided her to the bench beside the garden. Just having him near, holding her hand and listening, had calmed her as she recounted all Mama had told her. Somehow, sharing it with Diedrich had made everything right. He had even made her laugh with the comment about the name Mudpuddle.

The thought sparked warmth in her chest that radiated throughout her body. What a wonderful husband he would be. She had hoped to have a few minutes alone with him again today to assure him that she had recovered from the shock the jarring revelation had caused her and that her heart was now easy. But by the time she helped Anna with milking and cooking supper for the Rieckers clan, she would be fortunate to return home in time for Bible reading and prayers.

The sound of quick footsteps turned Regina's attention toward the house. Mama walked toward her carrying a glass jar as quickly as her Holzschuhe allowed. "Here, you must take this good, rich chicken broth to Frau Rieckers." She handed Regina the jar of still-warm broth, which she had covered with a thin scrap of leather tied with a length of twine.

"Ja, Mama." Regina smiled and nodded. The easy relationship she had always enjoyed with her mother had returned, almost as if this morning's events had never happened.

"Regina." Glancing down, Mama paused and her brow furrowed in thought. At length she lifted her face and met Regina's questioning look with a somber one. "Of course I understand you needed to tell Diedrich about how you came to be our daughter. But I will leave to you if you want Anna or anyone else to know of it." Her chin lifted a fraction of an inch. "I and your Vater do not care if others know. It was not for any shame in you that we never mentioned how you became our daughter. It simply did not matter to us. From the moment I took you in my arms, you have been our Tochter as much as Sophie or Elsie. We have nothing for which to be ashamed."

Regina grinned. Diedrich was right. God had blessed her doubly—more than doubly. She threw her arms around her mother's neck. "Of course you have nothing to be ashamed of. And neither do I." Then a thought struck, and she eased away from hugging her mother. "I do think we should add Eva to our daily prayers," she said, wondering why it hadn't occurred to her earlier. "If not for her good judgment, I would not have you and Papa or Sophie and Elsie." A smile she could not stop stretched her lips wide. "Or even Diedrich."

Her brown eyes welling, Mama cupped Regina's face in her hand. "Ja, Tochter. I think that is something we should do." She pulled the handkerchief from her sleeve and dabbed at her eyes. "Eva, I think, would be proud of the woman you have become." As was her way, Mama's mood brightened abruptly. Her lips tugged into a grin, and her tone turned teasing. "And I think she also would approve of your intended."

Mama's words made Regina long to see her sweetheart even more. An idea sparked. Perhaps she could see Diedrich before she left for the Rieckerses' farm. "I have not seen the new house since last week. Unless you think it *unpassend*, I would like to stop by there on my way to Anna's."

Mama paused for a moment, and Regina held her breath. Such a thing might not be considered exactly proper, but she and Diedrich *were* promised, and Herr Rothhaus should be there to act as chaperone.

Mama smiled and gave her a hug. "I think that would be all right." Then her expression turned stern. "But do not stay long, and be sure to get to Herr Rieckers's farm before milking time."

Her heart taking flight, Regina scrambled to the seat of the pony cart. Grinning, she gave her mother a parting wave and flicked the reins against Gypsy's back, sending her trotting down the lane. Despite the shock Regina had experienced this morning, she could not imagine a more perfect life or a more perfect world.

She glanced upward at the azure sky dotted with a few clouds like wooly lambs swimming in a tranquil sea. Did lambs swim? She laughed out loud at her silly thought. Gypsy kept up a fast gait, the clopping of her hooves on the packed dirt mimicking the quick thumping of Regina's heart in anticipation of seeing her sweetheart.

She'd gone about a mile in the direction of the new house when she spotted a figure striding toward her down the dirt road. Diedrich. Her heart bolted then settled into a happy prance. Would the sight of him always evoke the same excitement and joy she now felt? She hoped so.

Waving, she wondered why he was heading home on foot. It was too early for him to come home for supper. Since Herr Rothhaus was not with him, perhaps he was simply in need of a tool back on the farm. As she approached him, she realized he hadn't returned her wave, and now she could see that no smile touched his lips. An ominous sense of unease gripped her.

She reined in Gypsy. "Diedrich. I am on my way to Anna's farm, but wanted to stop and see all the work you and your Vater have done on the house this week."

Still no salutation. No smile or word of greeting. A look of pain crossed his grim features and the tiny yip of unease inside Regina suddenly grew to a growling dread. "Diedrich, what is wrong? Is your Vater injured?"

"Regina, we must talk." Without invitation, he climbed to the seat beside her and took the reins from her now trembling hands. "*Linke*," he called to the pony with two quick clicks of his tongue and pulled on the left line, turning the pony and cart around.

As they veered off the road and headed across a meadow, Regina's dread became a raging fear. She gripped his arm. "Diedrich, please tell me what is the matter."

Still he said nothing. At last, he reined Gypsy to a stop in the shade of a big cottonwood tree beside the meandering stream of Horse Lick Creek. Countless wild thoughts skittered every which way through Regina's mind. Surely if Herr Rothhaus was hurt they wouldn't be sitting here but heading as fast as Gypsy's little legs could carry them toward help. Unless. . . No. She wouldn't think such things. "Diedrich!" She said his name so forcefully she startled the pony, making the animal jump and jerk the wagon. "You must tell me this minute—what is wrong?"

For another long moment, the fluttering of the cottonwood's leaves, the gurgling of the stream, and the chirping of birds filled the silence. At length, Diedrich turned from gazing over the tranquil creek and took Regina's hands in his. His face looked drawn and almost as old as his father's. His eyes—those gentle gray eyes that usually looked at her with awe and love—swam with tears and sorrow. "Regina, I do not know how to tell you this, but Vater is not coming back to the farm."

Regina heard herself gasp. Her ears rang and her head felt light. For an instant, everything around them appeared to spin. If not for Diedrich's strong hands gripping hers, she might have fallen off the cart. With tears streaming down her face, she willed strength back into her weak limbs. Her poor Diedrich. Her poor Liebling. She must stay strong for him. "Oh Diedrich, your Vater is dea—dea. . ." She could not say the word.

"Nein. Vater is well." He shook his head and patted her hand, sending ripples of relief through her. "I did not mean for you to think that." Then his handsome features twisted in a look of anguish. "But what I must tell you is almost as painful."

For the next several minutes Regina sat in stunned disbelief as Diedrich recounted the incredible story his father had told him. A wave of nausea washed over her. Who was she? From what kind of terrible people had she sprung? She fought to keep from losing her dinner over the side of the cart.

Diedrich rubbed her arms in a comforting motion as he had done earlier on the bench beside the garden. "It is sorry I am to tell you this, my Liebchen. I would have rather cut off my own arm than tell you." He shook his head, which hung in sorrow. "But I did not want you to hear of it from anyone else, even your own parents."

Regina struggled to assimilate what he had told her. Herr Rothhaus must despise her. Though Diedrich had not used those exact words, Regina could surmise nothing less. Otherwise, Herr Rothhaus would not have vowed never again to step foot in her home. The ramifications of what this could mean to her and Diedrich and their future plans together hit Regina with the same force as if someone had struck her in the stomach with a wooden club.

Her head began to spin again. As if the shocking news about being adopted wasn't enough to discover in one day, now she must face another soul-jarring disclosure. *Dear Lord, how much more can I bear?* She now understood how Job in the scriptures must have felt. Suddenly a new thought struck, and with it, a new terror that grabbed her in its bloody, gnashing teeth. Her heart—no, her whole insides—felt as if they were crumpling in on themselves. Her lungs seized, and she struggled for breath. Diedrich had brought her here to tell her he no longer wanted to marry her. Herr Rothhaus was his father. Of course Diedrich would choose him over her. With her whole body trembling, she managed to muster enough breath to say, "So you do not want to marry me now." Her words came out in a desolate tone with no hint of a question. She hated the tears streaming down her face.

Diedrich's eyes widened. "Nein." He shook his head. "I mean ja." He slipped his arms around her waist and drew her closer to him. A tender expression softened the drawn lines in his stricken face. "I love you, Regina. I will always love you. And I want you to be my wife. You are mein Liebchen," he whispered, "mein Liebling, mein Schätzchen." His voice broke slightly over the last word. But Regina thought he uttered the endearment with a touch less conviction than he had six weeks ago when he first said those words to her.

A fresh deluge of tears cascaded down her face. "But your Vater will never sanction our marriage now."

Diedrich winced as if she had struck him. The muscles of his jaw moved then set in a look of determination. "Regina, my Vater is a gut man. All my life, I have known him as a kind and just man who tries to live as our Lord would wish. I am sure when he has had time to think on it—to pray on it—he will repent of his harsh words." He heaved a deep sigh. "But for now, I must gather his things and take them to him, for he insists he will live now in the new house, apart from your family."

With that, he turned Gypsy around and headed back home. They rode in grim silence until Diedrich reined the pony to a stop between the house and barn. He handed Regina the reins then cupped her face in his hands and pressed a tender kiss on her lips. Though his eyes looked sad, he gave her a brave smile. "Do not worry, Liebchen. Gott is stronger than any problem. If we pray, I am sure He will hear our prayers and have mercy on us and change Vater's heart."

Regina tried to answer his smile, but her lips refused to support it. She watched him jump to the ground, and her heart quaked. As much as she wanted to believe him, she couldn't help wondering if perhaps this was God's way of telling her and Diedrich that He did not want them to marry.

Chapter 19

"Honour thy father and thy mother: that thy days may be long upon the land which the Lord thy God giveth thee.'"

At the words from Exodus uttered in Pastor Sauer's resonant voice, the urge to emit a bitter laugh gripped Regina. The biblical edict seemed an impossible one for both her and Diedrich to keep. But laughing aloud in church and embarrassing her parents and Diedrich would not improve her plight. So she sat quietly, her head down and her hands folded in her lap while the silent misery that had held sway over her entire household these past nine days once again engulfed her.

Herr Rothhaus's stunning proclamation had shattered not only Regina's and Diedrich's happiness, but Regina's parents' serenity as well. Mama wept almost daily now, blaming herself for ever having disclosed the truth of Regina's parentage. Frustrated at his inability to soothe Mama, Papa seemed to stay in a nearly perpetual state of anger. Enraged that Herr Rothhaus considered him a liar and a sneak, Papa insisted that Diedrich keep his word and marry Regina. And though Diedrich's firm assurance that he had no plans to break his promise to Regina had somewhat appeased Papa, Papa's stormy mood remained.

And caught squarely in the center were Regina and Diedrich. Despite Diedrich's belief that his father's hard stance would soon soften, Herr Rothhaus showed no sign of moving in that direction. If anything, he seemed even more staunchly opposed to Diedrich and Regina marrying. As the days passed, Regina's hope of the man's attitude changing dwindled, especially since he refused to discuss the matter with either Papa, Diedrich, or even Pastor Sauer.

Morning sunlight streamed through one of the church's open windows and angled warmly across Regina's face. But neither the sun's rays nor the happy chirping of the robin perched on the windowsill could brighten her mood. The future that had once looked so sunny had now turned bleak. The commandment the pastor had read struck her as almost mocking. All her life she had tried diligently to keep God's commandments. Even when she and Diedrich had plotted together to avoid matrimony, they had not disrespected their parents. Instead, they had hoped to gradually—and respectfully—change their parents' minds. Ironically, now that they loved one another and wanted to marry, she could see no way for them to avoid breaking the commandment Pastor Sauer had just read.

Her gaze drifted to her left and the men's side of the sanctuary, and her heart ripped anew. Diedrich sat with his head bowed and his arms resting on his knees. As painful as Herr Rothhaus's rejection was for Regina and her family, she couldn't begin to imagine the agony it inflicted upon Diedrich. Her heart swelled at her darling's unwavering devotion to her. But his decision to defy his father and not cancel their wedding plans had come at a terrible cost to him. And it had proved a bittersweet victory for Regina. Daily she saw the toll that decision took on the man she loved. Though he kept up a brave face, she watched him grow sullen and gaunt. Not a day passed that he didn't assert his love for her, but rarely did she see him smile now. It was as if Herr Rothhaus had ripped a hole in his son's soul, and each day a little more of Diedrich's joy seeped out.

Guilt saturated Regina's heart. She had caused this rift between Diedrich and his father. If Diedrich sinned by defying his father's wishes, didn't Regina sin as well by allowing him to do so? But whether or not Diedrich saw his defiance of his father as a sin, Regina knew his honor would never let him break off their engagement. But if she broke it off, wouldn't she dishonor Papa as well as break her heart and Diedrich's in the bargain? A greater question loomed. Did she even have the courage to break her engagement and send away the man she loved?

Out of the corner of her eye, she caught Anna Rieckers exchanging smiling glances across the aisle with her intended, August Entebrock. To her shame, Regina experienced a stab of jealousy. She'd learned of her friend's engagement only minutes after Diedrich told her that his father had forbidden their marriage. Hearing Anna bubble with excitement about her engagement had driven Regina's hurt even deeper. She had tried hard to set her own heartache aside and rejoice with her friend but had ended up weeping in Anna's arms and spilling the whole awful story to her. And Anna had comforted her, faithfully following the apostle Paul's charge to "weep with them that weep." Sadly, Regina knew that her own concerns had prevented her from living up to the other part of the scripture and rejoicing with Anna as wholeheartedly as she should have.

More guilt. How many sins had Regina committed over the past two weeks? She didn't want to consider the number. *Dear Lord, forgive my transgressions.* But would He forgive her if she purposely continued to sin and to cause Diedrich to sin as well?

Despair settled over her like a dank fog. *Dear Lord, show me the way. Tell me what I should do.*

"'And Jesus said unto her, Neither do I condemn thee: go, and sin no more.'" Pastor Sauer's voice filtered into Regina's silent prayer. The words of the scripture echoed in her ears, and her heart throbbed with a painful ache. She'd asked for God's direction. And though she may not like the answer, He had given it. Now she just needed the courage to see it through.

The rest of the service passed as in a fog for Regina, the pastor's voice melding with the drone of the honeybees that buzzed around the hollyhocks blooming outside the church's open windows. At last the pastor invoked the benediction, and the congregation filed out of the church—the men first, followed by the women.

Regina's heart felt like a lump of lead in the center of her chest. Though everything in her screamed against it, she knew what she had to do.

Following Mama outside, Regina mumbled an absent pleasantry as she passed Pastor Sauer at the door. While

Mama went to talk with Frau Rieckers, who seemed well recovered from her bout of ague, Regina glanced around the crowded churchyard for Diedrich. She saw no reason to prolong the misery. Like the time last month when she got the splinters in her hands, the ones she and Mama pulled out quickly hurt much less than those they had to extract slowly. As Mama had said, "Better short pain than long pain." The same wisdom applied now.

Her gaze roved over the crowd milling about the churchyard. At last she spied Diedrich, and her heart clenched. He and Papa stood together talking with Herr Entebrock and Herr Rieckers and their sons. Regina knew that Papa's encouragement had meant a lot to Diedrich in the wake of his own father's rejection. And Papa had taken Diedrich to his heart as a son in a way he never had with Sophie's husband, Ezra, or Elsie's William. Papa would doubtless take the news of the broken engagement as hard as Diedrich would.

Regina's grip on her resolve slipped, and she swallowed hard. Drawing a fortifying breath, she started to take a step toward the men when someone grasped her arm.

"Regina." Anna's blue eyes were round, her face full of urgency. "I was hoping I would get a chance to talk with you." Tugging on Regina's arm, she pulled her to the side of the church. "I thought I should tell you. August said that Diedrich's father has been working this week on their farm." Glancing down at the ankle-deep grass as their feet, she caught her bottom lip between her teeth. "I thought. . .if you would like. . .I could ask August to talk to his Vater. Maybe Herr Entebrock could intercede—"

"No." Though her heart crimped at her friend's eagerness to help, Regina shook her head. She gave Anna's hand a quick squeeze. "I appreciate you trying to help, Anna, but I do not think such a plan would be wise—or necessary."

Anna gave a frustrated huff. "But you said Herr Rothhaus will not talk to your Vater or Pastor Sauer, or even to Diedrich as long as the two of you are promised." Her shoulders rose and fell with her sigh. "I know you said Diedrich still wants to marry you despite his father's objection." She frowned. "But you are so sad, and it is not right that you should be sad planning your wedding. We must do something to change Herr Rothhaus's mind so he will give you and Diedrich his blessing. Then you can be as happy planning your wedding as I am planning mine." Then her honey-colored brows slipped together and her eyes narrowed suspiciously. "What do you mean by 'not necessary'?"

Regina sighed. She'd told Anna everything else. She might as well tell her what she had decided to do. Bracing for the negative response she knew was coming, she blurted, "I'm going to break my engagement to Diedrich."

Anna's eyes popped to the size of tea saucers; then her face crumpled in a pained look. "But why, Regina?" She held out her hands palms up. "All you've talked about since the Tanners' barn raising is how much you love Diedrich and how you can hardly wait to marry him." The disappointment in Anna's anguished tone smote Regina with remorse. "We promised each other we would have both our weddings in September. You and Diedrich will stand up for me and August; then August and I will stand up for you and Diedrich."

It hurt Regina to disappoint her friend, but she might as well get used to the reaction. Telling Mama and Papa would be no easier. Yet as much as she dreaded telling her parents, that trepidation paled compared to the notion of telling Diedrich. Her heart quaked at the thought.

Regina clasped Anna's hands. "Didn't you hear Pastor Sauer? If Diedrich and I marry against his father's will, are we not dishonoring him?" The weight of her sorrow pulled her head down like an iron yoke. "I cannot make Diedrich sin by disobeying his father."

Anger flashed in Anna's eyes, and she snatched her hands from Regina's. "Are you daft, Regina? Don't be foolish. It is Diedrich's father who is wrong, not you or Diedrich. Didn't you hear Pastor Sauer read Colossians 3:21? 'Fathers, provoke not your children to anger, lest they be discouraged.'" Crossing her arms over her chest, she snorted. "I'd say that fits exactly what Herr Rothhaus has done."

Regina couldn't help a grin. She hadn't expected to get a double sermon this morning. And though it warmed her heart to see her good friend's willingness to leap to her defense with such fierce abandon, she couldn't entirely agree. "One sin does not cancel out another, Anna. Besides, how can Diedrich change his father's mind if Herr Rothhaus will not talk to him? And Herr Rothhaus will not talk to Diedrich as long as Diedrich and I are promised."

Sniffing back tears, she gave Anna a hug. "Diedrich still loves me, Anna, and I love him. Gott willing, our engagement will not stay broken long, and he will be my Verlobter again soon." She forced a smile. "Diedrich assures me that after his Vater has had sufficient time to think about it, he will repent. Just pray he is right and that Gott will help Diedrich change his Vater's heart." Anna opened her mouth as if to make another objection, but Regina held up her hand and Anna closed her mouth. "I know what I am doing is right, Anna. If it is Gott's will, we will both have our September weddings."

Giving a nod of surrender, Anna swiped at a tear meandering down her cheek. At the same moment, Regina glanced over Anna's shoulder to see a smiling August Entebrock walking toward them. Stepping away from Anna, she grinned and whispered, "Dry your eyes. August is coming."

To her credit, Regina felt only joy and not a speck of jealousy as she watched Anna and her tall, blond *Verlobten* walk hand in hand toward Anna's mother.

"They make a nice-looking *Paare*, do they not, mein Liebchen? Almost as nice looking as us." At Diedrich's soft voice and the touch of his hand on her back, Regina jerked.

"Ja. Almost." Her heart turning cartwheels, she pivoted to face him. Somehow she managed to muster a decent smile but wished her voice didn't sound so breathless. It was the first time since his father had disowned him that she'd heard even a hint of a tease in Diedrich's voice, and it did her heart good.

He slipped his arm around her waist, and from force of habit, she leaned into his embrace. Would the change in their formal relationship affect their familiar one? She prayed it wouldn't, but feared there was no way it could not. He began to guide her toward the wagon. "August tells me that he and

Anna are planning a September wedding as well." His voice, which had begun on a light tone, ended on a sad one. Had August also mentioned to Diedrich that his father was working on the Entebrock farm?

Stopping, she swiveled to face him. She might as well pull out the emotional splinter now. "Diedrich, there is something I need to talk with you about."

"Oh, there you two are." Mama bustled up and took hold of Regina's arm. "I would love to visit more, but we have that turkey Vater killed yesterday roasting in the oven. We must get home soon to see to it, or it will be as dry and tough as leather."

Instead of annoyance, Regina felt a rush of relief at the intrusion. She couldn't break her engagement to Diedrich with Mama, Papa, and half of St. John's congregation looking on. She needed time alone with him to fully explain her reasoning. Perhaps they could find a private moment together after dinner.

As they headed down the road toward home in the wagon, talk turned to the upcoming threshing of the wheat crops around Sauers and Dudleytown. Every summer the community came together, everyone helping each other harvest their wheat crop. And with the new threshing machine Herr Entebrock bought this spring, the work should go even quicker this year. In exchange for help harvesting his own wheat crop, he had promised the use of his machine to his neighbors as well.

Regina loved threshing time. It was like a big party that moved from farm to farm and went on for a month or more.

The women of the community gathered in the kitchen of the host farm and put together fantastic meals for their men, who labored long hours in the fields. She especially enjoyed when everyone came to her family's farm. Would she and Diedrich ever host a threshing at their own home? Her heart pinched at the thought. Not unless God changed Herr Rothhaus's heart and mind. And at this point, it was beginning to look like it might take a miracle.

Sitting beside her, Diedrich absently laced his fingers with Regina's as he talked with Papa. His thumb gently caressed the back of her hand, sending pleasant tingles up her arm. Her heart throbbed painfully. She fought the urge to cling to him and weep. They loved each other. It was not fair that she must let him go to have any chance of their gaining his father's blessing. She prayed she wouldn't have to let him go forever.

Blinking back tears, she lifted her face to the warm breeze as Papa turned the wagon into the long lane that led to their house. If Diedrich caught her crying, he would want to know why, and this was not the time or place to tell him.

As they neared the house, the sight of a wagon and team parked between the house and barn swept away Regina's anguished thoughts.

Mama gripped Papa's arm and gave a little gasp. "Ernst, is that not Sophie and Ezra's team? And why would they have chairs and feather ticks in the back of the wagon?"

Mixed emotions swirled in Regina's chest at the prospect of seeing her eldest sister. Though she itched to hold her baby nephew, Henry, she and Sophie could rarely share a room for a half hour without getting on each other's nerves. She had often wondered how she and Sophie could be sisters and yet be so different from each other. But since she had learned they were not blood sisters, their different personalities made a little more sense.

When they had all climbed down from the wagon, Sophie appeared from a wedge of shade beside the house. Glancing behind Sophie, Regina could now see Ezra playing with two-year-old Henry on a quilt spread out on the grass.

Mama beamed as she hurried toward the little family. "Sophie, Ezra, it is wunderbar that you have come. Where is my kleines Henry, my liebes Enkelkind?" But as Sophie neared, the distraught look on her face wiped the smile from Mama's.

Practically running the last few steps, Sophie threw herself into Mama's arms and sobbed. "Oh Mama, Papa. You must help us. We are desperate!"

Chapter 20

Feeling slightly awkward, Diedrich stood behind Regina, cupping her shoulders with his hands to silently lend his support. Obviously something was not well with her eldest sister and family. The last thing Regina needed was another emotional blow.

Frau Seitz hugged her eldest daughter and murmured words of comfort while alternately begging her to explain the cause of her distress. The woman's husband walked toward them, their young child perched on the crook of his arm. No hint of a smile touched Ezra Barnes's bearded face, which looked haggard and drawn.

Herr Seitz's frowning glance bounced between his distraught daughter and his son-in-law. "Sophie, Ezra, you must tell us now. What is the matter?"

Frau Seitz gently pushed Sophie away enough to look into her tear-reddened eyes. "Sophie, what is wrong?"

Sophie sniffed and for a moment appeared to get a better grip on her emotions. "We—we have been put out of our home." The last word dissolved into another wrenching sob.

Ezra, his eyes also red rimmed, approached his wife and rubbed her back with his free hand. In a gentle tone that held only a hint of scolding, he said something to her in English. Diedrich wished he had worked harder to learn the language.

The toddler, whom Frau Seitz had called Henry, whimpered and sucked his thumb so hard he made soft popping noises. Diedrich's heart went out to the little boy, who appeared at once confused and frightened. Fidgeting in his father's grasp, he began to whimper louder, and Regina reached up and eased him from Ezra's embrace.

Rocking the child in her arms, she whispered comforting hushes while brushing soft brown curls from his round cherubic face. "Shh, mein lieber Junge, shh." She bounced him in her arms and patted his back then kissed his rosy cheek.

At the sight, Diedrich's heart turned over. In a flash, he caught a glimpse of what their future might hold, and a sweet longing pulsed in his chest. What a wonderful mother she would make. How he would love to drive her back to St. John's Church this minute and ask Pastor Sauer to join them in holy matrimony. But too many things needed to be resolved before that could happen, including whatever plagued Sophie and her little family.

Herr Seitz harrumphed. "We must all go in the house and talk, I think." Moving as one, the group headed to the house. When everyone had situated themselves around the kitchen table, a slightly more composed Sophie, speaking in German, began to explain the family's plight.

"You know that Ezra's brother, Dave, brought him into his wheelwright business shortly before we married." Frau and Herr Seitz nodded, worry lines etching deep crevices in their faces. Sophie drew in a ragged, fortifying breath. "Lately, business has not been good." She sniffed. "A new wagon shop opened on the other side of town. Their operation is larger, and they began to undercut us in price." She gave her husband a brave smile. "Dave never liked it that Ezra fixed wheels for people on promise of payment. And when business fell off, it irritated him even more." Her fingers trembled across her cheek, wiping away a tear. "They argued all the time. Then Dave began to claim that money was missing from each day's till and accused Ezra of taking it."

Frau Seitz pulled the handkerchief from her sleeve and handed it across the table to her daughter, who wiped her eyes and delicately blew her nose. "Well, one thing led to another. Ezra and Dave got into a terrible argument, and Dave fired Ezra."

Regina shifted a squirming Henry on her lap. "But surely when Dave calms down, he will listen to reason. Perhaps you are being too hasty."

Diedrich couldn't help wondering if Regina was mentally comparing Ezra's situation with his brother to Diedrich's feud with his father.

Sophie shot Regina a scornful glare and snorted. "Don't you think we tried to reason with him?" she snapped. "He fired Ezra two weeks ago. We've been trying to reason with him ever since." Her face crumpled again, and she began to weep in earnest. "Because money was so tight, we had gotten way behind on our note for the house. By the time Dave fired Ezra, we had already missed three payments. So when Tom Pemberton down at the bank found out that Ezra had lost his position, he told us he couldn't float us any longer and said we would have to move out so the bank could resell the house."

Frau groaned. "Oh Sophie. Why did you not tell us sooner? Why did you let things get so bad?" She shook her head. "I was afraid something like this might happen. I knew you should not have bought such an expensive house."

Sophie sobbed, and Ezra gathered her in his arms. "We thought business would get better," she mumbled from her husband's shoulder. "We never imagined Ezra would be out of work."

Herr Seitz shook his head and put his hand on his wife's arm. "None of that matters now, Catharine. The past is the past. It is gut that Ezra has a skill. I am sure he will find work soon." In the midst of all the gloomy faces, his brightened. "For now, you will live here with us, and Ezra can help me and Diedrich with the threshing and putting up the hay."

He rose, and everyone followed. With a smile that looked strained, Herr Seitz glanced at Diedrich and Ezra. "Now we must give the kitchen to the *Frauen* so they can make us dinner." Lifting Henry from Regina's lap, he headed to the front room, and Ezra and Diedrich followed.

There, Herr Seitz and Ezra conversed in English with Herr Seitz translating in German for Diedrich. Henry played on the floor with a ball of yarn his grandfather had found in Frau Seitz's sewing basket. Though he didn't feel it proper to ask, Diedrich couldn't help but wonder where everyone would fit in the house.

Later, a somber mood reigned over the noon meal, lightened occasionally by Henry's rambunctious antics. Mostly the conversation was in English, which Diedrich assumed was for Ezra's benefit. Still far from proficient in the language, Diedrich struggled to follow what was being said. Between the little he could glean and what Regina translated for him, he gathered that the talk stayed mostly on the upcoming threshing. For each time Ezra's brother's name was mentioned, Sophie would begin to weep.

Diedrich understood Sophie's distress. But Regina's reticent attitude both perplexed and troubled him. She scarcely looked at him. And when she did, her eyes welled with tears. Even more worrisome was his sense that her sadness didn't entirely spring from her sister and brother-in-law's problems. In the churchyard she had said she needed to talk with him about something. Could whatever was on her mind earlier be the cause of her odd behavior? He was determined to talk with her privately after dinner and find out.

After the meal, Diedrich again joined Ezra and Herr Seitz in the front room while the women tidied up the kitchen. Sitting quietly, he only half listened as the other two men discussed the Barneses' financial problems. His mind kept drifting to Regina, wondering what she might have wanted to discuss with him.

"Diedrich, I—I need to talk with you." Her voice from the doorway surprised him, bringing him upright in his chair. He experienced a flash of alarm at her grim tone and the odd way her gaze refused to hold his.

His heart pounding with trepidation, Diedrich sprung from his seat. Mumbling an apology to Herr Seitz and Ezra, he carefully sidestepped Henry on the floor and followed Regina into the kitchen, where Sophie and Frau Seitz still worked. With her head bowed and her arms crossed over her chest, Regina stalked purposefully through the kitchen and out the back door. His concern growing with each step, Diedrich trailed behind, trying to think of anything he might have done or said to upset her.

Lengthening his steps, he caught up with her at the corner of the house. He put his hand on her shoulder, bringing her to a stop. "Regina, what is it? Tell me what is the matter."

Finally, she turned. The tears welling in her blue eyes ripped at his heart. Obviously he had misjudged the extent to which Sophie and Ezra's situation bothered Regina.

He drew her into his arms. "It will be all right, mein Liebchen. Your Vater is right. With Ezra's skills, he is sure to find work as a wheelwright soon. Until then, Sophie, Ezra, and Henry have a home here with family who love them." It felt good to hold her in his arms and comfort her.

To his surprise she pushed away from him. She shook her head, tears streaming down her cheeks. "I am not upset about Sophie and Ezra." She made impatient swipes at the wetness on her face as if angry at herself for crying.

Diedrich's bewilderment mounted along with his feelings of helplessness. "Then why *are* you crying, Liebchen?"

She stepped away, and fresh tears flooded down her face. "Please, you must not call me that."

"But why?" Diedrich took her hands in his. He couldn't guess what might be troubling her, but he couldn't comfort her until he found the cause of her anxiety. Her pain-filled eyes stabbed at his heart. He rubbed the backs of her hands with his thumbs. "Have I done something to upset you? If I have, I beg your forgiveness—"

"Diedrich, I must break our engagement." With that astounding declaration, she slipped her hands from his. Turning, she walked toward the garden bench he had begun to think of as theirs.

Feeling as if someone had punched him hard in the stomach, Diedrich stood stunned, unable to think or move. When his frozen limbs thawed and his mind began working again, his thoughts raced. He followed her to the bench and sat down beside her, praying she did not mean the words she had said. Surely they were simply a result of the several emotional blows she had suffered over the past couple of weeks.

He tried to capture her hands, but she pulled them away and folded them in her lap. Frustration tangled with the pain balling in his chest. "Why, Regina? Why would you say such a thing?" Had she decided she didn't love him after all? He couldn't believe it. Gripping her arms, he forced her to meet his gaze. His heart writhed. "Do you not love me, Regina? Is that what you are saying? You no longer want to marry me?"

The agony in her lovely eyes both tortured him and gave him hope. "Nein. That is not what I am saying."

Diedrich thought his head would explode. Having earlier watched Ezra Barnes deal with Sophie's tears, he felt a comradeship with the man. Mustering his patience, he blew out a long breath. "But if you still love me, why do you wish to break our engagement?"

Regina sniffed, making Diedrich regret the sterner tone he had taken. "It is not that I *wish* to break our engagement. I feel I *must* break it for now, if we are ever to have the chance to marry."

Diedrich's temples throbbed. He strove to keep a tight rein on his patience. "You are speaking nonsense, Regina. Either you want to marry me, or you don't."

New tears sketched down her face, smiting him with remorse. "Weren't you listening to Pastor Sauer's sermon?" She folded her arms over her chest as if to close herself away from him. "By defying your Vater and keeping our engagement, are you not dishonoring him?"

Diedrich winced at her words that reminded him of his painful separation from Father. Not a moment passed that their estrangement didn't gouge a fresh wound in his heart. Every day as he worked in the hay fields with Herr Seitz, he expected to look up at any moment and see Father striding toward them, smiling and waving his hand. But so far, it hadn't happened. More than once Diedrich had started toward the new log house with the intent to confront Father and try again to make him see reason. But each time he had turned back, fearing his efforts would only result in doing irreparable damage to their fragile relationship. Only Regina's love and his faith that God would eventually soften Father's heart had kept him going. It hurt him that Regina lacked the patience to wait for God to work.

Since her hands remained folded and tucked firmly against her body, he gently grasped her arms. "Regina, it has only been two weeks. I am sure that Vater will repent and give us his blessing soon. Besides, if we break our engagement, he will have less reason to change his mind. I have faith that Gott will change Vater's heart if we only pray and have patience."

Scooting back away from his grasp, she waved her hand through the air, barely missing a black and orange butterfly flitting past. "And you think your Vater will one morning wake and decide on his own that what he is doing is wrong, and he will then come and give us his blessing?"

Diedrich ignored the hint of scorn in her voice. "Perhaps it will happen that way. How can I know how Gott will work?"

She huffed. "But that is just it. Don't you see? Gott uses us to do His work. Your Vater loves you, Diedrich. When he sees that what he is doing is making you sad, there is a much greater chance he will change his mind about us marrying." She grasped his forearm, and her crystal blue eyes, which matched the sky behind her, pleaded for understanding. "But as things are, he is *not* seeing you. He can put you and me out of his mind and go on being stubborn as long as he wants. So if you can go to him and honestly tell him that we are no longer planning to marry, he will talk to you again. Then you will at least have a chance to convince him to bless our marriage."

Pondering her words, Diedrich rubbed his chin, already sprouting new stubble since his early morning shave. Her reasoning made some sense. But it also forced him to consider the possibility he had so far refused to face. What if Father never repented and gave them his blessing? No. He would not consider that. He trusted God to change Father's mind, and Regina needed to do the same. "You may be right. Perhaps I can more easily change Vater's mind if I can talk with him. But to me, breaking our engagement is like saying to Gott that I do not trust Him." Another thought popped into his head to bolster his argument. "Besides, I promised your Vater we would remain engaged. If we do not, are we not dishonoring *him*?"

For a moment, Regina's pale brows knit together in thought, giving him hope. But she shook her head. "I do not think it is the same thing. Papa would be sad if we broke our engagement, but he knows we cannot marry without Herr Rothhaus's blessing. He would understand."

Frustration built like rising steam in Diedrich's chest. He wanted to throw up his hands and tell her that none of this mattered because in a few days Father would doubtless change his mind. Instead, he couldn't resist trying another line of reasoning in an attempt to make her see things his way. "But by your thinking, we were dishonoring both our fathers when we decided not to marry after they had agreed between them that we would." He arched an eyebrow at her. "Yet as I remember, you had no scriptural objection to our plan."

Her face pinked prettily, and he couldn't stop a grin. What fun it would be to mentally spar with Regina for the rest of his life.

A challenge flashed in her blue eyes, and her unflinching gaze met his squarely. "And do you remember what our plan was?"

"To convince our fathers we should not marry." The words popped out of his mouth before he thought and was met by her triumphant and somewhat smug smile.

She nodded. "That is so. And if we convinced them, then

we would not be disobeying or dishonoring them by not marrying."

Blowing a quick breath of surrender, he gave her a sad smile. "You are a formidable opponent, Regina Seitz." Yet he was prepared to surrender only this one skirmish—not the entire war. "I still believe by remaining engaged, we will sooner turn Vater's thinking and win his blessing."

She swiveled on the bench and looked across the potato patch with its plants now sporting white blossoms. For a long moment, she seemed to focus her attention on a bluish-gray bird with a snowy belly perched on a fence post beyond the garden. The bird's head darted about as if following some unseen insect. Then, giving a bright whistling call followed by several chirps, he took flight. When he had gone, Regina sighed and pressed her clasped hands into the well of her apron between her knees. "So you do not believe you are dishonoring your Vater?"

"Nein." He blew out a breath. "I do not know." Why did she feel the need to force him to think of things he would rather not consider? He couldn't keep the irritation from his voice. "But Vater is the one who is wrong. It is not from any belief that we are poorly matched that he is against our marriage but because he refuses to forgive your birth Vater and Großvater." He gazed down at her lovely face, and his heart throbbed with love for her. He had to make her understand. Cradling the side of her face with his hand, he gentled his voice. "I know you want to do as our Lord commands, but I think you are wrong in this."

She shook her head sadly, and his heart plummeted. Her

eyes glistened with welling tears. "When you heard me tell Eli that I loved you, I knew you would give up your dream of going to California and marry me so as not to break my heart. That is why I lied and told you I didn't love you." A tear beaded on her lower lash then slipped down her petal-soft cheek. "I did not want to wake each morning wondering if that was the day I would see regret in your eyes."

Diedrich stifled a groan. Surely she didn't think he still harbored dreams of heading west. "Regina, I told you. All the gold in California means nothing to me now. You are all that matters to me."

She gave him a weak smile. "I believe you. But even if you are right about the commandment and we would not be dishonoring your Vater by remaining engaged against his wishes, you still need to mend the rift between the two of you. I want your Vater to give us his blessing, but I want him to give it with a full heart, not because he feels forced to give it. I want our family to be whole and full of love, not riddled with anger and resentment." She kissed him on the cheek, her warm breath sending tingles down his neck and spine. "I love you, Diedrich. But for now I must break our engagement. Go to your Vater and tell him so. Then pray that with Gott's help you can change his mind about us marrying. Because until your Vater gives us his blessing, I cannot promise to marry you."

Chapter 21

"These are some of the nicest cherries I have seen in a long time." Sophie smiled up from her work of pitting the bright red fruit at the far end of the table. "Did they come from that little tree at the east end of the barn?"

Using the back of her wrist, Regina brushed a strand of hair from her face before applying the rolling pin to a lump of pie dough. "Yes. Mama said she was surprised at how nice they are after we had such a cold winter." Her heart smiled with her lips. She couldn't remember spending a more amiable hour with Sophie. In fact, Regina noticed that her eldest sister's attitude toward her had sweetened considerably since Easter, when Sophie and her family had last visited. Regina couldn't have been more surprised when Sophie suggested that Mama play with Henry outside while she and Regina work together making pies for the threshing at the Entebrocks' farm Monday.

Sophie worked the paring knife's sharp point into another plump cherry and deftly plucked out the pit. "I did notice at Easter that the tree was covered with tight buds." She gave Regina a sideways glance, and her next words tiptoed out carefully. "That must have been just before Diedrich and Herr Rothhaus arrived."

At Diedrich's name, a painful longing pricked Regina's

chest. "Ja," she managed to murmur. She hadn't seen Diedrich since she broke their engagement almost a week ago. In fact, he had left shortly after their conversation. Papa and Mama had racked their brains trying to figure the best sleeping arrangement in order to make room for Sophie, Ezra, and Henry. They decided that Regina should give the young family her larger upstairs bedroom, which she had once shared with Sophie and Elsie. But that put both her and Diedrich downstairs, which would not be proper. Then Diedrich took Papa aside, informing him that Regina had broken their engagement and explaining why. Confident his father would accept him now that he was no longer betrothed to Regina, he suggested that Regina take his downstairs room and he would move to the new log house with his father.

At Diedrich's news, surprise, chagrin, and sorrow had flashed across Papa's face in quick succession. In the end, with a sigh of resignation and a look of profound disappointment, he had reluctantly agreed with Diedrich's suggestion. Regina sniffed as hot tears stung the back of her nose and filled her eyes. She smashed the rolling pin down hard on the dough. In one afternoon, she had broken the hearts of the two men she loved most in the world.

Sophie rose and came around the table to put her arm around Regina's shoulders, startling her with the tender gesture. "Forgive me, Regina. I didn't mean to upset you by mentioning the Rothhauses." She patted Regina's shoulder. "I know this has all been very confusing for you. I blame Papa." Irritation edged her voice. "He never should have made such a deal with Herr Rothhaus in the first place. Why, Mama says he didn't even tell her about it until the letter came saying Herr Rothhaus and his son were on their way."

Regina sniffed and gave her sister a brave smile. She knew Sophie meant well, but she could never make herself wish Diedrich had not come into her life. "It is all right, Sophie. I believe Gott will use Diedrich to soften Herr Rothhaus's heart."

Sophie stiffened and stepped away from her. "Hmm." She pressed her hand to her chest, and her voice turned breathless. "I must say, I am still stunned by it all myself. When Mama told me how she and Papa had adopted you, I nearly fell over." She shook her head and clucked her tongue. "And on top of it all, there is that awful business about the Rothhauses and your real Vater."

A flash of anger leapt in Regina's chest. A faceless man by the name of Hermann Zichwolff may have given her life, but in her mind, Papa would always be her real father. "Papa is my Vater just as he is your Vater." She hated the defensive tone in her voice.

Sophie gave an odd little giggle and waved her hand in the air. "Of course Papa is your Vater. You know what I mean."

Regina wasn't sure she did but decided to let it go. She hated to spoil the amicable mood she and Sophie had enjoyed together this afternoon.

Another little giggle warbled through Sophie's voice. "It is a bit funny though, since Elsie and I always thought you got your blond hair from Papa." She sashayed back to her end of the table. Dipping a tin cup into the sack of sugar, she scooped out a heaping cupful and poured it over the cherries she had pitted.

"I suppose." Regina wished Sophie would find something other than Regina's adoption to talk about.

Sophie reached into the sack of flour and grabbed a handful, which she sprinkled over the sugared fruit. "For a girl who was always a bit of a dull goose, you certainly have turned into a bundle of surprises. When we were here at Easter, Elsie was convinced you had set your cap for that Tanner boy." Another giggle. Shriller now. "Then two weeks later, I get a letter from Mama saying you are engaged to someone just arrived from Venne."

Regina hoped she was imagining the snide tone that seemed to have crept into Sophie's voice.

Sophie paused in mixing the flour into the cherries to shoot Regina a critical glance. "Be careful with that dough, Regina. Rolling it too hard will make it tough." Suddenly, her demeanor brightened. Her lips quirked in a sly grin, and her voice turned teasing. "Eli Tanner, is he not the miller's son? An exceptionally handsome boy, if memory serves."

Regina shrugged as she transferred the pie dough to two waiting pans. Once she would have agreed. But she had glimpsed meanness in Eli's character that now made him ugly to her. Regina was no happier with Sophie's new subject of conversation than her last. She almost blurted that Diedrich far surpassed Eli in both looks and character, but Diedrich was another subject she would rather not discuss with Sophie.

Humming gaily, Sophie picked up the crockery bowl

of prepared fruit filling and carried it to Regina. With the bowl tucked between the crook of her arm and her waist, she plucked out a cherry and popped it in her mouth. Her brows knit in deliberation as she chewed. After a moment, she picked out another cherry and held it out to Regina. "Here, taste this and tell me if you think it is sweet enough."

Regina couldn't remember the last time Sophie had asked her opinion on anything. Reveling in her sister's uncharacteristically congenial mood, she acquiesced, opening her mouth to accept the sugar- and flour-coated cherry Sophie dropped on her tongue. The earthy taste of the flour and the sugar's sweetness blended perfectly with the tart fruit to induce a pleasant tingle at the back of Regina's jaw.

Regina gave her sister a smile and nod. "I think you have it just right, Sophie," she said as she munched the cherry. "Ezra must think he married the best pie baker in three counties."

Sophie chuckled and raked the cherries into the dough-lined pans with a wooden spoon. "Well, whether or not he thinks so, he at least had better say so." She angled a grin up at Regina. "You learned from Mama, just like Elsie and I did. I am sure whomever you marry will like your pies as much as Ezra likes mine."

Whomever I marry. Regina stifled a sardonic snort. It was inconceivable to her to imagine making pies for, keeping house for, living with, and loving any other man than Diedrich. The past six days had crept by in agonizing slowness. The week she had spent helping Elsie, she had missed Diedrich. But then she had still guarded her heart, expecting him to leave for California. Since then, she had allowed him to claim her heart completely. So since their parting Sunday afternoon, the longing to see his face—to touch his hand—had become a palpitating ache in her chest. It burrowed ever deeper, intensifying by the day. Sunday she was so sure she had done the right thing. Now she wondered. Torturous thoughts darted about in her head like a hound after a warren of rabbits. Did Diedrich miss her, too? Did he lie awake at night trying to bring her face into focus in his mind? Had he yet broached the subject of Regina to his father? Did he even plan to? No. She must not think that way. *Please, Lord, give Diedrich the right words to change his father's mind and heart.*

At least tomorrow was Sunday. Surely he would come to services and she could see him then. But if his father came, too, it might be difficult for her and Diedrich to find a chance to talk.

Sophie looked up from cutting strips of dough for the pies' latticed tops. "I must commend you on your good sense, Regina. It was very wise of you to break off your engagement to Diedrich."

Regina swiped at the tears welling in her eyes. "Then you do not agree with Mama and Papa and Diedrich? They feel if I hadn't broken our engagement, Herr Rothhaus might be forced to examine his heart more closely and thus change his thinking."

Sophie dropped the paring knife to the table with a clatter. Turning, she took Regina by the shoulders and fixed her with a stern look. "Regina, I know that Mama and Papa do not agree with us, but they are just disappointed and are not thinking clearly. I am absolutely certain you did the right

thing. In that, you must believe me." Her brown eyes inten-
sified until they looked almost as black as coal. "Whatever
you do, you must not reinstate your engagement to Diedrich.
Nothing good can come of it."

"You mean I shouldn't reinstate it without his Vater's
blessing." Though she knew it was an oversight on Sophie's
part, Regina couldn't bear to leave the thought where her
sister had left it.

Sophie let go of Regina's shoulders and turned to face
the table again. With a flip of her wrist, she waved a flour-
covered hand through the air. "Of course," she said lightly.
"You know what I mean."

Moving to Sophie's side, Regina began placing the
strips of dough over one of the pies, weaving them into a
lattice design. It heartened her to know that she had an
ally in Sophie. At the same time, it caused an uneasy feeling in her breast. She had trusted her parents' guidance all
her life. The only time she had ever questioned a decision
of theirs was when Papa had chosen Diedrich for her husband. And now she could see that even in that, Papa was
right. In trying to prevent Diedrich from opposing his
father, Regina had no choice but to oppose her own parents. So although she was glad Sophie understood her
thinking and supported her, it didn't make her feel any bet
ter about her decision.

"Do not look so glum, Sohn." Father pressed his hand on Diedrich's shoulder and every muscle in Diedrich's body tensed.

Shrugging off his father's hand, Diedrich shifted on the low stool where he perched near the hearth with the open Bible on his lap. "I am not glum, Vater. I am but reading the scriptures." May God forgive his half-truth. His melancholy mood was far beyond glum. And gazing unseeing at a printed page while his mind was two miles away with Regina could not in truth be called reading.

The past week had proven a test of Diedrich's patience, faith, and fortitude. Facing Father and admitting that Regina had broken their engagement was hard enough. But seeing the look of relief and joy the announcement brought to his parent's face had torn his heart asunder. He would have turned on his heel and walked back to the Seitz farm that instant, if not for his father's happy tears and welcoming outstretched arms. It had irked Diedrich to be made to feel like the prodigal son when he knew he had done no wrong, but at least he and Father were talking again. And his and Regina's future happiness depended on his rebuilding a relationship with his father.

Father gave a sigh of contentment as he eased down on the seat of the rocking chair he had built during Diedrich's absence. Besides working each day at the Entebrock farm, Father's industry over the past weeks was evident in the several pieces of new furniture that now graced the house. "And which of the scriptures are you reading?"

Diedrich blinked and focused on the open book draped across his knee. A few minutes earlier, he and Father had endured another quiet supper during which the tension between them was thicker than the two-day-old stew they had dined upon. For the moment, their fragile and often uneasy truce seemed dependent on an unspoken agreement not to mention Regina. So in an effort to discourage conversation with his father and to be alone with his thoughts, Diedrich had simply opened the Bible and pretended to read. He glanced at the top of the open page and said, "Proverbs." He wished he had managed to keep the tone of surprise from his voice. Fortunately, Father didn't seem to notice.

Leaning back in the chair, Father emitted a contented grunt and folded his arms over his stomach. "Ah, Proverbs. *Prima.* There is much wisdom there."

Diedrich was tempted to say that perhaps Father could benefit from Solomon's wisdom. But he bit back the retort. To the best of his ability, he'd tried to stay respectful in his words and actions toward Father, trusting that God would bless his efforts and soften Father's heart toward Regina.

Father rocked his chair forward. "Read to me some of what you have been reading."

Caught unprepared, Diedrich scanned the open page. He angled the book to better catch the waning daylight streaming through the front window. His gaze lit on the thirteenth verse of the fifteenth chapter. "'A merry heart maketh a cheerful countenance: but by sorrow of the heart the spirit is broken.'"

Father's brow furrowed deeper with thought, and he absently grazed his chin whiskers with his knuckles. "Read more."

Diedrich dutifully sought the fourteenth verse and began reading. "'The heart of him that hath understanding seeketh knowledge: but the mouth of fools feedeth on foolishness.'"

Father flipped his hand in the air, indicating Diedrich should continue reading.

"'All the days of the afflicted are evil: but he that is of a merry heart hath a continual feast.'"

With a long sigh, Father rocked forward, his hands gripping the curved arms of the rocking chair. "I have been thinking, Sohn. This country we have come to is much bigger than the county of Jackson or even the state of Indiana."

Diedrich feared the direction his father's thoughts seemed to be taking. But he would let him have his say.

Craning his neck around, Father glanced out the front window. "There are many other German settlements besides this one in many other states." Looking down, he blew a quick breath through his nose. "The scriptures are right. It is not gut for a man to be sad. Because Herr Seitz did not deal with us honestly, your heart is sad." Hanging his head, he shook it in sorrow. "I did not bring you here to be sad."

Diedrich wanted to scream that he would not be sad if Father would only give him and Regina his blessing to marry. But quarreling with Father would not help his cause. So instead, he said, "I am not sad, Father." And at this moment, he told the truth. He was furious. Unable to sit and listen to any more of Father's musings, he stood abruptly, forgetting the Bible on his lap. The book dropped to the floor with a thud.

Father bent to pick it up, and a folded square of yellowed paper fluttered to the floor. He began to unfold it. "What is this?"

For an instant, Diedrich's heart caught with his breath. He knew exactly what Father held in his hand. He had long forgotten about the map to the California goldfields that he'd tucked in the pages of the Bible. Diedrich heaved a resigned sigh. "It is a map showing the way to the goldfields in California." None of it mattered now, so he no longer saw any reason to keep his earlier plans hidden from Father.

Father's eyes popped, and his jaw sagged as Diedrich told how he had secretly planned to avoid the marriage Father and Herr Seitz had arranged between him and Regina. Diedrich huffed a sardonic snort. "I was going to make us rich." His lips tugged up in a fond smile, and his voice softened with thoughts of Regina. "But then I found something far more valuable here." For a moment, Diedrich worried that Father might make an unkind comment about Regina—something he would never abide.

But the distant look in Father's eyes suggested he had stopped listening. His eyes wide, he perused the map. A smile crawled across his face until it stretched wide. With a sudden burst of laughter, he slapped his hand down on his knee. "That is where we should go, Sohn. I believe Gott put this idea in your head because He knew things would not go well for us here with Herr Seitz." His eyes sparked with a look of excitement Diedrich had not seen in them since they first embarked for America.

Diedrich was about to say he had no intention of going anywhere without Regina when Father popped up from his seat and pressed his hand on Diedrich's shoulder. His smile still splitting his face, Father gazed at the map in his hand

and bobbed his head. "Ja. When we have earned enough to pay Seitz for our passage, he can have back his land and this house. We will go to California as you planned."

Chapter 22

*C*oward. The word echoed in Diedrich's head as if hollered down a well. He bent and scooped up an armful of ripe wheat. Snagging another handful of the cut grain from the field, he absently wound slender stalks around the bundle he held in the crook of his arm, making a sheaf. Pitching the sheaf into the waiting wagon, he glanced up at the morning sky. Blue. Blue as Regina's eyes. The wheat reminded him of her hair. His heart ached to its very center.

Pausing, he dragged off his hat and ran his forearm across his sweaty brow. He glanced across the wheat field dotted with workers toward the Entebrock farmhouse situated beyond the barn. He could barely make out the white clapboard structure half hidden by several large maple trees that surrounded it. Somewhere in the kitchen, Regina worked with the other women of Sauers, preparing the noon meal. The moment he and Father arrived this morning, Diedrich began searching for her face among the gathering crowd. But just as he caught a glimpse of her climbing down from the Seitzes' wagon with her mother and sister, Father had stepped to his side and steered him toward Herr Entebrock's new Whitman thresher, eager to show him the workings of the machine.

Coward. Diedrich loathed the thought of branding himself with such an onerous label. Yet what else could he call himself when he had allowed the fear of his father's ire to keep him from the woman he loved?

He pitched another bundle of wheat toward the wagon with such force it almost sailed over it. Saturday evening when Father found the map on which Diedrich had drawn the route to the California goldfields and vowed the two of them should go, Diedrich had not disputed him. Not once since reconciling with Father had he stated outright that he still wanted to marry Regina. Instead, by his silence, he had allowed Father to think he had abandoned the notion of ever making her his wife. Although he realized the prudence of keeping his own counsel and not risking an argument and possibly another estrangement from Father, his reticence felt ignoble.

Anger and shame twisted in his gut like the straws he twisted around another bundle of wheat. "Coward." This time, he mumbled the word aloud in a guttural growl that sounded to his own ears like the snarl of a wounded animal. Surely the word fit his actions yesterday at church.

For days he had looked forward to Sunday and the opportunity to see Regina again. The two weeks Diedrich and his father were estranged, Father had not attended St. John's Church. He had even rejected Pastor Sauer's and Ernst Seitz's efforts to speak to him about his hard feelings toward Herr Seitz. So it had come as somewhat of a surprise when Father announced that he would be accompanying Diedrich to services.

Remembering his dismay at learning he would not be attending services alone, guilt nipped at Diedrich's conscience.

Although glad that Father would be in the Lord's house, he had hoped for an uninhibited opportunity to speak with Regina. Instead, he and Regina were forced to hide their affection for each other when in Father's sight. They had managed to exchange a precious few sweet glances during the service and later across the churchyard. The memory of those tender looks filleted Diedrich's heart.

But at least the pastor's sermon on forgiving neighbors seemed to have some positive effect on both Father and Herr Seitz. Immediately following the service, Herr Seitz had approached Father and asked his forgiveness. He vowed he had never intended to trick or defraud Father or Diedrich in any way. And claiming no knowledge of Father's feud with the Zichwolffs, he explained that having raised Regina from infancy, he had simply always considered her his daughter. Father had grudgingly accepted Herr Seitz's explanation and handshake, and the men had parted; if not exactly friends, then at least not sworn enemies.

At the sight, hope had sparked in Diedrich's chest that Herr Seitz might have actually cracked the wall of malice Father had built against Regina. But while Father forgave Herr Seitz for not divulging Regina's heritage, he had made it clear he still could not sanction a marriage between Diedrich and Regina. At that statement, Diedrich had seen anger flash in Herr Seitz's eyes—anger that had matched Diedrich's own emotion at Father's words. Yet both he and Regina's father had failed to champion her in voice. Diedrich understood Herr Seitz's reluctance to cause a row in the churchyard while his family and neighbors were within earshot. Diedrich, too, was hesitant to jeopardize the two men's fledgling reconciliation.

Diedrich's heart writhed in anguish and shame. Still, he should have gone to her as he'd wanted, taken her in his arms, and declared his love for her in front of Father and the entire congregation. He should have shouted his intentions to make her his wife regardless of the consequences.

In fact, he had tried to sneak a moment with her while Father was busy talking with the Entebrock men on the other side of the churchyard. But before he approached the spot where she'd stood huddled with her mother, sister, and Anna Rieckers, she had glanced up and spied him coming. Her face had blanched then turned crimson. Frowning, she had shaken her head and turned her back to him. She might as well have buried a knife to the hilt in his heart. But as much as it hurt to see her spurn him, he knew she was right. Antagonizing Father at this juncture would gain them nothing and would likely destroy any hope of earning his blessing.

How Diedrich wished that he and Regina could simply elope as young Tanner had tried to entice her to do at the barn raising. The thought of making her his wife and whisking her away from all impediments to their happiness was almost intoxicating. It reminded him of a poem Mama used to read to him when he was little. The German translation of a Scottish ballad, the poem told of a knight named Lochinvar, who stole away his lady love from beneath the noses of those who would keep them apart.

He crushed another armful of wheat against him so hard

he heard the stalks snap. Was he courageous enough to do anything so gallant? But even if he was, he knew Regina would never agree to leave behind her parents or this place she loved so well.

Blowing out a long breath, he tied another sheaf and slung it into the wagon. So far, he had failed Regina. He had failed them both.

A hard hand came down on his shoulder from behind. "Surely you are not already winded, Sohn." Father's chortle rasped down Diedrich's spine like a wood file. While Diedrich's mood had vastly deteriorated over the past week, Father's had greatly improved, especially since he began making plans for them to leave Sauers for California.

Reminding himself of the wise saying "A steady drip carves the stone," Diedrich forced a tepid smile. Though Father's heart had turned to stone toward Regina, Diedrich was determined to wear it down. And he would accomplish that only in little drips, not in one deluge.

Regina carried a large bowl of mashed potatoes to one of the trestle tables set up in the Entebrocks' yard. As she had done countless times today, she scanned the slice of field beyond the barn for Diedrich. But the distance was too great to discern the features of the workers who looked like moving specks on the pale background of the wheat field.

Heaving a sigh, she set the bowl on the table with a thud. What good would it do her to see Diedrich when she couldn't talk to him, touch him? None. How bittersweet to see him from a distance yet know that for him to come any closer would be to risk further angering Herr Rothhaus. Had she not tortured her heart enough yesterday at church?

When she had seen Papa and Herr Rothhaus talking and shaking hands in the churchyard, her heart had leapt in her chest. For one blessed moment, she'd thought surely Herr Rothhaus had repented and all would be well. But later, Papa's glum face had told her before his words that it was not the case.

Tears filled her eyes at the memory of her disappointment. Papa's cross demeanor later had not helped. All the way home he had scolded her for what he deemed her impulsive act of prematurely breaking off her engagement to Diedrich. Papa argued that if she and Diedrich had stood firm and shown their determination to marry, Herr Rothhaus would more quickly relent. He contended that since he and Mama continued to bless the union, it would put pressure on Herr Rothhaus to do the same. Though she saw some merit in Papa's argument, she still felt in her heart she had taken the correct route. Yet her longing to speak openly to Diedrich—to touch him—had grown so palpable that the temptation to acquiesce to Papa's wishes had been strong. Only Sophie's whispered encouragements to stay her course had given Regina the strength to remain resolute.

The sound of women's voices behind Regina jolted her from her reverie. In a moment, someone would ring the dinner bell and the men, including Diedrich, would head in from the fields. Her heart quickened at the thought. Hopefully the two of them could find a moment together away from Herr Rothhaus's sight.

"We have made a lot of good food, hey, Tochter?" Mama's bright voice broke into Regina's thoughts. "I must be sure to tell Diedrich that you and Sophie made the cherry pies."

Managing a sad smile, Regina turned and hugged her mother. Despite the many times she had begged her not to blame herself, she knew Mama still harbored guilt for her role in causing the trouble between their family and Herr Rothhaus. "Danke, Mama. I do think the pies turned out very nice."

Mama's expression and voice softened. "Regina." She took Regina's hand and gave it a pat. "Keep trusting in Gott and praying." Her brown eyes glistened with welling tears. "Your Vater is right, you know. Gott has bound your heart with Diedrich's. It is wrong of Herr Rothhaus to withhold his blessing for selfish reasons. And if we pray, I am sure in time he will see he is wrong." She gave her a coaxing smile. "Today, I think, would be a wunderbare time to tell Diedrich that you want again to be his *Verlobte*."

Regina sighed. She saw nothing to be gained in plowing this same ground all over again, but Mama seemed determined to do so. "Mama, did you not always tell me two wrongs do not a right make?" She took her mother's hands and gave them a gentle squeeze. "You know I love Diedrich and want to one day become his wife. You also know I pray every day Herr Rothhaus will repent and accept me as his *Schwiegertochter*." She hated the fresh tears welling in her eyes. "But what if he stays stubborn and will not change his mind? Would you have me wait until the day of our wedding to break our engagement?"

Mama shook her head. "Of course not. But the harvest is three months away. There is plenty of time for Gott to change Herr Rothhaus's mind."

Regina stifled the urge to scream. She must find a way to make Mama understand the folly in her and Papa's thinking without being disrespectful. "And it is only on how to help bring that about that we disagree, Mama. I love you and Papa, and I have always obeyed you. But to my thinking, remaining engaged to Diedrich without his Vater's blessing makes no more sense than if I would try to hitch Gypsy to the back of her cart instead of the front and ask her to push it rather than pull it. And Sophie agrees with me—"

The clanging of the dinner bell cut off Regina's words. When it had stilled, Mama glanced at the throng of women bustling about the tables, placing the last dishes before the men arrived. A look of consternation crossed her face. "We shall talk about this again later, Tochter." She patted Regina's hand again. "But I am believing Gott will hear our prayers and make a way for you and Diedrich to marry." Her countenance and her voice turned stern. "And my faith is strong enough to believe Gott can do that with you and Diedrich engaged just as easily as if you were not." With a brisk nod, she stepped away to relieve Helena Entebrock of one of the two pitchers of lemonade in her hands.

The jangling of teams and wagons brought Regina's gaze up to the barn and the wheat field beyond. On foot and wagon, the men began streaming around the west corner of Herr Entebrock's barn toward the house. Regina's heart quickened as she scanned the male faces for Diedrich's. When she found him, her heart skipped. Walking beside his father, he lifted his head and laughed then clapped his father on the back. Obviously, father and son had shared a joke. At the sight, Regina's heart throbbed painfully, and her resolve deepened. She prayed Mama was right, and God would soon change Herr Rothhaus's feelings about her. But despite her parents' wishes and her own yearning to reinstate her engagement to Diedrich, she couldn't risk causing another rift between Diedrich and his father.

Poking his fork beneath the golden layer of flaky piecrust, Diedrich snagged a cherry. He popped the fruit in his mouth and glanced down the long row of tables situated in the shade of four sprawling maple trees, praying he might catch Regina's eye. But he could no longer find her face among the women hovering around the table and assisting the diners. Disappointment dragged down his shoulders. By now most of the men had finished their main meal and, like him, had moved on to the desserts. Several of the women had begun carrying stacks of dirty dishes back into the house. Regina must have joined them when he wasn't looking.

Savoring the dessert, he couldn't help a secret smile, knowing Regina had helped to make it. The pie reminded him of her, both sweet and tart. Like yesterday at church, she'd kept her distance from him today. And again, they'd only managed to exchange a few smiles and glances. But he was glad, at least, that her mother had found a moment to stop him on the way to the dessert table and mention that Regina and her sister had made the cherry pies. Hopefully he would get a chance to compliment her on them before he had to head back to work.

Emitting a contented sigh, Father pushed back his chair. "That pie looks sehr *schmackhaft*, Sohn. I think maybe I will have a piece myself." Chuckling, he patted his stomach. "That is, if I can find an empty spot to put it in."

Diedrich pushed another bite of pie into his mouth to hide his grin. If Father knew Regina had made the pie, he wouldn't touch it. A flash of mischief he couldn't resist struck. "Ja, Father, you must taste the pie. Be sure to get a piece of the cherry. I know it is your favorite, and I have never tasted a better piece of cherry pie than this one." Knowing he spoke the truth helped to assuage his guilt for the trickery.

While Father headed to the dessert table, Diedrich gathered up their dirty dishes. He would risk being teased for doing women's work for a chance to see and maybe even speak to Regina.

Stepping into the house, he poked his head through the kitchen door. A blast of heat almost as intense as that from a forge slammed him in the face, nearly taking his breath away. Giving the room a cursory perusal, he could not find Regina among the shifting swarm of females squeezed into the small, stifling space. As hot a job as he and the other men had out in the field, Diedrich didn't envy these women their task. He would much rather be outside where at least he could catch a passing breeze to cool the sweat from his brow. It amazed him that anyone could breathe in here, let alone produce the wonderful meal he had helped to consume. Beyond that, the cacophony of chattering female voices resembled the buzz of a giant nest of angry hornets. After only a minute or so, his head began to pound from the racket.

Thankfully, he and Frau Seitz caught sight of each other at the same time. Somehow she squeezed through the crazy quilt of moving skirts and made her way to where he stood at the kitchen door.

He handed her the pile of dishes. "I would like to speak with Regina. Do you know where I might find her?"

Smiling, she pushed a sweat-drenched lock of brown hair from her forehead. "Ja. Henry was fussing, so she took him outside to show him some kittens. On the west side of the house, I think."

"Danke." He nodded his thanks and turned to go, but she grasped his arm, halting him. Her smile had vanished, and her expression held an odd mixture of sadness and hope. "Diedrich, Herr Seitz and I are praying you will yet become our Sohn."

"Danke, Frau Seitz. I am praying the same." Emotion thickening his voice, he gave her a quick hug then left before he embarrassed himself. Less than three months ago, he had prayed he might avoid becoming this woman's *Schwiegersohn*. Now to one day become her son-in-law was his fondest wish.

Outside, he hurried toward the west side of the house, his heart keeping pace with his quickened steps. As he approached the corner of the building, he heard Regina's unmistakable giggle. "Do not do that. You know better." Another giggle. "No, you are getting no *Küsse*. Now away with you."

Her words stopped him cold. For a moment he stood frozen as hurt and anger twisted in a putrid wad of jealousy in his chest. To whom could she be talking so sweetly and playfully denying kisses? Then he grinned at his own foolishness. Frau Seitz said she had taken Henry outside to play. She was obviously talking with her little nephew.

But when he rounded the corner of the house, his heart jolted. Out of the corner of his eye, he caught a glimpse of a male figure disappearing around the other end of the building. All that registered was a flash of auburn hair and a green shirt. Who had worn a green shirt today? His mind raced. He couldn't think.

"Diedrich." Regina's breathless voice yanked his attention from the now vacant end of the house to her flushed face. Her eyes were wide. Her hair had come loose from its pins and dangled in two braids on her shoulders.

"Who was here? I heard you talking with someone." Diedrich tried to keep his voice light but couldn't prevent an accusatory tone from creeping in.

She glanced over her shoulder. Did he imagine the flash of guilt in her eyes? "No one is here but me and Henry." No hint of guile tainted her voice, helping to ease the suspicious thoughts fermenting in Diedrich's mind. She walked over to where the toddler sat beneath a maple tree, digging in a loose patch of soil with a wooden spoon. A liberal amount of the dark, sandy dirt covered the little boy's face and hands, as well as his white cotton gown.

"No, Henry. I told you, do not do that. Your Mutti will

be angry with both of us for letting you get so dirty." Regina's laugh sounded a tinge nervous as she picked up the squirming child and swiped uselessly at the dirt and grass stains on his gown.

At her admonishment, remorse smote Diedrich's heart. Her chiding words to Henry now nearly matched what Diedrich had heard her say a moment ago. She had obviously been talking only to the child. Even her mention of kisses made perfect sense in the light of rational thought. As much as Regina loved her little nephew, Diedrich doubted she would have wanted the imp to kiss her until she could wash his face and hands. Shame sizzled through Diedrich for his uncharitable thoughts. He understood now what Solomon meant when he wrote in the sixth chapter of Proverbs, "For jealousy is the rage of a man."

"*Tante* Gina." Henry bopped Regina on the head with the wooden spoon.

She leaned away from the boy and rubbed the top of her head. "Henry, you must not do that." But the giggle warbling through her voice seemed to render the scold ineffective.

Laughing, Henry raised the spoon, poised to strike again, and Diedrich eased the utensil from the boy's chubby fingers. "Nein, you must not hit your Tante." He stifled a chuckle but couldn't stop his grin.

Whimpering, Henry squirmed harder in Regina's arms. He reached out a grimy hand for the spoon—now safely in Diedrich's possession—and made grabbing motions with his fingers.

"Nein. You can only have the *Löffel* if you do not hit your

Tante." Diedrich fought to retain a stern face as he had done so many times when disciplining his own nieces and nephews. He prayed that this grubby cherub would one day become his nephew as well.

Heaving a resigned sigh, Regina lowered the toddler back to the spot beneath the tree. "You might as well play there. I don't think you can get any dirtier."

Chuckling, Diedrich handed the spoon back to Henry, who promptly used it to attack a cluster of tiny anthills.

Regina turned a sweet smile to Diedrich. She put her hand on his bare forearm, sending pleasant tingles dancing over his skin. "I'm glad you found me. I hoped you would."

At her tender touch and longing gaze, Diedrich's heart pounded out a quick tattoo like the triple-time cadence of a military drumbeat. He ached to hold her. Instead, he captured her hands. "I have missed you."

"And I have missed you." Her blue eyes glistened up at his. Her soft, sweet lips—he knew how soft, he knew how sweet—tipped up in a sad smile.

The yearning to take her in his arms and kiss her grew so powerful Diedrich could no longer resist it. Dropping her hands, he slipped his arms around her waist.

She stepped back out of his embrace and a pained expression furrowed her delicate brow. "Papa said Herr Rothhaus has not yet relented."

"No, not yet." At the admission, Diedrich swallowed down a bitter wad of regret. He recaptured her hands. "We must give Gott time to work, Liebling."

She nodded, but her gaze drifted from his to where Henry

sat gleefully dispatching ants with his spoon.

The dinner bell began to ring, signaling it was time for the workers to return to the fields and the threshing machine. At the sound, Diedrich and Regina exchanged a desperate look. They would likely not see one another for at least another week and a half when the threshers moved to the Seitz farm. A determination stronger than anything Diedrich had ever felt shot through him. He would not leave her without the taste of her kiss on his lips.

He stepped toward her, praying she would accept his embrace. The next moment she surprised him by throwing her arms around his neck and pulling his face down to hers, now drenched in tears. For one blissful moment, nothing mattered to Diedrich but Regina's sweet caresses. A resolve to be her unfailing champion solidified in his chest.

With a sudden movement that jarred him back to reality, she let him go and stepped back away from him. "You must go. It would not be good if your Vater saw us together." She glanced nervously from one end of the building to the other. Then she snatched up Henry and, ignoring the child's whimpering complaints, turned and strode toward the back of the house.

A whirlwind of emotions swirled through Diedrich as he watched her walk away. He must no longer sit passively by and wait for God to change his father's heart and mind. *Dear Lord, show me how to soften Father's heart.*

With his prayer winging heavenward, he headed toward the east side of the house where the other men were gathering, some already making their way back to the wheat field.

As he glanced around for his father, a familiar, knobby hand gripped his shoulder, turning him around.

Father's eyes sparked with excitement, and his whiskered face beamed. "Where have you been, Sohn? I have wunderbare news to tell you."

Diedrich ignored the question. "What news, Vater?"

"The miller, Tanner, and his boy came for some bushels of last year's wheat that Herr Entebrock needed to move out of his granary to make room for the new grain."

Diedrich shrugged. "Ja. That is good news, I suppose. There will be plenty of room in the granary for the new crop of wheat." Could Father be entering his dotage at the age of fifty-six?

Father chuckled and shook his head. "Nein. That is not the good news. Herr Tanner mentioned to Herr Entebrock that he is looking to hire an extra man to work at his mill." He shrugged. "Sweeping up, seeing to the horses, those kinds of jobs."

Diedrich started walking toward the field, and Father fell into step beside him. "And did he find someone?"

"Ja. Is that not exciting?" Father bounced along with an extra spring in his step.

Diedrich grinned, indulging his parent's odd merriment. "Ja, that is gut. The scriptures instruct us to rejoice with those who rejoice. But I do not see why Tanner's success in finding a worker should be exciting to you."

Father stopped and took hold of Diedrich's arm, compelling him to stop as well. "I did not say? Why, because I am the man he has hired, Sohn."

While Diedrich struggled to digest what Father had just told him, Father nudged his arm. "There they go now." Grinning, he swung his arm in a wide arc as two men in a wagon passed them. Diedrich had not seen the older man before, but he had seen the younger one. It was Eli Tanner. And he was wearing a green shirt.

Chapter 23

Regina heard and smelled the town of Salem before she saw it. Tucked back in the stuffy confines of Sophie and Ezra's Conestoga wagon, she could see little in front of their team of horses. The arched frame supporting the wagon's canvas cover presented only a limited, thumbnail-shaped vista. But the noise of horse and wagon traffic, the halloos of passersby, and the smell of roasting meat told her they were finally nearing their destination. The distant sound of gunshots suggested some Fourth of July revelers had already begun their evening's celebration.

Leaning back against the wagon's side, she stretched and yawned. Beside her, Henry remained sleeping on his pallet, his rosebud lips making popping sounds around the thumb he perpetually kept in his mouth. Gazing at the sleeping toddler, she smiled fondly. The child's habit of sucking his thumb had built up a callus on the digit where his teeth constantly raked across the skin. At Mama's insistence, Mama, Sophie, and Regina had started rubbing the boy's thumb several times a day with bitter herbs to discourage his thumb-sucking habit. But for once, Regina didn't begrudge Henry his familiar comfort. The thirty-mile trip from Sauers to Salem had been a taxing one. They had left home at dawn, and now the lengthening shadows told Regina it must be at least five in the afternoon. Aside from the half hour they had taken near Vallonia to eat their midday meal and feed and water the horses, they had kept up a punishing pace in order to arrive in Salem before nightfall.

Ezra glanced over his shoulder into the wagon's interior. "We are almost there, Regina. Better wake the boy."

Beside Ezra, Sophie's shoulders rose and fell with her sigh. "Praise be to Gott! My whole body aches, and I am sure I must be bruised from bouncing for miles on this hard seat."

A moment before Ezra brought the horses to a stop, Regina had glimpsed the sign over William and Elsie's store. Reaching out to gently rouse her sleeping nephew, she had to agree with Sophie. Yet despite the grueling journey, she was glad for the chance to get away from home for a couple of days.

She had not originally planned to join Sophie and her family on their trip to visit Elsie and William. But after all that occurred at the Entebrocks' threshing two days ago, she needed time away from Mama and Papa and their constant insistence that she should reinstate her engagement to Diedrich. So when Sophie invited her to join them, Regina had jumped at the offer, though she suspected Sophie mainly wanted her along to help care for Henry.

But if she had hoped the trip would be a respite from her thoughts of Diedrich and her worries about their relationship, she soon learned she was mistaken. On the contrary, the long hours in the back of the wagon had provided ample time for her mind to wander to Diedrich and their parting kiss. Her heart fluttered at the memory. But as precious as their few minutes together were, that tender moment had made their parting again all the more painful. And as long as Herr Rothhaus forbade their marriage, such stolen moments, however sweet, were futile. Perhaps that was why Diedrich had not initiated the kiss. A finger of disappointment squiggled through her. After witnessing the congenial scene between him and his father, she couldn't help wondering if Diedrich had even mentioned her name again to Herr Rothhaus. Also, something about Diedrich's attitude when he first appeared around the corner of the Entebrocks' house bothered her. The way he had looked behind her and the suspicious tone in his voice when he asked who she had been talking with still rankled. For an instant, his demeanor had reminded her of Eli's jealous behavior. In fact, she later heard that Eli and his father were at the Entebrock farm that afternoon, though she hadn't seen them. Could Diedrich have imagined she'd spent time with Eli? At the memory of the kiss they shared, she dismissed the thought. Diedrich knew her heart.

Waking, Henry whimpered and began to cry. Regret smote Regina, and she turned her full attention back to her young charge. Helping him to sit up, she patted his back. "It is all right, my sweet Junge. Are you ready to see your Onkel William and your Tante Elsie?"

"I would say not." Irritation edged Sophie's voice from behind the wagon where she stood peering in at her little son. "With a soiled gown and diaper, you are not fit to see anyone, Henry. I would have thought your Tante Regina would have your diaper changed and a fresh gown on you by now."

Regina jerked. Lost in her own thoughts, she hadn't noticed her sister climb down from the wagon seat and come around to the back of the Conestoga. She hurried to untie Henry's soggy diaper and replaced it with a fresh one from the basket that held his clean clothes. She gave a little laugh. "I guess the wagon ride has made us both sleepy, hey, Henry?"

While Regina dressed Henry, Sophie stood looking on, her arms folded over her chest. "Ezra has gone into the store to let William and Elsie know we have arrived."

Buttoning Henry's fresh gown, Regina made funny faces until she had the toddler laughing. She couldn't understand why Sophie always seemed eager to let Regina, their mother, or even Ezra tend to Henry. She gently brushed the sweat-damp curls from the child's forehead. If God ever saw fit to give her such a sweet child, even Mama would have to beg to tend to him.

Handing a freshly dressed Henry to his mother, Regina climbed out of the wagon.

Sophie shifted the child to her hip, her mood seemingly as improved as her son's. "I am so excited to see Elsie. And I do hope Ezra can get a job here at the wagon factory."

In her letter inviting them to Salem's Fourth of July celebration, Elsie had mentioned that a new wagon factory had just opened for business here. Assuming they would need wheelwrights, William had suggested Ezra apply for a job. Of course, Ezra was eager to explore the possibility. Sophie, too, had gushed with excitement, saying how wonderful it would be to live near Elsie.

Regina gave her sister an encouraging smile. "I'm praying

for that, too." And she meant it. At the same time, guilt tickled her conscience. Of course she genuinely wanted Sophie and her family to be financially secure and happy in a home of their own again. But she couldn't deny that she also looked forward to them moving out of the home she shared with her parents. For the past three years, Regina had enjoyed a respite from her eldest sister's criticisms and bossy ways. And though Sophie had treated her more kindly since moving back to the farm, she still had a tendency to get on Regina's nerves. There was simply no denying that she and Sophie got along better with some distance between them. And though Salem wasn't quite as far from Sauers as Vernon, it *was* a full day's drive.

Sophie leaned toward Regina. "I must say, I was surprised that Elsie seemed in such good spirits in her letter." She shook her head sorrowfully. "Poor Elsie. Maybe seeing Henry will cheer her after her"—she glanced around as if to assure herself no one else was within earshot and lowered her voice to a whisper—"miscarriage."

Regina groaned inwardly. "I am sure Elsie will love getting to see Henry again, but you don't need to whisper, Sophie. Elsie had a miscarriage, not some sort of unmentionable disease." Why was Sophie so prudish about such things? Even when she was expecting Henry, it had taken her a full five months to admit she was in the family way. And then, she might have waited until the child's birth to reveal her happy news if Mama hadn't mentioned during one of the couple's visits that Sophie seemed to have gained weight since her wedding. At Mama's comment, Sophie had turned beet red. Then, taking Mama aside, she had privately whispered she was in the family way. Regina grinned, remembering how she and Elsie had jumped up and down upon learning of the coming blessed event. Clapping their hands, they had chanted, "Baby, baby, we are going to have a baby!" until their mortified sister turned purple faced and begged them to hush.

Sophie reddened and glanced around again. "Well, of course she didn't have a disease. But one must be discreet when mentioning"—she lowered her voice again—"women's problems."

Regina stifled a giggle at Sophie's priggish attitude. She was tempted to say that Elsie's miscarriage was not strictly a "woman's problem" since William had suffered the loss of a child as well. But antagonizing Sophie would not make for a good start to their Independence Day celebration.

At that moment, Elsie popped out of the store and came bounding toward them, her arms outstretched and happy tears glistening on her smiling face. It did Regina's heart good to see her sister's healthy glow.

Elsie hurried to hug Regina first. "Regina, I'm so glad you came, too!" Taking Regina's hands, she bounced on the balls of her feet and giggled. "I was so happy to get your letter saying your Diedrich chose you over California."

Regina returned Elsie's hug and gave her a tepid smile. Several times she had thought to write Elsie again and share all that had happened since Diedrich's declaration of love. But she couldn't bring herself to reveal in a letter the jarring news of learning about her adoption and the trouble it had caused for her and Diedrich. "I am glad to see you looking so well, Schwester."

Fortunately, in her exuberance, Elsie didn't seem to notice Regina's abrupt change of subject and immediately turned to hug Sophie and Henry. Easing Henry from Sophie's arms, Elsie swung her little nephew up in the air, making him giggle. "My, Henry, you have grown into such a big Junge since I last saw you!"

Regina smiled. Maybe Sophie was right. Seeing Henry did seem to cheer Elsie.

Perching Henry on her hip, Elsie headed for the store. "Come, *Schwestern*. While William and Ezra are gone to check on that wheelwright job for Ezra, we can catch up on all our news, and you can both help me prepare our picnic meal for later. Then when the men return, we can head to the Barnetts' farm for the pig roast and later the fireworks." Turning to Henry, her eyes grew big. "Do you want to see the fireworks, Henry?"

Henry nodded enthusiastically and clapped his hands, though Regina was sure the little boy hadn't the first notion what fireworks were.

A few minutes later, the three sisters were chatting away in Elsie's little kitchen as they assembled the picnic meal. Regina's recent familiarity with the room allowed her to work with speed and confidence, while Sophie fumbled through drawers and shelves, constantly asking direction from Elsie.

Bouncing Henry on her hip, Elsie moved about the kitchen offering her sisters one-handed assistance with the preparations. She stepped to the table where Regina stood mixing together the ingredients for potato salad and peered over her shoulder. "Mmm, that *Kartoffelsalat* smells wunder-bar, Regina."

Sophie turned from poking around in the shelves of El-sie's cabinet. Her face pinched up in a look of annoyance. "I am sure she makes potato salad exactly the way Mama taught us all to make it, Elsie." Her voice, if not exactly derisive, was as flat and dry as an unbuttered pancake.

"Perhaps." Elsie picked a snickerdoodle cookie from a basket on the table and handed it to Henry, who had begun to fuss. "But you should have tasted the broth she made for me when I was abed. Of the three of us, I do think Regina has most inherited Mama's gift for cooking."

Sophie turned from the cabinet. "But she's not—" If Regina didn't know better, she might have interpreted the quirk at the corner of Sophie's lips as a sneer. "Oh, you do not know, do you, Elsie?"

"Know what?" Elsie's expectant smile swung between Sophie and Regina.

Anger and dismay leapt in Regina's chest at Sophie's thoughtlessness. This was not the way she had wanted to tell Elsie what their mother had disclosed about Regina's birth. But she was determined that Elsie would hear it from her lips, not Sophie's.

Blowing out a resolute breath, Regina pulled a chair out from the table. "You should sit down for what I must tell you, Elsie."

With a quizzical look on her face, Elsie sat. Henry wriggled from her grasp and slid to the floor then toddled across the room to his mother. Elsie gave a nervous giggle. "What could you possibly have to tell me that I must sit to hear?" Suddenly her brown eyes grew large, and her voice turned breathless. "You are not married already, are you?"

Regina shook her head and gave her sister a sad smile. "Nein. I only wish that was the news I have to tell." Swallowing down the lump that had gathered in her throat, she recounted the fantastic tale Mama had told her when they had worked together on Regina's wedding quilt.

If possible, Elsie's eyes grew even wider. Her jaw went slack, and she looked at Regina as if she hadn't seen her before. Having never been close to Sophie, it hadn't bothered Regina so much for her eldest sister to learn they were not connected by blood, but Elsie was a different matter. Until this moment, Regina hadn't feared her revelation would diminish Elsie's love for her, or that Elsie would see her as anything other than her sister. But now she hated to think the news might weaken the special bond she and Elsie had always enjoyed.

Tears welled in Elsie's eyes, and she sprang from her chair to embrace Regina. "Oh my liebe Schwester, what an awful thing for you to learn." Then, pushing away from Regina, she took her hands. Her chin lifted, and her face filled with almost defiant loyalty. "I do not care how you came to be my sister. You are my sister, and you will always be my sister. Blood doesn't matter." She glanced over at Sophie, who was brushing cookie crumbs from the front of Henry's gown. "And I know Sophie feels the same way."

Sophie quirked a smile that vanished so quickly Regina

almost missed it. "Of course," she mumbled as she continued brushing at Henry's clothes. "But it is too bad Herr Rothhaus does not feel as you do, Elsie."

It stung that Sophie didn't enthusiastically reiterate Elsie's sentiment, but Regina dismissed the omission, considering it but another of Sophie's oversights.

Elsie gasped, and her forehead pinched in anger. "You mean Diedrich does not want to marry you because you were not born to Mama and Papa?"

Regina shook her head, eager to correct Elsie's wrong impression of Diedrich. "Nein. Diedrich still loves me and wants to marry me." But even as she said the words, a faint but insidious voice whispered inside her head. *Does he still love me?* And if he did, why hadn't he tried harder to change his father's mind about her?

Elsie blinked. "But Sophie said Herr Rothhaus—"

"Diedrich's Vater," Sophie said in a matter-of-fact tone as she reached into the cabinet. "Ah, here are the jars of sauerkraut."

Regina explained to Elsie the callous way in which her birth father and grandfather had treated Herr Rothhaus's family. The retelling stung the open wound on her heart as painfully as if she'd squeezed lemon juice into it. She sniffed back the tears. "So Herr Rothhaus has forbidden Diedrich to marry me. And unless Gott helps Diedrich change his Vater's mind. . ." Unable to finish the thought, she shook her head.

Elsie's expression turned indignant. "What those men did was terrible, but it happened before you were born. How can Herr Rothhaus blame you?"

Stifling a sardonic snort, Regina fought a wave of despair. "Because I am of their blood. And I cannot change that."

Elsie gripped Regina's hands, and her voice turned resolute. "Then we must pray that Gott will change Herr Rothhaus's heart. As our Lord promises us in Matthew 21:22, 'And all things, whatsoever ye shall ask in prayer, believing, ye shall receive.'"

At the familiar scripture, Regina's frustration burst free. She yanked her hands from Elsie's. "But I *have* been praying, and nothing has happened." Not wanting Elsie to see the flood of tears cascading down her face, she turned her back. She hated the anger in her voice but couldn't keep it out. "When Diedrich defied his Vater and refused to break our engagement, Herr Rothhaus disowned him. I did not want to cause Diedrich to sin by dishonoring his Vater, so I broke our engagement. I also thought if Diedrich could talk to his Vater again, he would have a better chance of changing Herr Rothhaus's mind about me. But so far, he hasn't been able to." *Or won't.*

Elsie marched around to face Regina. Grasping her shoulders, she forced her to meet her gaze. "Then for whatever reason, it is not Gott's time to change his mind. With Gott, all things are possible. He will give us the power to do whatever we need to do." She cupped Regina's face in both her hands as Mama might do. "Gott will give Diedrich the power to change his Vater's mind. If we pray believing that will happen, it will happen."

Swiping at her tear-drenched face, Regina nodded.

Despite the pain it had caused Regina to recount her heartache, sharing it with Elsie had also lightened her burden. Besides Mama, Regina knew of no one who could storm heaven with prayers on Regina's behalf more forcefully or with more sincerity than Elsie could. She sniffed. "At first I believed Gott would change Herr Rothhaus's heart. But nothing has changed, and I'm beginning to wonder if it will ever happen."

Elsie's mouth tipped up in an encouraging smile, and she patted Regina's hand. "You must have faith, Schwester."

Regina went back to mixing the potato salad that didn't need more mixing. Faith. Could Mama be right that Regina's lack of faith was hindering God's working? "Mama says by breaking my engagement to Diedrich, I am showing a lack of faith. She and Papa think if I reinstate our engagement, Herr Rothhaus would see how committed Diedrich and I are to each other and would soon relent and give us his blessing."

Sophie, who had remained quiet, crossed the room in three quick strides. "Nein!" Alarm filled her face. Elsie and Regina exchanged surprised looks. As if gathering her composure, Sophie squared her shoulders and cleared her throat. When she spoke again, her voice was tempered and her words measured. "I have told you, Regina, you are doing the right thing. And I am sure Elsie will agree with me." She shot their sister a look that defied contradiction.

Elsie blinked. "I—I can see virtue in both ways of thinking. . . ."

Sophie gripped Regina's shoulder, and her expression turned almost fierce. "Under no circumstances should you reinstate your engagement unless Herr Rothhaus grants you and Diedrich his blessing."

Her sister's repeated advice did not surprise Regina, but the passion with which she imparted it did.

Elsie ambled across the room to extract Henry from the bottom of the cupboard. A thoughtful frown creased her forehead. "Of course Diedrich should not defy his Vater. But I can see Mama's point."

Sophie crossed her arms over her chest and assumed a wide, dictatorial stance. Her stern look reminded Regina of the expression on Sophie's face when she scolded Henry. "To even contemplate marriage without the blessing of both families is inviting disaster, Regina."

Regina wondered if Sophie had forgotten Papa's reluctance to allow Ezra to court Sophie. Only Ezra's sound Christian upbringing and his unimpeachable work ethic had swayed Papa from insisting Sophie marry a German farmer instead.

Looking down her nose at Regina like a strict schoolteacher, Sophie tapped her foot on the floor. "Since Ezra and I married, I have heard of three girls—all from good Christian families—who married against the wishes of their parents or their husbands' parents." Her right eyebrow arched. "All ended very badly."

Elsie's eyes widened. "What happened to them?"

Regina stifled a groan. For the life of her, she could never understand why Elsie was always so quick to take Sophie's bait and beg for her to repeat gossip. Surely Elsie knew their sister was itching to tell the tale.

"Well," Sophie began, a smug look settling over her face. "I heard of one couple who married against the young man's family's wishes." She snapped her fingers. "Within one month, he had left her and gone back to his parents. The poor girl had no choice but to return humiliated and scandalized to her own parents' home." Her voice lowered. "Of course the girl was ruined after the divorce. No decent man would go near her."

Elsie shook her head in sorrow. It was enough to spur Sophie on.

Sophie's eyes sparked as if she relished the tale she was about to impart. "And then there was the girl who defied her parents and eloped with her young man." She clucked her tongue. "Her parents sent the sheriff after them all the way to Madison. They had the young man arrested for stealing their horse, though the girl said it was hers. The young man went to jail, and the girl was sent to live with a maiden aunt in Louisville." Bending down, she whispered, "They say the poor thing wasn't right in the head after that."

Regina couldn't figure out how people knew the state of the girl's mind if she lived as far away as Louisville. But she had no interest in encouraging Sophie by inquiring.

Sophie's brow scrunched, and she tapped her lips three times as if gathering her thoughts. "And of course there was the couple who—"

"Sophie, please. I'd rather not hear any more." Regina's nerves bristled. Though she was sure Sophie's intention was to save her and Diedrich from a similar tragic ending, her sister's gossiping made her skin prickle. Turning away from

Sophie, she swathed the bowl of potato salad in a linen towel and tucked it into a waiting basket.

Sophie sniffed, a sure sign her feelings had been bruised. "Well," she snapped, "they died."

Elsie gasped.

Fearing Sophie would feel compelled to recount grisly details of the grim story, Regina hurried to change the conversation to the possible job opportunity for Ezra. But although listening to Sophie's tragic stories had made her squirm inside, she couldn't deny the cautionary tales had made an impression. Sophie's words kept echoing in her head. *"Within one month, he had left her and gone back to his parents."* Diedrich had known Regina for less than three months. But he had known his father all his life. However much he loved her, she couldn't expect his allegiance to her to be stronger than what he felt for his parent. Sophie had solidified Regina's resolve. She must not reinstate her engagement to Diedrich until Herr Rothhaus found it in his heart to bless their union. And if not. . . No, she must not think that. If only she had the faith of Mama and Elsie. *Dear Lord, help my unbelief.*

Elsie covered a basket of dishes and eating utensils with a towel. "I do hope Ezra gets that job, Sophie. It might be a little crowded, but William's Mutter has two upstairs rooms she doesn't use. I'm sure she would rent them to you until you could find a home of your own here in Salem."

Just then, William and Ezra strode into the kitchen wearing wide smiles. Ezra snatched Henry from his spot on the floor and swung him up in his arms. "There is my little man." Giggling, Henry grabbed a wad of his father's shirtfront in his chubby hand and said, "Dada, Dada."

Sophie hurried to her husband, her face tense. She gripped his arm. "What did you learn?" Her voice sounded breathless.

Ezra's smile stretched so wide Regina feared his lips might split. "I start in two weeks."

"Praise Gott!" Sophie sank to a chair, all the starch gone out of her. Her hands trembled in her lap.

Regina and Elsie sent up their own prayers of thanks, and hugs and kisses were exchanged all around.

Ezra held up a hand palm forward in a gesture of caution. "The pay won't be nearly what I was making as part owner of my own shop. But if the factory makes a go of it here, there will be plenty of opportunity for advancement."

Sophie stood, and some of the tension returned to her features. "If they make a go? You mean the factory might not stay here?"

Ezra offered a nonchalant shrug, seemingly unfazed by his wife's concern. "Well, there is no guarantee, of course, but people are always needing wagons."

Appearing somewhat satisfied with her husband's answer, Sophie pressed her hand to her chest as if to suppress her jubilant heart. "At least it is a stable job for the present, and you can continue to practice your trade." Her lifting mood seemed to pick up steam, and she brightened. "Now if we can just find a house here, we could be moved within the month."

It was on this happy note that, a few minutes later, they all piled into Ezra and Sophie's Conestoga with baskets of picnic fare and traveled a mile's distance to the farm of a man named Jim Barnett.

At the end of a long lane, they pulled into a grassy expanse beside a large, weathered gray barn. Sitting in the back of the wagon, Regina rested her chin on her forearm draped across the wagon's backboard and gazed out at the deepening gloaming. The setting sun painted streaks of pinkish orange, purple, and gold across the darkening blue-gray sky. In a deep blue strip beneath the colorful hues, the first star of the evening winked at her like the eye of a playful angel. Was Diedrich back at the new house admiring the same view? At the wistful thought, warmth filled her. How she longed to share all the sunsets of her life with him—to stand beside him at twilight as they gazed together on the evening's first bright star. But unless God softened Herr Rothhaus's heart. . .

The wagon jolted to a stop, yanking her from her musings. Several other wagons and teams had already arrived, and dozens of people milled about the area. Roast-pork-scented smoke filled the air, teasing Regina's nose. As she climbed from the wagon, she spotted the smoke's origin. At the edge of a fallow field, two blackened patches of ground glowed red with smoldering embers. Above the embers stood iron spits on which two whole hogs roasted to dusky perfection.

Will jumped from the back of the wagon then helped Elsie and Sophie to the ground. "Mmm." He rubbed his belly. "Can't wait for a plate of that roast pork." Mimicking his uncle, Henry, perched on his father's arm, rubbed his own belly, drawing a laugh from his elders.

Regina helped Sophie and Elsie spread quilts over the

grass a few yards from the wagon, where they would have an unobstructed view of the fireworks later. As she headed back to the wagon for the basket that held their eating utensils, she noticed Ezra and William standing near the wagon and shaking hands with a scraggly bearded man wearing a fringed deerskin shirt.

"Zeke Roberts," the man said around the corncob pipe in his mouth as he pumped William's hand.

William introduced himself and then Ezra. "This is my brother-in-law, Ezra Barnes. He and his wife and baby and my wife's other sister have come down here from Sauers to join in our celebration this evenin'."

"Is that right?" Regina heard the man say as she reached into the wagon for the basket of utensils. He gave a throaty chuckle. "You fellers wouldn't know a young feller up there in Sauers by the name of Diedrich Rothhaus, would ya?"

At Diedrich's name, Regina froze. As far as she knew, Diedrich had never been to Salem. How could he know this man?

When Ezra explained that Diedrich was living on land owned by his parents-in-law, the man guffawed. "Well, I'll be switched!"

At his exclamation, a chilly foreboding slithered down Regina's spine. She stood as if paralyzed. A series of soft pops told her the man had paused to draw on his pipe.

A snort sounded, followed by Zeke's voice. "Why, young Rothhaus has agreed to join up with me and head to the Californee goldfields next spring."

Chapter 24

Regina pummeled the steaming bowl of potatoes with punishing blows of the masher. At least her frustration would make for some of the smoothest mashed potatoes served at today's threshing. Shortly after dawn, the threshers began arriving at the farm. She'd hoped to find a moment to speak to Diedrich alone and confront him with what she'd heard Zeke Roberts say. So far, she hadn't seen Diedrich today. But she had no doubt he was working somewhere in the field loading wagons with bundles of wheat and would appear in the yard with the other workers when the dinner bell rang. Diedrich still owed Papa a summer's worth of work on the farm, so whether or not his father decided to come, Regina was sure Diedrich would participate in today's threshing. And before the dinner break was over, she was determined to learn why he hadn't informed Roberts he was no longer interested in going to California. That is, if he *was* no longer interested.

She plopped another golden dollop of butter atop the potatoes then beat the melting lump into the snowy mound until it disappeared. In the week since Salem's Independence Day celebration, Zeke Roberts's words had tumbled around in her brain, tormenting her thoughts and robbing her of sleep. When she'd recovered from the immediate shock of hearing the man's claim that Diedrich planned to accompany him to California, she had confronted him, intent on learning the details behind his astonishing comment. But Roberts had seemed unable to remember the exact date he'd met Diedrich in the Dudleytown smithy. Regina surmised it must have been while she was in Salem caring for Elsie. But even if that were so, how could Diedrich promise Roberts he would travel with him to California next spring then a few days later pledge his love to Regina and promise to stay here in Sauers with her? Finding scant satisfaction in the man's vague answers, she'd leveled a relentless barrage of mostly fruitless questions at him until William finally took pity on Roberts and escorted Regina back to their picnic spot, little the wiser for her efforts. Wielding the masher, she punished the potatoes again.

"You have them mashed enough, I think, Tochter." Mama maneuvered through the shifting maze of cooks to stand beside Regina at the kitchen table. "We want mashed potatoes, not potato soup." She glanced across the room to where Sophie bent over the baskets of dishes and eating utensils Helena Entebrock had brought earlier. Sophie appeared to be sorting through the dishes and other tableware donated by all the families in the threshing ring specifically for use at threshing dinners like today's. She was likely gathering place settings to take outside to the makeshift sawhorse tables Papa and some of the other men had set up in the yard earlier.

Mama handed Regina a stoneware plate. "Here, cover those potatoes with this and put them on the stove to stay warm. Then help your sister set places at the tables."

"Ja." Regina nodded, happy for the opportunity to escape the hot kitchen for a while.

When she and Sophie had loaded four baskets with enough dishes and utensils for twenty-two settings, they gratefully headed outside into cool, welcoming breezes and the shade of the old willow tree.

Though reason told Regina that Diedrich was beyond her sight, she couldn't help turning her face in the direction of the wheat field.

"Have you talked with him yet?" Sophie's tone was matter of fact as she transferred a plate from the basket to the table.

"Nein." Regina didn't need to ask whom Sophie meant. All the way back from Salem, Sophie had railed about how inconsiderate it was of Diedrich not to have mentioned to Regina his conversation with Zeke Roberts. Regina had defended Diedrich, saying it was likely all a misunderstanding, but she couldn't help sharing a smidgen of her sister's sentiment.

Sophie placed a knife and fork at either side of the plate. "I do think you are sehr wise not to reinstate your engagement to Diedrich." She shrugged. "Who knows what is ever in men's heads?" With a light laugh, she tapped her own noggin.

Regina had thought she knew what was in Diedrich's head and his heart. But now she wasn't so sure. Yet she declined to comment, not wanting to encourage Sophie. For reasons that remained murky to Regina, Sophie seemed to have taken a negative view of Diedrich.

For the next several minutes, Regina and Sophie worked together quietly. After a while, Regina noticed her sister glancing toward the house. She assumed Sophie was checking to see when the women might begin to exit the back door with dishes of food.

Suddenly, Sophie gave a little gasp. "I'd better go check on Henry." With that, she took off toward the house at a quick trot.

Regina shook her head and gave a little snort. She would never understand Sophie. Regina herself had put Henry in his little trundle bed for a nap less than half an hour ago, leaving young Margaret Stuckwisch to watch over him. Usually Sophie never checked on Henry until he had slept at least an hour. And this morning, before the women began cooking, Sophie had handpicked Margaret to look after Henry, even commenting on how mature the girl seemed for twelve years old. So it seemed odd Sophie would suddenly become uneasy about Henry.

Abandoning her effort to decipher what had motivated Sophie's abrupt departure, Regina reached in the basket for another plate. The touch of a hand—a hard, definitely male hand—on her shoulder brought her upright. Whirling, she met Eli Tanner's smiling face.

His smile slipped into a lazy grin. "I was hopin' I'd get a chance to talk to you alone."

Regina frowned, wondering why Eli had decided to join the group of threshers. Or perhaps he had not come for that reason at all. Despite his reason for being here, he was not a welcome sight, and she couldn't think why she had ever considered him handsome or dashing. At the present, the only emotion he elicited from her was aggravation. "What do you want, Eli? I have work to do."

His jaw twitched, but his grin stayed in place. His green eyes held an icy glint. "Mr. Rothhaus—the old German man who works at our mill—said you gave his son the mitten." Cocking his head to one side, he lifted his chin, planted his feet in a wide stance, and crossed his arms over his broad chest. "So since you ain't promised now, I thought I'd give you another chance and ask your pa if I might come courtin'."

Had Herr Rothhaus encouraged Eli to come and make another offer for her hand? Fury rose in Regina's chest. How dare the man meddle in her affairs! Diedrich's father had obviously not changed his mind about her and was trying to get her out of his son's life for good. Well, she wouldn't have it. And she wouldn't have Eli now either, even if he offered her a mansion and untold wealth—which, of course, he couldn't. Though tempted to take out her anger on the silly young swain before her, Regina got a firm grip on her temper. Herr Rothhaus may have even led Eli to believe Regina would be open to entertain his attentions. She fought for a calm, dispassionate voice. "I am sorry if Herr Rothhaus gave you the wrong idea, Eli. But my feelings have not changed since your Onkel's barn raising. And it would do you no good to talk to Papa. He will tell you the same."

Eli snorted, and his grin twisted into a sneer. "Still stuck on the old man's son, huh?" He gave a derisive laugh. "Won't do you any good. Old Rothhaus ain't never gonna agree to you marryin' his boy. And accordin' to him, he and his son are headin' out west to the goldfields come spring." Another scornful chuckle. "He told me how you wasn't born a Seitz but come from bad people." With a slow, lazy look, he eyed her from head to toe, making her squirm and her stomach go queasy. Then he gave a disinterested shrug. "Don't matter none to me though. A German's a German, to my way of thinkin'. But I doubt if all the other fellers around Sauers would see it the same way." His smirk made her want to slap his face. "I'd advise you to give my offer another think, or you're liable to end up an old maid."

Any remnant of affection she might have held for Eli vanished. Eli Tanner was a slug. It seemed impossible that she had ever entertained the notion of marrying him. Her body trembled with the effort to contain the rage surging through her. She balled her fists so tightly her fingernails bit into her palms. Tears sprang to her eyes, but she quickly blinked them away. She would rather take a beating than have Eli think his words had hurt her.

Piercing him with her glare, she schooled her voice to a tone as dead flat and icy as a pond on a still January morning. "Like I told you before, my heart is already situated. And if I cannot have the man I love, I will have no one." She skewered him with an unflinching glare. "And I would rather live happily alone for the rest of my life than spend even an hour with you."

He winced, and for an instant his haughty mask crumbled. Regina experienced a flash of remorse for the satisfaction the sight gave her. Her words had found their mark. Eli might be a vain and cocky slug, but she *had* once encouraged his attention.

He sneered. "One day you'll be sorry." With another snort and a derisive parting look, he turned on his heel and stalked across the yard toward the barn and, she supposed, the wheat field beyond.

As she watched him walk away, a sob rose up in her throat. Not from regret for what she had said to Eli. She had meant every word. The anguish that gripped her sprang from Eli's claim that Diedrich and Herr Rothhaus planned to leave Sauers for California. Had Diedrich given up trying to change his father's mind? Could it be true they were planning to leave next spring? Zeke Roberts thought so.

Somehow she managed to finish her task as the dinner bell began to ring. With her head down to hide her tears, she started back to the house as a line of women streamed out of the back door, their hands laden with steaming dishes of food.

Panic flared. She needed time to think and compose herself before facing anyone, including Mama, Sophie, or even Anna Rieckers. Her mind raced to think of a spot where she might escape for a moment of solitude. On impulse, she headed toward the far side of the house and the half-log bench by the little vegetable garden. With the sun directly overhead, the short shadow cast by the house barely reached the bench.

Sinking to the hard seat warmed by the sun, she hugged herself, trying to still her shaking limbs. She had told Eli the truth, except for one thing. If she lost Diedrich, she would not live happily. She couldn't imagine her life being happy or even contented without him in it. New tears filled her eyes and cascaded down her face. Diedrich had accused her of not giving God time to work. Now it seemed he had given up on God working altogether. Or had the lure of the goldfields taken first place in his heart again?

"Regina." At Diedrich's soft voice, Regina jerked. Her heart jumped like a deer at a rifle shot then bounded to her throat.

Standing, she wiped the wetness from her face. "Diedrich." Her voice came out in a squeak.

He stepped closer, and she could see the pain in his gray eyes. "I saw you talking to Eli. Is it because the two of you had an argument that you are crying?"

He had obviously misconstrued the angry exchange he'd just witnessed between her and Eli. His insinuation that she cared enough about Eli for him to make her cry rankled. Did Diedrich think she and Eli were courting again? Had Herr Rothhaus suggested to Diedrich that was the case? Indignation flared in her chest. How could Diedrich believe such a thing, even from his father? It hurt that Diedrich could think her so fickle or her love so untrue that she would entertain attention from Eli or any other man. "Nein. . .sort of."

His gray eyes turned as hard as granite. "Then it is because of Eli you are crying."

She met his look squarely. "Nein. I am crying because Eli said you and your Vater are going to California in the spring," she blurted. The floodgates holding back her emotions burst inside her, allowing fresh tears to spill down her cheeks. "And Eli was not the first to tell me you are leaving." She told him what she had heard from Zeke Roberts at the Fourth of July picnic. "So when were you planning to tell me? Next spring?"

He groaned. Two quick strides brought him to her side. "Regina, I told you the truth when I said I had no more interest in going to the goldfields. I spoke to Zeke before I knew you loved me. And I never promised him I would leave Sauers." He frowned. "If he told you I did, he is wrong. There was no deal, no handshake." He glanced down. "Only if I knew I had lost all hope of winning your love would I have considered leaving Sauers for California." His voice softened with his gaze. "I could not bear the thought of staying here and being reminded of what I had lost every day for the rest of my life." A sad smile lifted the corner of his mouth, and he took her hands in his. "But Gott had mercy on me and granted me your love." Then his smile faded, and he let go of her hands. "Or has He?"

"What do you mean?" A finger of anger flicked inside her. So he did think she was encouraging Eli's attention.

His jaw worked, and he glanced toward the garden as if allowing himself a moment to gather his thoughts and perhaps rein in his emotions. At length he turned a blank face to her, but his voice sounded tight. "When I went looking for you at the Entebrocks' threshing, I heard you telling someone not to kiss you. Then when I reached the side of the house where you were, I thought I saw Eli disappear around the corner of the house. And just now, I see him talking to you again."

If she were not so angry and Diedrich's accusations were not so completely ludicrous, Regina might have laughed. Instead, she planted her fists against her waist to stop her body from trembling with fury and glared at him. "Diedrich Rothhaus! How dare you accuse me of consorting with Eli behind your back!" She hated the traitorous tears slipping down her cheeks. "I never saw Eli at the Entebrocks' threshing. I do not know what you thought you saw, but like I told you then, I was playing with Henry. He was trying to kiss me with his dirty face, and I was telling him to stop."

To his credit, Diedrich's expression turned sheepish. Then he glanced toward the side yard, and his Adam's apple moved with his swallow. "But Eli was here with you now."

"Ja!" She puffed out an exasperated breath. "Because your Vater told him we are no longer promised, he came again to ask if he could court me."

"And what did you tell him?" A muscle in his jaw twitched.

It took all Regina's strength not to stomp off in a huff. *Dear Lord, why did You make men with such hard heads?* Drawing a fortifying breath, she prayed for patience and searched his pain-filled eyes. "What do you think I told him, Diedrich? I told him the only thing my heart would let me tell him—that I love you. And if I cannot have you, I will marry no one. I sent him away and told him never to come asking me again." She stumbled back to the bench through blinding tears. Sinking to the wooden seat, she hugged herself with her arms and stared unseeing toward the garden. "But if you cannot trust my love, I do not see how we can marry—even if your Vater gives us his blessing." Her voice snagged on the ragged edge of a sob.

He came and sat beside her and slipped his arm around her. "Forgive me, mein Liebchen." His voice sagged with remorse. "It is just that we must be apart so much. We cannot talk and share what is in each other's hearts and minds." He lifted her chin with his forefinger and turned her face to his. "I am ashamed for questioning your love, even for an instant. But you also thought I was planning again to go to California. Because we cannot talk to each other, it becomes easier to imagine things that are not so and causes us to question each other's love."

What he said made sense, but his mention of California reminded her of another question that had niggled at her mind since her conversation with Eli. "It is hard for me to believe your Vater decided on his own that the two of you should go to California. Did you tell him about your earlier plans to go out west to hunt for gold? And if you did, why would you tell him if you are not still planning to go there?"

Turning from her, Diedrich blew out a long breath. Leaning forward, he gazed out over the garden, his arms resting on the tops of his thighs and his hands clasped between his knees. "I had forgotten about the map to the goldfields I put in the back of the Heilige Schrift. One evening Vater found it." He gave a short, sarcastic laugh. "Now he is convinced this is what Gott wants us to do."

Disappointment pinched Regina's heart. "And you let him think you would go to California with him?"

Diedrich winced. "At first." His voice dipped with remorse. "It was too soon after we had made amends. I did not wish to cause another argument. But after Herr Entebrock's threshing. . ." He shook his head. "I knew I must begin to fight harder for you. . .for us." He straightened then turned and took her hands. "That evening, I told Vater I still love you and hope to convince you again to agree to marry me. I told him if I could convince you to reinstate our engagement, I would not be going to California."

Regina's heart trembled, imagining Herr Rothhaus's angry face at Diedrich's admission. The thought stole the breath from her voice. "What did he say?"

Diedrich let go of her hands and turned back to the garden. "He laughed." A mixture of pain and anger crossed his scowling features. "Not a big laugh. Just a deep, quiet laugh, as if he pitied me. He said I would change my mind come spring."

At Diedrich's words, the hope Regina had nurtured that his father would soon repent and grant them his blessing to marry, withered. "So—so your Vater has shown no sign of changing his mind about giving us his blessing?" An errant tear escaped the corner of her left eye.

Diedrich shook his head. "Nein." He said the word so softly she scarcely heard it. He brushed the tear away from her cheek with his thumb. "That is why I came looking for you. We have tried this your way. But every time I try to speak to Vater about you—begging him to find some scrap of forgiveness in his heart for you, an innocent—he closes his ears and walks away."

He stood, and she followed. In the moment of stillness between them, she could hear the other men laughing and talking as they ate at the tables in the yard. Diedrich took her hands again. "I have tried, Regina. But I am now even more convinced your parents are right. I think the only thing that will change Vater's mind is if he sees we are determined to marry." He gave her hands a gentle squeeze. The plea in his eyes ripped at her tattered heart. "Please, mein Liebling, will you not reconsider reinstating our engagement? The scriptures tell us in Hebrews 11:1, 'Now faith is the substance of things hoped for, the evidence of things not seen.' And our Lord tells us in Matthew 17:20, 'If ye have faith as a grain of mustard seed, ye shall say unto this mountain, Remove hence to yonder place; and it shall remove; and nothing shall be impossible unto you.' I am convinced Gott will change Vater's heart. But Gott is waiting, I think, for us to show our faith in Him. Regina, can you not find in your heart faith the size of a mustard seed?"

The scriptures Diedrich quoted convicted Regina, pricking her with guilt. Like her parents, Diedrich seemed sure this approach would soon turn his father's heart around. But what if it didn't? How long could Regina and Diedrich wait on the Lord to work? And what if spring came and Diedrich was forced again to choose between her and his father?

Sophie's stern admonition echoed again in Regina's mind. *"Under no circumstances should you reinstate your engagement unless Herr Rothhaus grants you and Diedrich his blessing."* She thought again of the young woman Sophie had told her about whose new husband left her and returned to his parents' home. Not for one instant did Regina think her good and noble Diedrich would do anything of the sort. But if Papa, Mama, and Diedrich were all wrong and reinstating her engagement to Diedrich did not budge Herr Rothhaus from his position, next spring everyone would once again face the same impasse. No. Breaking her engagement to Diedrich the first time had nearly ripped her heart out. She wasn't sure she'd have the courage to break it a second time. Better to take Sophie's advice and wait for Herr Rothhaus's blessing.

Regina shook her head sadly. "Nein. I wish my faith was as strong as yours, but it is not."

Diedrich's Adam's apple moved with his swallow. A look of anguish darkened his gray eyes. "Then perhaps Vater is right. Maybe there is nothing here for me in Sauers. Maybe it is best if I go look for gold in California after all."

Chapter 25

Squinting against the rising sun, Regina trudged numbly through the dewy grass. Diedrich's parting words yesterday afternoon played in torturous repetition in her head. Each time his words flayed her heart as if scourging it with a briar cane.

She gripped the rope handle of the bucket filled with potato peelings until the rough fibers bit into her hand. If only she could have as strong a faith as Diedrich and Mama and Papa. Of course God could change Herr Rothhaus's heart. Of this, she had no doubt. But the nagging thought that lurked in the darkest recesses of her mind slunk out again to whisper its insidious question. *Does He want to?* Though she loved Diedrich with all her heart and he professed the same for her, what if, for reasons beyond their understanding, God opposed their union? In that case, nothing they tried would nudge Herr Rothhaus from his stubborn stance.

The scripture Papa read last night from the book of Isaiah joined with her own melancholy contemplations to fill her heart with doubt. *"For my thoughts are not your thoughts, neither are your ways my ways, saith the Lord. For as the heavens are higher than the earth, so are my ways higher than your ways, and my thoughts than your thoughts."* Gripping the bottom of the bucket, she slung the contents toward the chicken coop, scattering the vegetable peelings over the barren patch of ground. The chickens, which at first squawked and fled the barrage, batting their snowy wings in fright, now returned to greedily peck at the offering. Like the chickens, was Regina, too, unaware of what was good for her? Had God intentionally thrown up the impediment of her birth family to prevent her and Diedrich from marrying?

Her heart rebelled at the thought. Again she dragged out the question now worn and tattered from constant mulling. If God was against their love, then why did He bring Diedrich here to Sauers in the first place? And why, even against Regina's and Diedrich's own wills, did God allow their hearts to fuse so tightly?

She glanced up at the sky, lightening now to a pale blue as the sun faded the deep pink and purple hues of the waning dawn. "Dear Lord, why have You visited this heartache on me and Diedrich? Are You testing our faith as Mama, Papa, and Diedrich think, or are You telling us we should not marry?"

No answer came. Only the clucking of the chickens and the rustling of the maple trees' leaves stirred by a gentle breeze disturbed the quiet.

Heaving a weary sigh, she started back to the house, her Holzschuhe scuffing through the wet grass. How she longed for Elsie's levelheaded and unbiased counsel. Although Regina had enjoyed her time in Salem with Elsie and William, there had been no time for her and her middle sister to talk alone at length. But Elsie was thirty miles away. Perhaps she should talk to Sophie again. Although her eldest sister had made her opinion on the matter clear, she had on several occasions offered Regina a sympathetic ear. In fact, it still surprised Regina how interested Sophie seemed in Regina and Diedrich's situation. Perhaps it was the mellowing influences of marriage and motherhood, but for whatever reason, Sophie actually seemed to care about Regina and her future. After all, Sophie's advice *had* strengthened Regina's resolve, preventing her from giving in to Diedrich's pleas to reinstate their engagement. If nothing else, maybe Sophie could help ease Regina's mind about her decision yesterday.

As she approached the house, the sound of voices reached her ears. Another couple of steps and she was able to identify the voices as belonging to Sophie and Ezra. Glancing up, she realized she was standing beneath the upstairs bedroom that had, until recently, been hers. The morning air was obviously still heavy enough to carry the couple's decidedly intense conversation beyond the room's open window.

Not wanting to eavesdrop on what sounded like a spat between her sister and brother-in-law, Regina started to step away. But her sister's caustic tone of voice halted her.

"She is not even my blood sister! I tell you, Ezra, it is not right that that little pretender and a man who has been in the country less than three months should inherit Papa's land!" Sophie's words and resentful tone slashed Regina like a knife.

"You know your pa wants the land to go to a German farmer, Sophie. I am neither." Ezra's voice held a note of frayed patience.

Sophie snorted. "That is your problem, Ezra. Your view

is too narrow. Look, we have a son—Mama and Papa's blood grandson. It is Henry who should inherit this farm, not two people who have no blood claim."

Despite the warm July morning, an icy chill shot through Regina. She'd always known Sophie was not especially fond of her, but the vitriol in her sister's voice stunned her. So that was why Sophie was so emphatic that Regina should not re-instate her engagement. Her positive comments about Eli as well as her criticisms of Diedrich began to make sense.

Brokenhearted at her sister's greed and ugly words, Re-gina wanted to slink away, but the sound of Sophie's voice again kept her rooted to the spot.

"Eli Tanner assured me that Herr Rothhaus will never allow his son to marry Regina. So all we have to do is plant the idea in Papa's mind that there is no hope of a marriage between Regina and Diedrich Rothhaus, and that Papa would be far wiser to will the land to us to keep for Henry—Papa's blood grandson."

"But next week we'll be movin' to Will's ma's house in Salem so I can begin my new job. What good will this farm here in Sauers do us when we're clear down in Salem?"

Sophie huffed. "It is like you have blinders on, Ezra! You said yourself that job might not last. This land should be my birthright, and it will be here. Think. You could start your own wheelwright shop in the barn. Eventually we could even sell off some acreage and build a proper house—a big one like we had in Vernon. You could own your own busi-ness again. And when Henry gets old enough, he could help you." Her tone turned sweet, cajoling. "Barnes and Son,

Wheelwrights. It has a good sound, I think. Don't you want that one day, mein Liebchen?"

"Yeah, reckon I would, honey." Ezra's tone turned thoughtful then playful. "But I think Barnes and *Sons*, Wheelwrights, sounds even better." A soft chuckle.

Silence, then Sophie's giggle.

Regina's imagination supplied what she could not see. Her stomach churned at her sister's conniving treachery. Mama and Papa had taken in Sophie and Ezra when they were destitute. Now the couple conspired to use their baby son to steal her parents' homestead. Regina felt sick.

Moving as quietly as her wooden shoes and trembling legs allowed, she rounded the house then sprinted to the barn. There she searched and found an empty burlap sack and a shovel. Her parents and Diedrich were right. The time for inaction had passed. Regina needed to step out in faith and trust God with the rest.

Kneeling on the new porch floor, Diedrich took the nail dangling from his lips and pounded it into the next board. With the Seitzes' wheat crop threshed, cleaned, and stored and the corn crop months away from harvest, he'd decided this would be a good time to begin work on a porch for the new house.

Reaching in his shirt pocket for another couple of nails, he paused and took a moment to look behind him and assess his morning's work. Redolent with the smell of newly cut poplar, the porch extended two-thirds the length of the house's front. Washed in the morning sun, the boards gleamed like gold.

Gold. His heart contracted. The word reminded him of his angry parting words to Regina yesterday. The hurt in her blue eyes still haunted him. He shook his head to obliterate the memory then lifted another board from the pile on the ground beside him and fitted it into place. She still loved him. He saw it in her eyes and felt it in her touch. She wanted to marry him as much as he wanted to marry her. He glanced up at the front of the house. His heart told him she, too, longed for them to have a future here together. Why could she not see that as long as they remained formally uncommitted, they only encouraged Father's stubbornness?

He pressed the point of a nail into the board in front of him then wielded the hammer and drove the nail head flush with two powerful blows. But the exertion could not expel the anger and frustration roiling inside him. Despite telling Regina that he might leave for California in the spring, he knew it was a lie. As long as she still loved him, he could not leave. He felt trapped—unable to move forward, unable to move backward. The image of the Israelites gathered on the shores of the Red Sea came to mind. Diedrich understood how they must have felt with Pharaoh's army behind them and the impassable waters before them. Regina's love tethered him to Sauers. But until God provided a miracle and moved the impediment of Father's stubborn determination to cling to a decades-old grudge, Diedrich's life remained in limbo. Just as God provided a way for the children of Israel, Diedrich prayed He would grant Diedrich and Regina a like miracle.

At the distant sound of an approaching conveyance, he

turned his attention to the dirt path that ran between the house and Herr Seitz's cornfield. Father must be coming home early from his work at the mill for the noonday meal. As usual, emotions warred in Diedrich's chest at the thought of his parent. Every night Diedrich prayed the next day would be the one in which God stirred Father's heart to cast off his old rancor for the Zichwolffs and embrace both forgiveness and Regina. Yet each day brought only disappointment.

As the sound grew louder, the head of the animal pulling the approaching conveyance appeared over the gentle rise in the road. Diedrich's heart quickened, matching the lively pace of Regina's shaggy little pony's feet kicking up clouds of dust. Not since the day Diedrich told Regina of Father's opposition to their marriage had she attempted to visit the new house.

Standing, he dropped the hammer to the porch floor with a clatter. Could there have been an accident on the Seitz farm? At the thought, he hastened his steps toward the cart as she reined in the pony.

"Regina." Reaching up, he helped her down, reveling in the touch of his hands on her waist. His arms ached to embrace her, to hold her against him and never let her go. But with no one else here, that would not be proper. And by the intense look on her face, he sensed she had come on a mission. "Is something amiss? Has there been an accident?"

"Nein." A bright smile bloomed on her face, dispelling his fears. Walking to the back of the pony cart, she lifted out a burlap sack and handed it to him.

Accepting the sack, he grinned. "What is this?" Since

Father adamantly refused any food from the Seitzes' kitchen, Regina and her mother had stopped offering. So the sack's lumpy contents, which looked suspiciously like potatoes, surprised him. His curiosity piqued, he glanced inside. Sure enough, a dozen or so nice-sized new potatoes filled the bottom quarter of the sack. "Potatoes," he said unnecessarily.

"*Our* potatoes," she said with a grin. "We planted these together, and they have flourished, just as the love I believe Gott planted in our hearts for each other that same day has flourished."

She placed her hand over his, and Diedrich's heart caught with his breath. Did he dare believe the miracle he'd been praying for was unfolding before his eyes?

"Diedrich." Her eyes searched his. "Like the scriptures tell us in Galatians, 'Whatsoever a man soweth, that shall he also reap.' Gott sowed the good seeds of love in our hearts. And since we nurtured them and they grew, I believe our love is of Gott, and He will bless the harvest." She pressed her lips together and cocked her head, her eyes turning sad. "I am sorry that your Vater has decided to nurture the bad seeds of hate and bitterness. I continue to pray he will finally see how hurtful they are to him as well as to us and hoe them out of his heart. But until that day, he must reap what he has sown." She glanced down, and when she looked back up, her smile turned sheepish. "You were right. I need to show Gott I trust Him more. Today I will begin to do that. You asked me yesterday to reinstate our engagement. I am ready to do that now—that is, if you still want to marry me."

Diedrich fought to suppress the jubilation exploding

inside him like the fireworks some of the neighbors had set off last week. Grinning, he put one arm around her and tugged her to his side. A flash of mischief sparked by his unquenchable joy gripped him. "Of course I want to marry you. But you must say again what you just said."

She gave him a puzzled grin, her eyes glinting with fun. "And what was it I said that you would like to hear again?"

"That I was right. I fear it may be the only time I ever hear you say those words to me."

Giggling, she gave him a playful smack on the arm, and his resistance crumbled. He dropped the sack of potatoes to the ground and pulled her into his arms and kissed her. Somewhere in the midst of his bliss, he thought he heard the roar of a sea parting.

"Diedrich!"

At the angry voice, Diedrich and Regina sprang apart. Together they turned to see Father striding toward them, his face purple with rage.

Chapter 26

"What is this?" Herr Rothhaus's angry glower swung between Diedrich and Regina. "I thought you were done with this Zichwolff pup, Diedrich."

Regina felt Diedrich tense. He took a half step forward as if to shield her from his father's wrath. Yet his arm remained firmly around her waist, helping to still her trembling body.

"Be very careful, Vater." Diedrich's voice, low and taut, revealed his barely controlled anger. "Regina is my future wife. I will not allow anyone, not even you, to speak to her with disrespect."

Herr Rothhaus's fists balled and a bulging vein throbbed at his temple. Regina's nightmare had become real. Would father and son come to blows over her? *Dear Lord, don't let it happen.*

Now Herr Rothhaus focused his glare on Diedrich alone. "But you told me the two of you were no longer engaged. Have you then been lying to me all this time?"

Diedrich's back stiffened. "I have never lied to you, Vater. Regina did break our engagement. And it was for your sake she broke it. As I have told you, my love for her has not changed." He looked down at Regina, and the barest hint of a smile touched his lips. His voice softened with his tender gaze. "It never has, and it never will."

Confusion relaxed the older man's rage-crumpled face. "You call her your future wife. How can that be if you are no longer betrothed?"

Diedrich's arm tightened around Regina's waist, pulling her closer. "She has finally agreed with me that reinstating our engagement may be the only way to bring you to your senses."

Herr Rothhaus's face contorted, turning myriad shades of red and purple. Regina feared he might collapse in a fit of apoplexy. He glared at Diedrich, his gray eyes bulging nearly out of his head. "My senses? My senses?" His voice climbed in a crescendo of anger. "You go behind my back and defy my wishes and now have the audacity to suggest I am not in my right mind? It is you, I think, who have lost your senses!" His murderous glare shifted to Regina. "She is a Zichwolff! I told you what they did to our family. And still you are content to let this Jezebel Zichwolff lure you into a marriage that would mingle our family's blood with that of her reprobate Vater and Großvater?"

Diedrich let go of Regina and strode toward his father. "Enough, Vater!"

True terror gripped Regina. *Dear Lord, stop this! Please, Lord, intercede.* She clutched at Diedrich's arm, but he shook off her hand and focused his fury on his father.

Diedrich's arms stiffened at his sides, and his fists clenched. His face came within inches of his father's. "From my earliest days, you and Mama taught me the scriptures. Whenever my brothers and I argued or were unkind to each other, you quoted the words of our Lord, teaching us forgiveness." His arms shot out to the sides, his fingers splayed, while his body visibly shook with emotion. "How, Vater? How could you teach us Christ's words concerning forgiveness when your heart was filled with hate and unforgiveness?"

A look of shame flashed across Herr Rothhaus's face, but his defiant stance did not budge. He rose on the balls of his feet until he stood almost as tall as his son. His eyes blazed with anger. "You dare to call me a hypocrite? You insolent pup!"

In one sudden movement, Diedrich spun on his heel and bounded to the porch then disappeared in the house. For a second, the fear that had gripped Regina eased. Had Diedrich left to cool his temper? But her ebbing trepidation flooded back as she found herself alone to face Herr Rothhaus's angry glare. The thought struck that she should climb into the pony cart and head for home. But before she could move, Diedrich shot out the front door, his Bible in hand.

He stomped to his father and waved the book in his face. "Matthew 5:44. 'But I say unto you, Love your enemies, bless them that curse you, do good to them that hate you, and pray for them which despitefully use you, and persecute you.' Matthew 6:14 and 15. 'For if ye forgive men their trespasses, your heavenly Father will also forgive you: But if ye forgive not men their trespasses, neither will your Father forgive your trespasses.' Mark 11:25. 'And when ye stand praying, forgive, if ye have ought against any: that your Father also which is in heaven may forgive you your trespasses.'" He smacked the book's leather cover, and Regina jumped at the sharp report that split the air like a rifle shot. "I memorized them just as you taught me to do, Vater. I have tried all my life to live by these words, and I thought you tried to live by them, too. Now I find I am wrong. These words mean nothing to you."

In a flash, Herr Rothhaus reached out and struck Diedrich's cheek with the flat of his hand. Regina gasped. Diedrich's whole body seemed to shudder, but he held his ground. She was glad she stood behind him and could not see his face. But she could see Herr Rothhaus's. And for a fraction of a second, the older man's expression registered shock at his own impulsive action.

For a moment, Herr Rothhaus's eyes glistened but quickly dried and turned stone hard again. "I am your Vater! I never allowed you to disrespect me when you were growing up, and I will not allow it now." He shook his fist in Diedrich's face. "I will not tolerate being judged or called a hypocrite by my own Sohn!"

"I call you nothing but Vater." Diedrich's voice cracked, and his shoulders slumped. "I have bent over backward to remain respectful while you shattered my life and Regina's life with a laugh and a shrug. I do not stand in judgment of you. I will let Gott and your own heart do that." His voice sagged with his posture as his anger seemed to seep away, replaced by sadness. Pressing the Bible into his father's hands, he turned, and Regina's heart broke. His gray eyes held a vacant look, and three angry red streaks brightened his left cheek.

As Diedrich walked toward Regina and the pony cart, Herr Rothhaus stomped after him. "Do not call me Vater," he hollered. "You are not my Sohn! Now get out of my sight and take the Zichwolff whelp with you!"

Diedrich did not reply as he helped Regina up to the cart's seat then climbed up beside her and took the reins. They rode halfway home in silence.

At last, feeling the need to say something, Regina put her hand on Diedrich's arm. "I am sorry." Even to her own ears, the words sounded inadequate. "I should not have come. I—"

"Nein." Diedrich reined Gypsy to a halt. "You did only what I asked." As if unwilling to meet her gaze, he stared at the road ahead. "I am sorry you had to see that. And for the unkind things my Vater called you." He winced. "What you saw is not the man who raised me. I have never seen this man, and I pray I will never see him again."

Regina's heart writhed for her beloved. She prayed God would give her words to comfort him. "I know, my Liebling. Today, I did not see the Herr Rothhaus who came to our home in April. That man is kind, gentle, and caring. Today, I saw only hate. Hate is ugly, and it can make even those we love ugly." Turning to him, she reached out and pressed her palm against his wounded face. "I pray God will root out the hate from your Vater's heart so we can again see the gut man we know and love." Her words made her think of Sophie's treachery, and her heart experienced a double sting.

Diedrich's Adam's apple bobbed. He didn't reply, making her wonder if he didn't trust his voice. Instead, he touched her hand still on his cheek then turned his face against her palm and kissed it. Taking the reins back in hand, he clicked his tongue and flicked the line on Gypsy's back, setting the pony clopping along the road again.

As they turned into the lane that led to the house, he glanced over at her. "What made you change your mind?"

The memory of Sophie's hateful words rushed back to sting anew. Regina felt a deepening kinship with the man she loved. Today they had both experienced painful disappointment in people close to them. She fidgeted, reluctant to repeat what she had heard while eavesdropping. But since it affected Diedrich as well as her, she decided he had a right to know what Sophie was plotting. After recounting the conversation she'd heard this morning between Sophie and Ezra, Regina twisted the fistful of apron she'd been wadding in her hands. "I always knew Sophie wasn't especially fond of me, but I never imagined she disliked me so much." Rogue tears stung her nose, forcing her to sniff them back. "How could she act so sweet to me, when all the time she hated me?"

Diedrich shook his head and patted her hand. "I do not know, my Liebchen, just as I do not know how my Vater could let hate turn him into a man I do not recognize. But nothing is impossible with Gott. We must pray for Him to soften Sophie's heart as well as Vater's."

As they neared the house, Papa emerged from the big, yawning doors at the end of the barn. At the sight of Regina and Diedrich together, a look of pleased surprise registered on his face. He quickened his steps and met them between the barn and the house. Standing eye-level with Regina and Diedrich on the cart's low seat, he glanced between the two, his smile widening. "Has Herr Rothhaus changed his mind, then? Praise be to Gott!"

"Nein, Papa." Shaking her head, Regina reached out and gripped her father's arm to stifle his celebration. At Papa's puzzled look, Diedrich supplied the gist of what had just taken place outside the new log house.

Papa scowled and shook his head. "It is sorry I am to hear it." He pressed his hand on Diedrich's shoulder. "But you did the right thing, Sohn." A wry grin lifted the corner of his mouth. "It is never wrong to remind even a parent of Christ's commandments. Whatever your Vater may have said in anger, I know he loves you. In his letters to me, I could tell he was desperate to get you to America and out of reach of conscription. We must pray your words take root in his heart and that Gott will change him here and here." He tapped his chest and then his head. Turning to Regina, he patted her cheek. "It is happy I am that you have decided to trust Gott, Tochter. It is not always an easy thing to do." He glanced upward. "But Gott will reward your faith."

Regina smiled and hugged Papa. Though she had shared with Diedrich Sophie's selfish and deceitful plans, she prayed she could spare Papa and Mama ever learning of them.

Papa helped Regina down from the cart, and the three of them walked to the house together. "Your Mutter will be interested to hear of your news," he said as he opened the door for Regina. But when they trooped into the kitchen, Mama was not in sight. Instead, it was Sophie who turned from mixing corn bread batter in the large crockery bowl.

Upon seeing Diedrich with his arm around Regina, Sophie's eyes widened. To her shame, Regina experienced a flash of satisfaction at the dismay on her sister's face.

Papa crossed to Sophie. "Where is your Mutter? We have news to tell her."

Sophie blanched and opened her mouth, but nothing came out. She glanced toward the doorway that led to the interior of the house just as Mama emerged with Henry in her arms.

"What news?" Mama took in the three of them and gave a little gasp. With trembling arms, she lowered her squirming grandson to the floor. Her dark eyes swam with unshed tears, and she clutched at her chest. "Herr Rothhaus has repented. Praise be to—"

"Nein, Catharine." Papa stepped to her side and gently explained what had transpired.

The joy left Mama's face, and Regina was struck by the stark contrast between Mama's crestfallen expression and Sophie's hopeful one.

The starch returned to Mama's frame, and she lifted her chin. "But it is a beginning. Gott is working, I think."

"Ja." Papa nodded then turned to Regina and Diedrich. "When Georg sees you are determined to wed, he will relent and bless your union." He smiled, his countenance brightening. "And soon I shall have a gut German son-in-law to inherit my farm."

Everyone chuckled but Sophie. Whirling on the group, she stomped her foot, and her face turned stormy. "It is not fair!" She glowered at Papa. "Regina is not even of your blood, yet *she* gets the farm simply because she is willing to marry the man you handpicked for her?" Casting a scathing glance at Diedrich, she snorted. "Why, you scarcely know him." She stomped her foot again. "It is not fair, I say! I am the oldest and your blood daughter. *I* should inherit with my son—your blood grandson." With a flourish of her wrist, she gave Regina a supercilious wave. "Not that spineless little pretender." She wrinkled her nose as if she smelled something bad. "She's not even my sister!"

Though Sophie's sentiments came as no surprise to Regina, her sister's outburst and subsequent venomous diatribe stunned her. Regina and her sisters, including Sophie, had never before disrespected their parents in such a blatant manner. Diedrich stiffened at Regina's side. With his arm protectively around her back, he slid his hand up and down her left arm in a comforting motion. Regina was sure he understood little of Sophie's words, and wondered if Sophie had chosen to deliver her tirade in English for that very reason. Yet Sophie's angry demeanor and disdainful looks left little doubt as to the subject of her ire.

"Sophie." Mama uttered her eldest daughter's name with a disappointed sigh.

Papa stiffened, and his brow lowered in a dark scowl. "Enough, Sophie! Regina is my Tochter, the same as you are." He strode to Sophie, and for an instant, fear glinted in her eyes. But when he spoke, his voice was calm, and his words measured. "It is sad I am, Tochter, that you are so bitter toward the Schwester Gott has given you. Your Mutter and I have always tried to deal fairly with you and your Schwestern." He shook his head and held out his hands in a helpless gesture. "You knew when you married Ezra I wanted to give the land one day to a farmer—a farmer with ties to the Old Country."

Sophie's eyes welled with tears, and Regina's heart went out to her. She could see how Sophie must feel much like Esau of old when his mother and brother contrived to deprive him of his birthright. But as Papa pointed out, Sophie, like Esau, had willingly forfeited any claim to the land when she married Ezra.

Sophie lifted a defiant yet trembling chin. "But I fell in love with Ezra."

Papa put his hand on Sophie's shoulder. "And so it was right for you to marry him. But he is not a farmer. And Henry, too, may well decide to follow his Vater and become a wheelwright or practice another trade altogether." He gave Sophie a fond, indulgent smile. "Because your Mutter and I give the farm to Regina does not mean we love you and Elsie any less. Like now, you, Ezra, and Henry, as well as Elsie and William, will always have a home here if you need one. But Ezra and William are not farmers. It is sorry I am that you think your Mutter and I are unfair to want the land we bought and worked on all these years to go to a daughter and Schwiegersohn who will farm it as we have."

Papa's eye twinkled, and he quirked a grin at Regina. "I do not know what I would have done if Regina, too, had settled her heart on a merchant or a wheelwright or. . .a miller."

At the word "miller," Regina's heart jumped, and heat flooded her face. Had Papa suspected her earlier infatuation with Eli? She ventured a glance up at Diedrich's face. His lips were pressed in a firm line, and his gaze skittered to the floor.

"But praise be to Gott," Papa continued, "Regina has

settled her heart on Diedrich."

Sophie sniffed and folded her arms over her chest. Her rigid demeanor suggested she was not yet ready to surrender the argument. "But Herr Rothhaus may never grant them permission to marry. And Henry may grow up and decide to be a farmer. At least *he* is your own blood."

Mama, who had remained quiet but attentive to the exchange between Papa and Sophie, now glanced around the room, her attention clearly detached from the ongoing conversation. "Henry. Where is Henry?"

Chapter 27

Everyone stopped and looked around the kitchen, but Henry was not there.

Sophie shrugged. "He has probably crawled into Regina's bed again to take a nap. You know how he loves to do that. I'm sure I will find him there." She headed for the house's interior with Mama on her heels.

Papa checked the washroom without success, and fear flickered in Regina's chest. Though she suspected Sophie was right and Henry was fast asleep in her bed, she wouldn't be easy until she knew he was safe. She held her breath, expecting any second to hear her sister or mother announce they had found him.

Instead, Sophie's voice from inside the house turned increasingly frantic as she called her son's name. The next moment she burst into the kitchen, her face white and her eyes wild. "He is nowhere. I can find him nowhere." Her voice cracked, and she began to tremble.

Mama appeared behind her, looking as pale and shaken as her daughter. She turned desperate eyes to Papa. "Ernst, he is not in the house."

The flicker of fear in Regina's chest flared. It was not unusual to occasionally lose sight of the active toddler, but until this moment, they had always quickly discovered his whereabouts.

Sophie clutched her heaving chest. "My baby! My kleines Kind. Where could he be?" Her words came out in breathless puffs, and Regina feared her sister might swoon.

As Mama and Sophie embraced, Papa slowly pumped his flattened hands up and down. "Now, now, we must stay calm. He cannot have gone far. We will find him in a bit."

Despite Papa's assurances, Sophie began to sob in Mama's arms. At that moment, Ezra came in from cutting hay. His face full of alarm, he rushed to Sophie and Mama. "What is wrong?"

Turning from Mama, Sophie gripped her husband and sobbed against his neck. "He–Henry. We cannot find Henry. . .anywhere."

The alarm on Ezra's face grew as he patted his wife's back. "Has anybody looked upstairs?" The tightness in his voice revealed his concern. "I caught him climbing up there yesterday."

At his suggestion, Regina flew up the stairs, wondering why no one had thought of it sooner. But a quick perusal of the room revealed no Henry. She checked under the bed and in the wardrobe—every nook and cranny where a two-year-old could hide. As each spot revealed no Henry, Regina's heart began to pound, and rising panic threatened to swamp her. Downstairs, she could hear the others scurrying around. Soon the whole house rang with a discordant chorus of people calling the little boy's name.

Regina hurried downstairs, and Diedrich met her at the bottom step. Fear stole her breath, and she could only shake her head at his hopeful look. Now true terror gripped her, and her whole body began to shake. Both the front and back doors were propped open to allow a cooling cross breeze. While everyone was focused on the argument between Sophie and Papa, Henry had obviously exited the house through one of the open doors. But which one? She thought of Papa's bull, Stark. The well. Even her gentle pony, Gypsy, tethered beside the lane, could be lethal to a two-year-old if the child crawled between the pony's hooves and the animal impulsively kicked out. A shudder shook Regina's frame.

Diedrich grasped her shoulders and fixed her with a calm and steady gaze. "We will find him, Regina. Gott will help us find him. You must believe that."

Unable to speak, she nodded. Fear paralyzed her brain until she couldn't even fashion a coherent prayer.

"Everyone outside!" At Papa's booming voice, everyone jerked to attention then scrambled for the back door. Regina was glad for Diedrich's strong arm around her waist, lending support to her quavering limbs.

Sophie and Ezra stood fixed, their gazes darting around. They looked as if they would like to go in all directions at once, but their inability to do so kept them rooted in place.

Papa began suggesting places Henry might hide. Diedrich held up a hand. "Wait." At his quiet but firm voice, everyone turned to him. "I think we should first pray for guidance. Gott knows where Henry is. If we ask, He will keep the *kleinen Jungen* safe and lead us to him."

Papa nodded. "Ja. You are right, Sohn. We must first go to Gott in prayer."

Forming a circle, everyone joined hands, and Papa began in a strong voice, thickened by emotion. "Vater Gott, You know where our little Henry is hiding. We ask You to keep him safe and direct us as we go in search of our precious Kleinen." When he referred to Henry as their precious little one, Papa's voice cracked, and Diedrich stepped in to utter a hearty "Amen."

Even before the word had faded away, everyone scattered. Over the next few minutes, they checked the well, the chicken coop, and the outhouse. When they all gathered empty handed at the back door again, Sophie looked pale, shaken, and on the verge of collapse. Regina suspected she looked much the same as the terror in her chest grew to a growling monster.

Diedrich glanced toward the barn. "We have not yet checked the barn."

Mama sank, a trembling mass, to the built-up flat stones that edged the base of the well. At Diedrich's suggestion, she gasped and gripped her chest, rekindled fright shining from her worry-lined face. Her voice turned breathless. "The horses. The cow. Stark is in there." She lifted her terror-stricken eyes to Papa as if pleading for him to contradict Diedrich. "Not the barn, Ernst. Henry is only a baby. He surely could not have gone as far as the barn, do you think?"

Papa pressed a reassuring hand on her shoulder and shook his head. "Nein. I'm sure he is playing with us and hiding, or has fallen asleep in a place we have not yet thought of."

Despite Mama and Papa's denials, Diedrich continued to glance toward the barn, a look of urgency animating his features. "Still, it is worth looking, I think. Once when my little niece Maria was about Henry's age, she hid in the barn for two hours before we found her."

Regina sensed something was tugging Diedrich toward the barn. They had prayed for God to guide them. To ignore what could well be divine nudges seemed beyond foolish. She trusted Diedrich's instincts. "I agree with Diedrich, Papa. I think we should look in the barn."

Deliberation played over Papa's anguished face. He obviously questioned wasting time on a fruitless search in what he considered an unlikely spot. At the same time, she suspected that Papa also was wondering if God had planted the hunch in Diedrich's mind. At last he nodded. "Ja. We shall look in the barn." At his pronouncement, he and the others followed Regina and Diedrich to the large, weathered structure across the lane.

As they stepped into the building, Regina blinked, trying to force her eyes to more quickly adjust to the dim light. With trepidation, she turned her attention to the big bull's stall. To her relief, the large animal stood sedately munching hay and flicking away flies with the brushy end of his tail. The cow, too, was all alone in her stall, as were the two huge Clydesdales.

As she walked beneath the hayloft, a shower of hay dust filtered down, accompanied by what sounded like a faint giggle. She looked up and gasped as her heart catapulted to her throat. Perched on the edge of the loft with his bare legs dangling over the side beneath his gown, Henry looked down on them, his angelic expression keen with interest.

Afraid to speak or even breathe, Regina gripped Diedrich's arm. He followed her gaze and tensed. Mama, Papa, Sophie, and Ezra all gave a collective gasp.

"How on earth. . ." Ezra uttered the words Regina was sure filled everyone's minds.

The answer stood propped against the loft. Evidently, Henry had somehow managed to climb the long ladder either Papa or Ezra had left there. Regina cringed, imagining the toddler's precarious climb, his unsteady feet at times stepping on the hem of his gown in the course of his ascent. Her heart nearly stopped at the thought. But somehow God had helped the little boy to safely scale the ladder and reach the summit.

Sophie gripped Ezra's arm. "Do not just stand there, Ezra. Go up and get him!"

Ezra hesitated. "I don't know, Sophie. I don't want to scare him. He might. . ." Leaving the thought to dangle like Henry's legs, Ezra dragged his hand over his mouth. Beads of sweat broke out on his forehead.

Papa turned from Mama, who clung to his arm, and cupped his hands around Sophie's shoulders. He kept his voice low and calm, though it sounded brittle enough to break. "Ezra is right, Sophie. We must be careful not to frighten him."

Sophie huffed. "Oh, for goodness' sake! If no one else will go, I will." She headed toward the ladder. "Mama is coming, Henry."

"Mama." Henry leaned forward, evoking another collective gasp from the adults below. Sophie froze with her foot on the ladder's bottom rung.

Regina's heart stuck in her throat. She gripped Diedrich's arm and prayed. *God, please help us find a way to get him safely down.*

Ezra grasped Sophie's shoulders, gently moving her aside. "I'll go up."

With both hands pressed against her mouth, Mama leaned against Papa, who held her tight—ready, Regina was sure, to shield her eyes should the unthinkable happen. Regina clung to Diedrich as well, but he disentangled himself from her grasp. "Go to your Schwester." Confused and a little hurt that, unlike Papa with Mama, Diedrich had chosen to withdraw his support from Regina, she nevertheless went to embrace Sophie. With both her husband and son in peril, Sophie would need someone to support and comfort her.

As Ezra began to scale the ladder, Sophie's body shook even harder than Regina's. "Stay still, Henry," she called up in a tremulous voice. "Papa is coming to get you."

"Papa, Papa." Henry turned and drew his feet up under him, eliciting more sharp intakes of air.

Ezra quickened his steps. "No, Henry. Stay still."

Laughing, Henry pushed up to a standing position and toddled toward his father, his bare feet treading treacherously close to the loft's edge. Regina clung to Sophie, afraid to watch the proceedings and yet unable not to.

Now at the top of the ladder, Ezra reached out toward his son, curling his fingers toward him in a beckoning gesture. "Come here, Henry. Come to Papa."

Henry came within a fingertip's length of Ezra's reach.

For a moment, the fear gripping Regina eased its stranglehold on her throat. But instead of walking into his father's arms, Henry laughed and turned as if he thought Ezra was playing a game with him. He lifted a chubby foot. Time froze with Regina's heart as the little boy teetered on the loft's edge. A look of terror contorted Ezra's face. Lunging, he reached out and swiped at his son's gown. He missed. Collective gasps punctured the air. A strangled scream tore from Sophie's throat as Henry's little body tumbled over the edge.

Chapter 28

Regina's mind went numb. Turning Sophie from the sight, she pressed her hand against the back of her sister's head and drew Sophie's face against her shoulder. If she could do nothing else, she could save Sophie the memory of witnessing the death of her child. At the same time, Regina buried her own face in Sophie's shoulder. Weeping quietly, she held tightly to her sister's body, now racked with sobs. Then with sudden awareness, she realized the only sound in the barn was that of her and Sophie's weeping. She hadn't heard the dreaded thud of Henry's little body hitting the barn's dirt floor or a rush of footsteps toward the site of the tragedy. No one else was weeping or wailing with grief.

Pushing away from Sophie, Regina opened her eyes. Dread filling her, she peered hesitantly over Sophie's shoulder at the spot where she expected to find Henry's lifeless form. But to her amazement, instead of the gruesome sight she'd imagined, she saw Diedrich grinning with Henry cradled safely in his arms. She nearly collapsed with relief. Now she understood why Diedrich had pushed her away. He'd hoped to position himself to catch her nephew should Henry fall. Regina's heart swelled. Every time she thought she couldn't love this man more, he proved her wrong.

Ezra scrambled down the ladder. And as if in one

motion, he, Mama, and Papa all rushed to Diedrich and Henry. Only Sophie remained with her back to the group, doubled over and sobbing into her hands.

Regina gripped Sophie's forearms. "Sophie, look. Henry is safe. Diedrich caught him."

Sophie opened her eyes and blinked, disbelief replacing despondency on her face. She turned slowly as if afraid to believe Regina's words. Then, seeing they were true, she ran and snatched her baby son from Diedrich's arms.

"Henry," she mumbled against his curly head as she clutched her son's squirming form to her breast and rocked back and forth. "Don't you ever scare Mama like that again!" Her chide warbled through her sobs.

Ezra rushed to his family and enveloped them in his arms. Mama wept softly and caressed Henry's head, cooing comforting hushes to her grandson, who had also begun crying.

Papa gripped Diedrich's hand. "Danke, Sohn." His voice quivered, and his eyes watered. Regina couldn't remember the last time she'd seen Papa weep.

With red eyes and a soppy face, Ezra disengaged from Sophie and Henry then strode to Diedrich and grasped his hand. Sniffing, he ran his shirtsleeve under his nose. "I'm not good with words, but 'thank you' doesn't seem enough for what you did."

Papa translated, and Diedrich gripped Ezra's shoulder and grinned. "Bitte sehr, mein Freund. But it was Gott who dropped Henry into my arms. I am just the vessel He used."

Sophie finally relented to Mama's petitions and handed

Henry to his grandmother, who smothered the little boy with kisses. Henry, who had stopped crying but still looked confused about all the commotion, fussed to get down. But Mama shook her head and held tightly to him. Papa guffawed and tousled the boy's mop of brown curls as the three of them headed out of the barn.

With her head down and her shoulders slumped, Sophie scuffed over the straw-strewn floor to join her husband. Wringing her hands, she finally looked up to face Diedrich and Regina. Shame dragged down her features, making her appear old. "*Herzlichen Dank,* Herr Rothhaus, for what you did for our Henry." A flood of tears streamed down her face, but she paid them no mind. "If not for you, Ezra and I might be preparing to bury our son." The last word snagged on the ragged edge of a sob. Ezra put a comforting arm around her shoulders, but she shrugged it off. Straightening, she sniffed back tears and lifted her quavering chin. "There is something I must say to you both, and I must say it now," she said in German, her voice breaking. "I am so ashamed. I have been mean and greedy." A new deluge of tears washed down her face.

Regina's heart turned over at Sophie's agony, but it also warmed in anticipation of her sister's repentance. Her impulse was to tell Sophie an apology was not necessary. But she knew it was—not only for her and Diedrich's sakes, but more importantly for Sophie's.

Sophie's throat moved with her swallow. Apologizing had never come easily to Regina's eldest sister. "Earlier, I said some unkind things to you. I ask you to forgive me." Now she focused her gaze squarely on Regina's face. A fresh tear welled in her left eye and perched on her lower lid for an instant before trailing down her cheek. "Regina, please forgive me for saying you are not my sister. You *are* my sister. I was so awful to you. And you have been so sweet and kind to me. I realize now that blood is not important. Family is important, and we are family. I hope you can forgive me. I will try to be a better sister to you in the future."

At Sophie's penitent words and demeanor, Regina's heart melted. She knew what the admission must have cost her naturally unyielding sibling. She gathered Sophie in her arms. "Mein liebe Schwester. Of course I forgive you."

After a moment, Sophie pushed away from Regina and turned to Diedrich. "Herr Rothhaus, I said some very unkind things about you, too. I am sorry for them. Will you please forgive my unkindness?" Regina noticed Sophie's use of the courtesy title Herr in addressing Diedrich, an unmistakable token of regard.

Smiling, Diedrich took Sophie's hands in his. "Of course I forgive you, just as our Lord taught us to forgive."

Regina wondered if Diedrich was thinking of the scriptures he had quoted earlier to his father.

Wiping away her tears, Sophie stepped back into Ezra's embrace. "Danke, Herr Rothhaus." She glanced between Regina and Diedrich. "Ezra and I have not yet congratulated you on your engagement. We would like to do that now." She turned to Diedrich. "I look forward to having you as a brother. Please believe me when I tell you I will be praying that happens soon."

As Regina and Diedrich thanked Sophie for her kind sentiments, Regina was reminded of the scripture from the book of Hebrews that Mama liked to quote: "For whom the Lord loveth he chasteneth." Mama often warned, "When Gott wants our attention, He will get it one way or another. Those who ignore His whispered chide may have to feel the sting of His willow switch across their knuckles." God had obviously gotten Sophie's attention. And to Regina's mind, the fear of losing a child was quite a sting across the knuckles.

Over the next week, Regina and Sophie grew closer than Regina had ever imagined they could. And if she had harbored any doubt that her sister's repentance was genuine, Sophie squelched it as the two worked together in the upstairs bedroom, packing away the Barneses' things for their trip to Salem. Regina stopped her work to impulsively hug her sister. "I will miss you all so much."

At that, Sophie sank to the feather mattress and dissolved into tears. When Regina tried to comfort her, she confessed her scheme to convince Papa to will the land to her and Ezra instead of Regina and Diedrich.

"I don't know what came over me," Sophie said before blowing her nose into the handkerchief Regina handed her. "You and Diedrich are far more suited to farm life than Ezra and I. I would much rather live in town." She sniffed and mopped at her eyes. "I just wanted some security—a home no one could take away from me." With her head hung low, she twisted the handkerchief in her lap. "I know it doesn't excuse what I did, and I wouldn't blame you if you hated me."

Her heart crimping, Regina rubbed her sister's back. "Of course I don't hate you. You are my Schwester. I love you." Though cheered by Sophie's confession, Regina decided it might be best not to reveal her prior knowledge of the plan. "Everyone wants security, Sophie. But nothing in life is secure. That is why we must have faith in Gott. I had to learn that, too. Diedrich and I have no assurance Herr Rothhaus will ever give us his blessing to marry, but we have faith that he will."

Sophie hugged Regina and promised to pray fervently for God to convict Herr Rothhaus as He had convicted her.

But two days after Sophie, Ezra, and Henry left for Salem, Regina's own faith began to flag. Though she, Diedrich, Mama, and Papa prayed daily for God to soften Herr Rothhaus's heart, they still heard nothing from him. And he had not appeared at church yesterday.

Sighing, she bundled up the sheets she'd stripped from her bed and headed downstairs, where Mama had begun heating water for the wash. Regina had preached to Sophie about faith, and now she must listen to her own counsel. Even when it seemed impossible, God, in one stroke, had protected Henry and changed Sophie's heart toward Diedrich and Regina. If God could do that, He could also change Herr Rothhaus's heart. She remembered the scripture Pastor Sauer read yesterday from the third chapter of Ecclesiastes. "To every thing there is a season, and a time to every purpose under the heaven." Just as Monday wash day followed Sunday's day of rest, God surely appointed a specific time for each of His tasks as well. Still, she prayed He might hurry up and deal with Herr Rothhaus soon.

As she stepped into the washroom, a knock sounded at the back door. A man's shadow stretched across the open doorway. Papa and Diedrich were out cutting hay, but of course, neither of them would feel obliged to knock.

She dropped the sheets at the bottom of the stairs and stepped to the door. When the figure of the man came into view, dismay dragged down her shoulders. "Eli, I told you not to come around again. Diedrich and I are engaged—"

"I'm not here about that." His somber features held no hint of his usual cocky demeanor. "I'm here about Diedrich's pa—old man Rothhaus." He jerked his head toward the lane where Sam Tanner sat on the seat of a buckboard. "There's been an accident." Grimacing, he twisted his hat in his hands. "He's hurt bad. Real bad."

Chapter 29

Diedrich paused in his work with the scythe. Resting the curved blade on a mound of timothy hay he had cut a moment before, he leaned against the tool's long handle. Only one more half acre to cut. And if the weather stayed dry, he and Herr Seitz should be able to get all the hay put up in the mow by the end of the week.

Sighing, he lifted his sweaty face to the cool breeze and gazed at the fluffy white clouds the wind chased across the azure sky. He couldn't imagine a more idyllic scene. And indeed, to a casual observer, his life would undoubtedly seem ideal. He'd won the love of his life, and her entire family—even including Sophie—all wanted him to be part of their family. In the space of two months he could possibly claim Regina for his wife and at the same time become co-owner of the best farmland he'd ever had the privilege to work.

But the regret twisting his insides reminded him of the threatening cloud of uncertainty that still overshadowed his hopes for a happy future. Without Father's blessing, his dreams of a life with Regina on this land he had come to love could very well evaporate like the shifting clouds above him. Although Regina had agreed to reinstate their engagement, he couldn't expect her to wait forever. What was more, he knew his father's stubbornness. Father had never tolerated even a whiff of disrespect from any of his sons. And Father had undoubtedly seen Diedrich's outburst eleven days ago as a rank display of disrespect. Not since Diedrich was a child and received a disciplinary swat on the backside had Father struck him—and never before on the face.

He instinctively rubbed his unshaven cheek. The initial sting had long faded, but the memory of the blow still reverberated to his core. Diedrich's heart felt as if it were being ripped asunder. Thoughts of giving up either Regina or Father were equally abhorrent. *Dear Lord, don't make me choose. Please, God, don't make me choose.*

"Diedrich! Papa!"

At the sound of Regina's voice, Diedrich whipped his head around. The sight of her bounding toward him over the hay field lifted his glum mood while piquing his curiosity. It was too soon for dinner, so he couldn't guess what might have brought her all the way out here to summon him and Herr Seitz. And at the moment, he didn't care. He was just glad to see her. Though the distance between them still made it hard to discern her mood, he imagined her smiling face and his own lips tipped up in anticipation.

But the next moment her face came into clear view, wiping the smile from his face. Her blue eyes were wide and wild with fear. No hint of a smile brightened her terrified expression.

Dropping the scythe, he trotted toward her. He caught her around the waist, and her torso moved beneath his hands with the exertion of her lungs. "Regina, what is the matter?" He knew she and her mother were washing laundry today.

Could Frau Seitz have been scalded by hot water? "Has something happened to your Mutter?"

She shook her head then pulled in a huge breath and exhaled. "Nein. It is your Vater. Eli Tanner came to tell us there has been an accident at the mill." Her chin quivered, and her eyes glistened with welling tears, causing Diedrich to fear the worst. His insides crumpled at the thought of losing his father before they had the chance to reconcile.

He let go of Regina so she wouldn't feel his hands trembling. Though he longed to ask the dreaded question pulsating in his mind, her words had snatched the breath from his lungs. His chest felt as if he'd been kicked by one of the Clydesdales.

Herr Seitz loped up in time to hear Regina's news. "Tell us, Tochter. What has happened?" He grasped her shoulders, and she drew in another ragged breath.

"Eli said Herr Rothhaus was chasing a raccoon from the mill and slipped on some grain on the floor. He fell and hit his head on the millstone." A large teardrop appeared on her lower lashes and sparkled in the sun like a liquid diamond perched on threads of spun gold. At any other time the sight would have melted Diedrich's heart, and he would have pulled her into his arms to comfort her. But not now. Instead, an icy chill shot through him, and his arms hung helplessly at his sides.

"Regina, you must tell us." Herr Seitz's voice, though firm, turned tender—coaxing. "Does Herr Rothhaus still live?"

She nodded, and Diedrich's knees almost buckled with his relief. The plethora of questions crowding his mind tumbled from his lips as from an overturned apple cart. "Where is he? How badly is he hurt? Can he speak? Has anyone gone to fetch a doctor?" He hated the harsh, interrogating tone his voice had taken, but he couldn't keep it out. If Father died before he could reach him and reconcile, Diedrich would never forgive himself.

Regina blinked, and Diedrich glimpsed a flicker of fear in her eyes. It seared his conscience. Her forehead puckered as if in confusion, or was it pain? She narrowed a harder, unflinching look at him. "He is at the house. He is alive but not fully conscious. Eli has gone to Dudleytown for the doctor, and his Vater is helping Mama settle Herr Rothhaus onto the downstairs bed." Her voice sounded rigid—formal. It was as if they were suddenly strangers.

No one spoke as the three strode to the house together. Regina didn't look at Diedrich, and her father walked between them. In more ways than one, Diedrich could feel the distance between him and the woman he loved lengthening by the minute.

When they reached the house, Diedrich didn't stop to wash up but rushed to the downstairs bedroom he and Father had shared when they first arrived at the Seitz home. Father lay on the bed with the quilt pulled up to his chest. The clean white cloth encircling his head bore a crimson stain at the forehead above his left eye. Was it just the light, or had Father's salt-and-pepper hair turned even grayer in the week and a half since Diedrich last saw him? His eyes were closed, and his face chalk white. Frau Seitz sat at his bedside. Her expression anxious, she patted his hand while continually calling his name. If not for the tiny rise and fall of Father's chest, Diedrich might have thought his spirit had already left his body.

Diedrich rushed to his father's side and took his hand. A parade of memories flashed through his mind—his father's smiling face as he swung Diedrich up on a horse for the first time; his tender expression, compassionate voice, and gentle touch as he picked Diedrich up and brushed him off when he fell. The rancor in Diedrich's heart from his recent dispute with his parent faded. Father had always taken care of him. He would now take care of his father.

With tears blurring his vision, he knelt by the bed and rubbed his father's weathered hand. "Can you hear me, Papa?"

Father moaned and rolled his head on the pillow, igniting a flicker of hope in Diedrich's chest. But no amount of prompting evoked a more coherent response. For what seemed like days but was probably less than an hour, Diedrich stayed at his father's side alternately praying and trying to rouse him. Little conversation occurred. Regina and her parents and Sam Tanner hovered nearby, quietly praying. At last, Eli appeared with a middle-aged man in dress clothes carrying a black leather satchel.

With Herr Seitz translating, the man introduced himself as Dr. Phineas Hughes. He pulled up a chair next to the bed, displacing Diedrich, and handed Regina his dusty, short-top hat. First, he lifted Father's eyelids one at a time and peered into them. Then he removed the bandage from Father's head and examined the wound. Despite the bluish-purple lump rising on Father's forehead, the doctor pronounced the wound superficial and of no grave concern. The problem, he surmised, was any unseen damage that might have occurred to the brain in the fall.

Diedrich fought the urge to pepper the physician with a barrage of questions, deciding it best to wait and allow the man to make a full examination. So he held his peace as the doctor took a sharp instrument from his satchel and poked the bottom of Father's foot. At the touch, Father moaned, rolled his head, and drew up his knee. Though ignorant of medicine, Diedrich took Father's response and the doctor's "Mm-hmm" as encouraging signs.

Returning the sharp instrument to the satchel, Dr. Hughes then took out a wooden tube with a bell shape on one end and an ivory disk on the other. He placed the bell-shaped end on Father's chest and pressed his own ear to the ivory disk. Slipping his watch from his plaid waistcoat, he watched the face of the timepiece as he listened. At length, he put away both the tube and the watch. While Diedrich waited with bated breath, the doctor sat upright and emitted a soft harrumph. "Well, his heart sounds strong." He shook his head. "But that he has not yet regained full consciousness is troubling."

Standing, he picked up his satchel then retrieved his hat from Regina. "There is really nothing more I can do. His healing is in God's hands now. We know very little about the workings of the brain, and such injuries are unpredictable. All we can do is to wait and observe." He shot a glance at Regina and Frau Seitz. "Keep the head wound clean and bandaged, and someone should sit with him until. . ." Clearing his throat, he looked down. When he looked back up, he gave Diedrich a kind smile. "Just keep a watch on him. And it would not hurt to talk to him. It has been the experience of some physicians that such patients do seem to hear and understand in some way. It is thought by some who study these cases that conversation can actually help stimulate the brain and bring the patient back into consciousness." He plopped his hat on his thick shock of graying hair. "Let me know if there are any changes. We should know one way or another within forty-eight hours."

As Herr Seitz interpreted the doctor's words, a crushing dread gripped Diedrich. The doctor's prognosis seemed to be Father would either recover or die in the next two days.

Bidding the group good day, Dr. Hughes exchanged handshakes with Diedrich and Herr Seitz then left the house with young Tanner.

With the doctor's departure, a somber pall fell over the room, and an overwhelming sense of guilt and despondency enveloped Diedrich.

Regina's heart broke for Diedrich. Only the two of them remained in the room with Herr Rothhaus. Mama had left to gather more cotton cloths for bandages, while Papa saw Herr Tanner to his wagon. Seeing Diedrich slumped in the chair beside his father's still form, his face crestfallen and drawn, she was filled with a desire to comfort him. She pressed her hand on his shoulder. "Gott will hear our prayers and heal him. We must have faith."

He shrugged off her hand, sending a chill through her.

The cold look he gave her felt as if he'd stabbed her through the heart with an icicle. He gave a sardonic snort. "My faith is all used up, Regina. I prayed Gott would change Vater's heart—not stop it. When I asked Him to remove the obstacles preventing us from marrying, I never expected Him to answer by taking Vater from me." His lips twisted in a sneer, and his voice dripped with sarcasm. "But Gott has given us what we asked, has He not? Soon there will likely be no impediment to our marrying."

A pain more excruciating than any she had ever felt before slashed through Regina. Though reason told her Diedrich's hard words were born out of crushing worry for his father, she also knew they came directly from his heart. Diedrich blamed their love and, by extension, Regina, for his father's condition. Whether Herr Rothhaus lived or died, a marriage between her and Diedrich had become impossible. Tears filled her eyes and thickened her voice. "Pray for your Vater's recovery, as I will be praying. But there will be no marriage. I am releasing you from our engagement."

As she turned to leave the room, she harbored a glimmer of hope Diedrich might utter a word of objection. But he stayed silent, extinguishing her hope and plunging her heart into darkness.

For the next twenty-four hours, Herr Rothhaus's condition remained unchanged. Diedrich never left his side except when Regina came into the room to change Herr Rothhaus's bandage or feed him warm broth from a cup, which he oddly took only from her hand. She had insisted on shouldering much of Herr Rothhaus's care, initially out of a sense of scriptural duty. He hated her. And his hatred had robbed her of any hope for a happy life with Diedrich. But she did not want to hate him back. She had seen the pain hatred inflicted on Sophie and then later the freeing power of forgiveness. Though Herr Rothhaus could inflict an injury on her heart, she would not allow him to inflict one on her soul. Also, she hoped by caring for his father, she might earn back a measure of Diedrich's regard. But she hadn't expected to so quickly find her heart blessed by the moments she spent with Herr Rothhaus. She soon ceased to equate the gentle man she cared for like an infant with the angry man who had hurled insults at her. At the same time, Diedrich's altered demeanor toward her ripped at her heart. The moment he spied her coming, he'd leave the room with scarcely a word or a glance. It hurt to think he could not even bear to share the same space with her.

Despite Diedrich's rejection, Regina found solace in ministering to his father. Although Herr Rothhaus gave no sign of awareness, the fact he took the broth in a relatively normal manner with her holding the cup and wiping drips from his chin encouraged her. Remembering the doctor's advice, she talked to him, prayed, recited encouraging verses of scripture, and even sang hymns as she cared for him.

Two days after the accident, Regina had just finished giving Herr Rothhaus his supper of broth. As she dabbed the remnants from his mouth and chin whiskers with a cotton towel, she recited scriptures about healing. "'For I will restore health unto thee, and I will heal thee of thy wounds, saith the Lord.'" She bowed her head over her folded hands. "Dear

Lord, I ask You to heal Herr Rothhaus. Please restore him to full health—"

"Regina." Diedrich's soft voice halted her in midsentence. Opening her eyes, she looked up to find him standing in the doorway, gazing at her. His gray eyes—as soft as the morning mist—held a tenderness toward her she thought she would never see again. "I surrender."

She could only sit gaping, confused by his ambiguous comment. "Surrender what? I do not understand."

He stepped into the room. "I surrender to you—to my love for you." He crossed to where she sat and, taking her hands in his, knelt before her on one knee. "Regina, when I learned of Vater's accident, I feared he might die without us reconciling." He glanced at his father's face and grimaced. "I still do." He swallowed. "I blamed you. And I tried to close my heart to you. But it is no use. You have become too much a part of it—too much a part of me." He gave her a sad smile. "I could not bar you from my heart last spring when I thought I wanted to go to California. I should have known I could not do it now."

He glanced at his father again, and his eyebrows pinched together in a frown. "You were right. Vater made his choice. I have done much praying." His lips quirked in a wry grin. "Like Jacob of the scriptures, I have wrestled with Gott about this situation. In my own guilt, I blamed you for the rift between me and Vater. That was wrong of me—as wrong as it was for Vater to blame you for what your birth Vater and Großvater did against our family."

Regina held her breath. The lump of tears gathering in

her throat rendered her mute. What was he saying? Was he choosing her over his father?

Diedrich's thumbs caressed the backs of her hands, sending the familiar thrill up her arms. "You did not repay your sister's trespasses against you with meanness or spite but forgave her as our Lord bade us to do. In the same manner, I have watched you tenderly care for my Vater after the unkind way he treated you." He shook his head, and his eyes brimmed with emotion. "Where could I find another woman like you? I know now whatever happens"—he glanced once more at his father's face—"*whatever* happens, I must make you my wife. I cannot bear the thought of living my life without you. My Vater may be against our marriage, but I feel with all my heart Gott is for it. Please say again you will marry me."

Before she could answer, a faint voice intruded.

"Angel."

At once, Diedrich sprang to his feet and rushed to his father's bedside. But Regina stepped back. If Herr Rothhaus was truly rousing from his two-day stupor, Diedrich's face should be the one he saw first—not Regina's.

Diedrich sat on the chair beside the bed and grasped his father's hand. "Vater, it is Diedrich. Did you say something?"

Herr Rothhaus's head rolled back and forth on the pillow. "Angel," he murmured again. His eyelids fluttered then half opened. He peered at Diedrich from beneath drooping lids. "Diedrich, mein lieber Sohn. You are in heaven with me, then?"

Diedrich smiled and shook his head. "Nein, Vater. And neither are you. Two days ago, you fell at the mill and hit your head on the grinding stone. We feared Gott might take you, but He has heard our prayers, and you are still with us here on earth."

Herr Rothhaus scrunched his face, and his head rolled more fiercely on the pillow. "But there was an angel with me. She sang *schöne* hymns and spoke words from the Heilige Schrift."

At his words, Regina's heart pounded, and she fought the urge to flee the room. It appeared Dr. Hughes had been right when he suggested patients with head injuries like Herr Rothhaus's might actually hear and have some awareness. What would Herr Rothhaus think if he knew hers was the voice of the angel his muddled brain had heard?

Diedrich glanced at Regina then turned back to his father. "Vater, I believe the angel you speak of is Regina. She has cared for you since Herr Tanner and his Sohn brought you here to the home of Herr Seitz after your accident."

Herr Rothhaus's right hand clenched, wadding a fistful of quilt. For a long moment, he said nothing. Tension built in the room like a coming storm. Regina's breath caught in her throat, and she braced for his angry outburst.

Instead, when Herr Rothhaus spoke again, his voice was small, weak, even contrite. "Bring her, Sohn. I want to see her."

Turning to Regina, Diedrich curled his fingers toward his palm in a beckoning gesture. "Come."

Regina hesitated as fear gripped her. She did not want to ignite another ugly scene like the one they experienced in front of the new house a few days ago. But the steady look in Diedrich's eyes assured her of his unwavering protection, and she tentatively approached the bed. As she stepped into Herr Rothhaus's view, her heart thudded. How would he react?

To her surprise, a gentle smile touched his lips. His watery eyes looked sad, and his face appeared ancient, tired. "Forgive me, liebes Mädchen. I was wrong." His gaze shifted from her face to Diedrich's. "I must ask your forgiveness, too, Sohn. You were right. I had forgotten the lessons our Lord taught us in His Word." Reaching up, he fingered the bandage around his head. "It took you and Gott together to knock the sense back into my head." The quilt covering him eased down as he breathed out a deep sigh. "I am tired of carrying the burden of hate in my heart. It has grown too heavy," he murmured as if to himself. "Too heavy and too costly."

A tear slipped down his weathered face, touching Regina deeply and forcing her to wipe moisture from her own cheeks. Herr Rothhaus looked up at Diedrich, his eyes full of contrition. "I do not want to lose you, mein Sohn." He turned a sad smile to Regina. "Or the chance to have an angel Schwiegertochter." Then his gaze swung between them. "You have my blessing to marry." He grinned. "But you must wait until I am strong again. I want to stand beside my Sohn as he takes a wife."

Smiling, Diedrich rose from the chair and slipped his arm around Regina. "Do not worry, Vater. Regina and I will marry in September, as we agreed the day we arrived here. By then you will be stark, like Herr Seitz's bull." He shot Regina a knowing grin. At his veiled reminder of their first meeting, she couldn't hold back a merry giggle.

Herr Rothhaus's voice turned gruff. "Now both of you go

and let me rest so I can heal."

Diedrich grinned, and Regina bent and pressed an impulsive kiss on her future father-in-law's cheek. Her heart sang with anthems of thanksgiving for the answered prayers and miracles God had wrought over the past several minutes.

With his hand around her waist, Diedrich guided Regina outside. There they met Mama coming in from the garden with a basket of vegetables on her arm and shared the joyous news with her.

Mama wiped away tears. "Praise Gott!" Her expression quickly turned from relieved to determined. "After two days of broth, I must make Herr Rothhaus a proper supper."

When Mama had disappeared into the house, Diedrich led Regina to the garden. Regina gazed over the vegetable patch where bees buzzed and butterflies flitted around the verdant growth of potato and cabbage plants as well as vines of beans entwined around clusters of sapling poles. Her full heart throbbed with a poignant ache. Here she and Diedrich had shared so many significant moments in their relationship over the past several months, and now she sensed they were about to share another.

He took both of her hands in his, and she cocked her head and grinned up at him. "Why have you brought me here?" She gazed into his eyes—those same flannel-soft gray eyes that had made her feel safe last April in the bull's pen.

He didn't smile, but a muscle twitched at the corner of his mouth. "To hear your answer."

It suddenly occurred to her that Herr Rothhaus's awakening had distracted her before she could answer Diedrich's proposal. Mischief sparked within her, and a playful grin tugged at the corner of her mouth. Feigning weariness, she gave an exasperated huff. "Diedrich Rothhaus, I have agreed to marry you twice before. Must I say it again?"

"Ja, you must." He sank to one knee and lifted an expectant look to her, while an untethered smile pranced over his lips. "So, Regina Seitz, will you agree to be my wife?"

At his repeated petition, Regina's heart danced with happy abandon. Blinking back renegade tears, she fought to affect a bored pose while bursts of joy exploded inside her. "Ja," she drawled. "Since your Vater now agrees, I suppose I must marry you. But our Vaters promised us months ago, so my answer should be no surprise."

Grinning, he stood and let go of her hands. "Then this, too, should come as no surprise." Pulling her into his arms, he kissed her until her toes curled. Suddenly September seemed excruciatingly distant.

"Well," he murmured as he nuzzled his face against her hair, "did I surprise you?"

"Nein," she managed in a breathless whisper.

His voice against her ear turned husky. "Then I must try harder to surprise you."

Regina leaned back and smiled up into her future husband's handsome face. "Only if all your surprises are as sweet as the last one you tried."

He pulled her back into his arms and tried again.

Chapter 30

Regina bent and reached into the oven to extract the pan of freshly baked corn bread. The sweet aroma tickled her nose as she gingerly grasped the hot pan with the cotton pot holder. Noticing the quilted square of cloth's stained and singed condition, she couldn't suppress a smile. Over the past year, Sophie's wedding gift had seen much duty.

As she plopped the pan on top of the stove, strong arms encircled her waist. Twisting in Diedrich's embrace, Regina smiled up at her husband. She slipped her arms around his neck. Would his touch ever cease to send delicious shivers through her? She couldn't imagine such an occurrence. "I should make you wear your Holzschuhe in the kitchen so you cannot sneak up on me, *mein Mann,*" she teased.

Grinning, he nuzzled her cheek with his prickly chin, filling her nostrils with his scent and firing all her senses. "But then I could not surprise you, and you know how you love surprises." His lips blazed a searing trail from her jaw to her mouth and sweetly lingered there.

When he finally freed her from his kiss, she still clung to him, reveling in his closeness. No, she would never become immune to Diedrich's caresses. "You can no longer surprise me with kisses," she challenged breathlessly.

Stepping back, he reached into his shirt pocket and pulled out an envelope. "Ah, but I have other means by which to surprise you."

Intrigued, she plucked the already-opened envelope from his fingers. "What is this?" She looked at the name printed on the envelope's top left corner. "So what is so surprising about a letter from your brother Frederic?"

"Look at the postmark." His grin widened.

"Baltimore, Maryland?" It took a moment for the significance to register.

Diedrich beamed. "Frederic and Hilde and the Kinder are now in America. They should arrive in Jackson County within the month."

Regina's heart thrilled at her husband's joy. Separation from his beloved brother had remained the one spot marring Diedrich's otherwise flawless contentment. Her smile turned fond. "That is wunderbar, mein Liebchen. I am excited to meet my *Schwager* and *Schwägerin*." Not to be outdone, she decided to share her own piece of news. "Frederic, Hilde, and their children are not the only additions to our family we are expecting."

At Diedrich's puzzled look, Regina stifled a giggle. "Mama stopped by while you were gone. She got a letter from Sophie today saying Henry will be getting a little brother or sister soon." She laughed. "Mama wondered if helping Elsie with her and William's little Catharine made Sophie want another little one of her own."

Diedrich chuckled. "Soon our Vaters will have more

Enkelkinder running around than they will know what to do with. And since Ezra and Sophie bought Herr Roberts's big brick house in Salem, they will have plenty of room for even more Kinder."

Regina perused Frederic's letter. "Have you told Papa Georg yet about Frederic and Hilde?"

He nodded. "Ja. On my way back from Dudleytown, I stopped by the mill to deliver to Herr Tanner a letter from Eli." He grinned. "Vater is sehr excited about the news." His grin disappeared, and his gaze skittered from hers, signaling a measure of unease. "Eli and Herr Roberts believe they have discovered a rich vein of gold on their claim near San Francisco." The tiny lines at the corners of his mouth tightened. "Perhaps you will think you should have married Eli after all. You could be a *wohlhabend* woman now."

She cupped his dear face in the palm of her hand. "I am glad for Eli and Herr Roberts, but I married the right man. And I *am* a wealthy woman." She turned to cut the cooling corn bread. If his face held a tinge of regret, she would rather not see it. "And if you had joined Herr Roberts instead of Eli, the gold would be yours."

He grasped her waist and turned her around. His soft gray gaze melted into hers. "Gott has given me more treasure here in Sauers than Eli will ever find in the hills and streams of California." He bent to kiss her, but before their lips touched, a soft mewling sound that quickly became a full-throated cry halted them.

Regina sighed and slipped out of her husband's grasp. "I must see about our Sohn."

Diedrich followed her to the doorway between the kitchen and front room. "Perhaps he is hungry."

"Nein." Regina shook her head. "I just fed and changed him a few minutes ago."

By the time they reached the front room, the baby's crying had stopped, and the cradle was empty. As Diedrich and Regina shared a look of alarm, the sound of quiet singing wafting through the open front door turned Regina's sharp concern to mild curiosity. On the porch, they found Papa Georg in the rocking chair, cradling his swaddled grandson in his arms and softly singing a hymn.

Papa Georg stopped singing and looked up at them. "Jakob and I are just enjoying the nice day," he whispered, glancing down at the now sleeping infant. "So since we require nothing at the moment but each other's company, maybe the two of you could find something else to do." Grinning, he went back to rocking and singing, while Jakob's rosebud lips worked around his tiny thumb.

At the sight, Regina's heart melted. A little more than a year ago, she would not have imagined witnessing such a scene. Her eyes misted at the culmination of all her prayers. The words of Psalm 100:5 echoed through her heart then winged their way heavenward in a prayer of thanksgiving. *For the Lord is good; his mercy is everlasting; and his truth endureth to all generations.*

Diedrich and Regina shared a look, and their smiles turned to wide grins. Diedrich nodded. "Sehr gut, Vater. We will leave you alone with your *Enkel.*"

Inside the house, Diedrich took Regina's hand. He

glanced at the kitchen door then at the stairway that led to the loft. "The corn bread is baked, and you won't need to start dinner for at least another half hour. And I can't do any hammering, or I may wake Jakob. So what should we do?"

Her heart full, Regina grinned up at her husband. "Surprise me."

As he towed her toward the stairs, Regina knew that whatever surprises the years might bring, as long as she and Diedrich were together, life would be sweet.

About the Author

Even though Erica Vetsch has set aside her career teaching history to high school students in order to home-school her own children, her love of history hasn't faded. Erica's favorite books are historical novels and history books, and one of her greatest thrills is stumbling across some obscure historical factoid that makes her imagination leap. She's continually amazed at how God has allowed her to use her passion for history, romance, and daydreaming to craft historical romances that entertain readers and glorify Him. Whenever she's not following flights of fancy in her fictional world, Erica is the company bookkeeper for her family's lumber business, a mother of two terrific teens, wife to a man who is her total opposite and yet her soul mate, and an avid museum patron.

About the Author

Ramona K. Cecil is a wife, mother, grand-mother, freelance poet, and award-winning inspirational romance writer. Now empty nesters, she and her husband make their home in Indiana. A member of American Christian Fiction Writers and American Christian Fiction Writers Indiana Chapter, her work has won awards in a number of inspirational writing contests. More than eighty of her inspirational verses have been published on a wide array of items for the Christian gift market. She enjoys a speaking ministry, sharing her journey to publication while encouraging aspiring writers. When she is not writing, her hobbies include reading, gardening, and visiting places of historical interest.